The Varieties of Authorial Intention

John Farrell

The Varieties of Authorial Intention

Literary Theory Beyond the Intentional Fallacy

John Farrell
Department of Literature
Claremont McKenna College
Claremont, California, USA

ISBN 978-3-319-48976-6   ISBN 978-3-319-48977-3 (eBook)
DOI 10.1007/978-3-319-48977-3

Library of Congress Control Number: 2016963206

Cover illustration: Edgars Sermulis / Alamy Stock Photo

Printed on acid-free paper

This Palgrave Macmillan imprint is published by Springer Nature
The registered company is Springer International Publishing AG
The registered company address is: Gewerbestrasse 11, 6330 Cham, Switzerland

To Alex Rajczi

PREFACE

A little more than a decade ago, when I was in the middle of writing a book about the role of paranoid characters in modern culture (*Paranoia and Modernity: Cervantes to Rousseau*), I decided to offer an undergraduate course on the subject. The readings included books with literary figures notable for their grandiosity and suspicion—Don Quixote, Captain Ahab, Kafka's K., Charles Kinbote, and various Pynchon characters; it also included key philosophical contributors to the modern habit of suspicion—Luther, Hobbes, Rousseau, Nietzsche, Marx, and Freud. The enrollment was surprising. Forty students signed up, my largest class ever at Claremont McKenna College, and I had to request a bigger room. On the first day of class I went to the old room and wrote a note on the board that read something like this: "Lit 165 has been moved to Bauer 33." Then I went upstairs to wait for the students. But nobody came. Ten minutes into the hour and the room was empty. Could some prankster have erased my message that quickly?

Going downstairs to answer this question, I found a packed classroom, seats filled and some students on the floor, all staring at my message, which was still on the board just as I had written it. Baffled, I asked the students what they were doing and I received an answer I never expected: since it was a course on paranoia, they told me, they thought I was already trying to make them paranoid! "We thought you could see us from somewhere!" they said, a remarkable exaggeration of my powers.

The standard meaning of the sentence I wrote on the board was quite clear but the intention behind it was not, a reminder that mere words and their standard implications are hardly ever enough. Intentions are essential, but they can easily go awry, and in this case the mere association with paranoia was sufficient to deactivate the normal context and inspire mistrust, sending my intended meaning into the abyss. This episode provides an uncanny parable for the very phenomenon for which my book attempted to provide the historical background—how modern intellectuals, including scholars of literature, acquired the habits of suspicious decoding that have dominated the academy since the 1960s. Once the very notion of deception comes prominently into play, it easily effaces the ordinary context, leaving the interpreter susceptible to a mindset in which nothing can be taken at face value, strange powers come into being, and innocent intentions go unheeded. The author's action disappears behind a network of hostile influences.

In the era of Theory with a capital T, texts were ostensibly the one commodity that could be taken as given. But having been theoretically severed from their connection to authors and their intentions, they fell easily into other hands and became the avatars of hidden meanings and powers. And while the demise of Theory has been widely announced, the vocabulary and habits of suspicion have endured. As Lisa Ruddick nicely puts it, "what began as theory persists as style." Recently, however, mainstream scholars such as Ruddick, Eve Kosofsky-Sedgwick, Amanda Anderson, Rita Felski, and others have come to question the abstract, depersonalized discourse of the literary profession and its relentlessly suspicious character. Felski in particular has provided a trenchant analysis of the rhetoric of suspicion, which she calls simply "critique."

Felski's book *The Limits of Critique* (2015) is a landmark and a synthesis of the turn against scholarly paranoia and suspicious hermeneutics, and the analysis she offers is a powerful one. She has no regrets about the political work accomplished in the academy during the phase of critique and the opening up of new areas of inquiry accomplished under its banner, but she also recognizes that critique has had a drastically narrowing effect on the study of literature. Because it is entirely negative, it has nothing to say about what draws readers and scholars to literature in the first place. Viewed in this light, critique is now a self-protecting orthodoxy, a sterile routine that offers no resources for defending the value of the humanities, which in recent decades have come so acutely under attack. The style of critique as Felski describes it involves looking always beneath the surface of the text to find deep, hidden, never auspicious motives, or scrutinizing the text for cracks and fissures in its apparently innocent and consistent surface. For the gaze of critique, nothing is accidental; everything is a symptom of hidden power. Critics approach the text like a detective looking for clues to a crime, positioning themselves as superior, more knowing, than the text, which is always both naïve and corrupting. Critique is relentlessly hostile, employing a formidably technical jargon that nevertheless presumes to come from below and represent the interests of the oppressed.

The one element this analysis has been missing is a return to the question of authorship. *The Varieties of Authorial Intention* is my bid to reopen this question. It attempts to be, in a sense, the antidote to paranoia, treating the subject of non-suspicious interpretation and pointing directly at a key tenet of literary criticism since the mid-twentieth century—that reference to authorial intentions is out of bounds, literary works being constituted by the text alone. In Chapter 1 I provide an account of the origins and history of the turn against authors. In the chapters that follow I show that authorial intention is a natural and indispensable aspect of literary language as it is of language in general. I explain the difference this makes for our understanding of literature and for our practice as scholars. At stake is our understanding not only of meaning but also of value, and I have devoted Chapter 5 to that subject.

The concept of authorship offers an obvious resource to the critique of "critique," for, as Felski points out, critique always addresses a detached object, a "text," not an action, a work; as a result, the practitioners of critique relentlessly reduce text to context, seeing texts as unable to resist or deviate from the power relations that surround them. But the reason critique cannot separate text from context is that it has eliminated the obvious point of leverage between them, the authors who create the texts in context. Critique glorifies its own agency but occludes the agency of the author.

Opinions on these matters are deeply held, and readers will have to decide for themselves if my account of literary meaning and value are persuasive. At the outset, though, I will leave my fellow scholars with these questions. No matter how much importance we attribute to society, ideology, and other factors in the meaning and making of literature, can we really appreciate the works of the past without taking into full account the agency of the individuals who created them? Were they not just as strikingly enabled as determined by the conditions under which they wrote? And if we cannot give credit to their intentions, how can we account for our own? We too are authors, and to deny this status to authors in general is either to place ourselves irreparably under erasure or to indulge in an unjustifiable and privileged exception.

My debts to philosophers and critics who write about literature go far beyond what I have been able to acknowledge in the text, and that is true of debts to my friends as well. Jonathan Bolton, Leland de la Durantaye, Yoon Sun Lee, Seth Lobis, Jim Morrison, John Plotz, Alex Rajczi, and Bob von Hallberg provided helpful guidance and bracing resistance to the manuscript. They have saved me from many a pitfall. The dedication to my philosopher colleague and podcasting partner Alex Rajczi is in gratitude for over a decade of friendship and fruitful conversation on the issues of this book and so many others.

CONTENTS

CHAPTER 1

Introduction: The Origins of an Intellectual Taboo

In 1917, Marcel Duchamp, a French artist in exile in New York and a director of the Society of Independent Artists, famously decided to test the Society's commitment to artistic freedom by purchasing a standard urinal, giving it the title *Fountain*, signing it with the comic pseudonym R. Mutt, and having it submitted for exhibition. When the Society failed the test and rejected *Fountain*,[1] it was not the obscenity or the irreverence of Duchamp's work that made it unacceptable. It was its mere banality. *Fountain* was simply a urinal, no different from the ones that could be purchased in a shop. The artist's hand had done nothing to improve it. All *Fountain* had to recommend it as a work of art was the intentional gesture that brought it into view. It was a "readymade."

Fountain started as little more than a joke, though Duchamp had been experimenting with readymades for some time. Nevertheless, the joke's force and seriousness continued to grow. Once accepted as art, readymades became a tribute to the absolute freedom of the artist to transmute any object, even the homeliest or most rebarbative, into a work of art merely by virtue of the artist's power to declare it such. The reach of such an artist's ambition could be breathtaking; anything could now become a work of art. Duchamp considered making an artwork out of the world's tallest readymade structure, the Woolworth Building, simply by giving it a new name (65).

In addition to its inspiring vistas, Duchamp's action had its deflationary side. The artist had "cut off his hands," as he put it. His art would no

© The Author(s) 2017
J. Farrell, *The Varieties of Authorial Intention*,
DOI 10.1007/978-3-319-48977-3_1

longer be a matter of skill or mastery. It would be a purely cerebral activity. While its purpose was to demonstrate the freedom of the artist from the judgment of critics and administrators, it also had the effect of separating the artist from the work because the work no longer had a meaning or subject matter provided by the artist. It did not represent anything, conform to any style, embody any skill of hand or eye, cater to any taste. The artistic gesture was simply to say *voilà*, here is the object—a bracing display of naked intentionality.

At the point where the work of art becomes a work of art through mere intention, without any other distinctively artistic activity, the value of both art and intention come into question. Either of them can look like a fraud. Duchamp's gesture signaled the full arrival of the age of theory, for this was an art that simply could not be grasped without explanation. It was theoretical in its essence. Duchamp's reductio ad absurdum separated intentionality from the making of the object and allowed it to float in the direction of the observer and the theorist. By inviting the audience to look at a urinal as a work of art, he was asking it to share almost in its entirety the act of making it art, which consisted merely of seeing it in a certain way, guided by the artist's intent. Even this did not exhaust the degree to which the artist could erase the distinction between himself and his audience. In a famous work of music, *4'33"*, John Cage took the process one stage further, presenting mere time and place as an occasion of music and leaving the audience to fix its attention on whatever sounds might happen to turn up during the chosen interval. With such a work the artist does not even determine the object toward which intentionality is to be directed. The distinction between artist and audience has become thinner still.

The exposure of intentionality, in all its imperial nakedness, was an invitation to its overthrow. In the age of theory, the critic and the object (or in the case of literature, the text) would conspire to eliminate the middleman-artist. For an artistic culture in a state of constant revolution and crisis, intentionality was the last connection between convention and form to be stripped away. At the completion of this process, many visual artists would come to look upon what we might call their offerings entirely as the world would see them, without intending a resemblance to anything else. At this point the work is no longer *about* or *meant*. It is no longer a symbol or an act of communication. It stands as an object in itself, a mere find, an invitation to make of it what you will. The last vestige of the artist's skill becomes the ability to present an object that is somehow striking but does not fall into any familiar category or pattern, one that does not recall any previous artistic object or image. Audiences had always come to art looking for an impression of something other than the work itself, an impression of presence or significance due to the artist's skill and effort, but what the new audience got was the pure and simple *Ding an sich*, an attempt not to mean but to be—while somehow still being art.[2]

We can see some of the same tendencies at work in literary modernism. With its cult of individual styles, its freedom to experiment with the relation of form to content, and its inveterate whimsy and eccentricity, it also testified to the power and freedom of the artist, but here the emphasis tended to fall less on the nakedness of the artist's intention and more on the richness and proliferation of styles and meanings embodied in the work. There was, of course, a deeply skeptical aspect to a movement with Flaubert and Joyce among its chief exemplars, artists who tended to stand above their work and the entire tradition of Western literature they meant to culminate. In a different manner from Duchamp, this degree of detached virtuosity invited the dethroning of the author in favor of a proliferating textuality and a sense that form itself determines content. It is perhaps no coincidence that during this same period psychoanalysis was providing a new source of intentionality in the unconscious mind—a source of depth and meaning with radically anti-traditional implications. Escaping from conscious intentions began to rival, or even replace, the enacting of conscious intentions as an artistic pursuit. For critics and biographers, exploring the unconscious mind of the artist and reducing idealistic ambitions to egoistic wishes became a substitute for the Romantic cult of genius, a new way of relating author to work that allowed the critic to override surface intentions.

In English letters, it was religious and culturally conservative critics like T. S. Eliot and C. S. Lewis who took the first steps in the theoretical disenfranchising of authors from the position of responsibility for the meaning of their works. Like Duchamp, Eliot was a collector of reusable objects, lines of poetry that could be collected readymade under his own signature. But whereas Duchamp's aim was to demystify and make art ordinary, the aim of Eliot's artist, expressed in "Tradition and the Individual Talent" (1919), was to free art, and himself, from the ordinary life of emotions and practicalities—to elevate it, "by a continual self-sacrifice,"[3] into contact with an ever-changing yet ideal order, an order of significance above what can normally be expected of human activity but belonging nevertheless to "tradition." This was the beginning of a taboo aimed at the messiness of human thinking and feeling and grounded in a Brahmanical appeal for purification, part of what Ortega y Gasset presciently described as the modern "dehumanization of art."[4]

Lewis's attack on Romantic expressivism, delivered in a series of exchanges with E. M. W. Tillyard and published as *The Personal Heresy* (1939),[5] conveys a similar attitude toward literary language as possessing hieratic powers that separate it both from authors and from the language of ordinary life. For Lewis, the very act of writing separates the artist's life from his work, "and that is the beginning of a rift which will grow wider at every step we take from the vulgarity of confession to the disinfected and severer world of lyric poetry" (10). The disinfecting of poetry from the messiness of authors was codified, we shall see, in the landmark essay "The Intentional Fallacy" by the New Critic William Wimsatt and the philosopher Monroe Beardsley. And this was only the beginning of the disinfecting process. For Paul de Man, the theoretical project of New Criticism turned out to be not the "escape from personality" that the author of *The Waste Land* imagined but little more than an extension of the personality and ideology of Eliot himself. De Man diagnosed the contorted subtlety of Eliot's seemingly detached stance, describing it, with a contorted subtlety of his own, as "an Anglo-American blend of intellectual gentility not so repressed as not to afford tantalizing glimpses of darker psychic and political depths, but without breaking the surface of an ambivalent decorum that has its own complacencies and seductions." Thus, for de Man, Eliot's is not a true critical objectivity but a rhetorical one. "The normative principles of such a literary ambiance are cultural and ideological rather than theoretical, oriented towards the integrity of a social and historical self rather than towards the impersonal consistency that theory requires." For de Man the escape from the "social and historical self" into "impersonal consistency" would eventually be accomplished by linguistic theory.[6]

It is interesting to note that in the development of the visual arts, the separation of meaning and intention tended to undermine meaning and preserve intention, whereas in literary theory it was intention that was sacrificed to meaning as embodied in the text. This was owing no doubt to differences between the two arts themselves and in the different ways they experienced the pressure of other media. In both cases, though, the rejection of convention, with its bourgeois associations, was an animating motive, whether it drove an escape into tradition or its demolition.

So it is no surprise that the attack upon intentionality and the concept of the author, begun by cultural conservatives, was taken up and intensified by poststructuralists with a similarly anti-bourgeois and anti-capitalist attitude. Roland Barthes, for instance, envisions the author as a "peculiarly modern figure," an artifact of the recent discovery of the individual "emerging from the Middle Ages with English empiricism, French rationalism, and the personal faith of the Reformation." The emphasis on the centrality of the author was for Barthes the "epitome and culmination of capitalist ideology."[7] Barthes' implication was that such a recent development had to be reversible, and it was on the basis of new experimental artistic practices that he announced "The Death of the Author." In his account, authors such as Mallarmé had recognized "the necessity to substitute language for the person who until then had been supposed to be its owner. For him [Mallarmé], for us too, it is language which speaks, not the author." And in the most trenchant formulation, "only language acts, not 'me'" (142). After Barthes' announcement of the "death of the author," with its "destruction of every voice, of every point of origin" (141), all that was left was for Michel Foucault to make the argument that authors themselves had been nothing more than creatures of language, "discourse," in the first place.[8]

Among philosophers, by contrast, the notion of authorial intention as essential to the construction of linguistic meaning has had strong, though not unanimous, support following upon the work of the later Wittgenstein, G. E. M. Anscombe, and Paul Grice.[9] Among literary critics there were many powerful replies to the counterintuitive New Critical and poststructuralist teachings about literature and language, including landmark defenses of authorial intention by E. D. Hirsch and P. D. Juhl.[10] By and large, however, the protest on behalf of authors and intentions gathered little traction, while the rhetoric of textuality became irresistible. Authorship as a respectable concept was set out of bounds and has never fully recovered. In the early 1980s, Walter Benn Michaels and Steven Knapp made a bold reaffirmation of authorial intention as inseparable from textual meaning in their provocative essay "Against Theory," but the effect may have been blunted by their use of the issue as a weapon against the very concept of theory.[11] One of the aims of New Historicism, the most influential literary theory to emerge since the 1980s, was to restore the sense of historical agency to the intellectual vocabulary of literary theory,[12] but even this has not led to an explicit reconsideration of the intentional agency involved in the writing process. More recently, Seán Burke has shown in masterful detail how fully and freely the post-structuralist skeptics about authorship deployed the resources they called into question; the real object of poststructuralist critique was a certain conception of authorship as corresponding with the autonomous subject or transcendental ego, and it need not have applied to the concept of authorship per se.[13]

From the point of view of the twenty-first century, the old debate between intentionalists and textualists now looks extreme and tendentious. As with so many classic philosophical debates when they progress to their maturity, each side has now made enough concessions to the other that the criteria for judging the issue become hazy, with the skeptics appearing to have the more conservative position because they insist on holding the intentionalists to a more mentalistic standard than the intentionalists believe is required. (It is for similar reasons that in his polemics in favor of pragmatism, the late Richard Rorty was always insisting that the proper response to the skeptics was not to answer them but tell them to "get lost"—they were always upholding more traditional criteria for knowledge than Rorty would allow.) In this book I will be defending a position that I believe should count as intentionalist, but one that avoids the intentional fallacy as classically described and gives full recognition to readerly construction. As I will show, intentionality in language works in a way that depends as thoroughly upon the audience, the target of the utterance, as it does upon the maker of the utterance. Linguistic intentions are only valuable insofar as they can be deduced from the text in context. Both author and audience play a vital conceptual role in this process.

It is important to recognize from the start that not all of the critiques of authorship and intention, including Wimsatt's and Beardsley's, were fallacious. Intentionality is inherently complex; actions embody multiple intentions of different kinds, a fact that Wimsatt and Beardsley failed adequately to appreciate. The critics of literary intentionality aimed at different intentional targets and took up different questions. Some objected primarily to the notion that a literary work expresses the author's personal psychology, as Romantic critics tended to assume, while others were concerned to discourage the notion that the author's artistic intentions should be definitive of a work's value. There was also the natural desire to separate works from their authors' practical intentions, the ambitions, either egoistical or idealistic, that motivate the work of art. All of these concerns have obvious merit and do not imperil the basic notion of authorship. They belong to a set of familiar literary habits that can be usefully grouped together under the rubric of Romantic psychologizing. But the most radical critiques of intentionality denied the knowability of what I will call authors' communicative intentions, how authors expect the audience to understand the sentences, symbols, stories, and other features that make up a literary work. The upshot of this strain of argument is that texts and authors are little more than what we make of them. Whereas Eliot, Lewis, and the New Critics began by elevating language above its creators, making literary words the source of an inexhaustible semantic richness that stands as a rebuke to the mundane use of language, post-structuralists such as Barthes, de Man, and Foucault saw the text as containing much less meaning than a human author was traditionally thought to provide. For them, such meaning as a text possesses must come from inside, from language itself, in its self-enclosed, textual work-ings, cut off from authors and the world, or, if not, it must be imposed entirely from outside, either injected by the reader or generated through the functioning of various discursive practices, the manifestations of trans-cendent agencies such as Foucauldian "power." The author, once elevated to superhuman status by Romantic critics, was to be degraded in subordi-nation to the Word, which took on a new life, independence, and power of its own. Foucault himself pointed out that the Barthesian notion of *écriture* had a transcendent character, but his own conception of power and its erratically self-succeeding epistemes is also a transcendent one. It was not only authors that were in the process of disappearing; Foucault was looking forward to a transcending of "the human" itself. And with the same mid-sixties yearning for apocalypse, Jacques Derrida anticipated the overcoming of the tension that culminated the Western tradition of metaphysics—the tension between Rousseau's nostalgia for lost origins and Nietzsche's embrace of the void—as leading toward a transhuman birth of "the monstrous."[14]

The impulse to set up the text in place of the author, then, had multiple and overlapping sources: the modernist and postmodernist rejection of traditional literary and artistic forms, partly under the pressure of emerging media; the desire to establish a realm of art above or immune to practical considerations, the vulgar life of the bourgeoisie, and the reductive power of science; the appeal of modes of reading that pointed toward hidden rather than conscious intentions; and the utopian political hopes of the 1960s, which looked forward to a transcendence of capitalism and the human condition as embodied in Western metaphysics. Distrust of the very concept of mind also played a part, beginning in the positivistic and behavioristic mid-century, before cognitive science emerged to give the study of mental activity a naturalistic basis. This is just to scratch the surface of a subject whose full exploration would embrace the entire story of artistic and intellectual modernity.[15] It is important to remember that, as Seán Burke points out, the need for the control or regulation of subjectivity, the achievement of "negative capability," was already one of the persistent themes of Romanticism to which Eliot simply gave another turn in his discussion of impersonality.[16] Another element of the story is how the rhetoric of inspiration has persisted in modernity, based on the common experience of writers that, in their finest moments of creativity, a power not themselves, a voice not their own, seems to take charge—or, alternatively, that language itself is working rather than the conscious ego. The theory of inspiration—itself an intentional theory though the intention comes from elsewhere—has proven to be a remarkably durable resource for validating the authenticity of art.[17]

Taking an even broader view, fundamental problems of agency and authority are at the heart of the authorship crisis. The "death of the author" is only one of the more recent symptoms of art's fragile position in the modern world. Freed from its traditional masters, the rhetoric of art has veered between declarations of omnipotence and practical irrelevance. For modern authors, the putative power of art often appeared to be as much a hindrance as a guarantee of its freedom, while the stability of meaning often seemed threatening and confining rather than empowering. In this regard, the artist is a striking representative of modern intellectuals in general; detached from religious and metaphysical supports, their firmest claim to authority often lies in the vehemence of abdication. At such an impasse, literary language, detached from meaning and reference, could promise a domain of freedom by virtue of its emptiness–an untethered infinity to replace a disenchanted world.

To the non-specialist reader it might be hard to imagine how critics could in practice do without reference to authors, and in point of fact they don't. The taboo against intentions has always taken a highly ambiguous and only partial form. Given the talents and professional *élan* of its chief protagonists—Eliot, Lewis, the New Critics, Barthes, and Foucault—and given their broad coverage of the ideological spectrum, it is not surprising that their arguments had a powerful impact on the thinking of literary scholars, but that impact was not actually to reduce the currency of authorship or intention as guiding concepts for literary study. Whatever the attractions of that alternative locus of agency—words—to scholars who make their living from literary texts, authors and authorship have proven to be embarrassingly indispensable analytic resources. This is so in spite of the broader tendency among modern intellectuals—represented in figures as disparate in their concerns and attitudes as George Orwell, Martin Heidegger, and Walter Benjamin—to displace meaning and responsibility onto language. What the anti-intentionalist reformers accomplished was the establishment of the intentional fallacy argument as a merely theoretical taboo. Instead of abandoning concern with authorial intentions, literary scholars have clung to it as an indefensible peccadillo, not to be employed without disclaimers. As a result, scholars who pursue author-based practices like biography and textual editing suffered the loss of status that goes with not being "theoretical." But even for theoretical scholars, reference to authorial intention remained a constant if sheepish practice—a bourgeois habit impossible to break, a guilty pleasure too addictive to renounce, a form of naïveté that must be apologized for in ritual fashion but cannot be avoided. If there exists such a thing as a scholarly neurosis, this is it.

What difference does it ultimately make then if, presented with a literary work, we see the words before us as chosen words, the results of human work, or if we see them simply as marks on paper susceptible to our own interpretation? The most immediate difference is that mere marks on paper do not furnish us with the motive to make the inferences necessary to interpret them except insofar as they have human intelligence behind them. Every day we make the distinction between natural objects and humanly made ones; the natural ones we take simply as given but with the humanly made ones we can legitimately see purpose, design, and, with instruments of communication, meaning. What I will call *the textual fallacy*—the notion that the text is meaningful purely on its own—puts a literary work on the wrong side of the divide between natural and manu-factured objects. As a result, there is a pervasive asymmetry between the works produced by critics and the texts they address; the former are part of a project of scholarly investigation and political intervention while the latter are inert textual objects that require suspicious decoding. It is fascinating to see that the recent turn against the suspicious mode of critique has led some scholars to redress the asymmetry between analyst and text not by elevating the text to a work but by demoting the activities of human agents to the same status as non-human objects envisioned as having a role as "actors" in a social process. This is taking the textual fallacy to a new level.[18]

Of course the problem of demoting the text to an inert object is merely theoretical. In practice, advocates of the textual fallacy do not actually confine themselves to a mere text considered as a given set of marks. They persist in finding meanings associated with those marks. But the textualist attitude discourages them from being guided by the text in the right way. They either take up a linguistic theory that makes the text all-determining for meaning, in the structuralist vein, without leaving room for the reader's process of inference, or they take up a linguistic theory like New Criticism or deconstruction which does not place enough limits upon readerly inference. Deconstructionists in the Derridean mold recognize the importance of authorial intention but are excessively preoccupied with its limits. These are problems I will take up and explain at length in Chapter 2.

The final and deeper problem with the textualist attitude is one that can be appreciated without technical explanations. It is simply that to think of a literary work as a mere text is to neglect its impact and value as a human gesture made in a concrete historical situation toward a potentially identifiable audience. This is not to say that this gesture can be grounded solely or crucially in the personal psychology of the author, in the manner envisioned by Romantic critics; that is the full-blown intentional fallacy and it should be resisted. Writing of any kind is an intersubjective public practice, not the mere projection of personal subjectivity. But an intersubjective public practice requires a real practitioner and a real public, and to leave these out, to reduce either to a mere function of textuality, is to dehumanize the activity in question. It is to eliminate the once-living hand and voice.

One byproduct of such textual reification is that it eliminates the factor of risk that accompanies all human action. Any act of communication involves the possibility of being misunderstood, and any act of artistic making involves the possibility of failing to produce the intended impact. As readers of literature, we are attempting not only to understand the meaning of the literary work; we are also attempting to access the experience it offers and, as I will suggest, this always involves an assessment of the author's performance. To understand a literary work is to see how it accomplishes its effects, to see its elements as functional. This inevitably involves judgments of value. Literary scholars usually think of value judgments as applying post facto to works of art as a whole, and they often relegate such judgments to the domain of the merely subjective or see them as sociologically determined. But value judgments, I will suggest, are essential to literary understanding per se, and they play a role in our responses minute by minute. It is impossible to comprehend a work of literature without some appreciation of its match between means and ends. Literary scholarship inevitably involves making use of one's own reactions to literary works in the context of one's range of literary experience. It requires a combination of finesse and emotional receptivity, an engaged form of judgment. As we will see, the notion of the "aesthetic," which sees the experience of art as a response to a detached object, dovetails quite closely with the textual fallacy.

Finally, obscuring the human and therefore fragile, risk-governed origins of language and of literary works has allowed the writings of the past to be recruited into the "crushing system of domination" which, as Felski notes, has long been the rhetorical foil of the literary theorist (50). The evacuation of individuals' intentions has allowed hidden, transindividual sources of agency to flourish.

The goal of this study is to explain why the taboo on intentions is unnecessary and unhelpful—in fact impossible to abide by—and to suggest a way of thinking and talking about intentions that focuses properly upon the literary work and avoids the reductions of biography. Between the two wedges of anti-intentionalism—religiose aestheticism and poststructuralist prophecy—I discern a middle position, call it humanist, pragmatist, or naturalist as you will, which insists that literature need not be less meaningful or intentionally guided than the language of ordinary life and which refrains from connecting literature with higher sources of knowledge or making it a sacred, autonomous object. This view gives full space not only to the author's anticipation of readerly interpretation but the reader's ability to construct the work based on the text. In my view, there is no need to be discouraged from exploring this position just because the conservative critics of the 1940s and 1950s associated an early, extreme version of it with bourgeois vulgarity, the lingering indulgences of Romanticism, and the degraded language of business culture, or because the poststructuralist critics of the 1960s and 1970s associated it with capitalism, metaphysics, and oppression. Authorial intention is a straightforwardly naturalistic concept. It is essential to the definition of human action, and its application to the creation of literary works requires an assumption no more demanding than that writing is such an action—my starting point and basic theme. The deployment of the concept of authorial intention in literary criticism is grounded in a desire to understand what literary works are doing and saying, and how readers construct meaning from them. Such deployment is supported by the Darwinian sense that literature calls upon an evolved capacity for language too uncannily elaborate and useful to be an accident with no benefits for the creatures who possess it.

Intentionality is a capacity far too important to be relegated to the bourgeoisie. The attack on the intentional fallacy was once a mark of radical commitment, proclaimed with enthusiasm, but by now it enjoys such orthodoxy among literary scholars as to be part of common sense, so much so that the issues it involves have become difficult to understand. Misconceptions swarm around it—that authorial intentions are primarily to be discovered outside the text, that authorial intention conflicts with the interpretive freedom of the reader, that to accept the role of authorial intention is to cede excessive authority to the author as an artist or a thinker. These are just a few of the fallacies that have put reference to the author out of bounds. Literary scholars tend to associate intentionality—falsely in every case—with certainty, sanity, rationality, transparency, self-consciousness, authority, control, premeditation, and lack of spontaneity. There is also a sense that the notion of intention is linked with an undesirably metaphysical conception of truth or a Cartesian conception of mind, or that it suggests the embodiment of thought in communication in such a way as to ignore the slipperiness of language. I shall show why none of these associations is appropriate. The last one is particularly inapt since it is the very slipperiness of language that makes intention indispensable.

What I offer here is a broad attempt to provide the conceptual background literary scholars need to understand authorial intention and avoid the extremes of the classic debate, starting in Chapter 2 with an explanation of intentionality itself and the essential role it plays in defining human action and interpreting human behavior. I then explain how intentionality works in the use of language, stressing the need for inference on the part of the reader; speakers and writers provide us with remarkably exiguous cues for interpretation, and it is only knowing that they were intended by a speaker in a particular context that we can decipher them. With these discussions of intentionality and language in place, I proceed to the main point with an account of the complex intentional act that is the creation of a literary work. I stress the need to distinguish between communicative, artistic, and practical intentions and the very different conditions under which they are realized. This seems like a very basic point, but I have searched the vast literature on this subject without finding a discussion of it.[19]

In Chapter 3 I go on to show how the view I've proposed in Chapter 2 would alter our use of other items in the critical vocabulary, including terms such as "implied author," "poetic speaker," "omniscient narrator," and "linguistic indeterminacy." I move forward in a kind of dialogue with my imagined readers, anticipating concerns and objections and attempting to answer them. I occasionally provide some historical reflections beyond the ones given above, for instance about the changing role of the author in premodern, modern, and postmodernist literary cultures. In Chapter 4 I take up the issue of unconscious intentions (Freudian, Marxist, structuralist, and Darwinian) and whether Actor-Network Theory provides an answer to the problems they raise. In Chapter 5 I propose an account of literary value that recognizes the centrality of authorial performance as opposed to an "aesthetic point of view" which thinks of literary works as self-subsisting objects, another correlate of the textual fallacy.

In taking up issues such as intention, meaning, and value I am obviously getting into rather deep philosophical waters, but this is not a work in the philosophy of mind or philosophical aesthetics. I do not aim at definitive philosophical treatments or exhaustive exegeses of rival positions. What I am trying to do is get at basic intuitions and address stubborn issues in a way that will be clarifying and helpful to my fellow scholars of literature and to do so in a relatively brief and digestible form. If I can reopen minds to the centrality of intention in literary studies my own intention will have been realized.

I would be remiss not to express my indebtedness to the writings of philosophers such as Malcolm Budd, Noël Carroll, Gregory Currie, Arthur Danto, Donald Davidson, Denis Dutton, Alan Goldman, Nelson Goodman, Peter Lamarque, Colin Lyas, Frank Sibley, Robert Stecker, and Kendall Walton, to name just a few. Their work has made little impact on literary studies, unfortunately, because literary critics tend not to engage with them.[20] Monroe Beardsley, one of the authors of "The Intentional Fallacy," would seem like an exception, but he proves the rule, for even though Beardsley was one of the most prolific and influential philosophers writing about aesthetics in the twentieth century, literary scholars tend to be familiar only with that single co-authored essay and its companion piece, "The Affective Fallacy."[21]

There are reasons why philosophical aesthetics as it is currently practiced might look irrelevant to literary scholars. The philosophers who write about theoretical issues in literature tend to sidestep the proliferation of literary theories that have emerged since the 1960s, many of them depending upon "continental" philosophy rather than the analytic tradition. When aestheticians look for examples of literary critical practice, they often go back several generations to the tradition of literary scholarship as ethical and aesthetic evaluation represented by figures like F. R. Leavis. If we are going to judge theories about meaning and value by how well they account for the way literary study actually proceeds, as I intend to do, there will have to be some connection with current practices and concerns, however multifarious they have come to be. My sense is that literary scholars, before they go on to apply various theoretical modes of interpretation, still attempt to understand literary works in a way that is not radically unlike what occurred in the past, and that they make use of evaluative judgments in the course of their scholarship even while they are applying the theoretically inspired forms of reading provided by New Historicism or Cultural Studies. Readers will have to judge for themselves about whether or not the picture I provide of scholarly reading corresponds with their own sense of how it goes.

Before taking up the subjects of human action, linguistic meaning, and literary intention from the beginning, I would like to offer three preliminary observations. Firstly, about *meaning*. The trouble with the word is that it has too many. We use it to refer to the information that is transmitted in sentences, their "semantic content"—though I tend to avoid that phrase because it suggests that words contain meaning rather than providing a prompt for the audience's interpretation. The opposite of *meaningful* in this sense is *nonsensical* or *nonsemiotic*. In addition, we use *meaning* to refer to what difference a state of affairs makes to us. The opposite of *meaningful* in this sense is *trivial*. The sense in which a sentence is meaningful, therefore, is different from the sense in which a state of affairs or an event (say an increase in salary) is meaningful. The trouble is that when we learn about a state of affairs or an event by means of a sentence, the two senses of meaning easily run together. In this book I will use the word *meaning* to refer to the information communicated by the utterances of speakers and authors and *impact* to refer to what difference those utterances make to us. One of the ways in which sentences and words can have impact upon us is the skillful way they are composed.[22]

The second preliminary point is that there are many difficulties for those who would do away with the concept of authorship altogether and put the mere text in its place, but one of them is so simple and fundamental that it should be mentioned at the start; it is that the notion of the text can by no means be taken for granted. By making a complete identification of work with text, textualist critics ignore the fact that many literary works do not even exist as a single, unambiguously authoritative, or error-free text. Editorial intervention is often essential in establishing the text, and that intervention can only proceed on the basis of what the editor considers the author's intentions to have been. Even works created for the modern print media contain errors that need to be corrected. For earlier works there are typically multiple texts, multiple manuscripts, multiple sources of error, ambiguity, corruption, and confusion. In such cases, without the governing concept of an author as the original source of the text, there simply is no text. Modern editions of Shakespeare present a text that cannot be found in any earlier manuscript. Such texts are a composite of sources which editors have compiled, all with the aim of getting as close as possible to what the author originally intended. Even the twentieth-century masterpieces of Joyce, Kafka, and Proust present significant textual problems. Editions of these works put forward an already interpreted version of what the author intended. When there are multiple drafts or versions of a work each of which has authorial legitimacy, the editor has a choice either to select which of the author's intentions or sets of intentions should be honored or to leave the choice to the reader by presenting multiple versions. In either case authorial intention necessarily comes into play; authors' intentions play off against each other in rival versions, and the more drafts and versions of a work, the more re-gatherings and re-orderings it undergoes, the more salient is the intentional activity that produced it.

Since all information is subject to decay in the process of transmission, and since authorial intention is the only basis for refurbishing the text, there simply can be no stable text without the interpreted intentions of the author.[23] Those who come to the text as if it were an independently determined object forget that what they are reading is an already edited and interpreted version of someone's original attempt to put words in place. They are overlooking the physical instability of the text itself, which is a sign not of the absence but of the continuing need for the author as part of our reading and interpreting process. To make this mistake is to commit the textual fallacy in its most naïve and flagrant form.

Since the mid-twentieth century, textual editors have become more cautious about assimilating all available manuscripts of a work to a single "eclectic" version and more self-conscious about the problems of deciding which of an author's intentions should provide the crucial guidance—initial or final intentions, first versions or revisions, revisions made by the author or those made by others in the normal course of the editing and printing process.[24] The recognition of intentionality as an essential element of the literary work does not foreclose these issues; it enables them to be grasped and confronted. To invest all meaning in the text is to absolve the interpreter of the responsibility of identifying the actual content of the work. It is to forget that the distinction between editing and interpreting is an artificial one, and that the notion of authorial intention is indispensable for both of them.[25]

The instability of texts without authors also highlights an essential assumption, made throughout this book, about the nature of interpretation itself. The goal of interpretation is to understand what the work is saying. (Avant-garde works that do not make a statement, though they may reward analysis, thus do not require interpretation in the proper sense.) Interpretation enables appreciation, explanation, and analyses of all kinds by providing these activities with an object. But interpretation itself cannot be expected to enhance the interest of the work at the expense of its meaning. Not only would that turn it into a different work, authored by the critic rather than the author; it would also undermine a necessary basis for the preservation of the text itself. Once pleasure or interest replaces understanding as the aim of interpretation, there is no substantial reason to preserve the text. The differences between reading and writing, between author and critic, and between discipline and object of study would essentially have been erased.

Finally, part of the discomfort with the concept of authorial intention derives from the shift in the interests of literary scholars from issues of production toward issues of mediation and reception. It is important to see that while it may not always be possible to pursue all of these interests at the same time, there is no reason to think of them as rivals. The question of what a work meant for its originally intended audience is simply a different question from what it meant for those who read, edited, anthologized, or restaged it at a later time, including the present, and a good deal of the interest of the second question is in the contrast between earlier and later readings. As I have noted, Roland Barthes saw the "death of the author" as a necessary condition for the "birth of the reader" because for him the author was a limit on the freedom of the reader. But author and reader are both necessary conditions for literature—indeed, for written communication of any kind—and if there has been any limit upon reading it has been the limit that puts the author's activity out of bounds. Such limits curtail the healthy pluralism of scholarly interests. And this points toward another important consequence of the skepticism about intentions. Taking in view the whole range of activities that scholars are wont to investigate—writing, editing, anthologizing, repackaging, reviewing, interpreting—all of them are themselves intentional activities. By ignoring the role of intentions, we make all of these things uncanny and impossible to account for, including our own scholarly work.

NOTES

1. Francis F. Naumann, *Marcel Duchamp: The Art of Making Art in the Age of Mechanical Reproduction* (New York: Harry N. Abrams [distributor], 1999), 73–75.
2. As William A. Camfield observes, it was not long before interpreters of Duchamp's work began reinfusing it with aesthetic qualities. Alfred Stieglitz's photograph of *Fountain* was the first step in that direction. See Camfield, *Marcel Duchamp: Fountain* (Houston: Houston Fine Art Press, 1989), 35–60.
3. T. S. Eliot, *Selected Essays: New Edition* (New York: Harcourt, Brace & World, 1960), 7.
4. José Ortega y Gasset, *The Dehumanization of Art and Other Writings on Art and Culture*, trans. Willard R. Trask (New York: Doubleday, 1960).
5. C. S. Lewis and E. M. W. Tillyard. *The Personal Heresy: A Controversy* (New York: Oxford University Press, 1939).
6. Paul de Man, *The Resistance to Theory* (Minneapolis: University of Minnesota Press, 1987), 6.
7. Roland Barthes, "The Death of the Author" in *Image-Music-Text*, trans. Stephen Heath (New York: Hill & Wang, 1977), 142–43.
8. Michel Foucault, "What Is an Author?" in *The Foucault Reader*, ed. Paul Rabinow (New York: Pantheon Books, 1984), 100–20.
9. Ludwig Wittgenstein, *Philosophical Investigations*, trans. G. E. M. Anscombe, 2nd ed. (Oxford: Blackwell, 1967); G. E. M. Anscombe, *Intention* (Cambridge, MA: Harvard University Press, 2000); Paul Grice, *Studies in the Ways of Words* (Cambridge, MA: Harvard University Press, 1989).
10. E. D. Hirsch, *Validity in Interpretation* (New Haven, CT: Yale University Press, 1967); P. D. Juhl, *Interpretation, An Essay in the Philosophy of Literary Criticism* (Princeton, NJ: Princeton University Press, 1980). To get a sense of the more recent discussion see, for instance, David Schalkwyk, "Giving Intention Its Due?" *Style: A Quarterly Journal of Aesthetics, Poetics, Stylistics, and Literary Criticism* 44, no. 3 (Fall 2010): 311–27; Paisley Livingston, *Art and Intention: A Philosophical Study* (New York: Oxford University Press, 2005); Peter Lamarque, *The Philosophy of Literature*

(Malden, MA: Blackwell Publishers, 2009), chapter 3; and Richard Gaskin, *Language, Truth, and Literature: A Defence of Literary Humanism* (Oxford: Oxford University Press, 2013), chapter 7.

11. Walter Benn Michaels and Steven Knapp, "Against Theory," *Critical Inquiry* 8, no. 4 (Summer 1982): 723–42.

12. Stephen Greenblatt, *Learning to Curse: Essays in Early Modern Culture* (New York: Routledge, 1990), 164–66.

13. Seán Burke, *The Death and Return of the Author: Criticism and Subjectivity in Barthes, Foucault, and Derrida*, 3rd ed. (Edinburgh: Edinburgh University Press, 2008).

14. Jacques Derrida, "Structure, Sign, and Play in the Discourse of the Human Sciences," in *Writing and Difference*, trans. Alan Bass (Chicago: University of Chicago Press, 1978), 294.

15. The tendency of interpretation to become a battleground issue for large cultural struggles is exemplified with special vividness in *Truth and Method*, Hans-Georg Gadamer's grand account of the hermeneutic tradition, where the legitimacy of hermeneutic understanding vindicates the claims of the "human" versus the physical sciences, verbal versus mathematical reasoning (or even more archetypally, *mythos* versus *logos*), and philosophy versus history.

16. Seán Burke, ed., *Authorship: From Plato to the Postmodern: A Reader* (Edinburgh University Press, 1995), 22–23. Andrew Bennet provides an excellent collection of Romantic and modernist declarations of impersonality, expressions of the Baudelairean "moi insatiable de non-moi," in *The Author* (New York: Routledge, 2005), 202–03.

17. See Timothy Clark, *The Theory of Inspiration: Composition As a Crisis of Subjectivity in Romantic and Post-Romantic Writing* (Manchester: Manchester University Press, 1997).

18. The inspiration for this move, advocated by Rita Felski in *The Limits of Critique* (Chicago: University of Chicago Press, 2015), is provided by Actor-Network Theory. I will discuss the upshot in Chapter 4.

   For other diagnoses of the suspicious mode discussed in my preface see Eve Kosofsky-Sedgwick, "Paranoid Reading and Reparative Reading, or, You're So Paranoid, You Probably Think This Essay is About You," in *Touching Feeling: Affect, Pedagogy, Performativity* (Durham, NC: Duke University Press, 2003), chapter 4; Amanda Anderson, *The Way We Argue Now: A Study in the Cultures of Theory* (Princeton, NJ: Princeton University Press, 2005); and Bruno Latour, "Why Has Critique Run Out of Steam? From Matters of Fact to Matters of Concern," *Critical Inquiry* 30 (2004): 225–48. I trace the historical background of the suspicious mode in *Paranoia and Modernity: Cervantes to Rousseau* (Ithaca, NY: Cornell University Press, 2006).

19. See, however, Wendell Harris, *Literary Meaning: Reclaiming the Study of Literature* (New York: New York University Press, 1996), 101–02.
20. See, however, Terry Eagleton, *The Event of Literature* (New Haven, CT: Yale University Press, 2012).
21. The headnote to Wimsatt and Beardsley's essay "The Intentional Fallacy" in *The Norton Anthology of Theory and Criticism*, after giving background sources for the work of the literary critic William Wimsatt, baldly but correctly reports that "Other than the two classic essays he coauthored with William Wimsatt, Beardsley's work in philosophical aesthetics has had little impact in the field of literary criticism." *The Norton Anthology of Theory and Criticism*, second edition; general ed. Vincent B. Leitch (New York: Norton, 2010), 1232.
22. This discussion does not exhaust the meanings of meaning. We can also ask, for example, about a sentence whose semantic meaning is quite clear, did the speaker really *mean* it? Here *meaning* what is said is opposed to being *insincere*. The distinction is ethical and psychological rather than semantic.
23. Even the text of the law can be subject to "scrivener's error," requiring correction with reference to the authors' intent. Ronald Dworkin presses this argument to good effect against the textualist Antonin Scalia. See Antonin Scalia, *A Matter of Interpretation: Federal Courts and the Law: An Essay*, with commentary by Amy Gutmann, ed., Gordon Wood, Laurence Tribe, Mary Ann Glendon, and Ronald Dworkin (Princeton, NJ: Princeton University Press, 1997), 115–28.
24. For a provocative account of the problem of "multiple artistic intentionalities" (72) see Jerome J. McGann, *The Textual Condition* (Princeton, NJ: Princeton University Press, 1991), chapter 3.
25. For a striking exposition of the inseparability of interpretation from textual editing see G. Thomas Tanselle, *A Rationale of Textual Criticism* (Philadelphia, PA: University of Pennsylvania Press, 1989), chapter 1.

CHAPTER 2

Actions, Intentions, Authors, Works

ACTIONS AND INTENTIONS

My starting point is that the creation of a work of art is a human action, and it is by the presence of intention that we distinguish actions from other behavior. An action is what is done on purpose, as opposed to what is done by accident, by reflex, or through autonomic processes. To use a common example, a wink is an action while a blink is not. It is a mere reflex.[1] The fact that an action is performed on purpose doesn't mean that the purpose has been accomplished. A failed action is an action nonetheless.

The notions of action and intention are mutually dependent but not symmetrical. All actions have intentions behind them and all intentions envision some action, but not all intentions bring an action about. I intend to visit Venice again and I know how to do it, but I may never carry out my intention, even though I can specify exactly what it is. So while it makes no sense to talk about mere actions, it certainly does make sense to talk about mere intentions. For this reason the notion of intention carries connotations of unreality and even a certain irony. Proverbially, good intentions can lead you on a garden path down the road to hell. The apparent unreality of intentions is partly responsible for their disrepute.

Of course we never witness an intention directly, whether it is acted on or not, unless we can be said to witness our own intentions.[2] Because a wink may be physically indistinguishable from a blink, identifying it as an action requires a kind of interpretation, and once we have recognized an

© The Author(s) 2017
J. Farrell, *The Varieties of Authorial Intention*,
DOI 10.1007/978-3-319-48977-3_2

action as an action we still have the task of identifying the particular intention behind it, an operation that we carry out constantly and spontaneously in everyday life. During a class I see a student go over to the window and close it. I do not find her behavior mysterious. Instead, I instantly attribute to her certain desires and beliefs that explain it. I assume, for instance, that she wants the room to be warmer and believes that opening the window will make it so. In light of these intentional states, her beliefs and desires, the action becomes intelligible.

Further information about my student might alter my understanding of her behavior. If I later find her to be chronically antisocial, for instance, I might guess that she was only opening the window to make it uncomfortable for the rest of the class. Or if I learn that she has a settled hostility toward someone in the room, I might guess she was trying to make it warm for that person. Witnessing the student's action does not allow me to come to a unique and definitive explanation of it, only a set of more or less probable ones. What is consistent among these explanations, though, is that they preserve a kind of coherence, a certain rational fit, between her beliefs, desires, and actions. It is the fit among the elements of this triad that makes actions intelligible to the observer.[3]

Attributing an intention to another person obviously involves the application of a norm of rationality. Interpreting a person's behavior means recognizing that, given these goals, in this situation, under these conditions, understood in a certain way, it would make sense to do what the person is doing. This does not mean, of course, that interpreting someone's behavior intentionally requires that we regard it, all things considered, as substantively rational, for people can act upon beliefs and desires that are quite absurd given the circumstances in which they were formed. Madness itself can be internally coherent and exhibit a rational fit between beliefs, desires, and actions, for even when people are almost completely insane, we can still make out their intentions. This goes for fictional madmen too. When we see Don Quixote launching forth against the windmills, we know that he is mad, but we still understand the intentional character of his actions. He believes that the windmills are giants, he wants to vanquish giants, and so he attacks them. The belief–desire–action triad is intact, though Quixote's mind is not. He suffers from a radical detachment from reality, but his beliefs and desires maintain a certain rational fit with each other and with his actions, and it is this that makes them intelligible, however strange they may be. It might even be said that the identification of a person as mad, as opposed to catatonic or completely incoherent, requires that we understand his intentions and how the beliefs that constitute them depart from reality.

Being a good interpreter of other people's behavior often requires a shrewd sense of the compromises people make between coherence and substantive rationality. The set of constraints on the way we interpret other people's intentions is obviously very loose, and it is only in the most extreme cases that they become completely unintelligible. We may think of the mad Judge Schreber, the subject of one of Freud's case studies, who tells us in his *Memoir* that he spent several hours a day in the asylum where he lived sitting in front of a mirror dressed as a woman in order to keep the world from being destroyed.[4] This is absurd but, in a real though qualified sense, we understand it. Schreber is able to present his motives and actions coherently even though the assumptions behind them are obviously delusional because, given his admittedly absurd desires and beliefs, his actions make sense. There is an undeniable coherence, a rational fit, among them. His complex and brilliant exposition makes sense to us once we accept the absurd premises on which it is based.

It is worth pointing out that even when actions seem quite normal, ascribing to them the rational coherence that makes them intelligible does not guarantee that the subject is substantively rational because actions that look perfectly reasonable and ordinary may conceal unusual or irrational intentions. If my window-closing student happens to be an overly zealous or obsessed reader of Emily Brontë, for instance, she might be closing the window not to adjust the temperature but to keep the ghost of Catherine Linton, the window-haunting heroine of *Wuthering Heights*, from entering the room. In that case the student's action would be absurd, however mundane it might look. What we can say about it, though, is that once we have guessed her intention, it remains intelligible even in light of her ridiculous belief.[5]

Considerations such as these are important for ethnographers in the field. They cannot take the meaning behind any action for granted, however obvious or normal it may seem. Even in such hermeneutically challenging situations, though, the process of interpretation can only proceed by assuming a large degree of coherence among subjects' beliefs, desires, and actions so that each of these can be interpreted in light of the others. Once the beliefs and desires motivating unfamiliar customs or odd behavior have been made clear, they acquire a certain aspect of rationality—a method even within madness, strangeness, or superstition.[6]

Good storytelling depends upon preserving the proper fit between the characters' beliefs, desires, and actions and on giving the reader enough information to intuit what they are. It is typically unnecessary to spell out all three members of the triad. In *Pride and Prejudice*, when Elizabeth Bennet decides to walk to Netherfield to take care of her sister Jane, we do not need to be told that she undertakes this action because she wants her sister to get better and because she believes that by going to Netherfield she can help her do so. These desires and beliefs are too typical to require stating. But where issues of responsibility and blame are at stake, we often find it necessary to make intentions explicit. In doing so, we go beyond specifying what happened to take up the question of what it *meant*. What we need to do in such cases is to specify the proper characterization or description of the action in question. The same action may be deliberate in accomplishing one purpose but accidental in accomplishing another. Hamlet, for instance, stabs through the arras to kill what he thinks is an intruder, which is intentional, but instead he kills Polonius, which is not. It is important, then, to know why he did what he did, and that means explicating his beliefs and desires to reveal precisely what he intended. The divining of characters' intentions is a standard part of literary criticism, one aspect of what Eliot nicely called "elucidation."

It is also important to note that not all things that are done intentionally are done willingly even when they are deliberate. If I give you a hard shove to push you out of the way of an oncoming car, I do so knowing I am going to hurt you, and my action is intentional, but my hurting you is not intentional. It is not what motivates me or explains my action. It is imposed upon me by the situation as I believe it to be. A valid elucidation of an action must isolate the point it aims at from its accidental or contingent effects. In order to be valid, it must give the right description of the action in question.

With this account of intentional psychology I am not implying, of course, that whenever we act we are explicitly conscious of our intentions. Much of our daily activity is based upon habit, rooted in the standard routines and practices we share with others. Still, our habits typically begin as intentionally chosen actions that later become routine, and we are confident that, if asked, we can provide a rationale for our habitual behavior, which is to say, we can elucidate the intentions that gave rise to it in the first place. Some readers may associate being intentional with being disciplined, calculating, or manipulative, but there is no reason to endorse these associations. Intentional implies non-accidental, chosen, but many of our choices are quite uncalculated, and we can be intentionally generous in the same sense in which we can intentionally manipulate others for our own ends. Nor does intentionality conflict with spontaneity, creativity, the use of intuition, or the visits of inspiration. All of these things, in fact, require that we choose to direct our efforts toward a certain end. They are about *how* we carry out our intentions; they do not help make the distinction between intentional and unintentional. When we say "intentional," what we are excluding is the merely accidental, the things that do not belong to us as agents at all. Further, the presence of intentionality in no way implies that the agent in question has perfect self-knowledge or transparency. If we can recognize the intentions implicit in the speech and behavior of mad people like Quixote and Schreber, self-knowledge can hardly be at issue; neither can perfect deliberateness, control or self-control, planning, premeditation, or lack of spontaneity. All true actions are intentional, but no one can imagine that all true actions are perfectly rational or planned or that the people who perform them have a complete and infallible sense of what they are doing.

It follows from this that recognizing an intention by no means amounts to endorsing it. Once we have identified a particular intention as the best explanation of an action, we can subject that intention and the action it motivates to all kinds of other analysis and interpretation. We are by no means limited to the terms of understanding under which that action was taken by the agent. We can explain it in terms not available or even contrary to the agent's beliefs, and we can evaluate it in terms other than she would have endorsed. We can diagnose its effects in ways that the agent cannot. We can also use it as a clue toward understanding the agent herself and her situation in ways that she cannot do. We can read between the lines, and if we are willing to adopt the methods of decoding offered by Marxist or psychoanalytic theories, we can read beneath the surface of the action to find the workings of forces and structures unknown to the agent. This work of analysis can only begin after the action taken by the agent has been grasped as an action, and that can only happen by grasping its intentional character. Grasping the intention does not confine or put an end to analysis. It is just the necessary beginning. Without it there is simply nothing to analyze or interpret.

Is Intentional Psychology Legitimate?

It is a widely debated question as to whether intentional interpretations of the kind I have been discussing should count as genuine explanations or whether they are better thought of merely as "folk psychology," possibly to be replaced sooner or later with a set of categories provided by neuroscience. I will not enter here into the issue of what constitutes an explanation, but if we were to think of the ascription of rational coherence between intention and action as a kind of scientific theory, it might look rather weak. The case of Schreber in the asylum suggests that interpretations of this kind cannot fail no matter how bizarre the intentions we ascribe, so we appear simply to be assuming rational coherence rather than proving it. And while falsifiability may be too demanding a criterion for the adequacy of a theory, one might at least expect a theory of this sort to be revisable when it fails, whereas the theory of rational coherence seems to rebound intact from every misinterpretation only to be applied once more in its original form. If one of our interpretations of somebody's intention fails, we do not question the value of reconstructing the triad; we simply try out another triadic interpretation. Intentionality behaves like an idealizing model that cannot be adjusted no matter how often it fails.

What keeps this line of thought from being truly discouraging is that, first of all, without the ascription of intentions we have no other means of distinguishing actions from mere events. Intention seems to constitute the field of human action per se. There is no other way of marking the distinction between a blink and a wink, and without such a distinction not only would we be unable to function as denizens of everyday life, but as scholars we would also be unable to ascend from mere physical observation into the domains of psychology, history, social science, or literary criticism. Second, while we never abandon the assumption of rational coherence as long as we find a person's behavior intelligible at all, we do refine our understanding of individuals and groups through interpretive activity. The more we know about other people, the better we understand their actions and the more accurately we can anticipate their behavior. Our mistakes lead to adjustments. The relations between the terms of the triad may not change, but our expectations about individual cases are always in the process of developing. Ethnographers, for instance, do manage to learn their way around among the people they study in the field and so become able to understand and anticipate their language, thinking, and behavior in a variety of situations, and all of us experience the same progress of understanding in relation to the people we meet in everyday life. Indeed, we quite naturally take up a hermeneutic position toward our own desires, beliefs, and actions, trying to figure out what we really want, believe, and should do, and what our past actions may have meant. Entering a new discipline is partly an endeavor of this kind, in which we learn to pick out and exemplify the right kind of action given the discipline's common beliefs, motives, and practices. Assuming rational coherence among these allows us to predict what a properly trained professional will do in a particular situation. No other form of understanding works better at accounting for and predicting human behavior day to day.

Finally, the value of such fixed, idealizing models is not by any means limited to the discovery of intentions in everyday life. Such models play an important role in science. Charles Darwin's theory of natural selection according to fitness, for instance, is notoriously circular: fitness is what makes animals reproduce successfully, and what makes animals reproduce successfully is their fitness. The theory is true by definition. Its value lies not in successive refinements of the model itself but in expanding its application, discovering the meaning of fitness for each species and the nature of its adaptations. Like the theory of evolution through adaptation, the implicit theory of rational coherence in intention functions essentially through the development of its applications.

For all of these reasons, the view of intentions I have put forward is more or less proverbial among philosophers, psychologists, and social scientists. There are a few neuroscientists who would willingly do away with intentional or "folk" psychology altogether, claiming that intentions have no explanatory value at all,[7] but they are in the minority. Indeed, true abstinence from the inferring of intentions would deprive of us of what evidence we have that other minds exist at all. It is also important to note that we regularly apply intentional understanding in areas other than psychology strictly speaking—to the behavior, for instance, of transpersonal agents, institutions such as government bureaucracies, multinational corporations, or even nation states. There seems nothing odd about asking questions such as *Why did China invade Korea in 1950?* or *Why does Iran want nuclear weapons?* Thinking of institutions as "rational actors" provides an indispensable first approximation in understanding them; it can be refined but not replaced by input–output analyses of bureaucratic resources and routines or by breaking institutions down into lower-level internal competitors with their own rival intentions.[8]

Intentionality, then, is an indispensable cognitive resource. There is no alternative to the explanations it provides. We cannot even imagine doing without it. My account of intentionality is a deliberately minimal one and could be refined and enriched. "Desire," for example, is perhaps a stronger psychological term than is needed. It suggests an insistent form of craving. Then there is the fact that not all desires are endorsed by the agent; some of them are deliberately neglected or suppressed. A desire does not explain an action unless it trumps other desires, the fact that economists capture using the term "preference." The reason I am not on the way to Venice today is that, in spite of my real desire to go there and my knowledge of how to carry it out, my desire to finish this book, along with a range of other engagements, is more pressing at the moment. I may really want to go to Venice, but at this moment I prefer to do something else.

The model of intention might also be enriched with the notion of commitment. Having an intention implies not only the rational fit of our desires and beliefs with our actions but also our commitment to those intentions once we have made up our minds.[9] This point is quite relevant to the intentional character of artistic creation, which typically demands an unusual degree of commitment over an extended period of time. For the sake of simplicity I have chosen to confine myself to the belief–desire–action triad, but scholars of literature should keep in mind these additional aspects of endorsement, preference, and commitment.

And there is another element of intentional psychology that is worth keeping in mind. Because our beliefs and desires are complexly caught up with each other, so are our intentions. They are inherently multiple and we often typically carry out one intention in order to achieve another. We are always killing many birds with a single stone. A student comes to class on a particular day because she wants the value of what can be learned in that class. She is taking that class because she wants to become an educated person and obtain a college degree. She wants these things because she believes they will be a benefit in later life. The account could be extended almost indefinitely. And all of these nested and interlocking desires are accompanied by the appropriate beliefs, which are still more multiple and complexly interrelated. The number of implicit assumptions behind the action of coming to class on any particular day and the way in which it is carried out—that the universe will continue to exist, that the laws of physics are stable, that college degrees will retain their value, that shorts and sandals are still in vogue, and so on—is far too large ever to be specified. For this reason, providing a complete intentional explanation for any action may well be impossible even for the person who holds the intention. It is in the face of considerations like these that we recognize a certain benefit in the fact that our mental capacities are limited and can only cope with a few of our assumptions at a time—presumably the most salient ones—while leaving the rest to an indefinite background. In assessing people's intentions, we naturally gravitate toward the most locally relevant explanatory considerations. The ability to identify these is an important part of human intelligence. A supercomputer with infinite capacity and time would still need to be taught how to limit the field of explanations in order to comprehend human intentionality—whatever "comprehending" for a computer would mean.

In recent years, some cognitive scientists and evolutionary psychologists have proposed that human beings have a dedicated mental faculty or module, "Theory of Mind," which allows us to follow each other's intentions and enter into the psychology even of imaginary characters. The point behind Theory of Mind is to suggest that we wouldn't be able to accomplish such feats of mind-reading computation using nothing but our general intelligence. We must have some special equipment that accomplishes the job, some set of hard-wired assumptions that structure our thought process so we can understand each other.

The evidence for Theory of Mind is intriguing. In many domains of human thought we do see a tendency to overproject intentionality, to see intentions and intention-making beings where there are none. Human beings take a special delight in the discovery of hidden meanings and plans and their possessors—gods, angels, demons, enchanters, conspirators, bogeymen of all sorts. Our vulnerability to paranoia suggests the susceptibility to excess of a particularly well-developed apparatus. Also, there are some extremely intelligent people on the autism spectrum who, in spite of their unusual capacities, have difficulty with mind-reading, as if there were one particular piece of neurological equipment missing. This suggests that mind-reading is a separate faculty from the more general ones we use to cope with the world around us.[10] But whether mind-reading is made possible by means of a special, modular adaptation, whether its emergence has a cultural dimension, as some evolutionary psychologists argue,[11] or whether it is simply a function of general intelligence,[12] the fact remains that most human beings do have a ready and reflexive ability to make interpretations of each others' actions and that the ascribing of intentions is essential to the process.

I hope this discussion makes clear how radically the banishing of intentions would separate literary interpretation from our everyday mental habits and processes, where intentions play an indispensable role in the constitution of human action itself, including, as we shall see, the use of language. To carry out such a banishment consistently would amount to a kind of literary behaviorism. It would become impossible in principle to distinguish between an authentically meaningful text and an accidentally or artificially generated artifact in ostensibly verbal form.

INTENTION AND LANGUAGE

Now that we have seen how difficult it would be to remove intentionality from our understanding of human behavior in general, let us turn to the issue of language, where it is essential to recognize that communicating in language, like other actions, also requires the assumption of a rationally coherent intention. The simplest example will suffice. If I offer you a cup of tea and you say *yes*, you do so because you desire a cup of tea and you believe that saying *yes* will cause me to give you one. I instantly ascribe such desires and beliefs to you when you make this reply. Only such assumptions make your reply informative. Your belief that the word *yes* will work this way depends upon a convention—*yes* is generally what you say when someone offers you something and you want it. But this convention can be easily defeated because saying *yes* won't work if the context makes my intention ambiguous in some way. If I am being generally uncooperative, for instance, mockingly agreeing with everything you say, you might lack sufficient reason to believe I actually want tea. Or if for some reason I am so nervous or confused that I answer *yes* no matter what you say to me, or if I look disoriented or sound uncertain when I answer, my reply might not even count as an action, and it certainly would not count as an answer to the question. Finally, and most crucially, if my answer was physically involuntary—a symptom of Tourette's, for example—there would be no intention behind it at all, and the application of conventional meaning would be blocked. It would not be an action but a mere event. Conventions need intentions behind them to motivate their application.

Does this mean that *Yes* doesn't mean yes even when somebody says it? Here it is important to distinguish word meaning from utterance meaning. Word meanings of the type you find in a dictionary are the ready residues of prior usage. Enough people have used them the way they are defined in the dictionary to make them standing instruments for accomplishing their established range of communicative effects. "Yes" is one of the least polysemic and ambiguous ones. When deployed in a standard utterance it is an instant conveyor of assent. The person using it is calling upon the convention of its meaning established by previous users. But this convention is derivative from use and needs to be part of an actual utterance to have effect. Gottlob Frege famously remarked that words only have meaning in the context of a sentence, but it is necessary to add that the sentence must be uttered in an actual context. "Yes" can be a word, a sentence, and an utterance all at the same time. In the case of the Tourette's patient, no utterance is actually made even though a familiar word and a sentence with a typical meaning are pronounced. That, according to my understanding, is the strange and uncanny aspect of Tourette's disease, that the sufferer unwillingly emits sounds that if chosen as communication would be meaningful. They are uttered to relieve the urge to say them rather than to communicate.

Admittedly, creating a work of literature is a lot more complicated than saying yes when offered a cup of tea, and it is impossible to imagine one being uttered unintentionally. We view a whole work as an intentional structure, which is to say, an utterance, its composition and publication being complex and significant human actions, and inside a work there are many more intentional structures, patterns of rational coherence attributed to imaginary agents which make their actions and statements intelligible. Still, despite the greater order of complexity of a literary work, the essential distinction remains. If the words are not chosen words, words that convey an intention, then we simply have no reason to see them as having significance or being subject to interpretation. We have no motive for treating them as anything more than physical phenomena, no motive to resolve their ambiguities, for in fact they have none, being mere sounds or marks on paper. It takes no theory to guide our recognition of intentional actions and intentionally created artifacts. We do so all the time; we can recognize intentional activity as intentional prior to and apart from recognizing what the intention may be.

It is important to emphasize, however, right from the start, that a text's need for intentional grounding does not mean that evidence about intentions outside the text of an utterance must play a key epistemic role in literary interpretation. One of the great sources of confusion about this issue is the widely shared assumption that to accept the role of authorial intention would be to undermine the authority of the text as a bearer of the work's meaning in favor of an inaccessible mental construct notionally located in the author's mind. This, however, is hardly the case. The primary role of intentionality in the interpretation of literature is not to provide indirect access to the content of the work, even if seeking external evidence for an author's intention may have value as a last resort. Grasping the content of a literary work depends primarily upon our ability to interpret the linguistic structures of various kinds that compose the work itself in its peculiar context. What the notion of intention underwrites is the status of the text as a linguistic action that will bear interpretation as such and the existence of a proper context for doing so. In effect the author's intention is what the text allows us to infer, knowing that he intended us to recognize it.

This is powerfully brought out in Jorge Luis Borges's great story "The Library of Babel." Borges's imaginary Library is infinite and contains all possible books. It contains your true biography and mine, with the years after the hyphen filled in. It contains the book of all books and the complete history of the library itself. It contains all wisdom. But it also contains books that deny all of the statements in these books, books that are textually one character different from each of these books, two characters different, three characters different, and so on ad infinitum. It contains innumerable books that get your death-year wrong and many that place it before the year you were born. Almost all the books are gibberish.

It is the prodigality and abundance of the Library, ironically, that make it useless. These books could mean anything, and therefore they mean nothing. Meaning, after all, is not only a matter of inclusion but also a matter of exclusion and limit. Without a discernible intention behind any of these books to activate their strings of characters and make them worth thinking about, their relation to meaning must remain merely potential. The characters inside them have not been chosen or arranged by any author and do not bear the weight of a human action. They have no purpose or context. One has no reason to apply to them the search for coherence between belief, desire, and action. This is the point of Borges's brilliant epigraph from Burton's *Melancholy*, "By this art you may contemplate the variations of the 23 letters,"[13] for the entire Library contains no more meaning or value than the alphabet itself, which can also be arranged, by a competent author, to convey any possible message but is itself an inert instrument without an author to wield it. Reading in Borges's Library is impossible precisely because it contains every book and its opposite and everything in between, leaving it all to the reader to choose. The absence of the limit provided by choice is nihilating. To put it another way, in the Library of Babel reading a book would be exactly the same as writing one since you would have to supply all of the meaning yourself; and once you had chosen the sequence of characters that expresses your intended meaning, you would still have the extra and virtually impossible task of finding the volume that contains that sequence. No wonder many denizens of the Library take the extreme measure of eliminating meaningless books in the hope of finding the true ones. Taken to its conclusion, this process would eventually void the Library, exposing its original emptiness. Any books that were left over would have value only because some readers were able to provide an independent endorsement of an utterance composed of the sequence of characters they contain, having compared them with all possible alternatives. Such readers would have become authors.

The brilliant point of Borges' story, then, is the folly of our tendency to reify meaning in language, to see language as holding meaning, as if meaning were a substance that could be deposited in and extracted from a container. Language does not represent complete thoughts or meanings. It provides hints for their reconstruction in a particular context. The history of the Library, as Borges provides it, is the history of cults of the Word, the history of the search for the magical books and the urge to destroy the empty, useless ones in order to isolate the truth, while in fact all the books are empty and useless because without authors they cannot be interpreted as the results of an action which could prompt interpretation. To put this another way, Borges's library contains, in Saussure's terms, *langue* without *parole*, mere potential for meaning based upon past usage. To put *langue* before *parole* is to put language before its users, an unpromising strategy given that *langue* is nothing more than an abstraction from the behavior of those who employ it.

It is worth saying again that one of the reasons this issue has caused such perennial confusion is the ambiguity I mentioned in the notion of intention itself, an ambiguity caused by the asymmetric relationship between actions and intentions. We often form intentions in relation to actions that we have not yet carried out and, indeed, in relation to actions that we will never carry out—either because we were unable to do so, because the expected opportunity never arose, or because our desire never turned into an immediate preference that could motivate us to act on a particular occasion. This makes intentions seem to float free of actions, even though a person with a genuine intention must have some kind of action in mind. When it comes to an existing literary work, however, the action in question has always already taken place. The words have gone forth onto the page, and it is only by assuming that the author wanted to communicate something by them and that he believed the chosen words would accomplish that communication that we can ascribe meaning to them. The distinction between an intentional act of communication and a mere text is not an epistemic but an ontological one. A work is different in kind from a simple text, which on its own has no more value than a random set of marks. A work is a human gesture, not merely done but, as Stanley Cavell puts it, *meant*.[14] In this regard we should recall the full meaning of the word "work"—deliberate, often prolonged effort toward a determined goal. Among literary theorists of recent influence, only Mikhail Bakhtin has emphasized that language is not a mere matter of texts or grammatical sentences but of communicative utterances, spoken or written, involving complex relations of anticipation and response between speakers and audience based on a grasp of the utterer's intention or "speech plan."[15]

Authorial intention, therefore, is necessary to make a text into an act of communication. We can see this simply by recognizing the making of the work as an action. It also helps us to establish the type of work it aspires to be. Fictions, for instance, mimic other, non-fictional forms of discourse in a global way, so for many fictional works there is nothing in the text explicitly to indicate that the story is not meant as literal truth. To take it as fiction we need evidence (not necessarily external evidence) of the author's intention for it to be so. This is why many works of fiction bear the explicit label *A Novel*. It is also important to recognize that there are some elements of a literary work in which we seem to confront the author's hand more directly than others—for instance, when there is a question about which general category or genre a work is meant to fit. Is Defoe's *Shortest Way with Dissenters* satirical or serious? Does he really mean that dissenters should be violently done away with? Merely on the basis of the text, things could go either way. Is *The Turn of the Screw* meant to be a ghost story or a study in psychopathology? The text seems to license globally different interpretations. That in itself might be intentional or it might not. Sometimes we are deliberately left with unresolved alternatives, as at the end of Thomas Pynchon's *The Crying of Lot 49*. In other cases the ambiguity may not have been intentional. Such matters are crucial for our reading of the text. Similarly, when there is the issue of an allusion to another text or a reference to a historical event, something that gestures outside of the text, we have to ask ourselves whether or not the author would have expected us to recognize his intention to make such a reference or even whether he could have been familiar with the source in question. The text alone cannot tell.

It is important, though, not to overemphasize cases of this sort. The distinction between linguistic convention and authorial intention is not typically important for interpreting a literary work. It is mostly when authors fail to express their intentions clearly through literary means, or when they deliberately flout standard assumptions about the status of the work, that we find ourselves wondering if there is any external evidence about what they are up to. The recourse to external evidence is often the symptom of an aesthetic or communicative failure, though at times it can be the symptom of a particular literary strategy, when an author has chosen to be ambiguous. It could have been that Henry James deliberately designed *The Turn of the Screw* so that it could be read either as a ghost story or as a psychological thriller. In that case, to recognize his intention would be to see that either reading can be valid or that undecidability was the very effect James hoped to produce. The issue could only be settled if we had a contemporary record of James' intention, but even that might not be definitive, and there is a real sense in which it would not be desirable. *The experience of and engagement with the text of the work is the literary phenomenon par excellence.* To the extent that the author's intentions perplex us, it is to his chosen words that we should turn for a still deeper effort of questioning. As Cavell puts it, "the correct sense of the question 'Why?' directs you further *into* the work" (227).

THE VARIETIES OF AUTHORIAL INTENTION

As we have seen, the intentions behind any human action can be multiple and complexly intertwined and we often do one thing in order to do another. Our intentions can be complexly nested one within the other. I raise my hand at a meeting in order to vote for a certain candidate. I vote for a certain candidate in order to advance a policy. Advancing a policy depends upon voting. Voting depends upon raising my hand. These are intimately related but distinguishable intentions. The more distant ones depend entirely upon the accomplishment of the more immediate ones, and the more distant ones explain why I undertook the immediate ones; it is my desire to advance a certain policy and my belief that voting for a certain candidate will help accomplish that end which explains why I raised my hand when I did. Finally, it is important to see that the multiple intentions invested in a single action can suffer different fates. I may succeed in raising my hand and having my vote recognized, but the same action might fail to elect a candidate or adopt a policy, or it might succeed in all these things but the policy itself might fail. When we say an action succeeded we are almost always isolating particular intentional aspects.

All of this applies to authors and literary works. Authors' communicative actions are the most basic ones—they provide the meaning that comprises the work's information-content and make it a work. The artistic effects created by the work depend upon its communicated meanings. Only by grasping the meanings of the sentences and other semantic units of the work do we experience its artistic qualities; or it may be that we experience its artistic qualities by the way it eludes our search for meaning or balances between possible meanings. Finally, the practical effects of the work—for the artist and his audience—depend upon what is accomplished at these more basic levels. Some of the intentions behind the work can fail while others succeed. Communicative intentions are the easiest to accomplish, practical ones perhaps the most difficult. Saying, making, and doing all come together in the "structured hierarchy of intentions" which is the creation of a literary work.[16]

Applied to literature, this scheme of explanation is not as neat as my example of hand-raising/vote/policy would suggest. The communicative element of the work, which is its most basic, may not disappear entirely into its practical intentions the way raising my hand disappears into the act of voting, which explains it completely; and the practical aspects of the author's accomplishment, though in a sense the most distant from the original action, may not explain so comprehensively what happens at the earlier levels, especially the artistic one. Still, it is crucial to distinguish communicative intentions from the practical and artistic ones that motivate them because it is easy to make the mistake of thinking that if the author's intentions govern the meanings embedded in the work, this gives him the same authority about the effects that derive from those meanings at the more distant levels. But this is not at all the case. Intentions at these different levels are realized in different ways and cannot be equated. They can succeed and fail independently. The fact that the communicative meanings of the work are determined by the author's intentions does not mean that we are obliged to understand or assess the artistic or practical effects the artist brings about by means of his communicative action the way the author intended. Authors have authority over the meanings of their words because their words have value only when connected to the author's intention. But the value of the work as a work and as a human action, its success or failure, is no more determined by the agent-speaker's mere intent than the value of any other human action. In fact, as we shall see, the possibility of artistic failure is essential to artistic value.

For our purposes, the key fact that sets communicative intentions apart from the other kinds of intentions, practical and artistic, is that communicative intentions have a simple, fixed criterion of success. All that communicative intentions require is that a competent reader be able to recognize what they are. If you recognize what I intend by each of the sentences in this book, getting their drift in the light of the whole, my communicative intentions have succeeded. To the extent that you do not, I have failed.

Of course I would like to achieve more than merely have you grasp what I am saying. I would like to convince you with my words, or at least have you gain insight or find value in them, but that is a different matter; that requires more than simple uptake on your part. In fact, your very recognition of my intention to convince you may be counterproductive; it may cause you to resist and make my intention more difficult to fulfill. Not so with my communicative intentions. It is those which license you to bother trying to figure out what I mean in the first place. The same is true of literary works. If the reader can understand the sentences of a literary work in their local context, the symbolic dimensions of the work, and what the point of the whole roughly seems to be, then the author's communicative intentions have succeeded. The work itself is nothing more than the aggregate of these communicative intentions, though grasping all of them may not be possible given the complexity of literary works and the fact that ambiguity is a key artistic resource. But once the reader has understood the communicative intentions of the work, its artistic qualities become accessible to her, and she is free to respond to and evaluate them according to her own lights. This way of putting it, of course, sounds artificial because in practice understanding and experiencing the work are not temporally distinct processes. They happen concurrently. Still, they are clearly separate processes with separate ends. A literary work can be a complete success from a communicative point of view; we may know just what it was the artist was trying to convey with every sentence; yet the work may leave us completely disengaged. In this respect literature is no different from speech genres like the joke, which have both a communicative and an aesthetic purpose. Jokes can fail because we don't get them or because even when we do get them they fail to be funny. Mere recognition of the joker's intention is enough for success on the first level, but the second level requires much more.

It is important to recognize that when we talk about the communicative dimension of the work as being its basic level we are not implying that the overall aim of the work is communicative, that its purpose is merely to convey a message. Some literary works have messages but by no means all of them. What they all aim at is to create an experience through the medium of language, and that experience may be enhanced by the work's refusal to communicate as well as by its success in doing so. With nonsense verse and much poetry in the vein of Mallarmé, it is the experience of meaningful*ness* that is aimed at rather than meaning itself. Such verse highlights the separation of artistic and representational intentions in a manner akin to Duchamp's readymades. The communicative dimension of a work is also de-emphasized in highly stereotyped genres like the *carpe diem* poem, which depend not upon the value of what is being said but the manner of its expression.

At the opposite extreme from communicative intentions are the *practical intentions* that motivate the composition of literary works. By definition they seek some impact on the author's condition or the condition of the world around him that goes beyond the simple recognition of meaning by the reader. Authors compose with various egoistic or idealistic ambitions in mind: to impress others, give them pleasure, earn a living, gain status, sexual opportunities, the power to influence opinion, change the world, or keep the world the same. And, of course, they may compose just for the sake of it. Such practical intentions may have ethical significance. They may affect our attitude toward the author as a moral being and color our experience of the work. But they do not affect its meaning. Rather, they derive from its meaning and entirely depend on it. For this reason, though practical intentions are often of concern to biographers, they do not pose a theoretical problem regarding authorial intention. Few would imagine that the practical intentions behind a work must be intelligible in the work itself. There may be some practical intentions that are common to most dedicated authors—the intention, for instance, to achieve or sustain recognition—but even these may not be present in every case. Further, unlike meaning, the practical intentions embodied in a literary work can change. An author can undertake a work with one goal in mind, continue it for the sake of another, finish it in the hope of a third, and shelve it in despair of them all. None of this would affect its meaning as a work. They are not intrinsic to the activity itself. Knowledge of the artist's ulterior motives may affect our attitude toward the work. We may be deeply interested in the broad ethical significance of its creation. But these are not typically conveyed by the work itself.

Authors' *artistic intentions* are located in a zone somewhere between the communicative and the generally practical. By artistic intentions I mean the authors' attempts to provide a valuable reading experience by creating literary effects—to move, amuse, perplex, inspire, instruct, or infuriate the reader, using all means at hand—verbal skill, mastery of structure, imagery, metaphor, narrative forms and genres, or the flouting of any of these. We recognize artistic intentions in each and every particle of a work's construction—each choice of words, each decision to put this scene in front of that one, to describe one aspect of a story in detail and gloss over another, to treat one subject in heroic stanzas and another in blank verse. In all of these we can discern the author's desire to create a certain effect or set of effects and a belief in the efficacy of the means chosen, suggesting a rational fit between belief, desire, and action.

As I have mentioned, artistic intentions, like practical ones, differ from communicative intentions in that they do not succeed merely in being recognized by the reader; for artistic success, more than proper understanding is required. Obviously I can see that a poet is trying to move me deeply with a certain line at the end of a poem and yet it can fail to move me. There is so much more to artistic achievement than mere communication. Artistic intentions are like practical intentions in that they do depend upon the success of the communicative intentions which constitute the work, but they differ from practical intentions in being confined to what is visible in the work itself. Artistic activity, then, can be considered a subsphere of practical activity, but one that is internal to the fabric of the work.

Not only is it insufficient for the realization of an artistic intention that it be recognized by the reader; it is actually *not required* for the realization of an artistic intention that it be consciously recognized by the reader. The reader must be able to recognize that he is reading a work of art, but there is no necessary connection between understanding an author's literary techniques and being affected by them the way the author intended. A child, for instance, watching *King Lear*, can recognize that the action of the play is frightening, beautiful, and deeply sad, yet have little conception of how Shakespeare achieves these effects or even the genre he is working in.

This is not to say, of course, that the craft of a work cannot become part of its meaning. There is a dialogue of craft among artists, a competitive display of skill and technique, that is obviously intentional and can become part of a work's meaning. And the artistic features of one work may be highly relevant to the meaning as well as to the artistic features of another. Virgil's *Aeneid*, for example, is a grand reworking of Homer; it is not only an adaptation but a genuine interpretation of the *Iliad* and the *Odyssey*. In such a case the concept of allusion, or even "intertextuality," fails to suggest the broad structural and semantic relevance one work may bear to another. Artistic choices also bear meaning, of course, by the way they depart from previous ones. The decision to write in free verse in the nineteenth century was, as the name suggests, a means of revolt from tradition. In poetry, the abandonment of punctuation, the fragmenting of the sentence, and typographical innovations signal the reader that old literary habits are being discarded and new ones put in play.

The distinction between communicative and artistic intentions can at times become a subtle and perhaps not entirely pure one, and this is also true of the distinction between artistic and practical intentions. After all, the purpose of artistic choices is to produce an effective work, one that moves or shocks or amuses the reader in a certain way. It might seem, therefore, to be eminently practical. It seems preferable, however, to preserve the distinction between artistic effects, which are part of experience of the work, and practical ones, which are not. The moving, shocking, or amusing aspects of a work seem to belong to the work itself, even if they do not exist for all members of the audience. Appreciating them is directly connected with the value of the work as a work, whereas the practical aspects of a literary work exist primarily for the author.

THE "INTENTIONAL FALLACY"

Having established the distinctions between communicative, artistic, and practical intentions—the varieties of authorial intention highlighted in my title—let us turn to the famous article by William Wimsatt and Monroe Beardsley, "The Intentional Fallacy" (1946), which conjured up the venerable taboo against "intentionalism."[17] The subject of the article is the interpretation of poems, but its conclusions have been applied to literature quite generally. The first thing to be noted is that it focuses almost entirely upon artistic rather than communicative intentions and that it begins by locating these entirely in the mind of the author. "Intention is design or plan in the author's mind" (201). The authors take the "designing intellect" to be indisputably the cause of the poem, but this does not mean, they argue, that the author's design or intention provides a standard by which the poem is to be judged. In fact the separation between the intention and the poem seems to be rather complete. The article's next claim, however, qualifies matters. "If the poet succeeded in [realizing his intention], then the poem itself shows what he was trying to do. And if the poet did not succeed, then the poem is not adequate evidence, and the critic must go outside the poem for evidence of an intention that did not become effective in the poem" (202). Clearly Wimsatt and Beardsley do not deny that the author's intention can be found in the poem. It is, in fact, responsible for its design. What they deny is the relevance of authorial intention if it cannot be found in the poem. Thus their axiom number three: "It is only because an artifact works that we can infer the intention of an artificer" (202).

This is a perfectly sensible view even though it is expressed in a way susceptible to misunderstanding. It recognizes that authors are responsible for the design of their poems and that successful intentions inhere in the poems themselves in the sense that they can be inferred by qualified readers. So far so good. Nor is there reason to disagree with Wimsatt and Beardsley's contention that readers have the right to judge the poems by their own lights, regardless of what the author intended. It is also easy to endorse the essential point that it is not the author's psychology that is the object of the critic's concern but the poem as it exists on the page. It was only in the still partially Romantic and biographically obsessed culture of the 1940s that this argument could have seemed radical, and it is unlikely to have sparked perennial discussion had the article been titled "The Psychological Fallacy" or the "Biographical Fallacy," or had the authors borrowed C. S. Lewis's less successful coinage, "the Personal Heresy."[18] The choice of the phrase "Intentional Fallacy," however, was the article's most decisive gesture because it neatly and perhaps inadvertently implied that an author's relation to the *communicative* intentions embedded in the text are as loose as his relation to its *artistic* designs. This, as we have seen, cannot be true. It makes perfect sense to say about a poem that we recognize the author's artistic intentions but they fail. It does not make sense to say we recognize his communicative intentions but they fail; all that is necessary for the success of an author's communicative intentions is that we are able to recognize what they are.

Even in its treatment of artistic intentions, though, "The Intentional Fallacy" tends toward hyperbole. One of its key statements is that "the design or intention of the author is neither available nor desirable as a standard for judging the success of a work of literary art" (201). Reading this, it is easy to forget that Wimsatt and Beardsley do believe that the author's design usually is available by inference from the work itself. We might add that some works include an attempt to articulate it there explicitly. And it is also important to remember that while the reader is not necessarily obliged to evaluate the work by how well it carries out the author's design, that design might very well turn out to be quite desirable as a standard for judging the work; in fact, it usually does turn out to be the very one that most readers will decide to adopt, and they may adopt it partly because it belonged to the author. Wimsatt and Beardsley are so eager to exclude authorial considerations that they make the author seem like an intruder in the work.

"The Intentional Fallacy" had a number of other implications we should now be able to resist. One is the sense that intention typically takes the form of future planning. Their term "design" suggests an architect's fully worked out and conscious preparation for the erection of a building, but as we have seen, intentions need not precede an action and are not necessarily deliberate and self-conscious. Wimsatt and Beardsley also treat the intentions embodied in a work as if they were singular. In fact a literary work, we have seen, like most actions, is typically the product of a complex nexus of intentions. Again the emphasis upon variety is crucial. From the text of *Paradise Lost*, and without reading Milton's mail, we can infer quite a number of intentions in addition to the meanings of the sentences: to write an epic poem; advance Christianity; espouse an idiosyncratic version of it; dramatize the consequences of the Fall; portray love, ambition, pride, and vengeance; show the capabilities of blank verse; win fame and recognition for the author; and do all of this by creating a valuable reading experience for the audience, the one intention that literary authors have in common. Many of these intentions can succeed or fail independently of each other, and it is up to each of Milton's readers to judge and balance their relevance and importance. Milton's intentions were anything but single or simple.

These misunderstandings about intentionality are significant, but the most unfortunate legacy of Wimsatt and Beardsley's essay remains its failure to distinguish between communicative and artistic intentions. They see that "practical messages" succeed (communicatively) "if and only if we correctly infer the intention" (202), but they do not see that a message need not be practical to have a communicative character and be subject to the same communicative conditions of success. Not all poems, of course, have a communicative character; some use the instrument of language without making an actual utterance. But most poems do, and when they do, the utterance succeeds if and only if we can correctly infer what it is. Whether or not they succeed or fail in practical or artistic terms remains an open question, but as for communicative success, the author's intention has a special relevance. Authors sometimes fail to say just what they mean, so utterance meaning and speaker meaning are not absolutely indistinguishable; they remain usefully distinct concepts. But the occasional failure of communication stands out against the broad background of success. *Because Wimsatt and Beardsley did not distinguish correctly between different kinds of intention, the useful caution they fostered about the psychologizing of literary criticism became an obstacle blocking the necessary reference to authorial intentions in interpreting the language of the work.*

Wimsatt and Beardsley's failure to make a clear distinction between communicative and artistic interests is not all that surprising. It was not until the late 1960s that Paul Grice fleshed out his seminal account of intentionality in language, and only in 1962 would the publication of J. L. Austin's book *How to Do Things with Words* challenge the tendency to think of utterances as functioning primarily to make statements, a view that makes communicative utterances seem unsuited to the purposes of art. Critics of the mid-century, especially the New Critics, tended to think they needed a special theory of literary language to account for the fact that literature does something other than make statements, that its characteristic irony and ambiguity turn inward rather than outward and provide a counterweight to the practical language of science and business. This idealization of literary language, with its obvious professional motives, is one of the enduring reasons for the appeal of the textual fallacy. It ignores the expressive and dialogic character of everyday language and the variety of things we do with it.

Having removed the author and his intentions from the text, it was then necessary for Wimsatt and Beardsley to reanimate the text with a new dramatic character, the poetic speaker. This led to the reinforcement, and even tightening, of another already existing New Critical restriction—that poems should never be thought of as personal or general expression. "Even a short lyric poem is dramatic, the response of a speaker (no matter how abstractly conceived) to a situation (no matter how universalized). We ought to impute the thoughts and attitudes of the poem immediately to the dramatic *speaker*, and if to the author at all, only by an act of biographical inference" (202). The parenthetical phrases—"no matter how abstractly conceived," "no matter how universalized"—betray the authors' awareness that their claim very much goes against appearances. Nevertheless, just about all scholars of literature now teach their students to talk about poems as having speakers distinct from the author even in cases where there is no inferable dramatic situation, where the speaker has no distinguishable character, and where the author seems to be talking in his own voice. They do so, strange to say, even when the poem does not seem to make a coherent utterance at all. To complete the dramatic scenario built around the poem, Reuben Brower, one of the most influential of the New Critics, added to the poetic speaker an imaginary audience to be addressed. The conversion of lyric into dramatic monologue was complete. The entire situation of the author and his audience had been displaced from its original domain and made internal to the work.

The appeal to the dramatic aspect of poetry was a useful corrective to the nineteenth-century tendency, crystallized in the essays of the young John Stuart Mill, to see all poetry—even narrative poetry—as soliloquy, "overheard" rather than heard. The dramatic monologues of Tennyson and Browning were a contemporary reaction against this aspect of Romanticism, and Browning's dramatic mode was to exert a lasting influence.[19] Nevertheless there are poems that have no dramatic quality or suggest no speaker other than the author, even if it is the author in a particular mood or circumstance. Poems can make general statements without irony. The notion that they do not do such things is a disguised wish rather than a plausible claim. On the other hand, examples of "absolute poetry" and nonsense poetry may not constitute an utterance at all. The a priori requirement that a poem must be dramatic can only distract us from the task of determining how to read a particular poem.[20] (I shall return to the topic of poetic speakers in Chapter 4.)

One final observation needs to be made about "The Intentional Fallacy." Perhaps its chief concern was to discourage readers from appealing to evidence outside the poem. Even the identification of allusions seemed troubling to the authors, who suggest that the notes to *The Waste Land* should be considered part of the poem itself rather than external evidence. Wimsatt and Beardsley do not sufficiently acknowledge that external evidence can help readers discover meaning *in the text* that they would otherwise miss. This is particularly obvious when we are dealing with ancient texts, where both words and the things they describe can so radically depart from what we know. Here the failure to recognize a poem's communicative dimension is damaging. Further, the authors' failure to recognize the complexity of literary utterance keeps them from acknowledging another point, that knowing what the author intended but *failed* to say in one passage or section of a work may be a better help in understanding what he does say in other sections than knowing what he actually wrote. If we have external evidence to prove that Dante inadvertently misled his readers about what he was trying to say in one canto of the *Inferno*, it might be more helpful for readers of the *Paradiso* to take the canto in *Inferno* as Dante *intended* it to be understood rather than relying upon what he actually wrote because in writing the later part of the poem Dante would have been trying to preserve consistency with what he believed he had said earlier.

In order to see that recourse to external evidence for the meaning of a poem is not always unhelpful, consider W. H. Auden's poem "This Lunar Beauty," which seems to be about the virginal perfection of the moon, "complete and early," considered in its own beauty, so different from the inconstant and vulnerable state of its human lovers. The moon is featureless and changeless, unhaunted by the ghosts of desire, time, and change that trouble human beings. The final stanza is perplexing, though.

> But this was never
> A ghost's endeavor
> Nor finished this
> Was ghost at ease;
> And till it pass
> Love shall not near
> The sweetness here
> Nor sorrow take
> His endless look.[21]

Love has to wait till after the moon has passed—bringing the cover of darkness?—before it can near its own sweetness, which also brings sorrow's "endless look." What is this "sweetness" and what does sorrow "take" with "his endless look"? And why is sorrow explicitly male (*"his* endless look")? All of these questions are difficult to answer, though perhaps no more difficult than the questions posed by many of Auden's early poems, depending as they do upon a fragile, cryptic suggestiveness of imagery and mood.

Interpreting the poem becomes considerably easier, however, and considerably richer, when we learn from Edward Mendelson that this poem has a hidden context which cannot be guessed from the text.[22] It was written in 1930 at the beginning of Auden's days as a schoolmaster, and its subject is not the moon but the innocent, "lunar" beauty of Auden's young boy students. Mendelson takes the vision of childhood presented here to be a vision of Wordsworthian natural goodness, but the poem seems to focus not so much on the moral goodness of the child as on the moving beauty of untouched youth in the eye of the observer who is acutely aware that the child's innocence will not last, that it will soon be haunted by the ghosts of time and desire that belong to the adult world. Time, change, history, and lovers are all things that will come later, bringing sweetness but also sorrow's "endless look," a sorrow which is the inevitable companion of mortal pleasures. These pleasures are now pointedly identified as male. As Mendelson points out, Auden returned to this subject later in the thirties in "Schoolchildren," where he casts doubt on the innocence of schoolboys. Confined in the prison of a childhood they are too weak to resist, their perfection is "slightly awkward," as if already self-conscious. "The professor's dream [of their innocence] is not true."[23]

Only by setting this poem in its biographical context can we identify its intended subject and connect it persuasively with the wider themes of Auden's oeuvre, but there is no reason to apologize for doing do. Once we know what Auden is really talking about, the poem makes a good deal more sense than it did before; it becomes a richer and better poem, one more plausible for Auden to have written. The biographical key to the poem is not valuable because it leads us deeper into Auden's private consciousness. It is valuable because it makes the poem publicly accessible. It enables us to make the inferences that constitute the poem.

It is not hard to see why Auden didn't want everyone to understand this poem. It took considerable skill and contrivance to construct a poem that could properly be read as referring to the moon as well as to adolescent boys, but Auden was able to anticipate the inferences that would be made both by readers who had the key and by readers who didn't. We have here an almost Blakean contrast between innocence and experience, each producing its own reading of the work. What is not so clear, though, is whether the reading from experience leaves the reading from innocence intact. It seems to me that the well-informed Auden reader will see the sexual reading of the poem as mostly overriding the merely lunar one.

The lesson of this example is not a new or surprising one but it is worth stating—that any evidence, even personal evidence, that brings us closer to the communicative intentions of the author as they are embodied in the actual poem will legitimately help us understand it.

Interpretation and Ordinary Speech

Now that we have sketched the roles of intention in interpreting everyday behavior and the multiple kinds of intention involved in interpreting a literary work, let us deepen our perspective by examining how language works in everyday conversation, the domain linguists call "pragmatics." Literature, and especially modern literature, cultivates complexity and ambiguity, and ambiguity is clearly a resource that can enhance the effectiveness of a literary work. Things are different, though, when we are talking about ordinary communication. There we are interested primarily in finding out what the other person is trying to say, and ambiguity is a mark either of the breakdown of communication or the uncooperativeness of one of the parties. Still, it is important to see the continuities with as well as the differences between the reading of literature and the situation of ordinary speech. Whether the utterer is aiming at complex literary ambiguity or at conversational clarity, communication involves guesswork. The speaker or author makes a guess as to how the intended audience will interpret the words being spoken, and the audience recognizes the speaker's intention to communicate by means of these words and guesses about what the speaker expects it to understand by them. Anticipation works from both sides, and because both sides are aiming at convergence upon a single meaning or a finite set of meanings, they largely succeed. The interplay of anticipations might seem to threaten a vicious regress—*my* guess about *your* guess about *my* guess about *your* guess *ad infinitum*. The fact, however, that the speaker has been able to make an utterance in the first place, rather than stalling in hypothetical anticipation, guarantees that the anticipated process of interpretation will also be limited. And after a certain point, further levels of metaconsciousness beyond the speaker's and listener's awareness of each other's intentions add nothing new to the context. The listener applies to the speaker's words her notion of what context the speaker is assuming she will apply; the speaker anticipates the listener's guess about what the context will be and tries to satisfy it. Each recognizes the other's intent to communicate and the other's recognition of it. If the utterance is successful, the anticipations more or less converge. But uncertainty cannot be entirely removed; especially in literature, a knack for calculated uncertainty is part of the author's skill and the ability to appreciate it is part of the reader's sophistication and pleasure.

If this way of understanding communication applies as well to literature as it does to ordinary conversation, then clearly both are collaborative enterprises. Just as the interpreter of an utterance cannot do without the conception of an author to guarantee the communicative value of the utterance, the maker of the utterance cannot do without an anticipation of how the target audience will interpret it. Communication is like lightning. It cannot travel without being grounded in its target. This is not to say, of course, that we are conscious of our audience every time we form a sentence. With our default audience, which is often indistinguishable from ourselves, this is rarely necessary. The synaptic lightning is automatic. The moment we conceive ourselves as addressing a special audience, however—an audience of children, for example, or a hostile one that might twist our words—we do become conscious of the audience's particular characteristics and take them into account. And as listeners, when we recognize that we are not the target audience an utterance was originally made for, we are obliged to reconstruct what that audience would have had in mind.

Because intention doesn't necessarily imply forethought, the use of words such as "guess" and "anticipate" to convey the inherent uncertainty of linguistic communication is slightly misleading. They make it sound like the intention must be formed before the utterance itself is made. But the "guesswork" element isn't grounded in the temporal priority of utterance over interpretation. It derives from the fact that the speaker must rely upon the imagined competence of the audience. For his intention to be effective, the audience must be able to recognize that the utterance is intentional, that is it meant to be recognized as such, and that certain inferences properly follow based on its explicit content in context. We can imagine authors sometimes puzzling over whether or not readers will be able to make the leaps of inference or association their flights of fancy require. We can especially imagine poets caught between the sound of a phrase and the true rightness of its meaning and weighing what the audience will make of it. But this is by no means the default situation.

In spite of the considerable literature on reader response, the notion of a linguistic utterance or a literary text as a prompt for interpretation or guided inference on the part of a targeted audience rather than a container of meaning that anyone could extract will seem unfamiliar to literary scholars whose knowledge of linguistics tends to center upon the Saussurean concept of the sign, where a systemically delineated sound or marker, the signifier, is matched up with a systemically delineated content, the signified. This model does not recognize the need for norm-governed inference. Rather, the content of language is modeled as an internal system of differences articulated in the same manner and with the same stroke as the differential system of sounds. The problem with making the system of signifieds (or, we might say, concepts) as arbitrary as the signifiers that convey them, though, is an obvious one, and the structuralist model was so monumentally static that it demanded the deconstructive critique to restore some reasonable sense of the need for pragmatic interpretation.

It is not, however, the instability of the signifying system, as deconstruction would have it, that produces the uncertainties of interpretation, but the fact that there simply is no signifying system in the Saussurean sense. At bottom there are only guesses about guesses; the need for inference is fundamental. The elements of the communicative act that can be described abstractly as a system—the construction of the acoustical register, the lexicon of already existing meanings, and the syntactical permutations of the sentence—form only a part of the basis for communication. Guesswork, uncertainty, and the intuitive application of a norm of rational fitness are ineliminable. The speaker anticipates; the audience reconstructs that anticipation, looking for a fit between motives and performance. Even when we are writing for ourselves, as in a diary, we must distinguish ourselves as writers from ourselves as future readers and do everything we can to anticipate how, in the indefinite future, when memory has dimmed, we will construe the words we are choosing now. We can talk to ourselves as ourselves, without fear of misunderstanding even if we say the wrong thing, but when we are writing, we are always writing for someone else, even if the person we are writing for is only our self looking backward from the future. Things would be different only for a diarist who intended never to return and reread, who was writing just for the experience of the process. Aside from the manual activity, such writing would be no different from mere thinking or talking to oneself, and if a diarist of this kind slipped and wrote the wrong word, there would be no need to go back and fix it because the thought in the present would not have been affected and the word would have no future. Such a diary would not be communicative at all.[24]

It is important to emphasize that literary intentionality is richly layered, that a text has the potential for many levels of semantic investment and that these are bound to differ in their degree of explicitness. Communicative intentions occupy the same domains and levels as the interpretive activity of the reader, and the reader's confidence of interpretation naturally varies with the degree of explicitness of the author's practice. The layering of the text is easiest to envision from the reader's point of view. In order to construe a text as a literary work, the reader must first confront it as a sequence of sentences or sentence fragments. On the level of the sentence, even in literary works, we often enjoy that instantaneous, nearly instinctive grasp of meaning that typifies everyday conversation. Regarding the higher levels of organization that engage literary understanding—symbolic motifs, numerological schemes, patterns of allusion, and so on—the reader's interpretive confidence will naturally be weaker than the confidence with which she interprets the surface content of sentences. Recognition of the genre of the work is usually quite secure, though it may be less so in cases of mixed genres or when the genre is deflected in some way from its usual stance. But with symbols and allusions we are often putting ourselves consciously into the position of the author, trying to puzzle out whether or not he would have thought we would be likely to find a certain implication or allusion salient and clear enough to be recognized as intentional. Thematic interpretation is often still more speculative. And when it comes to the import of the work as a whole, the interpretive process can become even more difficult and tenuous—and therefore, paradoxically, more rich. Rather than a simple, unified, or straightforward message, what literary works tend to have is a distinctively blended tonality, a discernible general note, attitude, or impression. It is typically not in the author's interest to clarify the vision of a work to the maximum extent any more than it is in his interest to provide an authoritative paraphrase. As W. B. Yeats put it, "If an author interprets a poem of his own he limits its suggestibility."[25]

AUTHOR AND TEXT

The view I have been outlining here gives primacy neither to authorial intention nor to the autonomy of the utterance or text nor does it set these things against each other. What it points to is the fact that authors can only communicate what their readers will be able to infer based on the text and whatever knowledge of convention and context they can be expected to have. The author's goal, in other words, is typically to make the text as autonomous, and therefore as comprehensible to the audience, as possible. And the goal of readers is to interpret the text as much in its own terms as possible, since to do so is to give both the author and the text their maximum weight. The role of external sources becomes more important, of course, when the distance between the author's originally intended audience and later readers increases. Later readers may need to examine as many other documents of the time as possible in order to reconstruct what the contemporary audience would have been expected to use as the basis for inference. As historically informed scholars, we take it upon ourselves to reconstruct the contexts that authors took for granted in the minds of the original audience for which their works were intended. The further we get from authors in historical time, the less they are at fault for our need to open their mail. External evidence plays an especially decisive role, for instance, in the interpretation of allusions. As Frank Cioffi puts it, in such cases biographical facts "act as a kind of sieve" to exclude certain possibilities.[26] We can settle, for instance, the question of whether an author could have been referring to another author's work or to a historical event if we can arrive at an accurate dating of the texts.

It is worth mentioning that when we say that authors have a certain meaning in mind for their work, we are not implying that the text can be reduced to a nostrum, that it embodies a single overall message or attitude. Rather, authorial anticipation resides in every semantic element of the text, from the level of the sentence to higher-order symbols and structures to the thrust or direction of the whole. It is readers' meaning that authors are aiming at all the way through, and if they succeed, readers will find it in the text's every layer. Whether these meanings are to be gathered into a single overall message or whether the text aims at its own subversion and dispersal are questions that can only be decided by the reader based upon a reconstruction of the author's expectations. On every level the author's choices guide and constrain the reader to some degree, but that constraint may be the groundwork for calculated ambiguity, uncertainty, open-endedness, or even the simple presentation of words and phrases that do not make a statement.

Matters such as the autonomy of the text or, conversely, its degree of intertextuality, have much to do with the purposes for which individual works have been designed. They cannot be settled a priori. Some authors write with the expectation that readers will know their earlier work. Interpreting the works of prophetic poets such as Blake or Yeats involves giving oneself over to a process of critical thought that runs through their entire oeuvre. To take a small example, when the speaker of "Among School Children" says that he was "never of Ledean kind," we know he is admitting he was never as striking a physical presence as Maud Gonne, whom W. B. Yeats in earlier poems has mythologized as the daughter of Leda, Helen of Troy. Here an earlier poem by Yeats provides a privileged source of meaning for a later one. Many of the greatest literary works were meant to depend crucially on other texts and traditions. How much of *The Faerie Queene* is comprehensible without reference to the *Nicomachean Ethics* or *Paradise Lost* without reference to the Bible, Virgil, and Homer?

Textual autonomy, intertextuality, and degree of determinacy, then, are not properties of literature per se. They are artistic effects, three among many, and their importance must be determined work by work on an empirical and, indeed, historical basis. Paradoxical as it may sound, it is a matter of authorial intention as to how autonomous a work should be. Textual autonomy may or may not be a priority given the author's literary purposes or the literary institution within which he is working. It is not very valuable in satire, for instance, which cannot thrive without a clearly identifiable referent, an object of mock. Allegory cannot function without hidden doctrines, and epic by nature refers to history and memory. Skepticism about authorial intention has tended to obscure the historical dimension of this aspect of literature. For much of the literature of the past, the notion of textual autonomy is simply out of place.

Of course grasping the author's intention does not mean somehow getting in touch with his total psychology in the way envisioned by Romantic expressivists. That is the essence of the "Intentional Fallacy" attacked by Wimsatt and Beardsley and, before them, Eliot and Lewis. The author of a literary work, like other speakers and writers, can only take so much of his knowledge for granted in his audience, and this will not include a complete command of his personal psychology. When he uses the word "brother," for example, he cannot typically assume that the audience will know about his own brother or his relationship with him. In most cases that information will not be in the public domain. If he wants the audience to know about his brother he will have to convey the information to it in terms that will reliably produce the desired understanding. Authors must use the public resources of information and convention if they want to be understood. The authorial self, then, which speaks in the work, is much thinner than the biographical self who writes. It is not unknown, of course, for writers to use words with esoteric or private meaning, and the strategy has a certain aesthetic value, but it can only function against the background of communicative success based on meaning that is inferable from public information.

Another way to make this point is to say that, when the author envisions the reader whose understanding he is attempting to anticipate, he does not envision an individual but an abstraction embodying the common cognitive resources of his audience. And the audience, as the intended destination of the work's meaning, does not engage with the author personally except insofar as the author has made himself publicly known. The fact that the author cannot count on more than his audience knows is also a feature of conversational speech. Even there it is not the Cartesian substance of the author's mind, whatever that would mean, which expresses itself in chosen words, gathering together all of its past experience and projecting its hopes and dreams into the future. The person who speaks does so on a particular occasion with the resources of a particular audience in mind, speaking words that would have been differently chosen for different ears at another time. The process depends upon publicly shared resources and powers of inference. Compared to ordinary speech, literature may be more deeply expressive of an author's point of view because it has been constructed at greater pains for a more general audience and a more enduring occasion. To be a speaker on most ordinary occasions may be a thinner and shallower role than being an author, but the difference is a matter of degree.

It is also striking that literary characters sometimes seem to have as rich an interiority as real people even though in fact they have none—they are speakers only in the second order, imaginary beings uttering words to an audience of equally imaginary beings. There is no better way of establishing the fact that communication, the basis for artistic making, is an affair of inference and anticipation, not the sharing of private psychological states. We are able to imagine in everyday life what it would mean if so-and-so said such-and-such to so-and-so, and this same power of nested and embedded levels of intention is richly exploited in literature. And in reading works of literature we can interpret the meanings intended by the characters and read between the lines to grasp the author's own communicative intentions. The power to project imaginary utterances in imaginary contexts is an essential aspect of imagination.

The marginal character of authorial psychology hardly means that authors are of no interest. We cannot overlook the fact that there is a grand industry surrounding the lives of the artists, devoted to confronting the work with the life or, in the worst case, reducing the work to the life. Biographers pose potentially interesting questions that can be objectively answered, questions such as why particular authors chose the artistic means or held the views they did. The answers to such questions may alter a work's impact for us and change our assessment of its importance, sometimes for the better and sometimes for the worse. But they do not illuminate the meaning of the work, its informational content, unless they help us grasp the tacit understanding that the artist and his audience shared at a particular time and that contributed to the intelligibility of the author's words in the first place.

The key point is that communication is a public process and authors must constantly put themselves in the position that will be occupied by the expected listener or audience. This is a way of extending and deepening the common observation that artists must transcend a narrowly egoistical perspective in the process of creation in order to make the work attractive to the audience. The ability to do so is not only a condition for artistic success; it is essential to the communicative process per se. The process of artistic composition can be usefully envisioned as an oscillating movement between an "I" that fantasizes and creates and an internal critic that evaluates and shapes that creation according to his conception of the audience, what it will understand and respond to.[27] Here it may be useful to recall the distinction made by philosophers of science between the context of discovery and the context of justification. The discovery of scientific theories can be an activity as creative and unpredictable as the invention of literary works. It can involve hunches, aesthetic preferences, flashes of insight in the shower, personal animus against other scientists and their views, and even revelatory dreams. In the process of discovery, anything goes. Once the theory has arrived, though, it has to be justified, and that means giving it precise expression and imagining how it can be defended and tested to satisfy the scientific public. Literary creation has the same double aspect, of creation and evaluation. Both are going on all the time. However freewheeling the creative process, there must also be an evaluative consciousness that operates as a constraint (except, perhaps, for surrealists who hope to evade the censorship of conscious evaluation altogether). Just as the scientist has the process of justification in mind as the theory develops and is revised, so the artist has the audience's interpretations and responses in mind as the work develops and is revised.

The two aspects of creation, the generative and the critical, need not be consciously separate in the author's mind since, for many artists, the standpoint of the audience may be virtually indistinguishable from their own. It is probably fair to say about artists what we said for conversational speakers, that their default audience is indistinguishable from themselves. And even when authors are imagining a non-default audience, the conception of the audience will be only one factor in the process of composition. From a psychological point of view, the most important aspect of the creative process will be the author's task of discovering the substance of the work and choosing the words that will convey it. In that task the response of the audience functions as a constraint, and as with the constraints that govern all types of human performance, the accomplished practitioner obeys them for the most part subconsciously and often finds them enabling when he needs to think about them.

Some readers may fear that the notion of authorial intention limits the sources of a text to the products of consciousness, but this also need not be the case. As in so many areas of life, artists have a skill in accomplishing their purposes that goes beyond what they can explicitly articulate or consciously control. Nevertheless, once the work is complete, they must evaluate it from the point of view of its intended audience in order to gauge its fitness for its chosen purpose. They evaluate it as a whole and from a public point of view. Like God at the creation, they look upon their works to see if they are good, or at least good enough to be understood and appreciated.[28]

It is worth repeating that to recognize that the author is the original source of meaning for the text is not to ignore the fact that once the work has been issued, or indeed in the very process of its issuing, it is subject to intentional reframing by all kinds of intermediaries—editors, advertisers, anthologists, marketers, reviewers, librarians, book club jurors, reading group organizers, government censors, Christmas givers, and, last but not least, college and university course instructors whose activities collectively produce "the canon."[29] Among these influences we should include the way later works of literature reframe earlier ones and the way the extra-literary activities of the authors themselves contribute to their reception. Such reframing alters the way readers interpret works and affects how they value them, and their impact is an important subject of scholarship. But there is no reason to think of reception-history, which studies how works are actually interpreted by historically situated readers, as a competitor to the literary scholarship which studies their production. The task of the latter is to scrape away the overlay of intentional representations to reveal the original work; the task of the latter is to give full due to the historical experience of reading.

To sum up this discussion, I would like to enlist the eloquence of Roland Barthes, though stating a point of view quite opposite from mine. "A text is made of multiple writings," he explains, "drawn from many cultures and entering into mutual relations of dialogue, parody, contestation, but there is one place where this multiplicity is focused and that place is the reader, not, as was hitherto said, the author. The reader is the space on which all the quotations that make up a writing are inscribed without any of them being lost; a text's unity lies not in its origin but in its destination. Yet this destination cannot any longer be personal: the reader is without history, biography, psychology; he is simply that *someone* who holds together in a single field all the traces by which the written text is constituted."[30] Barthes is getting something very right when he says that "a text's unity lies not in its origin but in its destination" and that it is upon the reader that the meaning of the text is "focused." He is right, furthermore, to insist that this reader is not a single person with a concrete identity; actual readers are multiple. What he is missing, however, exploiting the vagueness of the passive voice, is that it is the author who does the focusing. The author focuses upon the reader, not typically with an individual but with a general conception of his audience, and readers focus upon the author's conception of the reader, an operation that is psychologically invisible in default situations but conscious when the author is historically remote. The anticipatory relation between the two sides is mutual, but for neither side is it personal in the full sense; both authors and readers are "without biography." But Barthes goes too far when he says that the reader is "without history [and] psychology." The author's conception of his reader will naturally be historically and psychologically specific and rich. It will provide important evidence for the decipherment of any work. Without the specification of an author, the conception of the reader is so indefinite as to be useless.

Meaning and Impact

At this juncture it is likely that my reader will be entertaining an obvious and important objection. If the structure of anticipation about the original audience's interpretation is fixed in the author's mind at the time of the work's creation, it follows that it cannot change. A work is, on this account, a single, complex utterance with a determinate range of meanings, a fixed quantity of information. This conflicts with our sense that the meaning of works of art can indeed change radically over time, that they have an inexhaustible quality, and that what they meant for their original authors was very different from what they mean for us. The conflict, however, is only apparent. Here I am going to introduce a distinction close to one made by E. D. Hirsch which has not had the influence it should—the distinction between *meaning* and *impact*. I begin with a real-world example. In 1953 millions of people across the globe heard a version of the sentence "Stalin is dead." As an utterance in context, all of them understood its meaning in precisely the same way; it contained the information that the body of the Soviet leader had permanently ceased to function. But its impact was various. For many, the world's greatest man had died; for many others, the worst. Literary works make their impact upon us in many different ways, all of them distinct from the way such factual statements as "Stalin is dead" do. But the distinction between meaning and impact remains. The information contained in the original utterance is limited and fixed, however much differing points of view may affect our reactions to it and however much those reactions may change with time.[31]

I have already observed that once a work survives the original audience for which it was written, a gap begins to open which it is our task as historical readers to close as much as we can in the hope of being able to get as near as possible to the author's intention. Now we can see that the passage of time opens another gap, the one that exists between the impact the work exerted upon its original hearers and its impact upon ourselves. To discover meaning, we look backward to the original scene of utterance; to discover impact, we look forward from that utterance as far as to the present day, often with the awareness of many intervening readers. The impact of a work might already have been multiple for its original audience and is not in control of the author or governed by his intention as is the case with the meaning of the work. It is, of course, of great interest to understand what impact the author hoped his work would have, and this is typically derivable at least in part from its intended meanings. But the creation of a literary work is like the performance of any other human action; its consequences may either exceed or fall far short of what the agent was aiming at, and, as with many truly important historical actions, its impact may never be fully accountable. The farther we get from actions in historical terms the clearer this becomes.

Stalin's survivors differed in their reactions to the news of his death because they had different interests and attitudes toward him, and such differences can indeed determine the impact of a literary work. Wealthy Victorian businessmen could not be expected to react in the same way to Dickens' *Hard Times* as literate working men because of the very different ways they are portrayed in the book. The presence of such differences in interest is what has led many critics to argue that only the test of time will establish the literary quality of a work—the test of time argument being based on the notion that we are not truly interested in works that owe their impact to transient factors. But differences of interest are only one of the factors that affect the impact of a literary work. They are as numerous and various as the ones that can inflect any human relation. Differences of culture and technological development play their role, and differences of intellectual opinion are often primary. Dante's *Commedia* cannot have the same impact for me that it had for a medieval Catholic who shared his religious and political opinions. This does not mean that it does not have a great and powerful impact, but the intervening centuries have left their mark. This would be true even if I happened to be a medievalistic Catholic of a later day. And of course there were many living Italians upon whom the work would have had a very powerful impact but one that was very much not what Dante would have hoped because they did not share his views or allegiances.

We have to stretch our powers of imagination to envision all the factors that can determine our relations to a literary work and affect the impact it has on us. It is not only changes in thinking that separate us from literary works of the past but changes in all the ways we can relate to their original production. When the *Iliad* was first sung, it was one epic poem among others, perhaps one of many that a particular poet, rendering a long tradition, had the capacity to sing on a particular occasion or set of occasions. It provided a magnificent evocation of events from a world that was already lost. At some point, let us guess, it was written down by a scribe and eventually, packaged together with the *Odyssey,* it became one of two surviving archaic Greek epics, replacing all others and outlasting the culture whose character it originally expressed. So one person's rendition of the story became one of two remnants of a long tradition. Possession of the *Iliad* fell to the rhapsode, an actor reciting from memory. For the Greeks of the classical period, the *Iliad*, together with the *Odyssey*, became a kind of encyclopedia, the canonical source of information about the Olympian gods and everything distinctively Greek. It then survived the Olympians to be taken over by worshippers of new gods who used it for new purposes. Imitations transformed it into the canonical example of a literary genre. In our century, more than two and a half millennia after its original invention, the *Iliad* appears in literature classes among the monuments of other past cultures—a great range of fixed, untouchable, ever-receding peaks. In order to do it justice, we must attempt to grasp the contingent quality it had in the minds of those original listeners for whom it was neither monumental nor inevitable but only one particular, fragile, and surprising expression of what its maker and his audience shared. And in order to grasp the historical impact of the *Iliad*, we have to recover all of the contexts through which it passed on its way to us, all of the roles it may have played, and all of the impacts it may have had.

Making a clear distinction between the fixed meaning and the almost infinitely variable impact of literary works brings into focus one of the crucial ironies of literary history, that while time can imperil the intended meaning of a work it can also enhance its impact. The very difficulty of getting back to original meaning makes that meaning seem more precious, and the relative impact of the great works grows ever stronger as they eliminate their rivals, becoming more and more representative of the age in which they were written. Time diminishes the contingency of literary works, enhances their aura of necessity. The farther away in time we get from an author, the less our differences with him seem to be moral or political in character (and so subject to moral or political censure), and the more they seem to be intellectual or cultural (and so less due to the author as an individual). Time contributes, then, to our open-mindedness and to our ability to regard an experience from an artistic point of view. It is in the matter of gauging the work's impact that the most vital cultural mission of criticism comes to the fore. The distinction between meaning and impact parallels from the reader's point of view the distinction between the author's communicative intentions and his practical and artistic intentions. Meaning and communicative intention are fixed within their original context; artistic and practical intentions aim at types of impact that transcend the original context and will be perceived differently by different recipients.[32]

COMMUNICATION AND THE POWERS OF INFERENCE

At this point the kind of action that goes into creating a literary work is becoming clear; like any other action, writing is defined by intention, but an intention of a very specific kind, a communicative intention based on a complex set of anticipations regarding how a particular audience will interpret the verbal performance being offered. The author assumes that this hypothetical audience will possess a general linguistic competence, background knowledge about the world, familiarity with a potentially extensive set of conventions and traditions, and an immediate sense of the context. And the actual audience for the work, its eventual readers, will do their best to reconstruct the author's original conception of his audience and its expectations so that they can play the interpretive role the author had in mind. This role does not by any means exhaust the possibilities of reading, but it is a first step, and without it there would be nothing further for interpretation to work upon.

When we think of a text as the focus of mutual anticipation between author and reader, it should be clear that the reader is an active participant in the process of interpretation, of making the text into a work, and that the text is not a kind of code that can be mechanically deciphered with a key.[33] The only key is the audience's knowledge that the speaker or author believes that the utterance was worth making and that he intends his attempt to communicate to be recognized as such. The same is true in conversation. There are many conversational elements that make the need for inference clear. Irony is an obvious one; an ironic sentence will have a meaning entirely different from its most typical one based upon the hearer's understanding of the speaker's intent. Indirect implications, which philosophers of language call "implicatures," provide another clear example. If you reply to my offer of a cup of tea by saying "Tea gives me a headache," you haven't really answered my question. Instead you've left it up to me to infer that, since we both know headaches are undesirable and you believe drinking a cup of tea will give you one, you don't want any tea.[34] Your indirect answer is actually more informative than a simple "no" would have been because you've suggested the reason why you don't want any tea. Now I know I shouldn't offer you any, not just today but in the future as well. Nevertheless, you left it to me to figure out the point of your reply. Without additional implicit assumptions (for example, that headaches are undesirable and you want avoid them), it is not logically implied by what you said.

The fact that we naturally and intuitively arrive at successful interpretations of other people's utterances, whether they are figurative, ironical, or straightforward, does not mean, of course, that this capacity is easy to explain. Sorting out the precise role of intention and inference in conversation has been a long-running and difficult task for philosophers and linguists. What seems hard to deny, though, is that whenever we recognize that a signal, a sentence, or a text has been constructed with the intent to communicate, we instantaneously seek out the right context in which to interpret it and look to identify an intention that could have made it worth saying. According to the most influential account, proposed by Dan Sperber and Deirdre Wilson, what we do is to maximize its *relevance*, that is to say the difference it makes to our current sense of things (our "cognitive environment"), while at the same time incurring the minimal processing costs.[35] In other words, the speaker attempts to hit upon the most economical way of achieving the desired cognitive effect for the audience, and the audience interprets the speaker's prompt in that light. The very fact that the speaker has bothered to make a statement and have it recognized as intentional conveys the presumption of its value. In most conversation, the convergence of the right interpretation happens instantly. We apply as many contextualizing or interpretive strategies as will make every aspect of the utterance relevant.[36] We seek relevance both in the explicit content of an utterance and in the way it is stated. For instance, if you ask a business owner how much he paid his employees last year, ordinary principles of expressive economy would lead you to expect a round number, perhaps in the thousands. But if you asked Scrooge that question he might answer it down to the shillings and pence. You would find the extra information irrelevant to your question, but you would recognize another relevance for it—that Scrooge is expressing his exasperation at having to pay wages at all. Of course it might also be the case that Scrooge is so obsessed with money that he thinks you would want your answer down to the last penny. In that case you would find that miserliness had altered his sense of relevance for the worse.

I am not implying, of course, that the search for relevance is a conscious one. Most successful utterances bring an interpretation immediately to mind, and the fact that they do so is an assurance that we have understood them as the speaker intended. Subconscious or "subpersonal" processes accomplish the job. Once again, as in the case of "Theory of Mind," it may be that the brain has a dedicated communication module which accomplishes these inferences, but whether or not that is the case, we do accomplish them with a remarkable degree of speed and success.

The theory of relevance provides a general account of communication emphasizing the power of inference even in non-linguistic forms of communication. Sperber and Wilson give the following scenario (abbreviated in my presentation) to suggest how tenuous the relation between sign and inference can be. At a tropical resort, a man standing on the pavement catches the eye of a lightly dressed tourist and glances meaningfully up at the one cloud in the sky. He is indicating that there is a chance it might rain in spite of the sunny day, hinting that the tourist is inadequately dressed. This is a scene whose plausibility we recognize, and it suggests how far our powers of inference can go just by having one element of a situation made more salient by recognizing someone else's intention to make it more salient and guarantee its relevance.[37] I will adapt another example given by Sperber and Wilson (55–56). You and I arrive at the seashore and you inhale with ostentatious pleasure. You are making salient for me the delightfulness of the sea air and the fact that you are delighting in it. Your gesture alters my awareness of the environment in a very slight way. It is what Sperber and Wilson call a "weak implication."[38] But in a sense it offers a very complete interpretation of the situation and expresses a subtle attitude that can be very personal and difficult to put into words. It is a form of showing rather than telling, or even suggesting rather than showing, and therefore germane to the novelist's craft. Fiction writers often show rather than tell using characters' gestures like these, and the importance of such weak implications extends well beyond the literary presentation of characters' behavior. Many aspects of a literary work have this delicate sort of implication, its value depending upon the sharing of sharing. An utterance may be worthwhile not because it tells us something new but because it strengthens belief in the already known or makes it more salient, casts it in a certain light, or simply draws attention to the fact that both the speaker and the listener are aware of it. The cognitive value of much literature has to do less with providing new insight than with reinforcing or shading the already known or signaling that a consensus is self-consciously shared. And so it is with everyday discourse. Hence the relevance of a wink or a raised eyebrow, which do not say anything but seem to ask, "Are you thinking what I'm thinking?" A wink can be a signal of pure relevance, leaving the interpreter to do all the work of inference, or it may cancel the relevance of what's already been said.[39]

It is not easy to grasp how the fact that an act of communication is intentional and mutually recognized as such can endow it with meaning it would not otherwise have, but here is a scenario that makes it clear. It so happens, let us say, that Sherlock Holmes has a distinctive and much valued pipe which has gone missing. Watson has often admired this pipe with conspicuous envy. Could he have taken it? Holmes is having these thoughts while reading a magazine, and he happens to glance at an advertisement illustrating a man smoking a pipe. The pipe is remarkably like his own and the man is remarkably like Watson! For a moment it almost seems as if someone is trying to tell Holmes who has stolen his pipe. But then Holmes reminds himself that this advertisement wasn't directed to him and that the intention behind it was to sell pipes to the general public, not to communicate with anyone in particular, so the resemblance to Watson must be accidental. In the next morning's mail, however, Holmes receives an envelope with no return address containing nothing more than the same advertisement clipped from another copy of the same magazine. *There is Watson smoking Holmes's pipe!* The resemblance to Watson is no longer accidental. Someone is telling Holmes that this image is relevant to him, and he can see why. The ad has not changed in the slightest. As a text it is identical. What has changed is the intention behind it, and this has charged it with new information. Holmes knows that someone wants him to recognize an intention to communicate with him personally through the advertisement and this makes its details informative and relevant, licensing Holmes to draw specific inferences in an expanded context. According to the informant, Watson has stolen Holmes's pipe.

The Holmes example makes it especially clear that recognizing an intention does not mean getting in touch with something private in a person's psychology, something "in the head" rather than out there in the world. Intentions reside neither in the head nor in the text. It is intentional activity per se that is detectable in the message and the fact that this activity has a point which can be predictably arrived at by the recipient. Intentionalists who add an inner, psychological dimension such as an act of "will" to determine the meaning are making a mistake, but so are those who want to deny the relevance of intention on the basis that such an inner psychological dimension is missing. The intention is the goal of interpretation and the message offers the basis for an inference about it. This example also makes it clear that the maker of a message need not be solely responsible for the character of the vehicle that is chosen. The utterance may be constructed entirely of standard usage or it may be significantly novel, including the invention of new words. All that matters is that the meanings are predictably inferable in context. In this case the message maker has chosen a drawing already in general circulation and added to it one more element of chosenness, thus providing a new level of implication and value.

It is sometimes said that, though intention is necessarily present, it has no active role in the process so the appeal to it is therefore redundant: what the interpreter works on is the patterns that become salient in the work in context, so all we need is an expanded sense of context. But without evidence of an intention, there is no definite context. As the Holmes example shows, Holmes can already make the inference suggested by the drawing before he knows it was sent to him, but until he knows the message was actually intended to be read from a Holmesian perspective he cannot take the message seriously. Without an intention behind it, the inference has no value. Of course the message does not tell Holmes everything he wants to know. He's not sure if somebody is telling him the truth or pulling his leg. Finding out more will mean identifying the sender of the message and establishing what he or she knows. Such information will further enrich the context of the original message. But without an identifiable intention there is no definite context and no license to infer one.

Of course there is also more than just meaning even in a message like the one received by Holmes in my imaginary example. It has a recognizable style even though the drawing itself is not original. There are many ways the informant could have transmitted the intended message, and this is one of the wittier ones. And it has an undoubted practical character too, though the full range of purposes the sender had in mind is yet to be determined. All of these are expressive of intention. This is what it means to be able to get in touch with other people's minds and recognize them as agents—not a direct contact with their mental processes but the ability to recognize a projected pattern of inference in a specifically conceived context and to compare the way that pattern was conveyed in contrast with other means that might have been chosen.

THE OPEN TEXTURE OF LANGUAGE

If a physically identical message can have different meanings when used by different speakers or in different contexts, obviously understanding messages involves more than simply decoding them—in other words, more than simply deciphering them character by character from coded into ordinary language. Decoding only leaves you with an original utterance that still has to be interpreted based on its intention in context. The discussion above may have done enough to dissuade the reader from the code theory of communication, but I want to dwell on this point a little longer—to make more vivid just how open-textured language can be, how radically dependent on context it is, and the license that the assumption of relevance provides. Linguists use the term "underdeterminacy" to refer to this aspect of communication, and it exists on more than one level.[40] In terms of simple meaning, the sentences chosen by speakers typically leave a great deal to the listener's interpretation. Such sentences underdetermine what is said. To start with the most obvious elements, pointing words such as *this* and *that, here* and *there,* known as "indexicals," refer to something in the local environment that must be deduced in each case. The same is true of pronouns such as *he* and *she, my* and *your.* Then there are many expressions that contain ambiguous elements. The sentence *Banks can be slippery* would typically express a different proposition when used among financiers or fishermen. The need to assign referents to pronouns and indexicals and to disambiguate slippery phrases is an aspect of underdeterminacy of which we are often quite conscious. Such ambiguities can be the source of wit; after a second car accident with an attractive person, you say "I like you better every time I run into you." Here the ambiguity is exploited for effect. Instead of fixing on one of the possible meanings we experience the unexpected relevance of both.

Other ways in which we complete or tailor the words people say to us are more difficult to spot. You meet a friend on the street and she says, *Have you had lunch?* You do not need to be told that she is talking about lunch *today.* That is part of what she intended, but it is nowhere to be found among her words. You infer it because the alternatives—a question, for instance, that meant *Have you ever had lunch?*—wouldn't be worth asking. Or take this sentence: *I hung up the phone, put on my hat, and left.* Reading it, you will have automatically assumed that the three actions were accomplished in the order mentioned and in close succession, but that is not explicitly stated. It is left for the interpreter to infer—unless the speaker "cancels" it by adding *not in that order.* It is a challenge for logicians that the simple logical operator "and" can add implicit information. Even worse, consider this sentence: *He read the note and gasped.* Here the implication is not only that one event occurred shortly after the other but that the first one caused the second. Again, though, no such fact is stated. All we have is "and" to connect the two verbs. But though the implication is underdetermined by the linguistic content, it is undeniably there for the audience.

If both teams score three goals, the game will end in a tie. This sentence is obviously true if we take it for granted that both teams will score *only* three goals. Strictly speaking, however—speaking more strictly, that is, than we typically do—both teams score three goals in a game that ends five to four, and there is nothing in the conditional clause of the sentence to exclude that possibility. Nevertheless, competent speakers naturally and effortlessly draw the proper conclusion—that both teams scored exactly three goals.

Some of the most interesting examples of our inferential dexterity involve the application of descriptions to objects. When we call a kettle black, for example, do we imply that every part of it is black? Must even the inside be black? Would it be disqualified if the trigger-like part that raises the lid was unpainted? Probably not. But a black veil would have to be all black. Such details are left to the reader's intuitive judgment based on their experience of the world and of language.[41] They constitute part of what is said and understood without being explicit in the sentence.

The underdeterminacy of language is a strong discouragement to the idea that language has a decisive power to determine how we think about the world, since we need to know so much else about the world to grasp what its users are saying. So firmly held, though, is the conviction among literary scholars that language determines our conception of reality that I would like to continue a little further on this underdetermining note. You are at the racetrack and you hear somebody say *My horse won!* In which sense was it *her* horse? Does she own the horse, ride the horse, train the horse, feed the horse? Did she bet on the horse or simply root for the horse without betting, or does she have some other special link to the horse? All this is underdetermined by the linguistic content of the sentence. Words of possession are strangely flexible and open-textured in this way.[42] In order to know what is meant, you need a speaker to provide an intention on a particular occasion, and you need more context than I have provided here.

You go to the butcher's shop to pick up a piece of meat. *It's ready*, you are told. You go home and start cooking it for your friends. When they arrive you tell them to have a seat in the living room because *It's not ready.* But at a certain point you ask them, *Are you ready?* The word *ready* means something very different in each of these cases. When the guests are *ready*, they are neither raw nor cooked. But we would not say that a different word is being used. Instead, words like *ready* need an intention behind them in a particular situation to be meaningful in the strict sense; they need to be uttered in order to activate a definite set of truth conditions for the sentence in which they appear.[43]

Then there is the matter of tone and emphasis. How many different thoughts can be expressed by the three little words *Don't do that* depending on how they are spoken? Readers of poetry are acutely aware of this problem since they have to reconstruct the tone and emphasis of each line based on the words on the page. This is especially important for English poetry given the role that stress plays in determining both English meaning and poetic rhythm. Only after you've interpreted an English poem can you know how it is supposed to sound.

> *Shall* I [or shall I not] compare thee to a summer's day?
> Shall *I* [or shall somebody else] compare thee to a summer's day?
> Shall I compare *thee* [or somebody else] to a summer's day?
> Shall I compare thee to a *summer's* day [or to a day from another season]?
> Shall I compare thee to a summer's *day* [or to a summer's night]?

The correct reading according to my ear is none of these but one that firmly emphasizes *summer's day* together. It is closest in meaning to the first reading given above, but whereas that one, stressing *shall*, poses the question of whether or not to make a comparison at all, stressing *summer's day* asks about its specific qualities as a candidate for comparison with the young man being addressed, ones that in the next line will be found wanting: *Thou art more lovely and more temperate.*

Now consider the verb *open* as used in the following expressions.

> open a jar
> open a door
> open a book
> open a store
> open a wound
> open a gap
> open a meeting
> open a debate
> open a mind[44]

Here *open* acquires a new meaning with every context in which it is used. At what point in the list have we reached the domain of metaphor? Awareness of the general underdetermination of language tends to weaken the distinction between the metaphorical and the literal use of words.

Language neither mirrors the structure of the world nor imposes its own structure. It is extremely malleable to the uses speakers make of it, and in using it speakers take an enormous amount for granted about the world and what their hearers know of it. World determines word at least as much as word determines world. The complaint has often been lodged against structuralism that it cannot cope with language's power of reference because it excludes word–world relations; for the structuralist, the only other of the signified—our repertoire of conceptual distinctions—is the signifier—our repertoire of acoustical distinctions.[45] This complaint misses the much more basic point that without what we know about the world, without the various assumptions our knowledge permits, we would not be able to make sense either of words or of sentences, not to mention each other's actions. Language, after all, does not come to us free of charge. We learn it at great pains. Acquiring a first language is inseparable from learning about the world surrounding us, including how to cope with other users of language. It is a process at once material, intellectual, and social, a triangulation between the way things are, the use of words, and how we relate to others and their speech.[46]

So far I have been stressing how the words that are actually chosen underdetermine what is said, but as we have seen in the example of "Tea gives me a headache," what is said also underdetermines what is actually meant by the speaker—in other words, what is the *point* of the utterance. Here is an example: Professor Wise is at a faculty meeting where Professor Quick has just made an intolerably obvious point which he, Quick, offers as profound. Professor Wise replies, *Yes, and two plus two equals four!* What is explicitly stated here is that Wise agrees with Quick and that *Two plus two equals four*, with the *and* between them suggesting a connection. But obviously the explicit, conventional content of *Two plus two equals four* is not sufficient to convey Wise's point. In fact it is precisely its very lack of relevance that Wise is exploiting in order to imply the irrelevance of Quick's remark. Wise is successfully implying that Quick's statement was no more worth making than a statement of simple arithmetic and that Quick is reducing complex matters to simple formulas. This example shows that not even the statements of simple arithmetic are immune to contextual drift.

Philosophers and linguists disagree about whether underdeterminacy is an essential aspect of language or whether it is only a matter of efficiency and convenience that makes it so pervasive. For our purposes, the key fact is this pervasiveness itself, which makes the need for inference impossible to eliminate from almost all communicative practices. One can hope to remove the need for inference from mathematical expressions and computer languages, and philosophers when they argue do their best to limit the room for readerly inference, but it is truly ubiquitous in ordinary speech and accentuated in verbal art.

The efficiency of our communicative process is most striking when different levels of underdetermination work together. I ask you to play tennis tomorrow. *They're saying rain,* you reply. This extremely terse statement requires a lot of filling in, but I have no difficulty doing it. *They* obviously refers to the weather forecasters, the people who are entitled to a hearing on the subject of rain; you wouldn't quote them if their opinion wasn't valuable. Their *saying rain* doesn't mean they are just saying the word *rain* but that they're saying *It is going to rain,* meaning that rain is going to fall, not just anytime but tomorrow, the time I proposed to play tennis, and not just anywhere but on the tennis court, the place where we usually play. All this is implied by your statement, with the further implication that, because *They're saying rain,* considered alongside a range of other facts, including the facts that tennis is no fun in the rain and that our court is not protected from the rain, we had better not count on playing tennis there tomorrow.

Examples like this throw into relief the extraordinary facility of our interpretive powers. As one linguist puts it, "What kind of inference is so powerful it can provide both the premises and the conclusion of an argument?"[47] In the example above, you, my imaginary tennis-playing interlocutor, gave me no more than a single premise of your argument and left all the other premises and the conclusion to be inferred. In cases like this our capacity for communication displays its remarkable efficiency and power. It can activate vast networks of implication based on the tersest of utterances. Calling the phenomenon *underdeterminacy,* rather than, say, efficiency or inferential power was a rhetorical choice on the part of linguists who were hoping to promote conversational pragmatics as a subject of inquiry. Underdeterminacy comes as a challenge to the traditional priority given by linguists to the fields of syntax and semantics, both of which focus on the sentence rather than the utterance. It is a hallmark of linguistics since Saussure to concentrate on our combinative linguistic competence rather than our use of language as a communicative tool. Calling the communicative incompleteness of sentences "underdeterminacy" emphasizes the inadequacy of semantics and syntax to account for the communicative functioning of language; from the point of view of the strictly verbal content of linguistic behavior, what we make of it in practice is radically underdetermined. But if we look at this phenomenon taking the importance of pragmatics for granted, it is the power and centrality of inference that stands out. Important as they may be, syntax and semantics look like attempts to find relatively local order within a much wider set of conversational phenomena.

Language is so malleable, multiple, and improvisational in use that one can seriously doubt the value of speaking about "a language" in the linguists' sense of a fixed set of codes and conventions. Donald Davidson, making this point in "A Nice Derangement of Epitaphs," observes that we are able to understand people like Sheridan's Mrs. Malaprop even when she is speaking apparent nonsense because we are able to divine her intentions in spite of her lexical eccentricity. What we do is to develop a new lexicon just for her, a "passing theory" of her idiolect based upon our understanding of her intentions in context. Davidson's point is that this is what we are always more or less doing, observing the relations between how the world is, how people talk about it, and how they behave, and looking for the explanatory links between them.[48]

One advantage of the view of language that I am presenting is that it allows us to understand rhetorical tropes, even master literary tropes such as irony and metaphor, in the same terms as we do standard usage.[49] Since the interpretation of utterances constantly requires that we go beyond what is presented to intuit the intention behind it, irony and metaphor are not exceptional or deviant in that regard. Instead, they are salient examples of the generally open texture and flexibility of linguistic intelligence. Scholars of language have typically assumed that we start with a presumption of literalness when we interpret the words of others and that tropes such as irony and metaphor cause us a moment's hesitation while we adjust to the deviation from ordinary usage. But if the theory of relevance is correct, irony and metaphor are as much at home in our usage as words and sentences that have their most common meanings; even those common meanings must be processed for their relevance before we settle upon them as giving adequate point to the utterance.

This sense of the ordinariness of rhetorical figures is deeply antithetical to the intellectual habits of literary scholars.[50] The classical tradition of rhetoric tended to see rhetorical figures as deviations from the literal and ordinary use of language, and in the twentieth century, Russian formalists and New Critics advanced conceptions of literary language that emphasized its difference from ordinary language partly based on its use of tropes. Deconstructionists also distinguished writing sharply from speech. But the identifying mark of so-called literary language, its reliance on various kinds of tropes, turns out to be a perfectly general aspect of communication. Metaphor, irony, and other tropes permeate both writing and speech and exploit the very same capacities as so-called literal usage.[51]

This does not mean, of course, that we process all language in precisely the same way. Even if Sperber and Wilson are right about the way communication works—that it involves an intuitive and automatic trade-off between the cognitive value of an utterance and the effort it takes to process it—obviously there is still a difference between the way we interpret unproblematic sentences and the way we interpret sentences that give us pause because there is more than one plausible interpretation for them in the context where they arise or because they have no obviously economical relevance. In such cases there is need for deliberate sifting and weighing, a conscious attempt to mimic the search for relevance that is usually automatic. The same need will arise when there is conflict between unambiguous sentences and larger units of meaning like the whole work. Our brains seem to be well equipped to find an immediate meaning in "To be or not to be" even though the expression is odd, but when we come to reflect on the mysteries of *Hamlet* as a whole, there is need for conscious judgment. Here enters much of the creativity of the interpretive critic. Let us take a poem by Emily Dickinson as an example:

> There's a certain Slant of light,
> Winter Afternoons—
> That oppresses, like the Heft
> Of Cathedral Tunes—
>
> Heavenly Hurt, it gives us—
> We can find no scar,
> But internal difference,
> Where the Meanings, are—
>
> None may teach it—Any—
> 'Tis the Seal Despair—
> An imperial affliction
> Sent us of the Air—
>
> When it comes, the Landscape listens—
> Shadows—hold their breath—
> When it goes, 'tis like the Distance
> On the look of Death—[52]

Let us pay particular attention to the last stanza. It begins with two brilliant conceits—the landscape that "listens," the shadows that "hold their breath"—and the reader of these words, even though they are fancifully metaphorical, instantly derives their meaning. The speaker's attention is portrayed as entering the landscape penetrated by the "certain slant," endowing it with her focused attentiveness, her sense of dawning mystery. But the next conceit is more elusive. What precisely does it mean that "When it goes 'tis like the Distance/On the look of Death"? What is the "Distance/On the look of Death" actually like? Here the reader has to puzzle out what the author could have meant, still being guided by some idea of her intentions but operating in a much more speculative vein. Certainly the tone remains serious. There is an idea of measuring, a reflectiveness upon one's proximity or distance from Death. Helen Vendler suggests that "when this last light goes, everything sinks into visual unreachability—as if one were to look on the face of a corpse and receive no answering gaze, only 'the look of Death', as the person is in an instant removed to an incalculable distance from life."[53] This is insightful and plausible, but its main effect is to underline how much has been left unsaid and how far we have to reach. Certainly closing on the word "Death" confirms the poem's subject and the theme of stillness. Yet there is a great deal left to be interpreted or divined, and even room for doubt that the poet succeeded in realizing a definite intention—or even that she meant to!

Notice that the trope of the listening landscape is a metaphor, typically thought to be the most deviant of tropes, though here it is instantly graspable, while the second trope, "like the distance," is an example of the homely simile, yet it is relatively obscure. The metaphor/simile distinction is not a strong one. Both are prompts for the same kind of inference. Nor is there room here for a strong distinction between literary and ordinary language. Both of Dickinson's conceits are equally literary and colloquial, just as ordinary language and literature are both permeated with metaphor. And as in ordinary speech so it is with literature: when the relevance of an utterance is unclear we try to broaden or deepen the context in order to guess what it might be.

Another implication of this discussion is that, in communication, as we have seen with action generally, a certain norm of efficiency is always in play, an implicit value judgment about what information would make the speaker's utterance worth making. The audience assumes that the author wouldn't have invested the effort to create every aspect of the message unless it was worthwhile for the reader to decipher it, and the author anticipates that judgment. The author's power to express always depends, then, upon the motivation of a particular audience; the author's style is in a sense the kind of relationship he can establish with the audience.[54] How much explicitness the audience needs will depend upon its sophistication, the amount of energy it is willing to invest in reading, and the richness of conventions shared with the author. The ability of the author to deviate from common information and literary forms is a sign of intimacy, but with literary works, that intimacy often has to be earned at considerable costs. Works for a "fit audience though few" leave more room for interpretation than is found in popular writing. However much uncertainty a literary work may generate, though, the fact that it was produced by an author, that its creation was a human action, means that in principle it is possible to understand.

To see this notion of rationality in action, let us now practice another small exercise in literary interpretation, taking as an example the famous first sentence of Jane Austen's *Pride and Prejudice*, which sets out a certain principle about marriage: "It is a truth universally acknowledged, that a single man in possession of a good fortune, must be in want of a wife."[55] This vertigo-inducing sentence, set in a position of authority at the beginning of a novel, has a surprising and contradictory quality. It is written with aphoristic succinctness and Johnsonian confidence, in an ostentatiously impeccable, educated style, announcing a universally acknowledged truth. At the same time, it is self-evidently false. A single man in possession of a good fortune *may* be in want of a wife, but he does not *have* to be, at least not at the moment. So the form of the sentence and its content are powerfully at odds. Such an injudicious thought cannot belong in the head of a respectable narrator, one who is in the habit of announcing universally acknowledged truths, yet for the moment, not having met any of the novel's characters, we readers have nowhere else to put it. We expect a story to begin with a problem of some sort—a "single man," a "fortune"—but in this case the problem comes to us off-kilter. It seems to be a problem not *in* the narrative but *with* the narrative. We could put the book down right here, concluding that the author is a pompous fool of just the type she actually loved to mock.

Of course we do not do that. When we see the author flouting the norms of common sense and rationality, we give her credit for doing so intentionally and use our own ingenuity to discover a better and more satisfying interpretation. Recognizing that this thought cannot be the author's, we take it lightly and move on to the rest of the chapter looking for an appropriately fatuous source for it. Even if we decide to pause here and take the sentence on its own terms, as its maxim-like character invites, it may well occur to us that certain excuses can be made for this errant principle about marriage. While it may not be true in the real world that a single man in possession of a good fortune must be search of a wife, it most certainly is true in the world of fiction, where few eligible bachelors can go to waste. It will turn out to be true in *Pride and Prejudice*, where Mr. Bingley, the young man soon to be in question, will indeed marry the first lovely woman he sets his eyes on, though not without the requisite complications. With this in mind, we might derive a new understanding of the word "must" as it appears in the first sentence. "Must" means whatever is necessary to make a good story, more particularly a good marriage plot. By gesturing toward the conventions of fiction, Austen might be pulling the ground out from under her imaginary world with the same wry gesture that conjures it up. *I am not going to be telling you about the way things happen in the real world*, she seems to be saying, *because you won't accept them that way. You need to believe in the marriage principle, and consequently I, as a novelist, can't do without it.*

At first glance, then, it might seem that the first sentence is introducing a kind of literary game in which the reader will be invited to recognize the distortions of intelligence imposed by literary conventions and laugh at them. Such diversions played an important part in Austen's artistic development, as reflected in her juvenilia. But here the marriage principle will not be so easily dismissed as a literary convention, for there is a reason that novels, as well as other literary forms, dwell on the complications of love and marriage, which is that readers never cease to be interested in them. So while the marriage principle needs qualifying, it has an undeniable force in the real world. One might even say that for Austen it is true for the most part and therefore close to being "universally acknowledged." As Chapter 2 of the novel continues, we find it "fixed in the minds of the surrounding families," then espoused most vigorously by Mrs. Bennet, a slave to the marriage principle whose fatuous simplicity makes it impossible for her to consider that the world might be anything other than what she wants it to be. Her husband lives on the pleasure of mocking her limited point of view, but he has no genuine means of opposing it, and though he teases his wife and daughters by refusing to open relations with the new arrival, in the next chapter we learn that he has already made the visit which will allow the marriage principle to begin taking effect. His resistance turns out to be nothing more than one of his many diversions—a diversion, if you like, from the more general diversion of the marriage principle itself.

For the reader of *Pride and Prejudice*, this is the first taste of Jane Austen's celebrated irony, an irony that tells us not to be foolish enough to think people's behavior can be predicted a hundred percent of the time but to recognize, nevertheless, that they are comically more predictable than not. Austen's irony thrives in the space between the necessary and the probable. It thus takes into view the predictability of novels, which are only slightly more predictable than human behavior in the round. Judging other people's minds is Austen's primary moral and literary game. To play it with her, we do our best to free her from the taint of literary predictability, finding a way to set her above her characters while holding them up to implicit judgment just as she does. And she anticipates our collaboration and makes good use of it, daring the reader to assign to her the fatuity of her own words. Austen gives us credit for playing the game along with her. Perhaps we may come to feel that in the end she gives in too readily to the literary and social determinism of the marriage principle, that her resistance to it is finally no more trustworthy than Mr. Bennet's. But we do not make this reservation until we have to because there is so much pleasure in the game.

How do we know that these were Jane Austen's intentions, that her attitude toward the marriage principle is the complexly ironic one I have described? Because we have intuitively grasped the standard by which she is operating and in doing so we can make the same judgmental use of it that she does. Not that we could invent the novel ourselves. What we can do, though, is participate in its inventiveness. Austen's writing makes this point more clearly than most because she so deliberately solicits the reader's participation in conscious superiority to characters whose powers of judgment fail. Many chapters later, we need not be told to laugh when, the marriage principle having been ironically vindicated, we hear Mrs. Bennet tell Jane, "I was sure you could not be so beautiful for nothing!"[56]

Our willingness to endorse the interpretation of Austen's novel that gives it maximum relevance and coherence corresponds with our sense that the more remarkable the achievement of the artist the less likely it could have come about by accident. We know that a novel is not a casual construction, that it takes enormous energy and effort to write one and, what is more, considerable energy and effort to read one, so we are unwilling to dismiss the value of the author's effort before we have given her the benefit of every doubt. Only by doing so can we justify the effort we expend in reading it.

By the same token, the fact that authors can expect this degree of charity and suspension of judgment on the part of the reader is what makes their more challenging techniques possible. As with so many displays of skill, it is the success with which authors flout the canons of ordinary practice that excites the audience's keenest appreciation.

It is enlightening in this regard to compare the opening sentence of Austen's novel with Tolstoy's equally famous one from *Anna Karenina*: "All happy families are alike; each unhappy family is unhappy in its own way."[57] To a reader who has just finished *Pride and Prejudice*, this sentence might look like a candidate for irony. Again we have an extremely confident observation couched in such general terms that we are tempted to raise an objection. Can it really be true that *each* unhappy family is unhappy in its own way? Aren't the sources of human misery actually rather common? Could there, in fact, be anything more common than the situation, described in Tolstoy's next paragraph, involving a wife, a husband, and a French governess, which had thrown the Oblonsky household into confusion? There are resources here that could allow us to see Tolstoy as making a comment upon the novelistic game, as we did with Austen. If it were true that all happy families are alike, that would be a good reason for the novelist to pass over them and move briskly on to the unhappy ones, which are bound to be more interesting.

But the manner of Tolstoy's sentence does not support a reading of that sort. His declaration is too straightforward, too wholehearted, and the sequel too serious in spite of what looks like its comic predictability, for us to detach him from his words. They have the ring of self-conscious profundity, a knowingness about the bitter arrangements of human fortune, that sets a tone for the grimness of coming events. If we were looking for mere truthfulness we might be ready to put the book down. We do not, however, because in spite of its empirical shortcomings, this sentence provides implications that are highly relevant and might turn out to be persuasive. It suggests a sad predictability even in the unpredictable realm of unhappiness and sets the stage for a sober examination of human fates. We move on having been warned not to expect too much out of life as it will be portrayed in this book.

The charity we invest in interpreting a novel is only an extension of our approach to all efforts at communication. The moment we recognize the intent to communicate, even with the barest signal like a wink, we instinctively do our best to grasp what made the effort worthwhile. The appeal of communicative value is irrepressible. And it is on the communicative level, not the level of artistic evaluation, that the reader's charity toward the author primarily operates. We do not change the meaning of the text in order to improve it, though we are sometimes tempted in that direction.[58] Our aim is to establish its communicative integrity so as to have the experience it offers. To take a famous example relating to this issue, Sophocles' Antigone, in her final speech, qualifies her commitment to the "unwritten laws" that command her to bury her brother no matter how he died in a way that seems to threaten the coherence of her character and motives. She would not take the same trouble, she admits, over a husband or a son, since one can take another husband and have another son. Thus Antigone's devotion to her ideal of familial piety, hitherto absolute, seems to be modified, tainted with a degree of subjectivity or even arbitrariness, and her conflict with Creon loses some of its principled significance. The play's central character seems to be diminished in her moral majesty by uttering these lines, and Hegel's grand reading of the play as representing the dialectical conflict between the religion of the family and the state no longer has the purchase it did. Goethe and many others have felt the urge to edit these lines from the play in order to restore its coherence, but the fact that Aristotle cited them makes the argument that they are a late interpolation hard to support.[59]

Yet it is not a concern with the play's artistic value that tempts us to edit these lines. It is not that we are willing to put ourselves in the place of Sophocles and say we can improve the play by deleting a speech in which his artistic judgment stumbled. Our urge to delete these lines stems from the fact that they threaten the communicative integrity of the play, its intentional coherence. Sophocles, we feel, could not have meant these lines to have been uttered by the same character who defends her actions only on the basis of an absolute rule. Far from being an artistic principle, the principle of charity in interpretation operates on the more basic, communicative level and comes into effect not when the play disappoints our artistic expectations or contravenes our intellectual preferences but when it frustrates our need for coherence—when we are having trouble understanding it as the coherent action of an author.

"INTERPRETIVE COMMUNITIES"

At this point readers may be wondering where my view of meaning and interpretation departs from that of Stanley Fish as presented in his classic work *Is There a Text in This Class?* since I have been emphasizing the same point he so often does, that chosen words do not adequately constrain meaning apart from the context in which they are stated, a point that Fish acrobatically demonstrates by devising, for even the most seemingly obvious, literal, or normal sentences, another context in which they would have a different but equally obvious, literal, or normal meaning.[60] So a sentence like the one in his title, "Is there a text in this class?", spoken by a student to a teacher at the beginning of the semester, can either mean something like "Will we be using a textbook in this class?" or "Is this one of those classes like Professor Fish's where we're not going to think of there being any such thing as stable texts apart from what we make of them?"[61] Fish's moral is that for people who share the same context or situation, what he calls an "interpretive community," a text can have a meaning that is completely unambiguous, yet its meaning would change radically in the hands of a different interpretive community for whom another unambiguous meaning would become available. So he deduces the folly of locating a fixed or determinate meaning in a mere structure of words apart from the readers who interpret it.

There is something magical about Fish's version of literary inter-pretation, in which indeterminacy reigns but ambiguity vanishes. Textual meaning becomes entirely relative to context. For each context in which a text might be interpreted, the relevant facts that govern the interpretation are constituted by the interpretive method itself. Yet Fish considers this relativity not to be a problem because we are always in some context, some situation. We are never outside an interpretive community, and so it is always perfectly obvious what will count as a correct interpretation and what will not. The contributions of inten-tions, readers, texts, contexts, and their relations to each other are all constituted by the community in the act of interpretation whose success is guaranteed by the like-mindedness of those who share it. For Fish this is a perfectly general fact about linguistic interpretation and about knowledge itself. The assumption behind Fish's point of view is that all interpretive communities are created equal, which means that the interpretive community for which the author created the work has no privileged position over any others that might engage with it. An interpretive community makes the meaning of the text clear and undeniable, but this clarity and force should not be seen as due to the persuasiveness of the interpreter, only as the natural effect of the arbitrary assumptions that constitute the facts of the case for each attempt at interpretation.

Fish would be right that all interpretive communities were created equal if all we wanted from interpretations was a satisfying match between a text and some context in which it could possibly be read. But we want something more. We want our interpretations to be explanatory. We want them to tell us how the text actually acquired the features that it has and what they were intended to mean. To make this point vivid, let us consider an intentional creation less complicated than a text. I am thinking of an everyday object like a screwdriver. It is at home in a fairly wide domain of practice, so wide that it would not be easy to delineate, but let us call it the domain of carpentry. Within carpentry there is a common understanding of a screwdriver's function, which is to drive in screws, another implement familiar in that domain. Screwdrivers have a number of distinctive features: grooved handles that make them easy to rotate; thin, elongated shafts for reaching into tight places; heads fitted to the heads of the screws they are intended to drive. Carpenters developed these feature intentionally, no doubt by gradual adaptation through trial and error, to make the screwdriver suitable to its task. And their suitability for that task explains why the screwdriver has the features that it does.

Now let us, in the manner of Fish, imagine this implement in the hands of a different interpretive community, acquiring new interpretations that would be just as obvious and even satisfying, fitting just as well with the evidence, as the one I've given. For the members of a cargo cult, for instance, a screwdriver might be interpreted as one of the gods' drumsticks, with its features adapted accordingly. Or to Martian archeologists of a distant future, it might be obvious given their assumptions about human life that the screwdriver must have been a weapon of war. Or it could be phallic symbol left over from a fertility ritual. Each of these interpretations might do very well in meeting the facts given the assumptions made, since each of the features I have mentioned would acquire a purpose in the light of the general function of the object being imagined. But in spite of their neat fit between theory and evidence, these interpretations would clearly be wrong. Only the first theory I offered would correctly explain how actual screwdrivers acquired their features, how they function in their domain, and what they mean for the people who use them. Driving in screws was the purpose for which they were intended and the reason why they continued in being. Both cargo cult and Martian interpretations might be reasonable given their assumptions, but their assumptions are incorrect. There is a fact of the matter they are aiming to explain and they get it wrong. All three interpretive communities want to explain the same object in the same way, but only one of them is right about it.

Now it would be open to Fish to say that these different interpretations of a screwdriver aren't really in competition with each other because cargo cult members and Martian archeologists aren't really looking for an explanation of the same kind that we are. But what could this mean except that they wouldn't be looking for an explanation at all? If they are playing a completely different game from ours, that fact casts no light on the one we are playing. To make this move would be to extract these presumably rational creatures from contact with the subject of rational action altogether. (If I seem to have excessive faith in Martian rationality, by the way, keep in mind that these are Martian *archeologists.*) Only by seeing tools like screwdrivers or words as the products of intentional actions can the members of any interpretive community make sense of them. Only in that practice can there be an *interpretive* community at all.

What shall we say, then, to the spectacular exhibits of literary confusion that Fish produces, in which distinguished scholars such as Kathleen Raine and E. D. Hirsch produce diametrically opposite readings of Blake's "The Tyger," one seeing the beast as an incarnation of evil, the other as an incarnation of good?[62] First of all, it is implausible to think of two such professional scholars as occupying different "interpretive communities" when they have very comparable training and the activity they are pursuing has the same explicit goal and takes place in the same institutional context. To do so is to stretch the notion of community beyond recognition. Where Raine and Hirsch differ is not in the context they are coming from but in the context in which they place the poem. It is not *their* context that is the issue; it is *Blake's*. They are aiming at the same context and so, however plausibly they argue, at least one of them, contra Fish, must be wrong. What Fish's example shows is the great difficulty of interpreting Blake, an author steeped in the Bible and its hermeneutic complexities but making idiosyncratic use of them, an author of self-conscious profundity, originality, and elusiveness, far removed even during his lifetime from the largely imaginary community for which he intended his works. Blake was virtually a community of one, and he was not excessively eager to admit readers into his confidence. Rather, he was determined to challenge his readers to struggle with the work. "The Tyger" itself is composed of nothing but a series of questions and, like God's questions to Job, it is not altogether clear that they can or even should be answered.

A glance at the scholarly bibliography on *Oedipus the King* would show that even a much longer and richer work than Blake's lyric can leave critics struggling to establish its point. Does the play dramatize Oedipus's guilt or his innocence? Is it a play of choice or a play of fate? Which of the many Greek conceptions of fate is relevant? The context that would supply answers to these questions has proven extraordinarily difficult to establish.[63] In the face of this situation, E. R. Dodds proposed the rule that things not mentioned in a play should not be evoked to explain it. Instead, we should pay attention to what is actually happening before us.[64] Unfortunately, such a limit is impossible to abide by since the text does not explain itself. Some context for it, some horizon, must be invoked. What seems hard to deny, though, is that Sophocles composed his version of this awesome story with a particular understanding or range of understandings in mind and this is what his interpreters are disagreeing about. The mystery of *Oedipus* perhaps will never be solved, but that is only a symptom of the deliberate elusiveness and indirection of art and the enormous distance in time and culture that separates us from Sophocles. Few literary works produce this degree of disagreement, though, despite Fish's implausible notion that any of them could just in the same way that any phrase can take on a new and obvious meaning in a new context. According to his way of thinking, we should not be surprised to see a perfectly convincing proslavery reading of *Uncle Tom's Cabin*.

Whereas Fish sees the malleability of the text to the interpreter to be a sign of its incurable indeterminacy, it looks to me like a sign of the impossibility of thinking that a text can have a stable meaning without ascription to an author, for once the author is gone the context goes with him and the reader is entirely on her own. Such a move would make all works of literature equally subject to multiple interpretation. "Twinkle, Twinkle Little Star" would become as indeterminate in meaning as "The Tyger," making it impossible to distinguish the prophetic mode of Blake from a nursery rhyme.

Consider the following poem, "The Song of the Old Mother," and, if you familiar with it, try to forget for the moment who wrote it:

> I rise in the dawn, and I kneel and blow
> Till the seed of the fire flicker and glow;
> And then I must scrub and bake and sweep
> Till stars are beginning to blink and peep;
> And the young lie long and dream in their bed
> Of the matching of ribbons for bosom and head,
> And their day goes over in idleness,

And they sigh if the wind but lift a tress:
While I must work because I am old,
And the seed of the fire gets feeble and cold.[65]

The "Song" presents us with a complaint by an old woman who is very much in the position of a servant. (In many contexts the fact that she is called "mother" would not guarantee anything more than her age.) How shall we take her complaint? It could be a mere object of curiosity, a prompt for amusement that such a servant can be given a voice. The language seems post-1700, but perhaps it is a late reflex of that detached observation of the condition of the lower classes which created some of the memorable genre paintings of early modernity, Georges de la Tour's *Hurdy-Gurdy Man*, for example, or Annibale Carracci's *Bean Eater*. Much of the pleasure offered by these images comes from the sense that these lower-class people too can be depicted, their undistinguished or grotesque familiarity can be uncannily reproduced as an aesthetic object. We can even imagine the complaints that govern their existence as part of their curiosity. The painter's expertise extends that far, and so, let us say, with the imagined author of the "Song."

Now let us project the poem forward to the 1910s in Britain. In this context of labor unrest, the suffrage movement, World War I, and the struggles for colonial independence, the woman's complaint, in spite of its confined setting, would be much harder to make into a merely aesthetic feature. Perhaps its intent is genuinely political. Setting it in the Irish context, we might even wonder if the "mother" is a figure of Ireland herself in her long misery and oppression.

In fact the poem was written by W. B. Yeats at an earlier stage, in 1894, and in that context it is meant to engage our sympathies in an imaginative way that is not immediately political even though it does not display the detached curiosity we imagined in our early modern reading. Rather, in Romantic fashion, it evokes a lost, simple world with perennial, elemental cares that trivialize the artificiality of our own. The old woman's sorrows are quaint and beautiful and without political resonance (though we may find political significance in the fact that they are treated this way). This exercise confirms Fish's point that once we have a context the interpretation naturally follows. It also suggest that imagining what a poem would look like in the context of a different age can help us understand its historical specificity, to clarify the differences in attitude that the same creation might evoke at a different time. But in the end, what the poem would have meant in other times and in other voices is not strictly relevant to its meaning, and as far as I know, exercises such as this have never been part of standard critical practice. What we have here is a poem written by Yeats in 1894. We need his identity to fix the poem in a time and place and link it to the interpretive community it was meant for. Without that its meaning would be truly indeterminate.[66]

If, as Fish would have it, the meanings of texts depended entirely upon the assumptions of those who read them, and these assumptions were constantly changing, with no practical criterion for choosing among them, the result would be that the voices of the past, and, indeed, of people other than ourselves and our "interpretive community," would simply cease to exist. What we thought were other people's voices would become nothing more than projections of our own concepts and interests. The possibility of listening to others, of seeing them as they are before we hold them up to criticism, and of having others do the same for us, would disappear. The otherness of others, our otherness from them, would be illusions, the arbitrary creations of a community that cannot itself actually exist because a community implies multiple individuals who are not identical with each other. Fish's interpretive communities permit no distance from their object of study and no internal discord. Meaning is always obvious and nobody can be wrong about it because the community simply constitutes the text's meaning. There is no possibility of misunderstanding the text because there is no possibility of understanding it.

Fish's vision of interpretation suffers the common fate of relativism. He offers the relativity of meaning to the interpretive community as a general truth that governs all communities, showing he cannot keep to his own rules. Further, he confuses difficulty in fact with impossibility in principle. It would be perfectly true to say that we can never know how completely we succeed in bracketing our own assumptions in order to adopt the context in which the original text was framed. We can never be entirely sure that we are close to the original spirit of the work. And this is why different readers come up with different readings based upon different understandings of the context. But this is only to recognize once more that risk and the possibility of failure are inherent to the communicative process. Fish's deepest error is that his description of interpretation deprives it of its goal-directed character. Interpreters necessarily aim at reaching not just any interpretation but a correct one. Without such a goal interpretation could not take place. An interpretive community that took Fish's account seriously would not actually be able to interpret because it would not be able to take any context as more relevant than any other.

Do Films Have Authorial Intentions?

I have often been asked how film fits into my view of intention. Few would contest that films have meaning, but if meaning is derived from authorial intention, where is the author of a film to be located? This question about film evokes a welcome clarification, and it also helps put into perspective a classic debate about the Aristotelian unities in the theater. Neoclassical critics up to the eighteenth century worried that a play whose scenes ranged across time and place would be disorienting to the audience and that such violations of unity constitute an artistic flaw. Had this been a valid concern, film would have taken it to the extreme. Movie viewers are presented with cuts back and forth from one place to another, dizzying montages, switches from black and white to color, moving or even shaking cameras, dream sequences, fantasies, hallucinations, flashbacks in which the same character is represented by a different actor, and every other kind of leap. And this is true not just in so-called "art films" but in popular entertainment as well. Obviously there is no reason to worry about the unities, but why is this? The reason is that films do not disorient us because we do not experience what happens in them as actual events in real time; that would make their phantasmagoria terrifying. Instead, we experience them as a sequence of messages in a medium of communication. Considered as slices of reality, all the things we see on the screen would be susceptible to a virtual infinity of interpretations, but because their construction is intentional, we are not looking for just any empirically plausible interpretation, only the one we are being guided to make. Thus we see in film both the underdeterminacy and the appeal to the audience's capacity for guided inference which we have observed in the verbal domain. No matter what we see in a film, we know it has been chosen for a reason. It obeys the principle of relevance. As introductory courses in film seek to explain, film is a language; the leaps of inferences it allows us to make are just as acrobatic as with the verbal medium.

When it comes to the communicative intentions of the film, the artist we are most primarily relying upon as we watch a film is the editor, though we may never think of her. When we see a character look off into the distance followed by a cut to a landscape, we understand that we are seeing what the character sees. Obviously this connection is not communicated explicitly. In a weak sense it is a convention, but such conventions, like the conventional meanings of words, arise because audiences have been able to make the right inferences in past cases. They are the residues of past communicative success. Guided by the assumption that the film is an intentional product, viewers can arrive at the implications of a bewildering variety of visual and acoustic information.

When it comes to assessing the artistic intentions behind the film, expert viewers are able to make discriminations among the contributions of many different participants—to assess the script, the camerawork, lighting, sets, music, and so on. Almost everyone is inclined to be conscious of the acting. Are all of these elements gathered up into the personal vision of the director just the way the author of a book is responsible for its unity and coherence, as the famous theory of *auteurism* in film would suggest? Or does the finished product emerge from the intersection of many different participants all being guided by a vaguely generic collective design ultimately governed by marketing? These are just two ways of describing the process, and most films will fall somewhere in between. Just where in between is another of those questions that can only be settled case by case. Some of the "great directors"—Hitchcock, Kurosawa, Bergman—have put their names to a large body of work with a distinctive style, which suggests they had some measure of artistic control. But on the whole the desire to make directors into *auteurs* reflects our impulse to personalize collective actions and to see more order and meaning in the world than is really there. Still, despite film's collective nature, interpreting one still means attributing to it a unified intention on the communicative level. Evaluating its artistic character is a different matter.

The Embodiment of Words

Because of the underdeterminacy of language and the constant need for inference I have been describing, it may seem that the integrity of words itself is being lessened. What we used to think of as their literal meaning now appears as nothing more stable or basic than simply the meaning they acquire in their default context, the one that is most common.[67] Even some of the simplest words, like *my* and *ready*, appear to have no predictable meaning until they are uttered in a particular context. As a result, we seem to lose some of our sense of the solidity of words, their palpableness and body, and the fixity of their relation to concepts. Such anxieties are underwritten by the long tradition in Western culture which saw meaning as invested in words before and apart from their communicative use, a tradition that tended to reify words as things with a power of their own.

It is a mistake to think that this tradition regarded words or signs or sounds as having a natural relation to the things they signify; no major philosopher, from Plato and Aristotle forward, held that view, though it is articulated in Plato's *Cratylus*.[68] But it has been part of the tradition to think of words as having a fixed relation to concepts which corresponded with real things. Part of the skeptical appeal of structuralism was its way of decomposing the unity of the word, of seeing both the system of sounds and the system of concepts as being constructed out of difference. In an intellectual environment dominated by the spirit of positivism, with its fear of reification, it was a metaphysical coup to arrive at an ontology composed entirely of differences and relations, with no positive terms. In the French context, the fact that this ontology was generated by a social instrument, language, made it all the more congenial to the optimistic, Durkheimian mindset of Saussure's day. Unfortunately this coup was achieved at the expense of another reification—the reification of language considered apart from its users, the relations of difference for Saussure being generated entirely within language itself and imposing their arbitrary structure upon the world of experience.

The instability and mutability of words can look like a foundational human problem—that our conceptual systems are richer than our linguistic ones, so that words wind up doing double, triple, or multiple duty in the complex and intricate blending of conceptual schemes;[69] but this difficulty arises mostly from the point of view of logicians some of whose tasks would be easier if the components of propositions had stable meanings so they could be predictably combined. From the point of view of the scholar of literature, however, it is here that we can locate some of the richness and suggestiveness, even the mystery, of words when employed by the most skillful artists. Words bring their multiple conceptual histories with them, memories of the many roles they have played, and when we use them in a particular way in the context of a unique utterance, we retain our sense of that history. Their previous uses are *felt*. Words bear the semantic and ethical weight of their typical values, and this weight seems present even in their physical being, for though the relations between sounds and the things they signify is indeed arbitrary, once they have been established, they become deeply integrated with our sensibility. They are no longer arbitrary *for us*. The neurophysiologist Stanislas Dehaene explains that "word meaning seems to be literally embodied in our brain networks. A string of letters only makes sense if it evokes, in a few hundred milliseconds, myriad features dispersed in the sensory, motor, and abstract brain maps for location, number, intention."[70] Take the word "bite," he suggests. "As you remember what it means, your mind briskly evokes the body parts involved: the mouth and teeth, their movements, and perhaps also the pain associated with being bitten. All of these fragments of gesture, motion, and sensation are bound together under the heading 'bite'" (112). This would be true even when you were using the word in a highly metaphorical or non-standard way.

Yuri Lotman once made the suggestion that the task of the verbal artist is to overcome the arbitrariness of the sign, to reconcile word and thing in a poetic effect.[71] This makes it sound like the poet has to start from scratch with a neutral medium that has only to be enhanced. It would be better to say that poetry works with an instrument that is not arbitrary *for those who have been educated in a particular language* and for whom the connections between sounds, thoughts, sensations, and feelings have become habitual and psychologically real. The depth and range of association between the sounds of words and "gesture, motion, and sensation" embodied in the brain give to language its poetic bite, an effect that poets learn to cultivate and enhance. They do not do so, of course, primarily by making up new words for things, or even by using unfamiliar words, but by looking for new combinations of words that evoke the way the world looks and feels. Poetry depends acutely upon a heightened sense of the acoustic value of words carefully patterned. The sensual aspect of our relation to language helps explain that peculiar sense of poetic value we gain in learning the vocabulary of a new language—the experience of new connections between sounds and ideas, a feeling of freedom from the words we know and power in acquiring new ones. In naming the world differently we seem to renew and enhance it.

This is a good place to go back to an issue I raised earlier about the stability in meaning of a text for different contemporary or historically distant observers as opposed to the variable quality of its impact. The worry it raises is, doesn't the meaning of a literary work change if the meanings of its words change, and isn't this a difference of meaning in the proper sense rather than impact? The answer is that, in cases of semantic drift, the communicative intentions invested in the work do not change, but their artistic value can change. Changes of this kind involve what we might call textual luck, a phenomenon analogous to what philosophers call "moral luck." Adam Smith famously pointed out that, though we claim to evaluate actions based on their intentions, our moral judgments are crucially swayed by an action's results. A person who drives negligently, for instance, but does not actually do harm is treated far more leniently than a person who actually kills someone, even if the risks they took were identical. This is an instance of moral luck. It doesn't make sense to judge the two drivers differently because there is no difference in character between them, but we do because one had more luck than the other.

Textual luck is about how the experience of a work changes when its words acquire new meanings apart from the author's intentions. When words change their meanings, the meanings of the utterances that used them are not affected because neither the author nor the original audience would have had these in mind. So as historical readers we do our best to filter out anachronistic readings. This is not only a scholarly or retrospective operation. Filtering out irrelevant meaning is part of just about all linguistic communication. Most of the words we use have multiple meanings, which is to say, multiple typical uses. The more common they are the more meanings and shades of meaning they have, frequently running up into the hundreds as the *Oxford English Dictionary* will testify. To use them in the construction or interpretation of a particular utterance requires hitting upon the meanings that are relevant and excluding the others. This being the case, excluding new, historically emergent meanings that have become attached to the words of an utterance after it was made is just a special case of the more general filtering process.

In works of art, however, there is another dimension that complicates the picture, one that is especially visible in poetry. The communicative dimension of artistic language does not aim to communicate for its own sake but to provide an experience in the reader's construction of meaning, and irrelevant meanings can affect that experience. Words themselves have a character, an emotional resonance, that derives from the full range of their meanings even when not all of those meanings are in play. Hence the emergence of textual luck, the effect on the experience of reading a poem that arises from the later-born meanings of its words. Like most luck, the textual sort can be either good or bad. When Andrew Marvell writes "My vegetable love will grow/Vaster than empires and more slow," neither he nor his audience would have thought of vegetables in our sense, but rather the process of vegetal growth. Nor it is likely they would have wanted to think of vegetables in connection with love. But readers in our modern, democratic, and more privately domestic world do not necessarily mind this association, which they cannot entirely ignore even when they know it isn't relevant. The cosy resonance of modern vegetables may even enhance the effect of the poem. On the other hand, when in his poem "Lapis

Lazuli" W. B. Yeats writes that "Hamlet and Lear are gay," meaning that however deep their sorrows they maintain the eloquence of art and "Do not break up their lines to weep," the modern connotations of "gay" seem intrusive. So with the figurine "Chinamen" climbing the mountain of lapis lazuli described in the last line of the poem—"Their ancient, glittering eyes are gay." This has nothing to do with sexuality, but though we understand what Yeats means by "gay," the overlay of more recent meanings is a distraction and takes effort to filter out. Textual luck has probably enhanced Marvell's poem for some modern readers, and for others it has probably harmed Yeats's.

I have stressed in this chapter the acrobatic process of inference that we use in order to makes sense of both literary language and one another's speech. I do not want to leave the impression, though, that inferences about verbal meaning are the only ones we make as readers of literature. The inferential character of verbal meaning stands alongside the wider set of inferences that make narrative possible. To take an example, consider the way Yeats begins his great poem "Leda and the Swan" with the phrase "A sudden blow" without, except for the title, telling us who dealt this blow or to whom:

> A sudden blow: the great wings beating still
> Above the staggering girl, her thighs caressed
> By the dark webs, her nape caught in his bill,
> He holds her helpless breast upon his breast.[72]

With the powers of inference which are quite normal to us we are able to assemble a terrifying scene out of these paratactic fragments—first the woman's shock, then her frantic resistance, and then the stasis amid the fury at the end of the sentence, when the repetition of the word "breast" brings the action of rape to a pictorial balance, underlined by the rhyme—from "caressed" to "breast" upon "breast." The action is vivid, immediate, and powerful even though our minds have been tasked with the job of envisioning its form. The fact that we are able to construct it from these fragments and suggestions does not mean, of course, that the words are left behind in the act of interpretation. Our experience is not simply of the action itself but of the action envisioned and expressed *this way*, activating our capacities with this level of succinct suggestiveness. We experience the rape of Leda *as* fragmentary, *as* sudden, *as* terrifying and mysterious even while we envision it from an observer's distance. The meaning comes to us with striking economy in the transparency of the artist's intention, but the artistic power of the poem resides not in the recognition of the artist's intentions but of his actual achievement. In that domain intentions are not enough; the poem has to work. It does so by exploiting our inferential and constructive capacities and by exploiting the limits of what we can infer.[73]

This example reminds us that the luck which effects literary reception is by no means limited to semantic drift. Many readers of the early twenty-first century will be less inclined than Yeats' original audience to take his choice of a woman being raped as a symbol of historical violence to be an innocent one, and this may be a source of resistance to the experience of Yeats' poem. Luck, of course, is not an adequate description of such a factor because the cause of the concern is far from accidental.

THE DIFFICULTY AND RICHNESS OF LITERARY LANGUAGE

If, as I have been arguing, there must be an intention behind every meaningful particle of a literary work, how can such works give rise to such a wide range of interpretive difficulties? This is an issue on which theoretical discussions about intentionality have distracted many of us from basic facts. Some of the diversity of interpretation arises from the application of literary theories which treat the texts as objects of suspicious decoding. This is a subject I will take up in Chapter 4. There are, however, more ordinary and obvious reasons why meaning in literary works is difficult to agree about. The first is the genuine difficulty of grasping the immediate or "surface" content. As Martin Heidegger pointed out, we interpret each detail of a work in the light of the whole, which we can only anticipate as we progress through it, and we interpret the whole in the light of each part. The movement from part to whole and back is sometimes called "the hermeneutic circle," with the implication that it may never end.[74] But it does end, at least for an individual reader at a particular time; it ends when the movement ceases to produce further understanding, when all the guesswork that the author has provided for the reader seems, for now, to be done. The process, however, in some cases obviously requires enormous expertise, and however achievable in principle may be the goal of recovering the author's intention, the nature of the process makes agreement difficult to attain. Indeed, understanding the whole and the intention behind the whole will generally be a more difficult accomplishment than understanding the local meanings of each of the parts. Grasping the whole requires literary as well as linguistic competence. And yet, as

Heidegger suggests, a notion of the whole plays a role in the comprehension of each particle of the text's meaning. "What is decisive," he says, "is not to get out of the circle but to get into it in the right way" (195).

Add to this dependence of the part upon the whole the fact that the meaning of every sentence of a literary work is grounded in a wider cultural and literary context. The same, of course, is true of the work considered as a whole—in other words, as a single utterance. Literary works need not have a single meaning but they do tend to have a point; they occupy a place in a conversation that exists outside them, and it takes a fine sense of the historical context to be able to recognize which aspects of the work would have struck its original audience as particularly salient and defining of the author's point of view and which of them would have been common property. To take an example, our reception of Wagner's *Ring* has been enormously colored by the future of the anti-Semitism it expresses and which was quite common at the time, but for its contemporary audience the more salient element was its glorification of sexual freedom.[75]

Adding to the difficulty of literary interpretation is the sheer size and complexity of some literary works, a factor that is hardly ever mentioned in critical discussions of interpretation. Compounding the problem is that, no matter how large it may be, a finished literary work still has the character of a single utterance, and this in some ways limits the degree to which it can serve as a guide to its own total meaning. If I am lecturing in front of an audience I can pause at any point, tell my listeners to forget what they have just heard, and give them a new and better formulation of what I have been trying to say. What I am doing is dividing my lecture into different utterances (or groups of utterances) and setting the later above the earlier in a kind of hierarchy, one speaking about the other. I may continue to do so at a still later point, adding metalevels, canceling and revising as I go. But in a literary work, which comes to us as a single utterance, such cancelation and division into separate utterances is impossible. Canceling gestures can be made inside a literary work, but the canceled materials remain to assert their value, if only as a stepping stone, and the gestures themselves will be subsumed into the hermeneutic process that governs the whole. The work remains a single utterance.

Literary authors can, of course, comment on their works at a later time, making a separate utterance, but the fact that such utterances are not part of the work gives them an entirely different kind of interest, one that, as we have seen, tends to rival or deflate the original utterance that is the work.

Literary structures do, of course, have a hierarchical dimension, so that they seem to comment upon themselves. Rhetorically speaking, certain moments—pre-eminently the beginning, the climax, and the end—have presumptive authority, but the possibilities of irony and playfulness can hardly ever be entirely excluded even there. It is in the nature of literature to be challenging, puzzling, and indirect, to balance parts against each other and against the whole, to flout its own conventions, and to leave much to the reader. Ironically, the very semantic playfulness and richness of literary texts, pushing language often to the brink of sense, contribute to the suspicion of its communicative powers. The effect is enhanced in modern literature, where authors so often aim at suggestiveness, indirection, irony, ambiguity, and even a calculated indeterminacy.

One of the ironies of literary history is that the difficulties of interpretation tend to be in a reciprocal relation to the richness of its possibilities. The history of literature can be thought of as a gradual absorption of interpretive possibilities from other areas of culture—from dream interpretation, for instance, from various kinds of inquiry, and especially from religion. The Hebrew Bible, to take the most obvious example, an anthology of sacred writings in a multitude of literary forms, posed for its readers many interpretive problems—its unity, its employment of tropes, and its internal contradictions just to begin with. Underlying these problems and guaranteeing their solution was the attribution of divine authorship. All of these problems made the work fruitful and productive of multiple interpretations, calling for a *Guide for the Perplexed*. The problem of interpretation became still more acute with the arrival of Christianity and the need to assimilate and reconfigure the Hebrew text so that it would harmonize with the New Testament. Thus arose the complex form of typological allegoresis that characterized the medieval synthesis. The two testaments were joined in a relation of promise and fulfillment, with an internal layering of both based on the scholastic model's four levels of meaning. Once this allegorical machinery had been developed, it could also work upon pagan literary ancestors like Homer and Vergil, who, according to this mode of synthesis, also made their proleptic contribution to the Christian truth. The typological mode was hardly confined to theology. It became invested in everyday life and the ongoing movement of history. Christian revelation looked forward as well as backward. The immediacy of its application was never more apparent than in the upheavals of seventeenth-century England and its colonial offshoot in New England. As long as an interpretive tradition maintains the confidence of its authority, every problem of interpretation becomes an opportunity for the extension of its reach.

The implications of this mode of interpretation for literature were of course profound, Dante's appropriation of it being a particularly crucial and interesting one, the idea of projecting one's own spiritual trajectory onto the cosmos of one's historical moment and endowing the narrative with the multiple levels of the sacred text—to read and to *write* one's own life allegorically as if it were scripture. The result was a brilliant literary version of the psychomachia that Christian moralism makes of the human experience. The *Commedia* thus models a thoroughly open-ended and inexhaustible mode of creativity and interpretation, a form not destabilized by its ambiguities or imperfect verifiability because it aims at something transcendent. Completeness and incompleteness, formal closure and semantic openness, both contribute to its power.

The stripping away of this totalizing mode of hermeneutics was one of the great modern projects but its secularization was another. The very notion of the modern was grounded in the rejection of what came before and the establishment of a new order and direction for history. Where as in Christian allegory the individual soul was re-enacting the cosmic struggle between good and evil, in the modern philosophy of history the individual soul was re-enacting the struggle between its irrational or less rational premodern ancestor and itself. Hegel saw this pattern as an ultimate vindication of religion, which left art behind as a merely symbolic manifestation, yielding in the end to the philosopher's grasp of his own arrival at the end of history and his realization of mind as the substance and agent of its own development. For Freud, on the other hand, the internal struggle of each modern person was to manage the transition from the premodern mode of psychic narcissism, invested in individuals in the pleasure principle, to the modern psyche grounded in the reality principle, and to do so at the least psychological cost. In this version, not mind per se but the scientific mind—indeed, the mind of the psychoanalyst—represents the heroic end state. The analyst's insight allows him to recover the psychic narrative of each patient as he or she attempts to pass through the sexual conflicts of childhood and adolescence without regressing into an illness historically linked to the human past.[76]

Freud's allegorical mode involved, of course, the recovery of mythic structures, especially the myth of Oedipus. In this regard he is an archetypal modernist, refiguring personal experience as the repetition of myth. The notion of the artist as the controller of all myths, the demiurge redivivus, was most fully realized by James Joyce. We can think of him as the person who fully and finally secularized Dante's allegoresis. The *Odyssey* plays a structuring role in *Ulysses*, but the main focus of its semantic fullness is internal. While achieving a remarkable evocation of Joyce's world, the text is self-referential to an extraordinary degree.

My purpose in retracing this history is to observe that, for this long sequence of developments, incompleteness and proliferation were a source of enrichment, not poverty. Difficulty was a benefit, not a drawback, because there was always something more. The final phase shows an ambivalence toward the figure of the author that prefigures later developments. He is the total creator of a world, but that world is so complete that it threatens to eclipse him. His creative gesture does not seem to set him in relation to other human beings. He withdraws, as Joyce's Stephen put it, like God paring his fingernails.

A DIGRESSION ON HUMPTY DUMPTY

If the enrichment of meaning in language is one of the significant directions of literary development, its breakdown and tendency toward nonsense is another. In a memorable episode of literary criticism from Lewis Carroll's *Through the Looking-Glass*, Alice finds herself in the presence of a mysterious book.

> There was a book lying near Alice on the table, and while she sat watching the White King...she turned over the leaves, to find some part that she could read, "—for it's all in some language I don't know," she said to herself.
>   It was like this.
>
> YKCOWREBBAJ
>
> *savor yetis eht dna͵gillirb sawT'*
> *ebaw eht ni elbmig dna eryg diD;*
> *sevogorob eht erew ysmim llA,*
> *ebargtuo shtar emom eht dnA.*
>
> She puzzled over this for some time, but at last a bright thought struck her. "Why, it's a Looking-glass book, of course! And if I hold it up to a glass, the words will all go the right way again."[77]

Like an archeologist confronting the remnants of an unknown script, it takes young Alice only a moment to recognize that she is dealing with the product of an intention in the form of language. Linguistic phenomena—and symbolic phenomena generally—can be identified by the signs that concerted effort has been invested in the making of a relatively orderly and salient but physically not very costly pattern. Of course Alice's best clue is that the characters are printed in a book—a sure sign of symbolic human action—suggesting that they are more than mere decoration. Alice's progress is the typical one; she recognizes the presence of intention, an intention that aims to be recognized, as the basis for discovering what that intention is, and she will always be more certain about the existence of the intention than about its precise character. It must mean something, then, but what?

Set in Alice's mirror, things appear the right way round, but the mirror text is still perplexing. Alice reads:

JABBERWOCKY

'Twas brillig, and the slithy toves
    Did gyre and gimble in the wabe;
All mimsy were the borogoves,
    And the mome raths outgrabe.

"Beware the Jabberwock, my son!
    The jaws that bite, the claws that catch!
Beware the Jubjub bird, and shun
    The frumious Bandersnatch!"

He took his vorpal sword in hand:
    Long time the manxome foe he sought
—So rested he by the Tumtum tree,
    And stood awhile in thought.

And as in uffish thought he stood,
    The Jabberwock, with eyes of flame,
Came whiffling through the tulgey wood,
    And burbled as it came!

One, two! One, two! And through and through
    The vorpal blade went snicker-snack!
He left it dead, and with its head
    He went galumphing back.

"And has thou slain the Jabberwock?
Come to my arms, my beamish boy!
O frabjous day! Callooh! Callay!"
He chortled in his joy.

'Twas brillig, and the slithy toves
Did gyre and gimble in the wabe;
All mimsy were the borogoves,
And the mome raths outgrabe.

"It seems very pretty," she said when she had finished it, "but it's *rather*
hard to understand!" (You see she didn't like to confess, even to herself, that
she couldn't make it out at all.) "Somehow it seems to fill my head with
ideas—only I don't exactly know what they are! However, *somebody* killed
something: that's clear, at any rate—" (114–16)

Alice's confession—that the work fills her head with ideas but she doesn't
"know exactly what they are"—is a beautiful description of the suggestiveness
of literary making and points to my distinction between communicative and
artistic intentions. The elusiveness of the poem's meaning does not detract
from the effectiveness of its artistic design. The reader's engagement with the
poem's meaningfulness provides a carefully contrived experience, and it is this
that makes for its literary character and value. Communication fails here, or
succeeds in a very slanted sort of way, while artistic intention succeeds beyond
measure. The brilliant linguistic surface of "Jabberwocky" achieves a definite
tone and range of suggestion. Its opening stanza, a parody of Anglo-Saxon
written many years before the Alice books were conceived, provides a whimsical, melancholy setting for the story, and the story recedes back into it at the
end. For the most part Carroll uses the standard grammar and syntax of
English but with a bizarrely childish vocabulary partly invented, partly borrowed from German (*brillig*), blended in with childish-sounding English
words such as *galumphing* and *whiffling*, and augmented with onomatopoeia
like *snicker-snack*. It is the familiarity of the story, with its boy hero facing a
world of funny monsters—Jabberwock, Jubjub bird, and Bandersnatch—that
makes it an apt support for the strangeness of the language. The effect is not
vague but vivid, the energetic character of the action rhyming, so to speak,
with the vivid physicality of the words.

Like pure or absolute poetry to which it is akin, nonsense poetry of this
kind depends upon the near-perfect reproducibility of modern printed

books because were any of the unorthodox words to be lost it would be impossible to repair the text based on authorial intention, the author having chosen them for sound rather than for meaning. None of these chosen words could be replaced with just any nonsense, for the pleasure of this poem and its value for the reader rests upon the inspired invention of its vocabulary. Each word is a work of art. The poem is deeply saturated with intentionality because so little of it is dictated by the conventional demands of communication; it is, however, intentionally directed toward artistic—artistically whimsical—rather than communicative ends. "Jabberwocky" perfectly illustrates the way literary works exploit our powers of inference both to provide meaning and to withhold it to the right degree, balancing message and mystery. Intentionalist critics are often thought to be excessively concerned with meaning, but as I hope I have made clear by now, works of art can embody many kinds of intention, not just communicative ones, and artistic intentions can override communicative ones or make them otiose.

Alice, of course, doesn't get this, so her struggles with the meaning of "Jabberwocky" are not over. She wants a clear explication. Later in the book she requests one from the autocratic Humpty Dumpty, who has just been explaining to her the advantages of "un-birthday presents." "There are three hundred and sixty-four days when you might get un-birthday presents—," he tells her, "And only *one* for birthday presents, you know. There's glory for you!"

"I don't know what you mean by 'glory'," Alice said.
Humpty Dumpty smiled contemptuously. "Of course you don't—till I tell you. I meant 'there's a nice knock-down argument for you!'"

"But 'glory' doesn't mean 'a nice knock-down argument'," Alice objected. "When *I* use a word," Humpty Dumpty said, in rather a scornful tone, "it means just what I choose it to mean—neither more nor less."

"The question is," said Alice, "whether you *can* make words mean so many different things."

"The question is," said Humpty Dumpty, "which is to be master—that's all."

This leads to Humpty's hilarious explication of the words in "Jabberwocky." On his account it turns out they are perfectly meaningful, but the meanings are known only to him.

Humpty's theory of language is, of course, absurd. Both he and his theorizing display a whimsical arbitrariness that matches the spirit of the poem itself. Alice's objection, that Humpty is making words mean too many things, isn't quite the right one, though, because words do mean many different things, and audiences typically manage to pick out the relevant ones for the utterance at hand. As we have seen, understanding is as much a process of eliminating meanings as it is discovering them, a point neglected by those who see authorial intention as an unnecessary limit upon meaning. Meanings, to be worthwhile, have to be limited. The trouble with Humpty's theory of linguistic mastery is that the meanings he ascribes to words are private, and there is no way for his interlocutors to infer them from the context. He does not see that meaning is communicative and public in nature.

Humpty is a crank, but he is not completely mad. When he explains his meanings they do become accessible because once the act of choice that connects a meaning with a word becomes public it can be the basis of real communication. Now that we know "glory" means "a nice, knock-down argument" we can use it in our own triumphs. Even more to the point, one of Humpty's own coinages, *portmanteau word*, has, based on his explanation, become a standard linguistic term for words formed by the blending of two existing ones. And the currency of "chortled," based merely on its undefined use in "Jabberwocky," shows how new words can emerge merely from their successful use in a context that allows their meaning to be inferred even when based on no prior acquaintance.

I have often stressed that authors need not be conscious of what they are doing when they anticipate the inferences made by their audience, but also that this is not true when the audience lacks the capacities we normally expect—when it is, for instance, an audience of children. When addressing children one does have to consciously consider what they are likely to know. The *Alice* books are notable in the history of children's literature for the way they enter into the child's perspective without moralizing or condescension, and their success with Victorian children suggests that Carroll excelled in anticipating how actual children would understand and respond to them. The difference between the adult reader's and Alice's perspective in *Through the Looking-Glass* is that adults are able to recognize—and enjoy—arbitrariness, silliness, and nonsense when they see them, whereas Alice tries to take them seriously. She is looking for logic where there is none. And this is where she is closest to Carroll the logician, for logicians and children do have something in common. The logician's art is to avoid the shortcuts, imprecisions, and inconsistencies of ordinary language, to eliminate the kinds of roughly guided inferences that we have seen to permeate both ordinary and literary language in order to arrive at what Frege called the "laws of truth." In a less systematic way, children also take things literally. They look for more logic than is there in human language and behavior. They must take pains to acquire the experience which will allow them to convert the exiguous cues provided by words into correct inferences, and one of their difficulties in doing this is that adults constantly disguise the illogic, arbitrariness, and deceptiveness of their behavior with the appearance of reason. The *Alice* books show adult readers the madness and arbitrariness of their own world—its illogic, willfulness, and plenitude of nonsense—and they show us how fully we have accommodated ourselves to it. Thus we take pleasure in the truth of its strangeness. We regain contact with the innocence of childhood and some of its terrors as well as with the venturesomeness of children who can experience the strangeness of Wonderland as fun and the absurdities of the mirror world as something to adapt to. Alice's dreams present us with a world in which language and communication go astray, and this is what gives them their supreme literary quality, for the artistic value of literature depends upon its ability to exploit the limits as well as the powers of language. Indeed these two things are really the same.

One of Carroll's best critics has argued that language in the looking-glass world conforms more rigidly to logic than in our world and that, "by being more logical, it *seems* more true."[78] In fact, the language in the looking-glass world, considered merely as language, is just as little governed by mere logic as in our world. The difference is that the characters behind the looking-glass always take the logical ambiguity or indeterminacy of words in an absurd direction, ignoring the principle of relevance. Either they are being arbitrary and sophistical or they are talking the way you talk when you are assuming a contextual world completely different from one we can recognize—usually a sign of insanity. Take the phrase "every other day" in the famous dictum of the White Queen, elicited when Alice tries to refuse her offer of jam.

> "It's very good jam," said the Queen.
> "Well, I don't want any to-*day*, at any rate."
>
> "You couldn't have it if you *did* want it," the Queen said. "The rule is, jam to-morrow and jam yesterday—but never jam *to*-day."
>
> "It *must* come sometimes to 'jam to-day'," Alice objected.
>
> "No, it can't," said the Queen. "It's jam every *other* day: to-day isn't any *other* day, you know." (147–48)

"Every other day" could mean every *second* day, which is how Alice takes it, or every day *but today*, which is how the Queen means it. The Queen's meaning is just as logical as Alice's if you happen to be living in the looking-glass; if you are at home in such a counterworld, the White Queen's rule may be valid and communicable. But in our world no one, logician or otherwise, would be able to infer the Queen's meaning without her absurd explanation; and even when we understand it the queen's explanation comes off as a ridiculous piece of sophistry, if not a product of insanity. The lesson is that we are relying on a lot more than language and logic to make sense of each other. We are relying upon a shared world. Only knowing what is plausible and relevant allows us to pick out what is valuable from the farrago of possible meanings for our words.

Alice and Humpty nicely represent two opposite extremes in their approach to language. One sees meaning as arbitrary and imposed by the user based on mere private fancy. The other expects objective precision and logic where they cannot and should not be found. The adult middle ground is to recognize that communicative language involves a myriad of inferential leaps that turn a logician's world comically upside down and that writers love nothing more than to exploit.

CONCLUSION

Up to this point I have tried to show intention to be definitive of human action, how it is essential to understanding human behavior, communication of every kind, and verbal communication in particular. To think of a work of literature as a mere text is to overlook the massive underdeterminacy of the language that constitutes it. When words are considered apart from a particular occasion of use, they have so many possible meanings as to be effectively useless. We need the recognition of an intention in order to guarantee their relevance, allowing us to use our remarkable powers of inference to narrow down the meanings of the author's words, fill them out, and derive their unstated implications. Only because they have been chosen by an author are they worth our attention and effort. We do not always interpret them successfully or completely. The more esoteric or remote in time, the more we need scholarship to help us establish the proper context and background.

The creation of a work of art is a nexus of complexly interwoven intentions of different kinds, and these different kinds of intention crucially have different conditions of satisfaction. The communicative intentions that underlie an artistic work succeed simply if the reader is able to recognize what they are, motivated by the knowledge that they were intended to be recognized. These intentions effectively constitute the work. They also allow us to distinguish it as a work of art and to establish the text itself in the presence of multiple manuscripts or readings. The artistic and practical aims of the author succeed or fail on the basis of what is communicated by the work, but the author is always aiming at something beyond mere communication. He is at least trying either to provide a valuable experience or to instruct the reader in a way that goes beyond the simple transfer of information. Many works aim to do both, delight and instruct. An understanding of what ulterior purposes the author was aiming at in the production of his work can be interesting and valuable, but it is not definitive in the way that a knowledge of his communicative intentions is definitive for the work's meaning. The author's intentions constitute the meaning of the work but not its impact or value. The impact of a work, like that of any other linguistic act, depends upon the position of the observer and is subject to change, but the communicative intentions are fixed in the act itself. We may never be able to understand it fully, and even the author himself, in the moment of composition, might not be able fully to specify all of the background he was taking for granted. Nevertheless there is a stability of meaning here that allows us to gauge the way the multiple and changing world responds to the original act.

My discussion of language as it appears in literary works has strongly undermined one of the ways that literary critics have often defined the literary—with reference to a specifically literary language, with its peculiar reliance upon tropes such as irony and metaphor. Such tropes and the kinds of inference they require are no less common in ordinary language than in literature. Literature is special not on account of the instrument it uses but upon the uses to which that instrument is put. It is the presence of the artistic dimension itself that defines the literary, while the communicative level of intention is what literature shares with all other forms of language. The distinctiveness of literature is not so much a matter of meaning as it is of value, a theme to which I will return in Chapter 5.

NOTES

1. Alexander Rosenberg, *The Philosophy of Social Science*, 3rd ed. (Boulder, CO: Westview Press, 2008), 31.
2. For a long time philosophers largely derived the concept of intention from the way we make sense of other people's speech and behavior, applying Davidsonian "principles of charity" or Daniel Dennett's "intentional

stance," but in the last decade there has been a resurgence of interest in the direct, first-person experience of our own intentionality, which arguably does not require inference. See, for example, Uriah Kriegel, *The Sources of Intentionality* (New York: Oxford University Press, 2011).

3. My example may suggest the Humean picture that desires provide the ends which reason, the "slave of the passions," seeks to implement, but the account I have given does not necessarily exclude the Kantian view that beliefs may incite the desire that leads to action. See Allen Wood, *Kant's Ethical Thought* (New York: Cambridge University Press, 1999), 29.

4. Daniel Paul Schreber, *A Memoir of My Nervous Illness*, trans. Ida MacAlpine and Richard A. Hunter (London: Wm. Dawson and Sons Ltd., 1955).

5. The economist's interpretive model for the behavior of corporate bodies and individuals, which renders beliefs and desires as "preferences" and "expectations," does tend to assume that the agent is substantively rational, and it is vulnerable to skepticism on that account.

6. In order to understand other people, we also have to assume that their beliefs correspond to a significant extent with our own. As Donald Davidson has argued, only against a background of largely shared beliefs can we make sense of behavior based on assumptions we do not See "On the Very Idea of a Conceptual Scheme," in *Inquiries into Truth and Interpretation* (Oxford: Oxford University Press, 1984), chapter 13.

7. For example, P. M. Churchland, "Eliminative Materialism and the Propositional Attitudes," *Journal of Philosophy* 78 (1981): 67–90.

8. Graham T. Allison and Philip Zelikow, *Essence of Decision: Explaining the Cuban Missile Crisis* (New York: Longman, 1999). Along the same lines, Ronald Dworkin, in *Law's Empire* (Cambridge, MA: Harvard University Press, 1986), makes a powerful case that we can make sense of the way the law functions as an institution in a particular community only by endowing it with the integrity, the striving for coherence, that belongs to persons.

9. See Michael Bratman, *Intention, Plans, and Practical Reason* (Cambridge, MA: Harvard University Press, 1987). Bratman would replace the focus on beliefs and desires with a more unified concept of planning. For a helpful synthesis in the context of aesthetics, see Paisley Livingston, *Art and Intention: A Philosophical Study* (New York: Oxford University Press, 2005), chapter 1.

10. Simon Baron-Cohen, *Mindblindness: An Essay on Autism and Theory of Mind* (Cambridge, MA: MIT Press, 1995).

11. Kim Sterelny, *Thought in a Hostile World: The Evolution of Human Cognition* (Malden MA: Blackwell Publishers, 2003), chapter 11.

12. See David Buller's strictures on theory of mind in *Adapting Minds: Evolutionary Psychology and the Persistent Quest for Human Nature* (Cambridge, MA: MIT Press, 2006), 190–95.

13. Jorge Luis Borges, *Labyrinths: Selected Stories and Other Writings*, ed. Donald A. Yates and James E. Irby (New York: New Directions, 1962), 51.
14. Stanley Cavell, *Must We Mean What We Say? A Book of Essays* (New York: Cambridge University Press, 1976), 227–28.
15. M. M. Bakhtin, *Speech Genres and Other Late Essays*, trans. by Vern W. McGee, ed. by Caryl Emerson and Michail Holquist (Austin, TX: University of Texas Press, 1986), 77.
16. As Donald Davidson observes, the "structured hierarchy of intentions" embodied in a single sentence has often been overlooked in discussions of literary intentionality (176). See *Truth, Language, and History* (New York: Oxford University Press, 2005), 176.
17. Wimsatt, William and Monroe C. Beardsley, "The Intentional Fallacy," in Virginia Jackson and Yopie Prins, eds., *The Lyric Theory Reader: A Critical Anthology* (Baltimore, MD: Johns Hopkins University Press, 2014), 201–10. It is worth remembering that, along with their attack on intentions, Wimsatt and Beardsley erected a second taboo, against the critical appeal to a work's effect upon readers, which they labeled "The Affective Fallacy." This taboo was also effective but has long been dispelled.
18. C. S. Lewis and E. M. W. Tillyard, *The Personal Heresy: A Controversy* (New York: Oxford University Press, 1939).
19. See Herbert E. Tucker, "Dramatic Monologue and the Overhearing of Lyric" (1985), in *The Lyric Theory Reader*, 144–56.
20. T. S. Eliot attempts to counter this attitude in "The Three Voices of Poetry." See Jackson and Prins, *The Lyric Theory Reader*, 192–200. This anthology provides rich sources and a running commentary on the lyricization and de-lyricization of poetry. Regarding the nature of the lyric speaker, see especially Jonathan Culler, "Lyric, History, and Genre" (2009), 63–76.
21. W. H. Auden, *The English Auden: Poems, Essays, and Dramatic Writings, 1927–1939*, ed. Edward Mendelson (New York: Random House, 1977), 52.
22. Edward Mendelson, *Early Auden* (Boston, MA: Faber and Faber, 1981), 82–83.
23. Auden, *The English Auden*, 216–17.
24. Theorists of language call the guessing about guessing I have been referring to "recursive mind-reading," and if the Theory of Mind thesis is correct, we accomplish it so easily because, like the data-processing that makes vision possible, it occurs in a dedicated "module," a part of the brain developed just for this purpose. The evolutionary bases of recursive mind reading and its developmental implications regarding the cognitive capacities of young children are still matters of dispute. For a recent discussion see Thom Scott-Phillips, *Speaking Our Minds: Why Human Communication Is Different, and How Language Evolved to Make It Special* (New York: Palgrave Macmillan, 2015), esp. 63–75.

25. W. B. Yeats, *Letters*, ed. Allan Wade (New York, Macmillan, 1954), 840–41.

26. Frank Cioffi, "Intention and Interpretation in Criticism," *Proceedings of the Aristotelian Society*, New Series 64 (1963–64): 90.

27. Peter Bournedal, *Speech and System* (Copenhagen: Museum Tusculanum Press, 1997), 53.

28. As John Shoptaw puts it speaking of poetry, the quintessential artistic gesture may not be *fiat* but *stet, Let it stand*. "Lyric Cryptography," *Poetics Today* 21, no. 1 (Spring 2000): 224.

29. For exemplary work of this kind see Leah Price, *The Anthology and the Rise of the Novel: From Richardson to George Eliot* (Cambridge: Cambridge University Press, 2000); Virginia Walker Jackson, *Dickinson's Misery: A Lyric Theory of Reading* (Princeton, NJ: Princeton University Press, 2005); and Michael C. Cohen, *The Social Lives of Poems in Nineteenth-Century America* (Philadelphia: University of Pennsylvania Press, 2015).

30. Roland Barthes, "The Death of the Author," in *Image-Music-Text*, trans. Stephen Heath (New York: Hill & Wang, 1977), 148. When using the word *text* in his writings, Barthes tends to oscillate strategically, referring at times to a peculiarly recent conception of writing as a repudiation of authorship and at other times to the general condition of literary language—language, that is, being used in an "intransitive" or "symbolic," which I take to mean non-referential, mode. In this passage it seems clear that he is referring to literary language in general.

31. Hirsch uses the terms *meaning* and *significance*, both of which can normally refer to the semantic content of an utterance or to the importance of what it conveys, making his distinction between them seem difficult and hard to remember. See *Validity in Interpretation* (New Haven, CT: Yale University Press, 1967), 8–10. *Impact* is a broader term than *significance*. It includes the effects that utterances, including works, may have on account of the information they convey, the fact that it has been conveyed, and the way it is conveyed. Hirsch's version of the distinction has raised skepticism about whether it could be implemented in practice, a reaction I believe was prompted in part by his choice of terminology. The mere difficulty of separating other people's meanings from our own reactions to those meanings, however, is somewhat beside the point, for as Hirsch himself observes, the fact that a practice is difficult and cannot be carried out with perfect certainty is not an objection to its value and importance (17). We make difficult distinctions between what is intentional and what isn't every day; our legal and political systems are based on our ability to do so. Only in the context of literary reception, where the information content often matters less than its aesthetic impression, could the difference between meaning and impact seem difficult to discern.

32. The double movement I have described, toward original meaning and away from original impact, is obviously quite different from the "fusion of horizons" described by Hans-Georg Gadamer as the goal of the hermeneutic process. For Gadamer, interpretation seeks not the author's meaning but the truth of what he is saying, a truth guaranteed by tradition and by the nature of language itself, which, like Hegel's Absolute Spirit, has an inherently speculative and therefore truth-relevant character. Ultimately there is only one horizon, that of the truth as sought by present understanding, since "understanding," Gadamer says, "is, primarily, agreement"—as if one could not understand what one could not accept as true, a condition that would make even one's own past errors unintelligible. Gadamer's most fundamental mistake is to believe that we can assess the truth of a statement or a work before we can understand what it is saying, whereas, until we have done that, we have no idea under what conditions it *would* be true. Only when we know that can we experience the impact of its truth or falsity. See *Truth and Method*, second, revised edition, trans. Joel Weinsheimer and Donald G. Marshall (New York: Continuum, 1975), 180 and *passim*.

33. As Michael J. Reddy has explained, our common way of talking about language implies that it is a conduit which we can put thoughts into and get them out of. See "The Conduit Metaphor—A Case of Frame Conflict in Our Language about Language," in Andrew Ortony, *Metaphor and Thought* (New York: Cambridge University Press, 1979), 284–324. On the limited value of the code model for linguistics see Dan Sperber and Deirdre Wilson, *Relevance: Communication and Cognition*, 2nd ed. (Cambridge, MA: Blackwell Publishers, 1995), 1–15.

34. Sperber and Wilson, *Relevance*, 36.

35. For a recent summary see Dan Sperber and Dierdre Wilson, *Meaning and Relevance* (Cambridge: Cambridge University Press, 2012), chapter 1. Relevance theory builds on Paul Grice's account of conversational maxims, which is still a viable alternative and does not depend upon a modular conception of the mind. I have chosen the relevance model here because of its simplicity and because it seems to be more influential at this point. See Paul Grice, *Studies in the Way of Words* (Cambridge, MA: Harvard University Press, 1989).

36. As Sperber and Wilson put it, "the rational way to go about interpreting an utterance, or any other ostensive stimulus, is to follow the path of least effort and stop at the first interpretation that satisfies one's expectations of relevance." Sperber and Wilson, *Relevance*, 272.

37. Sperber and Wilson, *Relevance*, 51–52.

38. Poetic effects are often of this kind. Sperber and Wilson, *Meaning and Relevance*, 118–22.

39. For a lucid account of relevance theory in comparison with its alternatives see Betty J. Birner, *Introduction to Pragmatics* (Chichester, West Sussex: Wiley-Blackwell, 2013), chapters 2 and 3.

40. Robyn Carston provides a detailed account in *Thoughts and Utterances: The Pragmatics of Explicit Communication* (Malden, MA: Blackwell Publishers, 2002), chapters 1 and 2.

41. For a similar example see Seana Coulson, *Semantic Leaps: Frame-Shifting and Conceptual Blending in Meaning Construction* (New York: Cambridge University Press, 2001), 161.

42. Sperber and Wilson, *Relevance*, 188.

43. Coulson, *Semantic Leaps*, 28.

44. I am unable to provide the source of this example.

45. Fredric Jameson, *The Prison-House of Language: A Critical Account of Structuralism and Russian Formalism* (Princeton, NJ: Princeton University Press, 1972), 211–14.

46. This point of view has been developed in great depth by Donald Davidson. For a late synthesis see the essays in *Subjective, Intersubjective, Objective* (New York: Oxford, 2001).

47. Stephen C. Levinson, Review of Relevance: Communication and Cognition by Dan Sperber and Deirdre Wilson (Oxford: Basil Blackwell, 1986), in *Journal of Linguistics* 25, no. 2 (September 1989): 464.

48. Donald Davidson, "A Nice Derangement of Epitaphs" (1986), in *Truth, Language, and History*, 89–108.

49. Sperber and Wilson, *Meaning and Relevance*, chapters 4–6.

50. Sperber and Wilson, *Meaning and Relevance*, 84–85.

51. Though one can disagree about the implications, the virtual ubiquity of metaphor in our use of language has been amply demonstrated by Lakoff and Johnson and many others following in their wake. See George Lakoff and Mark Johnson, *Metaphors We Live By* (Chicago: University of Chicago Press, 1980), and especially Gilles Fauconnier and Mark Turner, *The Way We Think: Conceptual Blending and the Mind's Hidden Complexities* (New York: Basic Books, 2002). Relevance theory would tend to undermine the sense that metaphor determines thought in the way some of these authors claim.

52. Thomas H. Johnson, ed., *The Complete Poems of Emily Dickinson* (Boston: Little, Brown, and Company, 1960), 118–19.

53. Helen Vendler, *Dickinson: Selected Poems and Commentaries* (Cambridge, MA: Harvard University Press, 2010), 128.

54. Sperber and Wilson, *Relevance*, 217

55. Jane Austen, *Pride and Prejudice: An Annotated Edition*, ed. Patricia Meyer Spacks (Cambridge, MA: Harvard University Press, 2010), 29.

56. Austen, *Pride and Prejudice*, 389.
57. Leo Tolstoy, *Anna Karenina: A Novel in Eight Parts*, trans. Richard Pevear and Larissa Volokhonsky (New York: Viking, 2001), 1.
58. Cf., for instance, Alan H. Goldman, *Aesthetic Value* (Boulder, CO: Westview Press, 1995), chapter 4.
59. See the discussion in Bernard M. W. Knox, *The Heroic Temper: Studies in Sophoclean Tragedy* (Berkeley: University of California Press, 1966), 104–06.
60. For Fish's most virtuosic performance see "Normal Circumstances and Other Special Cases," in *Is There a Text in This Class? The Authority of Interpretive Communities* (Cambridge, MA: Harvard University Press, 1980), chapter 11.
61. The student's reported gloss on her own words is "in this class do we believe in poems and things, or is it just us?" Fish, *Is There a Text*, 305.
62. Fish, *Is There a Text*, chapter 15.
63. For a striking illustration, see the essays collected in the Norton Critical edition of *Oedipus Tyrannus*, trans. and ed. by Luci Berkowitz and Theodore F. Brunner (New York: Norton, 1970).
64. E. R. Dodds, "On Misunderstanding the *Oedipus Rex*," in Berkowitz and Brunner, eds., *Oedipus Tyrannus*, 218–29, rptd. from *Greece and Rome* 13 (1966), 37–49.
65. Peter Allt and Russell K. Alspach, *The Variorum Edition of the Poems of W. B. Yeats* (New York: Macmillan, 1957), 150–51.
66. In the introduction to *Is There A Text in This Class?* Fish describes the process by which, in the course of his career, he has shifted the locus of meaning from the authorless text of the New Critics to the activities of the reader, and then to the all-subsuming interpretive community. More recently, having done his best to make sense of the alternatives, Fish has taken what I hope will be the final step of returning to intentionalism, though in doing so he insists that intentionalism is uninstructive because it doesn't tell you whose intention is at stake or how to find it—as if the author of *Surprised by Sin* and *How Milton Works* leaves us in any doubt about whose intentions govern in *Paradise Lost*, where, according to his account, the "epic voice" of Milton harasses, shames, surprises, tempts, and above all educates his fallen reader with an astonishing battery of manipulative techniques. See the introduction to *Versions of Antihumanism: Milton and Others* (Cambridge: Cambridge University Press, 2012), 5–6.
67. Coulson, *Semantic Leaps*, 27.
68. Paul de Man makes the remarkable claim that Cratylic thinking is fundamental to aesthetics and to the reliability of language in general and that the absence of Cratylic correspondence between sign and thing gives language "considerable freedom from referential restraint, but…makes it epistemologically highly suspect and volatile, since its use can no longer be said to be

determined by considerations of truth and falsehood, good and evil, beauty and ugliness, or pleasure and pain." I can think of no one who has attributed more importance to the way individual words look and sound or who makes all cognitive, aesthetic, and ethical claims depend upon it. See *The Resistance to Theory* (Minneapolis, MN: University of Minnesota Press, 1986), 10.

69. Fauconnier and Turner, *The Way We Think*, 277.

70. Stanislas Dehaene, *Reading in the Brain: The Science and Evolution of a Human Invention* (New York: Viking, 2009), 113. Ellipsis in the original.

71. Yuri Lotman, *The Structure of the Artistic Text* (Ann Arbor, MI: University of Michigan Press, 1977), 55.

72. Allt and Alspach, *The Variorum Yeats*, 441.

73. There is no end to the subtlety of the distinctions artists can count on readers to make. Readers of Browning's poem "Porphyria's Lover," for example, grasp that the character is mad and that he is an eminently unreliable narrator, but this judgment is based upon details we accept from him as accurate. How do we know what we can trust and what we can't? Why shouldn't we take the speaker for a prankster who is pulling our leg rather than for a madman narrating the enactment of his delusion?

74. Martin Heidegger, *Being and Time*, trans. John MacQuarrie and Edward Robinson (New York: Harper and Row, 1962), 191–95.

75. Laurence Dreyfus, *Wagner and the Erotic Impulse* (Cambridge, MA: Harvard University Press, 2012), 117.

76. For a reconstruction of Freud's bio-historical account of human development, see John Farrell, *Freud's Paranoid Quest: Psychoanalysis and Modern Suspicion* (New York: New York University Press, 1996), chapter 1.

77. *Through the Looking-Glass*, in Lewis Carroll, *Alice in Wonderland*, ed. Donald J. Gray, 3rd ed. (New York: Norton Critical Editions, 2013), 113–14.

78. Patricia Meyer Spacks, "Logic and Language in Through the Looking-Glass," in Robert Phillips, ed., *Aspects of Alice: Lewis Carroll's Dream Child as Seen Though the Critics' Looking-Glasses, 1865–1971* (New York: The Vanguard Press, 1971), 274.

CHAPTER 3

Uncertainty, Indeterminacy, Omniscience, and Other Matters

In Chapter 2, I set out the basic reasons not to forget the chosenness of words, the fact that every utterance, in art and in life, represents an intention, not proleptically but in the act, and that our recognition of this intention is what makes our inferential efforts worthwhile. Communicative intentions are not infallible. A theory describing them as such would be obviously false. But risk is part of the value of the process and contributes to its remarkable efficiency and subtlety. Language working as a mere code, without implication or inference, would be more reliable but have little potential for art. The possibility of misunderstanding is inseparable from the possibility of more than understanding.

Even though chosen words only partly determine the meaning of the utterance, they communicate it reliably and predictably in context and with the potential for rich implications. The key ingredient is the recognition on the part of the audience of the author's intent to communicate and to have that intent be recognized in order to motivate the audience's search for relevance. It is worth saying again that in default conditions all of this can go on without conscious deliberation and without either side having to think specifically about who is speaking or listening.

In this chapter I will pursue some of the implications of this view. I begin by taking up the difference between the underdeterminacy I ascribe to language and the indeterminacy found there by some prominent critics. Again I do not aim at full-dressed explication and refutation. Rather, I aim to evoke basic intuitions and provide a way of responding to them.

© The Author(s) 2017
J. Farrell, *The Varieties of Authorial Intention*,
DOI 10.1007/978-3-319-48977-3_3

Uncertainty, Indeterminacy, and Underdeterminacy

The uncertainty and consequent need for anticipation and mutual guesswork which I have been attributing to the process of communication are different from the textual indeterminacy that is sometimes ascribed to literary discourse or to discourse in general by literary theorists like Fish, Derrida, de Man, and others, and it is important to see the difference. Uncertainty is a state observers may find themselves in with relation to an object of knowledge. For instance, I know that right now I am more than two thousand miles away from Providence, Rhode Island. I don't know precisely how many miles, but I could easily look it up, thus going from uncertainty to knowledge. Like certainty and ignorance, uncertainty is a subjective state. It can differ from one observer to another with respect to the same set of facts, and it can change. There are some things we are all uncertain about—for instance, how many people there are on earth at the moment. Being uncertain about this is still a subjective state even though all of us share it.

You can be uncertain *about* things, but you can't be indeterminate about them because indeterminacy is an objective condition; if something is indeterminate for you it must be indeterminate for me too. Indeterminacy is not the state of an observer. To say that something is indeterminate is simply to say that there is no fact of the matter to settle the relevant question about it. The paradigm case is from quantum mechanics; if we know the position of certain subatomic particles then we cannot specify their velocity, not because we are uncertain or ignorant about them but because they simply cannot have a specific velocity and position at the same time.

Literature provides more accessible examples of indeterminacy. In *Hamlet*, for instance, is the number of rooms in the Castle of Elsinore odd or even? Because the text of the play does not tell us the answer and because the world of *Hamlet* exists only in the play, there is simply no fact of the matter to settle the question. It is indeterminate. We could go to the real-world Kronborg Castle, Helsingør, and count the rooms, but Shakespeare never did so, and there is no reason to think he would have been interested in the result. For the reader of *Hamlet*, Elsinore is a prototypical castle. It must have more than five rooms, I would venture, to count as a castle, and it cannot have five thousand, but beyond that there is simply nothing to say.

In a sense, indeterminacy is rather like situational irony, which we feel when the normal implications that we associate with a situation are unexpectedly suspended. We are inclined to say that something is indeterminate in cases where we usually can have more complete information. When we know something's location, we generally think we can find out, at least in principle, how fast it is moving, but on the quantum level that proves not to be true. And when we are talking about castles, we generally assume we can know precisely how many rooms they have, provided we have a definite enough idea of what should count as a room, but with fictional castles this also turns out not to be true. Fictive objects, it has often been observed, have a strange immunity from the law of excluded middle, the logical principle which tells us that meaningful statements must be either true or false. It is either true or false, for example, about human beings, that they are either at least as tall as or not as tall as Jamaica Kincaid. Absent quantum considerations, Jamaica Kincaid has a definite height which can be measured, and everyone is either at least that tall or not. It cannot be said, however, whether or not Hamlet is at least as tall as Jamaica Kincaid. When reading the play, we attribute to Hamlet's height a default value—it would be odd for Shaquille O'Neal or Mickey Rooney to play him—but that height can only roughly be specified. There is simply no fact of the matter to settle the question of Hamlet's precise stature.

When an action such as writing a play has been performed, the intentions behind it may be matters of uncertainty, but for the most part there is a fact of the matter to determine them, however inaccessible that fact may be and however irremediable our uncertainty. The temptation to say that the meaning of literary texts in general is indeterminate is based either on a confusion between uncertainty and indeterminacy or on the blanket rejection of authorial intention, which keeps the question of relevance from coming into play at all. It is only when we attribute a sentence or a literary work to a person who originates it that we are able to ascribe to it a particular meaning. Otherwise it is truly indeterminate, if it can be said to have meaning at all.[1]

That is not to deny, of course, that words have a typical range of potential meanings; that is what dictionaries provide. Many whole sentences have a default meaning too. "Have a nice day" typically means have a nice day. But only when a particular speaker or author has chosen an utterance for a particular audience in a particular context does its meaning become fully determinate. Thus we can be certain or uncertain about what is being said in a literary work, but the fact that it was created intentionally means that in principle our questions do have answers, however difficult it may be to arrive at them. And the fact that some elements of the story are left indeterminate presents few mysteries. No author could specify the world of a work in full detail, and none would want to.

Indeterminacy can also be an artistic effect or theme and cultivated as such. At the end of Thomas Pynchon's novella, *The Crying of Lot 49*, four possible interpretations of the heroine's situation are presented and the matter is left in the air. Unlike with *The Turn of the Screw*, where we feel that there must be a right answer about whether there are ghosts in the story or not, Pynchon is deliberately making a display of indeterminacy at the heart of his story, which is largely about problems of information. Pynchon refuses his reader the typical solution provided by detective novels, where all but one of the possibilities which have been deliberately kept in play are finally excluded. The irony, of course, is that this display of indeterminacy and incompleteness is perfectly clear and to the point and brings the story to an appropriate end.

Some metaphors exploit indeterminacy in an artistically evocative way. When Romeo answers his own question *What light through yonder window breaks?* by saying *It is the east, and Juliet is the sun* he does not specify precisely which attributes of the sun are relevant to Juliet—though he does add *fair sun* in the next sentence. We could analyze the metaphor in the Aristotelian manner as a ratio—what the sun is to the east, Juliet is to Romeo's vision, that is to say, the most beautiful object in view. But Romeo's, and Shakespeare's, meaning is not necessarily limited to the beauty that prompts the comparison. It has a broader sensual suggestiveness the further relevance of which cannot be made explicit as we did with the examples of underdeterminacy in Chapter 2. Still, the range of associations of Juliet as the sun is quite limited. We certainly do not think of her as a ball of gas ninety-three million miles away, and it is not only fear of anachronism that keeps us from doing so. Our broad sense of what Juliet herself is like and of Romeo's love-struck attitude toward her constrains our associations while still leaving them impossible to specify fully. One of the advantages of metaphor is its ability to evoke the presence of an object in a way that is not strictly delimited.[2] In some vague sense Juliet reminds us of the sun or is sun-like; our tactile or synesthetic receptivities are activated by her in a manner reminiscent of the sun. So if there is indeterminacy involved here, it is a calculated indeterminacy, gratifyingly intentional and dependent upon the author's expectations about how the audience will respond both to the import and to the experience of the image. Its calculated vagueness does not keep it from being just right.

Here the reader may recall W. V. Quine's famous argument about the indeterminacy of translation. Quine imagines a native informant pointing at what we would call a rabbit and saying *gavagai* (an unfamiliar word from the informant's language). Quine goes on to make the point that the interpreter will have a wide range of choices about how to translate *gavagai* in addition to invoking our familiar concept of rabbit. He might translate *gavagai* as *time slices of rabbit* or *undetached rabbit parts*. Quine need not have used the word *rabbit* in his examples. *Gavagai* might mean *long-floppy-eared dinner candidate*. Quine is repeating a point made by Frege, that the meaning of the term for a thing takes up a certain point of view regarding that thing. He is adding that there is no right point of view, and no way to be sure we are all taking up the same one. Hence arises the specter of "ontological relativity," the possibility of an unlimited number of different vocabularies dividing up the world in different ways but being ultimately indistinguishable in practice. This makes the concept of meaning itself unreliable for Quine's epistemological purposes—to explain how our knowledge is grounded in our experience. What he concludes is that other psychological processes are involved in the way we narrow down the meaning of other people's words in addition to the ones that are useful for philosophical and scientific inquiry—that this, in fact, is where psychology has to take over from philosophy and logic.[3]

Readers who have come this far with me will see that the missing psychological principle Quine mentions is of the kind we have been talking about, the principle of relevance which depends upon our more general sense that human action, to be understood, has to exhibit a rational fit between means and ends. It is not only the world that constrains our interpretation of language but its origin in the activity of a speaker. We are fairly confident, when we see our native informant point to a rabbit and say *gavagai*, that he means more or less what we mean by *rabbit* even if he would say some things about rabbits that are different from what we would say. (He might say, for instance, that rabbits are sacred, while we might say that rabbits are mammals.) *Undetached rabbit parts* simply isn't relevant or efficient enough to be the meaning of *gavagai*, and not just because it replaces one word with three.

Quine is not claiming that indeterminacy is fatal to communication. What he is concerned with is how we should explain the way inquiry works. Philosophers have struggled mightily to settle how meaning and reference function—whether the meanings of referring terms are in the world or "in the head," whether or not they must be the same in all possible worlds, and so on. The matter is of great interest, but it has little import for literary theory. The intuitions upon which philosophers attempt to settle these matters cannot be as firm as our everyday sense that our anticipations about other people's words and actions function smoothly enough to make communication both cognitively worthwhile and aesthetically effective.

It is rather beside the point, then, to argue, as Paul de Man does, that the inadequacy of grammar and logic to fix meaning leaves us in a situation of radical indeterminacy in the reading of literary texts.[4] De Man gives as an example the difficulty of grammatically defining the genitive *of* in the title of Keats' poem "The Fall of Hyperion." Does it define the poem's subject as the "story of the defeat of an older by a newer power," Keats' original subject, or could it better be rephrased as "Hyperion's Fall," suggesting the god's fallenness as the subject, a fallenness he seems to share with his replacement, Apollo. "Does the title tell us," de Man asks, "that Hyperion is fallen and that Apollo stands, or does it tell us that Hyperion and Apollo (and Keats, whom it is hard to distinguish, at times, from Apollo) are interchangeable in that all of them are necessarily and constantly falling? Both readings are grammatically correct, but it is impossible to decide from the context (the ensuing narrative) which version is the right one." De Man goes on to say that we could also read the title intertextually, making "Hyperion" refer to Keats' earlier poem of that name, and, since that poem is also unfinished, the fallenness of intertextual reading can even be generalized to textual being itself: "are we telling the story of why all texts, as texts, can always be said to be falling?" The trope of "falling" now widens out to infinite proportions. "Faced with the ineluctable necessity to come to a decision, no grammatical or logical analysis can help us out."

About that de Man is quite correct, but that is because he is asking for more than grammar and logic can provide. What is more striking is that he doesn't actually turn to logic or grammar to help him decide the question. Instead, he resorts to the context as a key to the author's intention, but when he does so, instead of being constrained by it in a normal way, he considers a gamut of logically possible meanings most of which are completely implausible. Of course there is a lot that is indeterminate about the meaning of this poem simply because it is unfinished. That is why there is no "ineluctable necessity to come to a decision" on our part about the true meaning of the title. In fact, even if Keats had finished the poem he might have left the title ambiguous. Nevertheless, it is very likely, as de Man says at the outset, that the title originally referred to the replacement of Hyperion by Apollo and that Keats never thought beyond that point. Looking for other meanings than that, de Man takes up authorship of the poem himself and makes it an expositor of his own theory.

The inadequacy of language that de Man discovers in the poetry of Keats does not, of course, derive from its literary qualities. For him it is a general deficiency of language per se, and in his influential early work, *Blindness and Insight*, he describes the entire project of mid-century continental criticism, "whether it derive its language from sociology, psychoanalysis, ethnology, linguistics, or even from certain forms of philosophy," as an attack on the notion that "literary or poetic consciousness" can "pretend to escape, to some degree, from the duplicity, the confusion, the untruth that we take for granted in the everyday use of language." De Man goes on to provide a remarkably confident form of skepticism as if it were common sense. "We know," he says, "that our entire social language is an intricate system of rhetorical devices designed to escape from the direct expression of desires that are, in the fullest sense of the term, unnamable—not because they are ethically shameful (for this would make the problem a very simple one), but because unmediated expression is a philosophical impossibility."[5] The reason for this impossibility is, as de Man explains a few pages later, that "sign and meaning never coincide" (17). It turns out, however, that literature, and by extension the literary critic, does after all have a privileged position over "everyday language"; it knows its own fallenness. It is "the only form of language that is free from the fallacy of unmediated expression." In this knowledge, all—even ancient—literature, knows itself as fiction (17).

It is odd to think that we are all using deceptive rhetoric to conceal "unnamable" desires that never could have been brought to light in the first place. But de Man is right, in a sense, to say that "sign and meaning never coincide." They are not, after all, the same thing. The sign is a medium, a symbol. It points, giving a prompt for interpretation, and this prompt will be only as determinate as it needs to be to accomplish its purpose. But when we read that literary language is "free from the fallacy of unmediated expression" and that even in ancient times it knew itself as fiction (17), we recognize the textual fallacy in its purest form—that it is language that speaks, not the human being speaking in language. Language falls short for de Man, and literary language acquires its special self-demystifying authority, on account of the failure of a metaphysical desire for (or is it a metaphysical fear of?) unmediated expression which, de Man himself admits, cannot be satisfied and which I would suggest was misbegotten in the first place.

At the end of this chapter I will scratch the surface of the deep metaphysical considerations which motivate the willingness of critics like de

Man to assert the predominant indeterminacy of meaning, among them Jacques Derrida's concerns about the Western legacy of metaphysical presence. Here I will note, though, that Derrida also presents more empirically based arguments for the indeterminacy of writing as opposed to everyday speech. Readers might wonder if I am not missing the importance of what he calls *dissemination*—the distance that opens up between the immediate context of a written utterance and its voyage on the way to undetermined readers; to ignore *dissemination* would, from a Derridean perspective, be to fall into the myth of the self-present voice, which denies the drift and deferral of signification Derrida calls *écriture*. I do not believe there is any reason to think this is the case, for, as Derrida recognizes within the terms of his own argument, the original notion of the self-presence of word and consciousness in the speech situation is already a symptom of excessive confidence about knowledge. Rather, what I am pointing to is merely the uncertainty and guesswork that are already part of the original speech situation and that may or may not be intensified in writing. Genuine communication is never immune from the possibility of failure. Literary composition in particular is a situation of risk—not a roll of the dice but a calculated risk—and risk by its very nature implies the possibility both of failure and success. In fact, the failure of communication can only be meaningful against a background of successful communication. It would have been impossible for language to develop if communicative failure were systematic or complete. Derrida, on the other hand, takes the mere possibility of risk to be fatal to our confidence in the power of language. In critiquing J. L. Austin's conception of the speech act, with its setting in a unique context and conveyance of intention, Derrida asks "What is a success when the possibility of infelicity [*échec*] continues to constitute its true structure?"[6] On such a basis, only foolproof communication would count as successful. This criterion for success is much too demanding, and it misses the fact that foolproof or fully explicit and unambiguous languages like the languages of mathematics pay a price for their precision which would not be worth paying in everyday conversation. When it comes to literature, the undesirability of a fully explicit language is even more obvious. Literature cannot do without the ambiguity, polysemy, calculated indeterminacy, and riskiness that make even ordinary language too slippery for the purposes of logicians and mathematicians. The element of risk and the need for the author to count on the reader's powers of inference is especially important in one of literature's most compelling qualities—its power of intimacy.

The "Omniscient Narrator"

The use of terms like "indeterminacy" adds a certain glamour to discussions of literary meaning, but it would be easier and less confusing simply to say that the number of rooms in Elsinore, not being relevant to the action of the play, went undecided. After all, the number could in principle have been given, while the velocity and position of an electron cannot be given at the same time. It was up to Shakespeare to decide how many rooms there are in Elsinore but, real estate being far from his concern, he had no reason to bother, and what he left undecided is undecidable for us, though if we are staging the play we will have to make some of the decisions Shakespeare didn't. Shakespeare was largely borrowing Elsinore from the real world in the same way he borrowed Verona, Venice, and ancient Rome, with the vagueness that comes of prototype or cliché.

This casts a certain light upon the accuracy of the term "omniscient narrator," for it is clear that even the most elaborately descriptive realistic novelists—Tolstoy, for example, or George Eliot—leave many details about their characters' lives and worlds undecided. They neither know nor tell all. Strictly speaking, it isn't a matter of knowledge at all. How tall is Conrad's Marlowe? It's not just that we don't know but that Conrad didn't determine the point. For us this may feel like a matter of knowledge—that Marlowe has a height to be known is part of the fiction—but for the artist it's a matter of fiat. The author appears to select the facts to be told out of many that exist, but that is simply the nature of the pretense. What is actually happening is that the author is selecting the facts of the story out of the many possible ones, some of which happen to obtain in the real world and some of which don't.[7]

Wayne Booth defined the omniscient narrator by contrast with the "unreliable narrator," an indispensable term of literary criticism which points to the fact that there are many stories where the teller belongs to world of the work and so his or her point of view is subject to scrutiny by the reader within the larger framework of the story.[8] The unreliable narrator's point of view must be checked against the background of the tale which readers infer based on their broader understanding of the world projected by the work. Unreliable narrators must always be assessed for their epistemic slant.

The unreliable narrator, then, stands in contrast not with an omniscient one—a narrator who is epistemically perfect or whose knowledge is complete—but with a narrator whose point of view is simply not subject to epistemic scrutiny. The opposite of an unreliable narrator is an unimpeachable one—unimpeachable not merely in the sense that one cannot successfully impeach him but that the whole notion is incoherent, there being no higher court to which one could address the charge. Perhaps the most accurate terminological choice in this case would have been "questionable" versus "unquestionable" narrators, the distinction being that some narrators can logically be questioned because they are characters in the story while others have authorial immunity from questioning. Objections that arise in the latter case can only be applied to the author himself. (For practical purposes, "reliable" versus "unreliable" seems to be the best terminological choice, the reliable narrator being the author of the work in question.)

That the unimpeachability of authorial intentions really has nothing to do with narrators can be seen from the fact that authors play the same role in determining the world of a novel that they do in determining the world of a play, where there is no narrator. Authors don't *know* their worlds. It is not a matter of science, omni- or otherwise. Rather, like an Ockhamite god, they *invent* them, except when they are co-opting large tracts of ontological real estate from the world they live in. For the most part they borrow from the real world only vaguely. Not even Balzac's Paris, Dickens' London, or Joyce's Dublin would make good blueprints of their originals, and there is no easy or objective way of checking them for accuracy. They belong to their authors more essentially than they do to the world.

The most inept storyteller has a fiat that can't be challenged because there is no appeal beyond the author's say-so. Consider a story that begins, "There once was a boy with seven heads. On his birthday his mother bought him seven hats." This is a ridiculous story, and few of us will want to read more of it. We are being asked to contemplate a world that has no interest because of the empty spirit with which it has been conjured up. But we cannot challenge the fictive existence of this world or the truth of these statements within it. Unless the story changes direction and an unreliable narrator emerges, we cannot challenge the narrator any more than we can challenge what happens in a play, where there is no narrator. The author's fiat cannot be impeached on epistemic grounds.

THE "IMPLIED AUTHOR"

Wayne Booth, in what seems to me an attempt to accommodate textualist assumptions, tried to give authors a back door into the picture by suggesting that a fictional work has, in addition to its narrators, an "implied author" whose presence is part of its meaning.[9] When, as readers, we spend time in the imaginary company of Henry James or Virginia Woolf, we are learning to see, feel, and judge the way they do, and, Booth would argue, this element is intrinsic to the structure and meaning of the work. This seems to me a mistake. We can indeed learn, when reading Henry James, to think like Henry James, and James, like many authors, is certainly attempting to teach us to see, think, and feel the way he does. He has a vision of the world he wants us to share, and understanding his work will demand, temporarily, that we imaginatively inhabit that vision. But all of this is the normal activity of the real author. No purpose is served by attributing an "implied author" to the work itself. How is the implied author different from the author per se? If there is no difference, let us be wary of multiplying authors without need.

Consider this analogy. I get up in the morning and decide to dress in a certain way based on what I think is appropriate for the day. When people see me, they will know I've dressed this way for a reason. My choice implies that it is good to dress this way in the settings I expect to traverse and the roles I expect to play on this kind of a day. This type of commitment belongs to most of my choices. When I do something or say something I license the inference that, under the prevailing circumstances, I consider it good to do or say this kind of thing. I am also aware of what others will conclude about me from my choices. With everything I do or say, I am aware of what it says about me. I am aware of what others will make of it; I may even be able to divide those others into different audiences who will have different views. Erving Goffman has provided a lovely term for the theatrical presentation of self in ordinary life—"impression management."[10] The management of impressions is universal and may apply to every publicly observable choice I make, including my choice of clothes in the morning. But would there be any point in attributing the qualities suggested by these impressions to an implied wearer rather than to me? Even if I am not the wearer I pretend to be, even if I am Don Quixote putting on my armor for a joust with giants, is it not to me that the audience justifiably refers my pretense?

It might seem appealing to be able to look at an author's oeuvre and say that the implied author of the early works is different from the implied author of the later works, but this would be to suggest that such differences are merely artistic choices. It is more likely that the difference in maturity of perspective, not to mention gloom of perspective, we find in moving from, say, Thomas Hardy's early work to his last novel, *Jude the Obscure*, should be attributed to the development of Hardy himself rather than to a decision on his part to imply a different author. In the same way it would be strange to say about someone that today he is implying a different wearer than he was yesterday rather than that today he is dressing differently and that we are simply seeing an additional element in his range of self-display.

The notion of the implied author is also singularly unhelpful when it comes to actual artistic failures, which ought to be attributed directly to the author. As a matter of meaning, for instance, it is impossible to disagree with the narrator of *Vanity Fair* that Becky Sharp turns out to be a murderer. That is strongly implied in the text, even if not explicitly stated. But it is possible, and in fact quite reasonable, to disapprove of Thackeray's decision to make her one. If the author's activity were merely "implied" as part of the meaning of the work, this latter judgment would not make sense. It would not penetrate past the textual function of the implied author to reach Thackeray himself. But in fact it is open to us to judge that Thackeray himself erred and hurt his novel by making Becky a murderer because this kind of behavior seems like an unmotivated change in her character, especially coming just after her unselfish intervention facilitating Dobbin's marriage to Amelia. Up to this point in a very long novel she has been tricky and unmotherly but not absolutely evil. When we say that the Becky Thackeray has been describing in the rest of his novel can't be a murderer, we are disagreeing with Thackeray himself, not his narrator. We are complaining about his novel's failure of coherence, and we may wonder if some bias was behind it. Our complaint cannot be addressed to some intermediate construction of Thackeray as an authorial function of the text. It applies to the man himself.[11]

Another odd consequence of the implied author theory is that works with unreliable narrators would seem to have no implied author at all, or at least no author one can say something about. Reading *The Adventures of Huckleberry Finn*, one is getting to know Huckleberry Finn, not Mark Twain. Clearly it is best to recognize that the author has a character but he cannot be a character, at least not one of his own.

By drawing attention to the close relationship between reliable narrators and authors, I do not want to deny the conceptual difference between them. To be a fiction writer in the default mode is simply to pretend to narrate when one is actually inventing a story. A narrator is not an inventor; an author is. So there is a difference. The narrator is the author's guise, we might say, in the role of author. The author plays him. But if the author is not making the mode of narration part of the story, he is not inventing a character in addition to himself. He plays narrator as himself, we might say, rather than assigning the role to someone else. The logical slipperiness of this position furnishes some of the resources of metafiction; some authors use it to feed themselves into the narrative machine by appearing inside their novels under their own names. But the functional role of the narrator cannot be abrogated, so the effect is always one of paradox and deflation, a reductio ad absurdum of fiction or a breaching of its logical limits; thus arises the need to posit a meta-level to articulate what is happening. It is impossible for authors to pass through the mirror of their own invention into the story. Reliable narrators cannot merely pretend to believe in their stories, nor, as Descartes might have warned, can authors merely pretend to believe in their own existence.

It is important to note that narrators can be marked out for significance and made part of the story in other ways than by giving the point of view of an unreliable character. Authors like Pynchon or William Gaddis who imitate the novelistic voice as if it were an autonomous linguistic machine make us aware of the form of the narration, but in doing so they are obviously not creating a character. Rather, they are portraying a way of seeing that is not personal but has a distinctive ethical and aesthetic nature recognizably not the same as the author's. In the case of Pynchon's *Gravity's Rainbow*, the narrator's voice seems to imitate the blank point of view of a camera as envisioned in the present-tense unfolding of a screenplay.

Having separated the author from the narrator as decisively as possible, I would like again to underline the point that in spite of the difference between the roles of narrator and author, there are indeed aspects of an author's mentality which do have an intrinsic relation to the works he creates. The author's intellect, as it shapes the whole meaning and impression of the work, cannot be displaced onto a mere textual function. A work's "controlling intelligence," to use Colin Lyas's felicitous phrase, can only belong to the person who made it. So it is with qualities like sensitivity, maturity, subtlety, perceptiveness, and sense of humor. A work can only have these things insofar as the author has them. This is even true if the author's personal behavior outside the work does not make these qualities particularly evident. In works with reliable narrators there may be no significant distinction between authorial and narrative point of view, and no matter how many levels of unreliable narration a work contains, the controlling intelligence that keeps them in play can only belong to the author.[12]

Further along the same lines, there is a level of dissonance between author and work that can impede our response to the work. Were we to learn, for instance, that the humanitarian sympathies of authors like Dickens or Whitman had been calculated for effect with the scientific detachment advocated by Poe, some of our response to their writing would be deflated. Certainly the appeal of Trollope's novels has not been enhanced by his account of the workmanlike manner in which they were produced. So while sincerity may not be a properly artistic virtue, being much more common than artistic skill, the appearance of insincerity can be an artistic liability.[13]

One further point about authorial presence is worth making. Our judgment about the author's capacities does not only affect our overall perception of the story; it plays a role in our interpretation of minute details, for instance in the way we interpret the first sentence of *Pride and Prejudice* discussed in Chapter 2. If we imagine one of Austen's original readers, cutting the pages of the newly arrived book, the first thing she observes is that the opening sentence seems to have been born in the mind of a silly person. This reader has three choices as she proceeds. She can suppose that the author herself is a silly person; that the story is being told by a silly person, an unreliable narrator; or that the sentence is ironic and the silliness is elsewhere than in the mind of the speaker. It is only by excluding both the author and the narrator as silly people that the reader will be able to arrive at the third conclusion. In this case, clearly, it is not the author as an implied function of the text but the actual author of the text that is being evaluated.

We do not have to insist, then, on the deep sympathy and intimacy between author and reader that was part of Romantic culture and its attempt to escape from classical dignity and decorum to admit that there remains a definite ethical and psychological connection between author and work which affects the meaning of the work as well as its impact and therefore conditions our aesthetic response. The values that govern this connection may vary widely, but the connection is there. Probably the closer the reader is to the author in attitude and sensibility, the more the author's sincerity matters. If we want to feel the way Dickens feels about his characters and world, we will naturally resist the notion that his feelings are insincere. On the other hand, if we can stomach Céline's anti-Semitism enough to read him at all, the possible insincerity of his repugnant views might actually be an advantage.

Can Fiction be Defined Without Reference to Authors?

I have been arguing that, even though the distance between the narrator and the author is a constitutive part of the game of fiction and cannot be erased, neither can the narrative function be delegated to an implied author. Often what we have is simply the author playing his role as narrator. I have also made the point that fiction poses a problem in that it often mimics other forms of discourse without any internal markers to establish that it is fictive. Here I would like to treat the nature of fiction a little more closely. Scholars of literature often think of fiction as primarily a literary phenomenon, but this is a mistake. There are non-literary fictions of all kinds, from legal fictions to outright lies. Counterfactual thinking, which deploys fiction, is an essential part of everyday life; we make use of fictions about what did not happen to explain what did. Just about every time we use the word *if* we engage in a fiction. As Hume pointed out, counterfactual thinking is one of our primary ways of making sense of the idea of cause—if X had not happened, Y would not have happened. When we say that Hitler was responsible for the Holocaust, we are not saying that he accomplished it singlehanded; we are saying that without his contribution it would not have occurred. Such judgments of responsibility depend intimately on the juxtaposition of fiction and fact.

It is natural to think that this ordinary sense of fiction should be helpful in understanding the status of literary fiction, but there are reasons to doubt it. Defining fiction in contrast with the truth or in relation to it slides easily into the old idea that fiction is a form of lying. Now a lie, of course, is a full-blooded act of communication. When the lie succeeds, the liar gives the victim every reason to believe that some state of affairs is the case even though the liar knows it isn't. But obviously this is not what happens with fiction. So truth and fiction are not the opposites they may seem.[14]

To see the upshot more clearly, let us start by imagining a storyteller giving a truthful account of an experience. This is not fiction; it is history, though it may contain many of the embellishments that writers of fiction employ. Studies of vernacular storytelling show that they use the same arsenal as literary composition—subtleties of narrative structure, figurative language, and ways of shaping audience response; novelists often cast themselves in the role of such storytellers, or of their literary equivalents, the memoirist and the biographer, without having to give up the use of literary means.[15]

Now let us imagine a second case identical to the first except that the events of the storyteller's narrative are entirely invented and never happened. It is easy to see that this does not make them fictive in a literary sense because the audience is actually being deceived by the performance. It is taking the events as true. This is fiction in the everyday sense, which is indeed akin to lying rather than fiction in the literary sense. What needs to be added to make the invented story into fiction is the mutual understanding shared between author and audience that what is being offered is not truth but an invitation to imagine, a set of prompts for the reader's experience.

In every act of communication there is an implication about what Frege called *force*, in other words the type of action that the speaker intends—asserting, questioning, promising, and so on. The attitude that one takes toward fiction is a matter of force in this sense. Though the superficial signs of assertion are present, we take up a different stance toward them than we do towards assertive speech. We adopt the *fictive stance*. It may not be visible in the text, but it is part of the mutual understanding between author and reader. It is the mark of a distinctive kind of activity, a game of "make-believe," as Kendall Walton calls it.[16] We can think of it as the invocation of a literary institution, but my own sense is that the enjoyment of stories, novels, fables, and tall tales, like jokes and other forms of verbal amusement, goes beyond the conventions of literature and reflects a more or less universal human interest in storytelling, which is to say in extending the pleasures that come from truthful narration into the realm of shared fancy.[17]

To say that fiction cannot be defined in relation to truth is not to say that it contains no truth; that is the inference which would come from defining fiction as a kind of lying. This is where the distinction between the fictive and non-fictive narration becomes most telling. Both kinds involve a general sense of faithfulness to the facts and, as John Searle pointed out, fictions contain a good deal of factual discourse;[18] fictions need factual discourse in order to accomplish their illusionistic purpose. But though fiction and non-fiction typically contain a good deal of generalization based on the facts conveyed by the narrative, they do so in a different way, and the difference is crucial. In non-fiction, the evidence and the interpretations it gives rise to can be separated by the author and the reader. So when the non-fiction author speculates about the meaning of the events he has presented, he is doing so in a way that is open to second-guessing by the reader or, in other words, to other ways of telling the story based upon the same facts. But this gap between the facts and their meaning does not exist in fiction. The two have been tailored to each other in the act of creation. We can criticize the truthfulness of the work in comparison with our own view of the subject and even say how we would rewrite it, but in rewriting it as fiction we would be altering the facts as well as their meaning. They come from the same source, the author, and point toward truth at a higher level of generality than the empirical detail of factual narrative.

This may seem like an unflattering characterization of fiction, but I believe it illuminates many of its attractions, its vocation for the typical and the general being one of the chief among them. Another is that it allows characters and their actions to be observed more clearly and definitively than they appear most of the time in real life. Fiction can present not just good and bad people but heroes and villains, and even its mediocrities are mediocre all the way through. And when it turns away from such absolutes, it can portray lucid ambiguities based upon opposing but equally perspicuous facts. Thus it can isolate ambiguity and ambivalence from the circumstantial uncertainties with which they are typically surrounded in real life, making them stand out as more intelligible and poignant than they appear in factual narration.

The notion of a fictive stance understood by author and reader allows us to distinguish fictive from factual narrative on a different basis than truth; it also reminds us that literature is a much wider category than fiction, and that there are great works that lie in between. The epics of Homer and many books of the Bible, for example, have an obvious historical character and do not employ the fictive stance. Instead, they are presented as inspired historical narration. But the relation between evidence and judgment implied by the narrative often seems closer to the fictive than the factual, and with the Greek tragedies it is even clearer that transmitting and interpreting the old stories involves the license to alter facts as well as themes and interpretations and to tailor them to each other. So even if fictive tale-telling is a practice to be found at all times and places, as I believe it to be, its relations with other forms of discourse can be extremely complicated to sort out, and the attempt to do so merely by discerning the relation of the work to the truth of the world, eliminating the fictive stance of the author and its understanding by the reader, seems doomed to fail.

Do All Poems Have Speakers Distinct from the Author?

My discussion of Auden's "This Lunar Beauty" in the previous chapter made it clear that some poems are deliberately contrived to deflect all but a clued-in coterie from guessing its true import. In such a case, it would be strange to attribute the poem's hidden meaning to a speaker other than the poet, especially when, as with "This Lunar Beauty," the poem clearly presents its insight into innocence, beauty, and sorrow as touching and profound. Yet under the influence of the textual fallacy, generations of scholars and classroom teachers have made the poetic speaker—that is to say, a dramatic speaker different from the author—a necessary element of every poem.[19] Given this assumption, the notion that a poet would give a powerful assertion of an idea or sentiment becomes extremely difficult to cope with. Some of the most famous New Critical essays try to show how we can take statements such as "Beauty is Truth, Truth Beauty" not as expressions of dogma but as dramatic or ironic. Deconstructive critics would also work to undermine the force of such statements; for them, language itself becomes the speaker, and, true to its nature, it always says both less and more than the author can have intended.[20]

Let us consider a poem by Emily Dickinson that obviously makes a statement and goes on to exemplify and dramatize its import.

> Success is counted sweetest
> By those who ne'er succeed.
> To comprehend a nectar
> Requires sorest need.
>
> Not one of all the purple Host
> Who took the Flag today
> Can tell the definition,
> So clear of Victory
>
> As he defeated—dying—
> On whose forbidden ear
> The distant strains of triumph
> Burst agonized and clear![21]

It would be not only fatuous but irrelevant to read this poem as an expression of Dickinson's personal despair. She herself warned Thomas Wentworth Higginson against too biographical a way of reading her. "When I state myself," she says, "as Representative of the Verse—it does not mean—me—but a supposed person."[22] But that does not mean we should seek another "supposed person" in whose mouth to put these lines so that we can ironize the poem's statement, make it eccentric, dramatic, or self-enclosed, offering a detached spectacle of deviant consciousness. Rather, it is far more reasonable to accept the fact that it is the poet who is speaking, but speaking poetically, framing an utterance at a certain distance so that it can be experienced for its imaginative qualities and its intellectual value. It would be possible, of course, to look for psychological eccentricities in "Success is Counted Sweetest" that would separate poet and speaker. The phrase "purple Host" might tempt therapeutic ingenuity, and the strangely intellectual way the appreciation of life is framed—"comprehending" a nectar and "tell[ing] the definition" of victory—might be interpreted as signs of an oddly clinical detachment. To read in this way, however, would be to impose an eccentricity of our own.

Accepting the poem as a statement does not mean, of course, that we are left with the mere banality of the idea behind it. The fact that success means more to those who lack it than those who have it is one of those frail half-truths nobody really needs to be told, but what Dickinson offers in this poem is an interesting contemplative formulation of it which is valuable more for the experience than the insight. When she writes "comprehend a nectar," for example, we need not invent a ventriloquist's dummy to take the blame for these lines. As poetry they have a whimsical strangeness that is part of Dickinson's style, a strangeness whose appeal would be diffused by attribution to a misguided, ironic, or psychologically deviant speaker.

This does not mean that there are no complexities, ironies, ambiguities, or ambivalences here, only that they belong to the poet. In the first half of the first quatrain Dickinson states the poem's idea in its most proverbial form, with the contracted "ne'er" adding a note of old country wisdom ("Gather ye rosebuds while ye may"), while in the second half of the quatrain she restates the idea with aphoristic astringency and in a vivid image—"To comprehend a nectar/Requires sorest need." The contrast is striking. The first version is simply ethical in its import while the second suggests a veritable aesthetics of failure, with the suggestion that failure offers a more intense "comprehension" of life's nectar than success. This impression is reinforced by the amplification of the word "clear," from the intellectualist connotation of its first appearance in the telling of "the definition/So clear of Victory" to its fuller sensual and intellectual impact upon consciousness at the end of the poem when the "distant strains of triumph/Burst agonized and clear." The value of failure as an aesthetic enhancement to life—and its value as a subject, indeed a basis, for poetry—has its own ironies, and it is perhaps here, with its reflection upon the nature of poetry, that the poem's attitude is most indubitably the poet's own. At this point the devotees of the textual fallacy might be tempted to displace the tensions and ironies of the poem onto language itself; in the New Critical style we would find a balance between opposing attitudes toward failure that was richer than any statement could be, while from a deconstructive vantage we might see that Dickinson had started out to write a poem about failure and, through the binary instability of language, had been brought around to writing a poem that can just as well be taking failure as a form of success.

Instead, it seems more reasonable to say that there is an undercurrent of ambivalence in the poet's attitude here given that the "forbidden ear" turns out to be the sharpest, subtlest, and clearest by virtue of being the most "agonized," but it is this very ambivalence that Dickinson offers as the poem's point and the basis of the its experience. She is speaking in her own voice and in her own style as the poet who offers this observation for what it is worth to an audience who will read it as poetry. To ascribe it a priori to a distinct speaker or character would be to underestimate its seriousness; to ascribe it to Dickinson like a statement made under oath would be to take it seriously in the wrong way; and to attribute it merely to the text would be to defuse it altogether. Under the influence of the textual fallacy, all poems turn out to be about the same thing—they repeat and enact the ironies of language with tedious predictability; whereas questions about how seriously to take a poem and how to take poems seriously have to be decided poet by poet and poem by poem.[23]

Emily Dickinson is an apt subject for close reading, but it was the "metaphysical" poetry of Donne, Herbert, and Marvell which New Critical readers, following Eliot, took as the paradigms for the complexity, irony, and ambiguity that separate poetic from ordinary language. Unsurprisingly, it was these poets they interpreted best; there was no need for a special theory of poetic language to find wit, irony, and complexity in "The Flea" or "To His Coy Mistress." The rejection of the "intentional fallacy" freed the New Critics from the excessive concern with clarity and sincerity which had made poets like Donne and Marvell, with their violent images and acrobatic wit, unsympathetic in different ways to neoclassical and Romantic readers. The best New Critics—Cleanth Brooks, for example—avoided the temptation to make the metaphysicals into ironized speakers or mere exempla of the power of literary language. They understood metaphysical wit as a conscious artistic strategy and were able to appreciate near-blasphemous poems like "The Canonization" as self-conscious displays of rhetorical fireworks. They did add a certain pathos to metaphysical wit, for in their view great poems cannot be entirely playful or cavalier because poetry, even the wittiest poetry, has a deeply serious cultural mission—to counteract the dulling, logical language of science, which has been undermining the coherence of culture since the seventeenth century. Hence the therapeutic value of the logical distortions supposedly produced by the major poetic tropes, including Donne's favorite, the paradox. It is not clear to me even now that the playfulness of seventeenth-century poetry as an aristocratic diversion has been fully registered by academic critics.

The New Critics were right to say that some of the great metaphysical poets strain the resources of language almost to the breaking point, but this is a good place to remember that, though metaphor, irony, and even paradox use words in surprising ways, they are typically the components of successful and quite transparent utterances. When Oscar Wilde says "I can resist anything but temptation," we know precisely what he means even though our ordinary logical habits are being flouted; when we hear "anything but" we expect a narrow restriction to follow, and here we get anything but—which is exactly the point. New Critical aesthetic value was based on the idea that literary tropes and literary works avoid actually saying anything, whereas actually they allow skillful users to say a great deal.

The challenge for the New Critics was to show how the effectiveness of apparently unparadoxical poetry could be explained in the same terms as Donne without undo strain on the part of the interpreter. Here Brooks leans especially heavily on the notion of paradox. "The language of poetry," he says, "is the language of paradox,"[24] and at the beginning of his Donne essay he gives an example. In the sonnet by Wordsworth that starts "It is a beauteous evening, calm and free./The holy time is quiet as a nun/Breathless with adoration," Brooks sees paradox in the fact that the word "breathless," which he says is a word normally connected with excitement, is being used here at the end of a sequence that describes a hushed evening—"beauteous, calm, free, holy, quiet, breathless" (9). Using the breathless adoration of a nun to convey the quiet of the evening certainly intensifies that quiet and gives it a delicately poised, watchful quality, but there is no paradox. "Breathless" can mean out of breath or panting, but it can also mean simply not breathing or holding one's breath, and that is the meaning that is activated by the phrase "breathless with adoration." The qualification "with adoration" filters the meaning down to a small set of connotations that are relevant, whereas Brooks's search for paradox deactivates this filter. If there is tension between the quiet of the evening and the breathlessness of adoration it is not a tension derived from language. There is no paradox or logical strain, just a precise and beautifully chosen simile.

THE "DEATH OF THE AUTHOR" AND THE "AUTHOR FUNCTION"

In this chapter I have attempted to develop a sense of the author as a working concept in literary studies, building upon the discussions of intention in the previous one. Now it is time to turn to the more radical rejection of the author as a key literary concept. From the mid-1930s to the mid-1960s, the debate about intentionality had a largely theoretical character. It focused on the nature of language or of literary language. In its later phases, though, the debate took on a new, historical dimension under the influence of Roland Barthes and Michel Foucault. When Roland Barthes announced the "Death of the Author" and asserted that authors are mere functions of language, projections of the first-person pronoun, citing linguistics as providing the evidence that "the whole of the enunciation is an empty process" (145), he also gave a clue as to who had killed the author, that supreme representative of the bourgeois order and its constraints upon signification. The perpetrators, it turned out, were authors themselves, canonical ones such as Mallarmé, Flaubert, and Proust who had chosen to reverse the relationship of life and work so that, in a Wildean manner, it was life that imitated art and not the reverse. Mallarmé, Barthes tells us, was the first to "see and to foresee in its full extent the necessity to substitute language itself for the person" and to realize "it is language which speaks, not the author." So the "death of the author" was itself the result of an intentional action and, for Barthes, a historically decisive one. In place of the author there emerged the text—infinite, playful, irreducible, "stereographically plural," "always *paradoxical*," and "*radically* symbolic."[25] The utopian implications of this litany are obvious. But the fact that this utopian program was a deliberately chosen one, a program that Barthes himself was striving to advance, never comes to the surface. Barthes' own agency remains curiously under erasure.

When Barthes tells us that Mallarmé was the first to "see and to foresee" the need to extirpate the author, he provides a key to his own method, which is part observation and part prophecy. He offers no arguments as to why the author should be thought of as dead in the way he describes, only that some artists have wanted it to happen and that it would be a good thing. "The Text," he says, "participates in its own way in a social utopia; before History (supposing the latter does not opt for barbarism), the Text achieves, if not the transparence of social relations, that at least of language relations" (164). Barthes imagines that if the author can be displaced in favor of language itself, the result will be a perfectly transparent signifying system without limitations. This is just the reification of the Word that Jorge Luis Borges so tellingly mocked.

Like "intentional fallacy," the "death of the author" was a brilliant slogan which had more influence than the arguments supporting it. Yet it was not as bleak as the death it was modeled on, Nietzsche's "death of God," because it also led to a compensatory birth, the "birth of the reader." Without authors to exercise constraints on the meanings of texts, readers would be liberated to make of them what they would—to redouble the original effect of writing by projecting a meaning of their own. It is perhaps this implication that gave Barthes' slogan its enormous force. Along with the historical sense of crisis that it generated there was a liberation—a replay, in a sense, of the liberation of art from patronage culture in favor of markets that began in the seventeenth century. The emergence of market opportunities for the artist was accompanied by a gradual shift away from production in the understanding of art toward consumption and "criticism." The production/consumption pendulum has swung more than once, and the shift toward consumption, toward the effects of art rather than its causes, has been pronounced over the last two generations of literary scholars. Amid the enthusiasm for the figure of the reader it is sometimes easy to forget that this figure is often merely an idealized incarnation of the academic critic.

About the issue of intentionality Barthes had little to say. His thinking about language worked almost entirely within the Saussurean concept of the sign and the way it arbitrarily impresses form and meaning on the world. He raises no question about the communicative efficacy of language. The "*Doxa*" or Code imposed by society through language—"the Voice of Nature, the Violence of Prejudice"—functions, in his view, all too effectively.[26] Still, it was the status of his own speech-acts that troubled Barthes. The problem was how to escape from the linguistic code without simply imposing another equally arbitrary one. "Unfortunately," he writes, "I am condemned to assertion: we lack in French [and perhaps in every language] a grammatical mode which would speak *lightly*" (55)—without, in other

words, making a claim to truth. His remedy against "this kind of embarrass-
ment," he states in the third person, is "reminding himself that it is language
which is assertive, not he. An absurd remedy, everyone would surely agree, to
add to each sentence some little phrase of uncertainty, as if anything that
came out of language could make language tremble" (48).

For Barthes, the standard conception of authorship is closely connected
with the sense that the author writes what is true, that his life determines the
nature of his story, rather than the other way around. That language
is grounded in its source, that it has a power of representation, is the mythology Barthes is most concerned to discredit. As he writes about himself, again in
the third person, "He wants to side with any writing whose principle is that *the
subject is merely an effect of language*. He imagines an enormous science, in the
utterance of which the scientist would include himself—the science of the
effects of language" (79). As Seán Burke has pointed out, this means that
those authors Barthes sees as being like himself, authors who undermine or
abandon the myth of representation and see their writing as a mere performance of the effectivity of language rather than an attempt to express a pre-
existing reality, retain their authority and value for him as authors. "When a
text no longer speaks the language of representation," Burke explains, "the
death of the author becomes gratuitous."[27] Paradoxically, the imputed intention of such authors to renounce conventional authorship is decisive. So
whereas in *S/Z* Barthes expended enormous labor undermining the referential
claims of Balzac's fiction, disassembling the Balzacian text into a mesh of codes
and clichés, he can endorse authors such as Joyce, Proust, and Bataille because
he believes they undermine rather than express the subject. They write out of
the insight that it is language that speaks. The same presumably applies
to Barthes' autobiographical reflections. If we take him seriously, we should
not read *Roland Barthes by Roland Barthes* as an attempt to retrace the life and
career of the historical person Roland Barthes but rather as the author Roland
Barthes' construction of his own career, which owes nothing to his biographical past and everything to the language in which he works. We could see
Barthes in his autobiographical writings as an attempt to become a "founder
of language" like Sade, Fourier, and Loyola, those great disciplinarians who,
in his account, withdrew from the world in order to escape from the received
meanings of language, enabling them to impose a new order on the basis of
language itself. "If Sade, Fourier, and Loyola are founders of a language,
and only that, it is precisely in order to say nothing, to observe a vacancy."[28]
But to accept this this would be still to take Barthes more seriously than he asks
to be taken—to take him, in other words, as specifying a correct attitude.

Barthes' project was pursued in a more elaborate fashion by Michel Foucault in "What Is an Author?"[29] Foucault does not argue that understanding authors as functions of discourse is the best way of making sense of the phenomena of authorship in general but rather that authorship as a phenomenon has changed its character and imposed this new conception upon us. Unlike Barthes, however, Foucault thinks it is too soon for us to know precisely what the new conception will be. He follows Barthes, however, in taking his bearings from the revolt against bourgeois psychology among the great modernists, quoting Beckett's words, "What does it matter who is speaking." Foucault identifies indifference to the question of who is speaking as "one of the fundamental ethical principles of contemporary writing," providing the basis of a governing "immanent rule" (101). Two developments follow from this rule of indifference to who is speaking—the banishment of the notion of art as expression, embodied in the new dominance of the signifier over the signified, and the "voluntary effacement" of the writer in his work, which no longer functions as a hedge against the author's death; instead, the author now sacrifices his life to the work. "The work," Foucault says, "which once had the duty of providing immortality, now has the right to kill, to be its author's murderer, as in the cases of Flaubert, Proust, and Kafka" (102). Thus Foucault portrays the Barthesian "death of the author" as a long-accomplished and long-acknowledged historically decisive fact. This argument is closely akin to Fredric Jameson's arguments about postmodernism; both Jameson and Foucault take the procedures and attitudes of elite and avant-garde artists as definitive of their historical era and a reliable index of its ability (or inability) to represent reality.[30]

Already the historical implausibility of Foucault's "immanent rule" should be obvious. There are some modernist authors—Mallarmé may be the best example—who might be thought to give the signifier, in other words the flow of sounds, precedence over the signified, what the sounds say. The trouble is that such authors are clearly in the minority, and Proust and Kafka are certainly not among them. If Foucault can find a single example of obedience to his rule, that is enough for him to attach that rule to an entire phase of culture even when most of the artistic figures of the era—indeed, even the most artistically advanced figures—do not follow it.

As for the claim that Flaubert, Proust, and Kafka sacrificed their lives to their art rather than vice versa, need we believe there is anything modern about that? Art, like any accomplishment, requires sacrifice, the giving up, at the very least, of other things one might be doing. And as for the rewards of art, the great modernists have lived on in their works as much as anyone can be said to do. Art may not have allowed them to overcome death, but it has kept them from being forgotten, which is all that fame ever promised. The need to state such banalities seems odd, but it is the only way of responding to Foucault's remarkable confidence in the face of the obvious.

It is perhaps with a sense of the weakness of his characterization of modernism that Foucault declares the "death of the author" still to be incomplete because authorship as a principle of unity for literary work has migrated into the concept of the work itself and into the Barthesian and deconstructive notion of writing, *écriture*, which "seems to transpose the empirical characteristics of the author into a transcendental anonymity" (104). "To imagine writing," Foucault says, "as an absence seems to be a simple repetition, in transcendental terms, of both the religious principle of unalterable yet never fulfilled tradition, and the aesthetic principle of the work's survival, its perpetuation beyond the author's death, and its enigmatic *excess* in relation to him" (105). One might wonder why the notion that the work survives the author's death is a religious principle, but for our purposes the more important point is that while Foucault sees the "death of the author" as an accomplished fact, he also sees it an incomplete development which has encountered "transcendental barriers" and which he would like to push to its proper conclusion.

Clearly Foucault is attempting to marry historical necessity with his own normative commitment to abolishing bourgeois individuality. Thus his next section begins with a kind of exhortation: "It is not enough ... to repeat the empty affirmation that the author has disappeared.... Instead, we must locate the space of his disappearance, follow the distribution of gaps and breaches, and watch for the openings that this disappearance uncovers" (105). The "death of the author," apparently, is not a fact after all but a project—not a historical reality but a goal of individuals in history. Ironically, with this sequence of metaphors Foucault provides a surprisingly robust portrayal of his own authorial activity—that of the vigilant observer looking for the subtle signs of historical displacement, *locating, following, watching for openings*, in a manner hardly compatible with the immanent rules of the dominance of the signifier over the signified and the necessity of authorial self-effacement.

The rest of Foucault's famous essay is a description of how authorial discourse functions, with an eccentric discussion of proper names and an emphasis on the fact that not all texts are considered to be "authored" in the same sense—that private letters, for example, aren't "authored" in the manner of literary works (107–08).[31] This may be true but it does not mean that there is a conventionally or discursively imposed distinction between what is written for private purposes and what is written for the public. It seems more reasonable to think that everybody's letters are authored in the ordinary sense but that some privately written letters become "authored" in a literary sense if we find it worthwhile to read them with literary interests in mind. The letters of Kafka and Keats have an authorial quality because they were written by people who successfully took up an authorial stance in public. That, in fact, is primarily why we read them at all. And reading their mail does not always help us comprehend their literary works. It will be a matter of judgment as to whether the correspondence between Robert Musil and his tailor bears tellingly upon our understanding of *The Man Without Qualities.*

Foucault also makes the claim that "the author function does not affect all discourses in a universal and constant way," that in the past scientific texts like those of Hippocrates were marked with the names of authors and "literary" ones were not, whereas in the seventeenth or eighteenth century matters got reversed; literary texts were marked by an author whereas as scientific ones were not (109). Again the implication is that some profound change in discursive functioning has occurred. But once more Foucault's presentation of evidence is patently weak. In the same way that the name of Hippocrates served to unify a body of medical texts, the names of whose authors were lost, so the names of Homer, Aesop, and Anacreon functioned in poetry. And as for the anonymity of modern science, here Foucault is perhaps being confused by the fact that our interest in, say, the works of Newton does not relate as directly to the totality of Newton's personal experience as is the case with the works of Milton, natural philosophy being by its nature more impersonal than poetry. But the notion that modern science has become anonymous is the prejudice of a layman who cannot tell the differences between scientists until they win the Nobel Prize. It would come as a great surprise to the highly competitive scientists themselves. Again Foucault is looking for historical rupture where there is none. Notions of authorship vary over time, and some of them—divine inspiration, for example—go out of circulation, but the discontinuities and ruptures are not as extreme as Foucault, looking forward to the completion of a great rupture in the near future, would like to think.

Foucault's most interesting rhetorical turn comes with his discussion of the "complex operation which constructs a certain rational being that we call the 'author',," a being endowed with a "'deep' motive, a 'creative' power, a 'design'" (110). Here we are finally dealing with the concept of the author on a level where there are historical differences to be found, and one may certainly wonder, for instance, about the psychological plausibility of assumptions commonly made by modern critics, especially when we see biographers, who know the facts of their subjects' lives from cradle to grave more fully and accurately than the subjects themselves, discovering connections between life and work that stretch over decades of time. It is not, however, the exaggeration of the rational coherence and sheer powers of memory of the author but his existence at all that is the subject of Foucault's complaint. In a manner reminiscent of Paul de Man, Foucault argues that those "aspects of an individual which we designate as making him an author are only a projection, in more or less psychologizing terms, of the operations we force texts to undergo, the connections that we make, the traits that we establish as permanent, the continuities that we recognize or the exclusions that we practice" (110). In the context of "What Is an Author?" this comes as rather a surprise. Whereas earlier in the essay we have been told that the notion of the work was a holdover from the "death of the author," now it seems that the author is a projection of the work itself as we create it through our own (unquestionably authorial) operations. Then we go on to read that the author serves as a constraint upon "a series of texts," "a point where contradictions are resolved, where incompatible elements are at last tied together or organized around a fundamental or originating contradiction" (111). This is mystifying because, without a common author to bring them into relation with each other, how could there be contradictions or originating elements in any "series of texts"? Without a common author they would not be related at all.

The notion of the author as a limit on meaning is clearly Foucault's central concern. "The author is . . . the ideological figure by which one marks the manner in which we fear the proliferation of meaning" (119). It is with reference to this fear that Foucault moves from the historical triumphalism of the "death of the author" to the prophetic mode in which he envisions the disappearance of the "author function," though in his account the author and the "author function" are supposed to be identical. Foucault speculates that "as our society changes, at the very moment when it is in the process of changing, the author will disappear, and in such a manner that fiction and its polysemous texts will once again function according to another mode, but still within a system of constraint—one which will no longer be the author, but which will have to be determined or, perhaps, experienced" (119). This prophecy is in line with other prophetic moments in Foucault's writings, including his proclamation of the disappearance of the human, and of his own desire to "write in order to have no face."[32] It is important to acknowledge that, unlike Barthes, Foucault is not inviting us into the Library of Babel. He recognizes that meaning requires constraint. But he is akin to the mystic in seeking that constraint in some unspecifiable source or experience rather than the author's intention.

Like "The Death of the Author," "What Is an Author?" hangs uncertainly between diagnosis and prophecy, between the descriptive and the normative. It gestures toward an important subject, the history of conceptions of authorship and artistic activity, but its arguments are strangely ill-informed. Foucault reduces that history to the mere transformations of a concept, and the history of a concept is not the same as the history of the thing itself unless you are the kind of idealistic philosopher who believes that mind—or one of its substitutes (discourse, culture, power)—is the prime mover of history. Foucault does seem to be that kind of philosopher, for "discourse" in his employment has all of the agency he would divert from the author and all of the transcendental autonomy he would strip from *écriture*. Whereas Barthes saw in the "death of the author" the birth of the reader, Foucault sees the power of discourse itself, and that power beckons as the subject of more academic discourse as it charts its own scissions, ruptures, and discontinuities.

In the attacks on the author as a representative of the bourgeois subject we find always the same argumentative structure, the disenfranchisement of the person who speaks in favor of the medium—in other words, the promotion of *langue* over *parole*. It is always language that speaks. The Word comes before its user. So we are either drawn upward toward a realm of power and profundity that is always there, liberating us from the competitive domain of the individual, or we confront a system of concepts and mythologies that imprison our thoughts, leaving us with irony as our only resource. For both the left and the right, the myth of *langue* may be the quintessential myth of the modern. The trouble, again, is that *langue* does not exist without *parole*. It is an abstraction drawn from the empirical reality of individual speech and writing. *Parole* is human activity, *langue* a somewhat useful term for its analysis. From the individual point of view, words seem to have a power of their own, but this is because of the efforts of previous speakers to establish ways of describing, explaining, and communicating about the world. The influence exercised by an existing language is not merely cognitive or semantic. It is social.

The "linguistic turn" and the elevation of *langue, écriture,* and discourse in the mid-twentieth century provide one of the great ironies of modern culture, which was founded crucially on the mistrust of words. The attempt to escape from the seductions of language has been one of modernity's signature themes, from Bacon and Hobbes to Wittgenstein and Quine. Yet in its latest turn backward upon itself, language has once more come into its own, alienated from its origins, purged of its human imperfections, its natural inadequacies, and, through the inadvertent agency of skillful authors, doing its best to eclipse its human source. Supremely fearful of reifying words, the textualist mode culminated in the reification of language itself.

The promotion of *langue* over *parole* was in a sense the culmination of the decentering and transgressive impulses of avant-garde culture from the late nineteenth century forward, but it also had its ascetic and transcendental aspect. It proposed limits to discourse which discourse itself seemed by nature to transgress, and it was an insight so seemingly profound that it inevitably possessed its advocates as something more than verbal. It was always tempting for the devotees of *langue* to proclaim its dominance with a prophetic *parole.* The prophetic temptation in both Barthes' and Foucault's writing about the author appears in the exceptions they make for certain founding figures. Barthes promoted Fourier, Sade, and Loyola as "founders of language" who instituted its use in full awareness of its non-referential freedom. In *The Order of Things,* Foucault repeatedly presents Nietzsche as a grand transgressive and discourse-destroying author who transcends the limits of existing language. And in "What Is an Author?" he identifies Freud and Marx as "founders of discursivity," authors who initiate a form of discourse that remains connected to its source even when it is being augmented and modified by the contributions of others.[33] Clearly neither Barthes nor Foucault can resist endowing their chosen precursors with extra-discursive authorial force.[34]

DECONSTRUCTION AND THE METAPHYSICS OF MEANING

At this point it should be clear to the reader that I agree with advocates of linguistic indeterminacy such as Stanley Fish that, once we rule out intentions, strings of words can mean anything and nothing, and readers must construe them to discern their meaning. Where we differ is that these implications seem to me like a good reason *not* to rule out authorial intentions, whereas they embrace the idea of linguistic interpretation as mere play and see this attitude as providing a salubrious form of demystification. None of them, of course, loses confidence in the usefulness of language in everyday life or in the ability of readers to decipher their own extremely demanding works.

Not all advocates of the indeterminacy thesis do rule out the availability of authorial intentions, however, and certainly not the most influential of them, Jacques Derrida, whose method typically begins with the uncovering of the author's intended meanings followed by the demonstration that the author is not in full control of his instrument.[35] As Seán Burke points out, Derrida's practice embraces psychobiography, history, textual scholarship, intention-guided hermeneutics, as well as deconstruction proper.[36] Derrida is famous for the textualist mantra, "Il n'y a pas de hors-texte," which sounds like an exclusion of intentions. By "text," though, what Derrida means is the conceptual vocabulary which is neither the vocabulary of the world nor the vocabulary of the author but resists being assimilated to either: such "absolute" or "natural" presences as "Nature" in Rousseau's writing have "always already escaped, have never existed."[37] The problem, then, is not that the author's intention cannot be understood; it is the inadequate grounding of his vocabulary, or the fact that the inadequacy of its grounding itself cannot be adequately registered. This is because the writer (Rousseau in this case) is confined, "*held within*" his language so that his sentence says "more, less, or something other than what he *would like to say* [voudrait dire]"; "the writer writes *in* a language and in a logic whose proper system, laws, and life his discourse by definition cannot dominate absolutely. He uses them only by letting himself, after a fashion, be governed by the system" (158).[38]

The reader who has followed my discussion of the inferential character of linguistic activity will not expect, as Derrida does, that language or discourse will have "laws," "logic," or a "proper system" or that its patterns and regularities will stand alone and "govern" the meanings to be conveyed. Language cannot impose its shape or "logic" upon the world because the guidance it provides is much too exiguous to accomplish such a task; to become intelligible, it requires the background of a world and those who communicate about it. If we feel that the language of the past constrains our present thinking that is because the assumptions that support that language are difficult to recognize and dislodge, not because language imposes them on its own. Compare Derrida's anxious and excessively perfectionistic attitude about the power of linguistic systems with Mikhail Bakhtin's account of how we cope with the fact that our words have been invented and already used by others: "Our speech, that is, all our utterances (including creative works), is filled with others' words, varying degrees of otherness or varying degrees of 'our-own-ness,' varying degrees of awareness and detachment. These words of others carry with them their own expression, their own evaluative tone, which we assimilate, rework, and re-accentuate."[39]

As I pointed out earlier, Derrida's doubts about communication are also based upon the notion that the use of language should be without risk. The expectation that the author's discourse should dominate "absolutely" the resources of his language is equally naïve. Authors are dependent upon the information they share with their audience, that which is mutually manifest to them in the act of communication. For the purposes of communication, the fact that they share assumptions and ideas about the world is more important than the ultimate validity of those assumptions and ideas. This does not mean that new thoughts cannot be communicated, but they must be communicated on the basis of shared linguistic resources and information. Only a god, or a transcendental subject, could expect to dominate language "absolutely." Derrida wants to negate the possibility of such a transcendental subject, but he fails to negate the negation. In other words, he fails to recognize that since transcendental domination is a false and misguided hope, it should be abandoned as a standard for judging the efficacy of language.

The easiest course from here would be to set aside ultimate metaphysical questions about the nature of truth and knowledge and leave the reader to assess the importance of intentions in the interpretation of literature on the basis of the practical demonstrations I have provided regarding communication as guided inference. But since important philosophical concerns have motivated the participants in the intentionality debate all along, I will offer some indications about the difference in attitude that separates my own position from those who embrace textualist and indeterminacy arguments regarding the foundations of truth and knowledge. These issues have been advanced by poststructuralist authors in a peculiarly dramatic form—as the critique of Western metaphysics grounded in the presence of Being. The indeterminacy they discover in language does not betoken the empirical or contingent failure of a practical instrument but is the disappointment of a metaphysical expectation that cannot be satisfied. The critique of metaphysics exists in many different and brilliant versions, offered by such figures as Nietzsche, Heidegger, and Lévi-Strauss, but the basic pattern of argument goes back to Greek skepticism. It starts with this question: What does it take to let us to say that one of our beliefs is true or, alternatively, that we know something? The common-sense answer is that there have to be a number of other things we believe to be true and these things taken together make the belief in question true (or highly probable). In other words, we have reasons for what we believe to be true. To say that something is true, then, is typically to see it as the conclusion of an argument.

Evidently, though, we cannot be any more confident in the conclusions we draw than in our premises for them. The moment we come to question these premises, we must question the conclusion as well. So it seems that, if we are rational inquirers, we will want to seek the premises of our premises. There lies the problem, for no matter how many layers of presupposition we uncover and justify, we will never get to the starting point; we will never find the grounds of our first premises, because to call something true is to make it the conclusion of an argument, and a first premise is by definition a proposition that has no prior reasons to support it. It cannot be a conclusion and a premise at the same time.

This line of thinking seems to lead quite directly to a very disturbing conclusion—we ought not say that anything is true, or that we know anything, because our conclusions rest upon premises which cannot be validated or even, in fact, fully identified. Ancient philosophers had another way of putting the matter. To identify the truth you need a criterion of truth, but to identify the criterion you need a separate criterion for that one, and on again into infinity. Taking this line of thought to its logical conclusion, we cannot say that anything is true or that we know anything.

This conclusion, though, is a hasty one, for the moment we say even these things we have to take them back because we are continuing in the very mode we have just admitted to be groundless. We are still making a statement, implying that we have reasons to do so, that those reasons have reasons, and so on. The logical upshot is, we cannot say we have the truth and we cannot say we don't have it. Both are equally groundless. Truth has the strange quality of being at once both uncertifiable and undisclaimable. You can't embrace it but you can't get rid of it, rather like a stray dog who won't stop following you home. Unable to avoid saying either too little or too much, we are stuck in mid-air. Attempting to come down, we only flap our wings more helplessly.

This impasse has, of course, produced a number of celebrated responses. One was Descartes's search for a foundational thought that validates itself: *I think, therefore I am.* This is still a live idea. It seems to allow us make a statement that is undoubtedly true. Unfortunately the path from validating that statement to validating the rest of the things we tend to believe is a difficult one. In Descartes's treatment it depends upon assumptions about God—his existence and unwillingness to deceive us—that are less prevalent and plausible than they were when Descartes made them.

Empiricism was another important response to the impasse. Instead of rebuilding the world from the top down, as Descartes did, it attempts to build from the ground up. Empiricism is based on the idea that we have discrete experiences or sensations ("sense date," "impressions") that, considered one by one and apart from anything else we know, constitute knowledge and, individually or combined, are a basis for true statements. This approach dominated Anglo-American philosophy from the mid-seventeenth century till the mid-twentieth, but in recent decades its currency has weakened. The trouble is that mere sensations by themselves, considered apart from any context and independent of our conceptual vocabulary, don't seem adequate to count as knowledge or the basis of truth. Further, when we say something is true we may be responding to a state of affairs in the world but we are also responding to a state of the vocabulary in which we think about the world, and these two things are difficult to separate and establish independently.

Now we come to a third way of responding to the impasse, the one that has been most attractive to avant-garde literary theorists, which is to take that impasse itself to be foundational, just as Heidegger took Schelling's ontological question—"Why is there something rather than nothing?"—to be foundational for his conception of being as lived experience. It is a neat trick to make skepticism itself a foundation, but that is the best way to describe the approach of deconstruction as it was practiced by Jacques Derrida.[40] Derrida makes language the focus of his inquiry, discovering in each statement both an excess of metaphysical confidence and an awareness of that excess. Characteristic of Derrida's practice is his borrowing of Heidegger's gesture of putting key terms in the philosopher's lexicon *sous rature*, which is to say, "under erasure," writing the words and crossing them out to signify both their ability to play their roles and their deficiency in playing them. Thus Derrida is able to dramatize the impasse as a form of play between unstable positions.

It might seem improbable that skepticism about the meaningfulness of language could provide the basis of Derrida's enormous interpretive productivity, not to mention that of his many followers, but Derrida had a crucial resource, Saussurean linguistics, which holds that every sign is a bonding of differences within two unlike systems—the system of sounds (signifier) and the system of concepts (signified). The key notion here was that in the same way the sounds which a language fixes upon to be significant are arbitrary and therefore meaningful only in relation to each other, so the repertoire of concepts is also equally arbitrary and the concepts meaningful only in relation to each other. Take the natural numbers as an example. They begin with the number 1 and you might think that 2 is 2 of 1, 3 is 3 of 1, and so on. A deconstructive reading, though, would point out that the notion of a single unit cannot exist outside the system of difference. So 1 depends upon 2, 3, and the other natural numbers as much as they depend upon it. It would be a typical deconstructive strategy to argue against the notion that 1 is primary by saying that 2 actually comes before 1 because 1 can only establish its identity in contrast with 2. Similarly, a text that takes *male* as a primary category must ignore the crucial role of the concept *female* in distinction from which *male* establishes its identity; *female* is now revealed as the hidden primary term. Semantic hierarchies are thus overturned, and what was once in the margin is revealed to be at the center insofar as there is a center in this unstable process.

This way of reading became the modus operandi of deconstruction. It starts by identifying semantic features of the work that appear to refer to the world outside them but always turn out to be defined internally within the work as mere features of difference, thus allowing the junior partner in every binary opposition to be rescued from the margin because only in opposition to it could the primary term be defined. It was an ingenious way of tapping into the anti-essentialist appeal of Saussure's model, for which concepts are purely relational: there are no positive terms—no entities, quiddities, essences, or species. Concepts maintain what stability they have not in relation to the world they refer to and the speakers who use them but only in relation to the system of differences in sound, to which they in turn lend stability. Our conceptual vocabulary thus turns out to be an arbitrary social construction.

Here, however, we come back to the impasse and find ourselves saying too much, for once we try to assert that "language is everywhere" or that there is "nothing outside the text," or the discourse or structure or sign, we seem to be forgetting that these things are themselves only figures of discourse which do not exist outside the differential system which itself cannot be constituted as a separate entity. The moment we try to say "X is only a Y" we have endorsed the existence of a Y and thereby invented another term demanding deconstruction. Derrida speculates that what ultimately indicates the "quality and fecundity" of a discourse is the "rigor" with which it works out this set of problems with relation to the history of the metaphysically loaded concepts it deploys (282). "Rigor" here, it seems, turns out to be more or less an aesthetic value since the explanation of one term in relation to another can never succeed. Every attempt to come to rest in a set of analytic terms must be eventually abjured since no endorsement of a conceptual vocabulary can either be sustained or definitively rejected. This is what I mean by saying that the impasse I described above became for deconstructionists a kind of foundation. It is a surface you can ride along but never get off. The moment you try to declare the limits of your discourse you find you have stepped beyond.

At the end of his early, rhetorically brilliant programmatic essay on Lévi-Strauss, Derrida poses two attitudes toward the "interpretation of interpretation" he has offered. One is the Rousseauistic sense of the loss of origins, "saddened, *negative*, nostalgic, guilty," the other a Nietzschean "joyous affirmation of the play of the world and of the innocence of becoming, without truth and without origin" (292), the latter aiming, with the renunciation of the metaphysical hopes that define the human species, "to pass beyond man and humanism" (292). These are obviously two forms of desperation, and the essay ends on an apocalyptic note that takes us back to the mid-sixties moment it was written. There was no possibility of choosing between Rousseauistic nostalgia and Nietzschean affirmation, Derrida says, but he finds himself, like many members of his society, turning his eyes away "when faced by the as yet unnamable which is proclaiming itself and which can do so, as is necessary whenever a birth is in the offing, only under the species of the nonspecies, in the formless, mute, infant, and terrifying form of monstrosity" (293). Like Barthes and Foucault, Derrida in his understanding of language looked forward to a decisive rupture with the human past, a disappearance of the human and the arrival of something monstrous.

If it seems absurd to define the human species by the unsuccessful attempt to grapple with a problem made by a single Eurocentric philosophical tradition, there is something genuinely disturbing about the fact that our perfectly everyday insight that we cannot be more sure of a conclusion than we are of the premises supporting it leads to the impasse I've described. So let us return to that problem. I have surveyed only three of the responses it has evoked and cannot deal with all of them. The attempts to redefine truth in minimalist or deflationary terms or to reduce it to practical consequences, justification, or warranted assertability while still doing justice to the role it plays in our thinking lead to logical complications and subtleties I cannot pursue here even if I were qualified to do so. Instead I will take up another response to the impasse, which is to say that if the notion of proving your first premises seems to be a contradiction in terms, then it would be best to give up the attempt altogether. I am suggesting a position that is not so much anti-foundationalist as non-foundationalist.[41] This approach emphasizes the fact that language is a natural instrument for thinking and communicating, that we are always developing and adjusting it, and that there is no way of harnessing its individual elements to a foundation apart from the workings of the whole. Donald Davidson's writings on the subject provide an example of how to think about truth and knowledge which requires no further metaphysical commitments than the ones we need to understand the act of communication itself.

Davidson argues that we should not try to define truth. It is too closely caught up with other primary notions like meaning and thought, and they are too closely caught up with it, for any of them to provide a foundation for the others. But looking to its use, we see that it is primarily a notion that helps us interpret each other as well as to understand the world, those two tasks being in essence one. Truth is a semantic concept. To know the conditions under which people take a sentence to be true is to know what it means to them. When we are trying to learn a language by interacting with its speakers—the situation Davidson calls "radical interpretation"—we must assume as much as possible that they think along the same lines we do, and we use this presumptive agreement to guess at the meanings of their words. Our theory of meaning is thus also a theory of belief. As we translate, we trade off between what we think our informants ought to be saying about the world in a particular situation and the way they ought to be using their words given the meanings we've ascribed to them. We apply, in other words, what he calls a "principle of charity."[42]

The appeal of this theory is that it provides a substantial and informative account of how the concept of truth functions without implying that the elements of language stand in some special relation to the elements of the world unmediated by the speakers who use it. "Truth" is a tool of interpretation. One needs it to cope with other people and to proceed with one's own efforts of thought, which cannot get along without the distinction between being right and being wrong. And though we can use it to think about things that don't involve other people—particle physics, for example, or the reproduction of fungi—when we think we are always operating with a social instrument which has a certain fit between meaning and belief as an indispensable norm.

Davidson's conception of truth permits an interesting response to the Cartesian skeptic who imagines the possibility that an all-powerful demon might be keeping him from having any actual knowledge of the world outside his own mind. Davidson's move is to remind the skeptic that he would not have been able to learn enough language to understand the demon-argument in the first place if he were not connected to an actual world and other speakers who are also in contact with it. My understanding of words depends upon no bare assignment of word to object; rather it is a theory about how people use the word, a theory that tries to optimize both the rationality of their linguistic behavior and their thinking about the world. No world, no people; no people, no language; no language, no doubt, and no demon.[43] This does not mean we can't be wrong about things, but we can't meaningfully say we're wrong except against the background of a generally successful process of thought, communication, and interaction with the world.

For the purposes of literary theory Davidson's philosophy of language is instructive for its essential use of intentionality,[44] its refusal of skepticism without short-circuiting normal uncertainty, and for the three-way relation it establishes between language, speakers, and world. While Davidson insists, perhaps too confidently, that we have no power to think about the world without language, he equally insists that we have no power to use language without access to the world and without the people with whom we share it and communicate about it. This perspective frees us from the notion that language is a frictionless medium which imposes its own arbitrary structures upon the world in the manner of an Ockhamite God, a view that is hard to reconcile with the underdeterminacy of language I have been emphasizing. It also discourages the notion that mind functions free of what it thinks about, imposing its own internal order upon the world. And finally it discourages a notion of culture that could serve this role, as Davidson argued in his well-known essay on "The Very Idea of a Conceptual Framework."[45] For the same reasons it would relieve us of Kuhnian paradigms, Foucauldian epistemes, and the "discourse of power." Davidson takes words as part of the world; we learn to use them as we learn our way around. So if the world does not impose its meanings upon our language, neither does language impose its structure on the world.

The upshot of the position I have outlined here is that we should not expect to ground our knowledge in an indubitable foundation nor seek to define the most basic terms of our vocabulary and use them as the basis for understanding everything else. These are expectations we are better off without, and to insist on them is to oscillate, just as Derrida describes, between the sense of loss and the embrace of emptiness. Such an abandonment of the foundationalist attitude was tirelessly preached by Richard Rorty under the banner of pragmatism. Rorty was right to say that we should not expect philosophy to provide a ground for the methods and procedures of other fields and that the disciplines should simply go about their business without deferring to philosophy's general theory of knowledge. But he was wrong, and self-contradictory, to insist that the absence of foundational Truth is itself a great philosophical lesson we all must take to heart. Rorty frequently wrote as if he wanted to reform our everyday sense of the meaning of truth and knowledge, thus remaining just the kind of philosophical prophet he set out to discredit. Also, one could easily interpret Rorty as implying that philosophers have nothing useful to say about the quality of arguments in other disciplines and that the absence of metaphysical foundations for our knowledge means that all other philosophical issues are now moot. These need hardly be the case. It is ironic that the advocate of inquiry as a kind of conversation often sounded like he wanted the conversation to end.

These brief remarks are designed to provide a context for one of the motives of skepticism about literary meaning. I will make one more observation about the benefits of renouncing the hopes of metaphysical grounding for our knowledge and the discomfort that comes with it. There are many aspects of our thinking besides the ones I have been discussing here which we have to take on faith. The principle of induction is a well-known example. The list of basic but unprovable assumptions in physical science is impressive, including the assumption that the laws we derive from observations made in our tiny quadrant of the universe can reliably be extended beyond it.[46] Barry Stroud has added the concepts of cause, necessary cause, and value to the list of things we can neither renounce nor find reasons to support.[47] We cannot explain anything without them, according to Stroud, and therefore we cannot explain them. We cannot coherently occupy an intellectual space in which we have not already taken them for granted. Therefore we will never be able to understand them in terms of anything else or reduce them to anything else we already understand.

Take the concept value as an example. In order for us to endorse a statement—about value or any other subject—we have to pronounce that statement worthy of belief. We have to assign it, therefore, a value. So evaluation is inseparable from the process of thought itself. We cannot think without it. And if we cannot think without it, we cannot think about it, not in the full sense of being able to question its value. We can call the problem to mind, be bothered by it, imagine resolving it, but we cannot set the operative concept at a sufficient rational distance from ourselves to consider giving it up. It is simply *too close* for us to do that. The tension between these two senses of "thinking about"—calling to mind versus genuinely questioning—can give rise to a feeling of entrapment in our own thoughts. It's not necessarily that we have a preference for skepticism and questioning. It's just that if we can't coherently question something in the full sense of assessing its validity, it seems as if we cannot fully make it our own. Stroud calls this "metaphysical dissatisfaction." But this is just the point where it is an advantage to say that our concepts show their validity not by withstanding a foundational critique but by guiding our interaction with the world and other users of language. Without this acceptance of our limits, our metaphysical dissatisfaction will be severe indeed.

PREMODERN, MODERN, AND POSTMODERN

The burden of the foregoing exposition has been to explain why the vocabulary of literary study cannot function without the concept of authorial intention. Without this concept we simply cannot make sense of the way literary language, or any other kind of language, works. The mere text is not enough. Most of the arguments that made textualism fashionable were extremely weak and hard to pin down—those of Roland Barthes being notably so. But as the foregoing discussion of deconstruction would suggest, the generally skeptical turn of modern literary scholarship also played a part. For modern intellectuals, the very discovery that a belief can be questioned is often sufficient to discredit it. Perhaps our greatest credulity has been our reflexive openness to doubt.

As I mentioned in Chapter 1, however, the allure of textualism and the disenfranchisement of authors cannot be understood in purely theoretical terms. It also has much to do with the differing social positions of art during the succeeding phases of modernity. It is within the context of this story that we must ultimately understand the urge to put authorship into eclipse, so here I digress from the theoretical pursuit of my theme to suggest in the broadest possible strokes its historical aspect in connection with postmodernism. The eventual rejection, in the upper echelons of literary culture, of practices based on the expressive self and the individual vision of the artist is best understood as the exposure and exhaustion of the modern solution to the artistic challenges of cultural modernity.

The tale of modernity can be told in many ways, but for our purposes, certain very basic details of classical—or better, premodern—literature bear special emphasis, especially the stance of the premodern artist and the role of literature in relation to its content. First and most obviously, before modernity literature was not under the obligation to discover the truth but rather to convey the already known. If artists are closer to the truth than their audience, that is only because they have labored to acquire an erudition and a wisdom that in theory are available to others. The epic poet and courtly maker retell a familiar story with an accepted religious, moral, or political (often Platonic) significance. There is no suspense or mystery involved, no difference, as Coleridge pointed out, between reading and rereading. The story itself, as he observed, is no more than the pre-existing canvas upon which the artist paints his vision.[48] The artist's sincerity or insincerity is little in question because the truth of his vision is not in question. It is already known. The artist's claim to merit is not in the content of the story but in how it is told. The truth may be well established, but the stories that hold it are infinitely malleable, recombinable, and repeatable. For the premodern artist, the truth is already a story. There is no tension between the literary determinism of the genre and the intellectual value of the truth it expresses—no tension, in other words, between form and content. The challenge for the artist is to discover the most powerful version of the truth and those conventions which offer the best resources for expressing it. Artists do not stand alone; they do not write only as individuals. They provide an enhanced version of a set of truths that everyone with a certain degree of access to culture can see.

I am offering here a Weberian type, the artist in the premodern mode of truth, which is clarifying partly in virtue of all that it leaves out. What is easy to forget about the position of the artist in the premodern mode, as opposed to its modern successor, is that while the modern artist may be more visible as a subject within his work, the premodern artist displays his activity and skill with greater abandon. He is in a position of freedom with regard to his activity and participates to no little degree in the heroic values of the aristocratic culture he glorifies and promotes. (We who have largely renounced these heroic values still find it embarrassing to see premodern, especially Renaissance, artists cringing before those patrons with whom they had to share the credit for their accomplishments and without whom they would have been unable to work.) The artist is not embarrassed to remind us that he is turning already existing truth into art. In fact he is eager to do so. He puts on display the entire armamentarium of rhetoric— grand digressions, heroic similes, far-fetched conceits, and invocations to the muse. His activity is a part of the truth that he conveys. He is a servant and creature of the muse, and as such has his place in the story.

Modern works of art and literature, so persistently focused on expressing the sovereign individual rather than being the servant of truth, emerged with the rejection of the heroic artist and his patrons. We move from the mode of truth to the mode of experience, an essentially passive dimension— one that constricts theological speculation and underwrites liberal politics but also confines the artistic subject, making it both essentially private and passive. To come onto the modern stage, the artist had to take off his laurel crown and become the subject rather than the maker of his art. There were two primary roles—the poet, who presents his own experience, and the novelist, who presents the experience of others, including that other who is himself in society. The first was the domain primarily of male authors while the second admitted women, who made up a substantial part of the audience and who figured in its Richardsonian origins as the bourgeois subject personified.

Gradually the modern artist achieved a cultural status rarely hoped for by artists in the premodern world. Freed from patronage and served by mass markets, he became the privileged articulator of private experience and its connections to things beyond itself, moving hopefully between those two problematic and incompatible unifying factors, nature and society. But in order to function in this position, the artist had to do without the freedom that belonged to the artist in the mode of truth. In the mode of experience, the artist becomes a figure of necessity and takes the world as a given. The more obviously his work is shaped by literary choices and rhetorical skills, the less persuasively it renders experience, either the experience of others or his own. Whereas the courtly maker stood perhaps only a little closer to the truth than his audience, the artist now becomes the very locus and guarantee of the truth of experience. The origins of the maker's truth were absorbed into the work itself, whereas the artist's truth, the truth of life, is now the very substance of the work. The maker has no reason to conceal that he is a particular individual exercising choice in retelling a familiar story to which he attributes a general or universal significance. But for the modern writer, to repeat a familiar story is to divorce the work from the uniqueness of experience. To advertise choice in the shaping of materials is to deprive the work of its authenticity, which derives from necessity. To let a general message shine through the particulars is to detach the work from its lived origin in experience. The mode is essentially genetic, focused on origins instead of ends, history instead of verity. This genetic mode gave license to a wholesale reinterpretation of the art of the past in its own image, to see the writings of the past—of Dante, Shakespeare, and Milton—as autobiography writ large, the products of psychological struggle.

The ambiguity of the author's position is beautifully encapsulated in the claims of art to "realism." While art can legitimately claim to offer what is universal and true (at least for those who believe that the truth exists), it can never offer what is real. What it offers as reality is actually an illusion—an invitation to a shared illusion. But every reminder of the author's presence behind his words detracts from the illusion, which depends upon particularity rather than universality and the concealment of creation. It is the writer's concealment of the universal and willed dimension of art that gives point not only to autobiographical reduction but also to ideological critique. For writers who deny the typical character of the experiences they present, the latent purposes and universalizing implications of their work become a hidden point of vulnerability. Ideology critiques unmask the hidden universal and the moral beneath the writer's claim to be authentic and unique. Suspicion looks beneath the surface of difference to discover the identity of the same.

The modern conceptions of art and of the aesthetic reflect the change in perspective I am attempting to sketch. As Paul Kristeller argued in his groundbreaking essay "The Modern System of the Arts," we owe our unified conception of the "fine arts" to the eighteenth century. Before that, the term "art" served mostly to contrast with nature and referred to excellence in any endeavor, including what we now call science. It was synonymous with skill and craft, our versions of the Greek *techné*, and closely linked, in the case of literary making, with rhetoric. Only in the course of the eighteenth century do we see a separation of "art" from science—part of the victory of the ancients over the moderns—and with it the emergence of the "fine arts," part of the promotion of the status of art that came with the arrival of the market. It was in this period that the theater became respectable and other modern institutions for the popular consumption of art were established: periodicals, coffee houses, lending libraries, public concerts, and museums. The key text, Kristeller argues, is Charles Batteux's *Les beaux arts reduits à un même principe* (1746), where the most common grouping of the "fine arts" appears—poetry, painting, sculpture, architecture, and music. Kristeller speculates that the grouping of the arts together in terms of the kind of experience they offer represents a shift of perspective from the maker to the consumer that is part of the emerging culture of the market.[49] The final step in this process would be the Kantian concept of the aesthetic, which applies equally to nature and to art, defining its object entirely in terms of the consumer's experience.[50]

Modernism was, in many ways, the gradual repudiation by elite culture of the regime of experience and the cult of the aesthetic, while postmodernism was its final abolition.[51] In the mid-nineteenth century we see artists such as Flaubert pushing experience to its extremes, while investing new significance in the literary form and in the artist as maker. Looking for a new, more elite audience, artists sought to highlight their own originality and powers of innovation, and even the whimsicality and arbitrariness of their intentions. *Intentions*, it is interesting to note, was the title of the volume by Oscar Wilde that included "The Decay of Lying." Such demonstrations of whimsy were responsible for the aura of scandal surrounding modern art noted by Stanley Cavell, its habitual way of courting accusations of fraudulence,[52] a signal of the eventual disenfranchisement of the author. It is at this point, from a number of different directions, that the cult of literary language arises. Literary language itself acquires powers that are not of artists' making but inherent in their very medium. It takes away the artist's privileged relation to experience. Its quality transcends the individual. Literary language belongs at least as much to the critic as to the artist since the critic is the one who has the technical knowledge to explain its special qualities. Art for art's sake is another step in this direction.

Finally, by the 1960s, we see the mode of experience displaced altogether, with the most authentic-seeming art and literature addressing the world as already written over, already transformed by imagination. The social pressure of the mass media upon art and other forms of cultural activity now becomes a primary subject of art. Literary authors find themselves too far behind the information curve to make their impact by bringing new experience to market. Whereas Balzac's Paris and Dickens' London offered vast unexplored territories with hidden social enclaves of all kinds, now newspapers, television, and the internet bring experience to the public too quickly for the novelist get there first. Unlike truth, which is not limited to time or place, unfatigued by repetition, and unmarked by individual difference, experience is limited and personal and can become a commodity, its rate of market turnover having increasingly accelerated with the ever-decreasing costs of communication. And commodities of course can be exhausted or the market for them taken over by other suppliers.

To speak of the exhaustion of the mode of experience, then, is simply to say that artists no longer have the monopoly they once had upon the conveying of experience as a commodity. They can continue to strive for new and extreme experiences, as some performance artists do, but the fact that such experiences have to be pursued beyond the limits of the normal and the average guarantees their marginal character. They lack the necessity and indeed the passivity that belongs to genuine "experience" in the modern mode. Their works are too clearly gestures of will. The compensation for the loss of unmediated experience is the opportunity to make mediated experience part of the subject of art, but this is also a resource that art must share with the mass media, which are also much preoccupied with themselves.

What is the moral of this story for literature and the other arts that have passed through the phase of postmodernism? It is certainly not that literature or visual art or music has come to an end. If the most advanced classical music has become an esoteric pursuit, pop music is everywhere. It had its renaissance in the 1960s and 1970s and has its own cadre of historians, experts, and fans with wide knowledge. It sometimes acquires the aura of profundity. Photography and film have their own artistic development. And just about every kind of modern literature is still being written, from nature poetry to postmodern metafiction. What has disappeared is the special frisson that belongs to a work which is grounded in either a truth beyond the artist's making and to which he leads his audience, as in premodern art, or a new and authentic experience of necessity which he shares with his audience, as in modern art. The aura of power that comes of being able to provide those commodities has either faded or moved to other media which do not package them as literature. Much of the vitality of contemporary literature has depended upon the contributions of writers from less economically and technologically developed countries which have not yet reached the level of media saturation that characterizes advanced modernity, writers from the periphery of modernization who have not yet been deprived of the ability to reinterpret familiar experiences and recombine them in interesting ways. The recent popularity of memoir, which catalogues the particularities of individual experience without a claim to art, is another symptom of these changes.

It is a mistake, then, to say as Fredric Jameson does in his essay on postmodernism, that Nature and History have now moved out of reach and that literary language no longer has a referent just because realistic representations of them now seem less authentic than works that call attention to their own fictiveness.[53] If anything, Nature and History are now too close to us to depend upon art for our appreciation of them. They are more vividly and continually accessible through other media, embodied in other forms than the ones we associate with the phenomenology of spirit or the Western literary imagination.

It is in this context that we can see most clearly the impulse to reject authorial intention. On the one hand, the desire to detach authorship from works was a product of the early twentieth century's nostalgia for an ideal religious and political order that is no longer credible for the majority of university-educated people in the West. Nurtured in a Romantic culture that personalized everything and surrounded by a democratizing and, for them, vulgarizing mass culture, Eliot and Lewis tried to get behind the bourgeois artist in order to let art and, indeed, language speak for itself. But there was also the sense that the strategies of bourgeois art had reached a dead end and wreaked a dispossession on the artist, so that Eliot and his fellow modernists were making a virtue of necessity. Later, radicals such as Barthes and Foucault took the exhaustion of bourgeois individualism in art as a sign of utopian possibilities. They also wanted to separate language from author so that it would be free of human limitations, and they were willing to surrender agency to the medium of language—to *langue*. Instead of looking to the past and to an ideal order they looked forward to an unknowable future. Their proclamation of the author's death betrayed a regicidal enthusiasm—"The author is dead, long live the reader!"

Both the conservative and the utopian critics of the author missed their targets, confusing a historically local set of strategies of literary production with authorship itself. In doing so they marginalized an essential resource for understanding literature. The author is a more mundane figure than either of them realized, with a connection to language no more magisterial than the user of ordinary speech. Authors are authors whether they write well or badly, whether the invitations they offer to their readers are worth answering or not, whether they achieve originality or merely reproduce the already known. The emergence of newly impersonal forms of literature does nothing to remove them from the special relation where writer and reader meet. Writing is a human, all-too-human action, and it must have an agent behind it. To deny that is to mislocate both the powers and the failures of writing, to remove the flesh and blood in the toil of writing and obscure the social nexus of the meeting of minds.

NOTES

1. There are, of course, sentences which have not yet become utterances, so we can say their meaning is indeterminate because they have no definite context. Take for example those signs one sometimes sees in furniture stores: *This item not for sale*. They serve to distinguish between the furnishings that belong to the store and those that are being sold. The full meaning of such a sentence, like all the ones that contain pointing expressions like "this," is indeterminate until it is actually used in connection with a particular item. It means something different when attached to a couch, a chair, or a lamp, and one can imagine rogue utterances, perhaps as a plaque sitting on a politician's desk.

2. See William Lycan's interesting attempt to bring together the semantic aspect of metaphor stressed by John Searle with the sensual aspect stressed by Donald Davidson, in "An Irenic Idea about Metaphor," *Philosophy* 88 (2013): 5–32.

3. See especially "Epistemology Naturalized," in *Ontological Relativity and Other Essays* (New York: Columbia University Press, 1969), chapter 3.

4. Paul de Man, *The Resistance to Theory* (Minneapolis, MN: University of Minnesota Press, 1987), 16. All the quotations in this paragraph are from this page.

5. Paul de Man, *Blindness and Insight: Essays in the Rhetoric of Contemporary Criticism* (Minneapolis: University of Minnesota Press, 1983), 9.

6. Jacques Derrida, *Limited Inc.* (Evanston, IL: Northwestern University Press, 1988), 15. Brackets in original. Derrida's concerns about "iterability" are based on equally weak reasoning, as John Searle brought out in his unpleasant set of exchanges with Derrida which cemented the split between literary theorists and analytic philosophers of language. See John Searle, "Reiterating the Differences: A Reply to Derrida," in *Glyph: Johns Hopkins Textual Studies* (Baltimore, MD: The Johns Hopkins University Press, 1977), 1: 198–208.

7. In Canto Four of the *Inferno*, Dante the explorer-narrator plays on the fiction of the author's real world when he ostentatiously truncates his account of the great spirits in the first circle because there is so much more of the journey left to tell. See *Inferno* 4: 145–47.

8. Wayne C. Booth, *The Rhetoric of Fiction* (Chicago: University of Chicago Press, 1961), 158–59.

9. Booth, *The Rhetoric of Fiction*, 70–76. Booth's strategy has been adapted by a number of other critics who discover hypothetical or postulated author or writers. For a useful gathering of examples see Part 2 of William Irwin, ed., *The Death and Resurrection of the Author?* (Westport, CT: Greenwood Press, 2002).

10. Erving Goffman, *The Presentation of Self in Everyday Life* (New York: Doubleday, 1959), chapter 6.

11. Readers who disagree with me about Thackeray and Becky will be able to provide their own examples of authors who take their characters in the wrong direction. Many, including Unamuno, have accused Cervantes (wrongly I would say) of not being worthy of his own creation, Don Quixote, subjecting the worthy man to ridicule. It seems to me that William Faulkner erred in a late addition to *The Sound and the Fury* when he gave Caddy Compson a future with a Nazi officer. See the Appendix to *The Sound and the Fury* in Malcolm Cowley, ed., *The Portable Faulkner* (New York: Viking, 1946).

12. Colin Lyas, "The Relevance of the Author's Sincerity," in Peter Lamarque, ed., *Philosophy and Fiction* (Christchurch, NZ: Cybereditions, 2000), 32–54.

13. Lyas, "Sincerity," 50.

14. For a detailed account of the "fictive stance" and the non-truth-related concept of fiction to which I am indebted see Peter Lamarque and Stein Haugom Olsen, *Truth, Fiction, and Literature: A Philosophical Perspective* (New York: Oxford University Press, 1994).

15. Drawing on the pioneering work of the linguist William Labov, Mary Louise Pratt shows the common means and strategies shared by literary and vernacular storytellers in chapter 2 of *Toward a Speech Act Theory of Literary Discourse* (Bloomington, IN: Indiana University Press, 1977).

16. Kendall L. Walton, *Mimesis as Make-Believe: On the Foundations of the Representational Arts* (Cambridge, MA: Harvard University Press, 1990). Walton neglects the author's role as the proposer of this game.

17. It is worth adding here that, if a fictive narrative turns out unexpectedly to be true in fact, that does not alter the stance with which it was originally composed.

18. John Searle, "The Logical Status of Fictional Discourse," in Peter Lamarque and Stein Haugum Olsen, eds., *Aesthetics and the Philosophy of Literature: An Anthology* (Malden, MA: Blackwell Publishers, 2004), 327.

19. As we have seen, Wimsatt and Beardsley included this as one of the axioms in "The Intentional Fallacy": "Even a short lyric poem is dramatic, the response of a speaker (no matter how abstractly conceived) to a situation (no matter how universalized). We ought to impute the thoughts and attitudes of the poem immediately to the dramatic *speaker*, and if to the author at all, only by an act of biographical inference" (202). William Wimsatt and Monroe C. Beardsley, "The Intentional Fallacy" (1946), in

Virginia Jackson and Yopie Prins, eds., *The Lyric Theory Reader: A Critical Anthology* (Baltimore, MD: Johns Hopkins University Press, 2014), 202. Eight years earlier, Cleanth Brooks and Robert Penn Warren, in their highly influential textbook *Understanding Poetry*, left a little more room for the poet's voice. "All poetry, including short lyrics, or descriptive pieces, involves a dramatic organization. This is clear when we reflect that every poem implies a speaker of the poem, *either the poet writing in his own person or someone into whose mouth the poem is put*...." Emphasis added. "Introduction to *Understanding Poetry* (1938), in Prins and Jackson, *The Lyric Theory Reader*, 191. T. S. Eliot's essay "The Three Voices of Poetry" (1953) was an attempt to discourage the reduction of lyric to dramatic poetry.

20. See "Keats' Sylvan Historian," in Cleanth Brooks, ed., *The Well-Wrought Urn: Studies in the Structure of Poetry* (New York: Harcourt, Brace, Jovanovich, 1975), 151–66. In his superb article "Dramatic Monologue and the Overhearing of Lyric," Herbert F. Tucker shows that the development of the dramatic monologue by Tennyson and Browning in the 1830s was precisely contemporaneous with Mill's hyper-Romantic theory of poetry and can be seen as a form of resistance to theories of this type. Tucker suggests that the dramatic monologue was supremely fruitful for the development of modern poetry, but at a high theoretical price: "Upon the establishment of Yeats' mask, Pound's personae, Frost's monologues and idylls, and Eliot's impersonal poetry, it became a point of dogma among sophisticated readers that every poem drama-tized a speaker who was not the poet" (151). Tucker sees the problem of this ahistorical assumption, but writing in 1985, still close to the high tide of deconstruction, he can only recommend a greater stress on textuality in reading as a remedy, though he recognizes that this can only be the beginning of a solution (153). See Jackson and Prins, *The Lyric Theory Reader*, 144–53.

21. Thomas H. Johnson, ed., *The Complete Poems of Emily Dickinson* (Boston: Little, Brown, and Company, 1960), 35.

22. Emily Dickinson, *Selected Letters*, ed. Thomas H. Johnson (Cambridge, MA: Harvard University Press, 1986), 176.

23. Jonathan Culler, in *The Theory of the Lyric* (Cambridge, MA: Harvard University Press, 2015), has argued on a grand scale that our understanding of lyric must go beyond the models of lyric subjectivity and dramatic monologue to include the epideictic range of truth-telling, praise, and blame, the ritualistic aspect of poetry, and magical forms of address, especially the apostrophe.

24. Brooks, *The Well-Wrought Urn*, 9.

25. As described in Roland Barthes, "From Work to Text," in *Image-Music-Text* (New York: Hill and Wang, 1971), 158–59.

26. *Roland Barthes by Roland Barthes*, trans. Richard Howard (New York: Farrar, Strauss, and Giroux, 1977), 47.

27. Seán Burke, *The Death and Return of the Author: Criticism and Subjectivity in Barthes, Foucault, and Derrida*, 3rd ed. (Edinburgh: Edinburgh University Press, 2008), 45.

28. Roland Barthes, *Sade, Fourier, Loyola*, trans. Richard Miller (Berkeley: University of California Press, 1976), 6.

29. *The Foucault Reader*, ed. Paul Rabinow (New York: Pantheon, 1984), 101–20.

30. Fredric Jameson, *Postmodernism, or, The Cultural Logic of Late Capitalism* (Durham, NC: Duke University Press, 1991), chapter 1. See the discussion in John Farrell, *Paranoia and Modernity: Cervantes to Rousseau* (Ithaca, NY: Cornell University Press, 2006), 320–24.

31. Foucault argues that the proper names of authors function differently from other proper names because they serve a classificatory function, permitting us to establish a certain relation among texts (107). But proper names function this way generally, not just for authors. They allow us to group together the poems of Villon but also the children of Genghis Khan, the fans of Oprah Winfrey, the fights of Muhammad Ali, and the loves of Don Giovanni (an imaginary person) as well as the faculty of Princeton and the ships of the U.S. Navy. Foucault follows John Searle's account of proper names, but there is no need for us to go into the issue of whether, as Searle would have it, the descriptions that are associated with a proper name define its meaning and serve to pick out the objects it refers to or whether the proper name refers to a thing independently of its descriptions, as the now more popular account by Saul Kripke would suggest. Either way, proper names function as a means of classifying many other things beside authors.

32. Michel Foucault, *The Archeology of Knowledge & The Discourse on Language* (New York: Pantheon, 1972), 17.

33. Michel Foucault, "What Is an Author?" in *The Foucault Reader* (New York: Pantheon, 1984), 113–17.

34. Once again Seán Burke has provided a detailed explanation of the inconsistencies and problems surrounding the concept of authorship in Foucault's work, and particularly his elevation of Nietzsche, Marx, and Freud above the normal limits of discourse. See *The Death and Return of the Author*, 60–100.

35. Again the most illuminating discussion is by Seán Burke. See *The Death and Return of the Author*, 133–44.

36. Burke, *The Death and Return of the Author*, 119–24.

37. Jacques Derrida, *Of Grammatology*, trans. Gayatri Spivak (Baltimore: Johns Hopkins University Press, 1976), 159.

38. Spivak translates "voudrait dire" as "would mean."

39. M. M. Bakhtin, *Speech Genres and Other Late Essays*, trans. Vern W. McGee; eds. Caryl Emerson and Michael Holquist (Austin: University of Texas Press, 1986), 89. Chapter 2 of *Marxism and the Philosophy of*

Language, a book which appeared under the name of Bakhtin's colleague V. N. Vološinov but may be by Bakhtin himself, provides a powerful critique of the notion of language as a fixed system of signifiers, the
symptom of a "philologism" that depends upon the status of dead
languages. The work lays great stress upon the Bakhtinian theme of
utterance meaning, not sentence or word meaning, as the primary
phenomenon of language. "In actuality, we never say or hear *words.
We say or hear what is true or false, good or bad, important or
unimportant, pleasant or unpleasant, and so on."* V. N. Vološinov,
Marxism and the Philosophy of Language, trans. Ladislaw Matejka and
I. R. Titunik (Cambridge, MA: Harvard University Press, 1973), 70.
On the problems of authorship regarding Bakhtin and his collaborators
see Katerina Clark and Michael Holquist, *Mikhail Bakhtin* (Cambridge,
MA: Harvard University Press, 1984), chapter 6.

40. Still the best place to start with deconstruction is Derrida's classic essay
"Structure, Sign, and Play in the Discourse of the Human Sciences," in
Writing and Difference, trans. Alan Bass (Chicago: University of Chicago
Press, 1978), 278–94. Page numbers in the text are from this essay.

41. The distinction I have in mind is rather like the distinction between the
atheist whose commitment to atheism is of the same scale and urgency as
religious belief and the nonbeliever who does not necessarily see nonbelief as
a personally defining characteristic or a crucial practical imperative.

42. These themes are pursued in "The Folly of Trying to Define Truth" and
other essays gathered in the "Truth" section of Davidson, *Truth, Language,
and History* and the "Objective" section of *Subjective, Intersubjective,
Objective* (Oxford: Oxford University Press, 2001).

43. See Davidson, "A Coherence Theory of Truth and Knowledge" (1983) and
the "Afterthoughts" (1987) in *Subjective, Intersubjective, Objective*, 137–58.

44. This is especially brought out in Davidson, "Locating Literary Language" in
Truth, Language, and History, 167–81.

45. Donald Davidson, *Inquiries Into Truth and Interpretation* (Oxford: Oxford
University Press, 1984), 183–98.

46. Nicholas Maxwell provides a detailed and challenging account in *The
Comprehensibility of the Universe: A New Conception of Science* (Oxford:
Clarendon Press, 2003).

47. Barry Stroud, *Engagement and Metaphysical Dissatisfaction: Modality and
Value* (New York: Oxford University Press, 2011).

48. Samuel Taylor Coleridge, *Biographia Literaria*, eds. James Engell and
Walter Jackson Bate (Princeton, NJ: Princeton University Press, 1983),
2:187.

49. Paul Oskar Kristeller, *Renaissance Thought and the Arts: Collected Essays*
(Princeton, NJ: Princeton University Press, 1980), 224.

50. Kristeller's argument has been usefully developed in L. E. Shiner, *The Invention of Art: A Cultural History* (Chicago: University of Chicago Press, 2001), especially chapters 5–7.

51. We can already see an impatience with the limits of the mode of experience (and the empirical philosophy that underwrote it) among the more promethean figures of Romanticism, particularly Blake, Shelley, and the later Yeats.

52. Stanley Cavell, *Must We Mean What We Say? A Book of Essays* (New York: Cambridge University Press, 1976), 214–15.

53. Jameson, *Postmodernism*, chapter 1.

CHAPTER 4

Unconscious and Transindividual Intentions

Is There a Single Correct Interpretation of a Literary Work?

As I pointed out in Chapter 2, the fact that an action is intentional does not mean that the intention is conscious or that the performer of the act can give a complete account of it. Nor does it mean that the intention has been formed ahead of time rather than being embedded in the act itself. For users of language, the act of communication is often indistinguishable from the act of thought, and in default conditions there may be no need even to consider the audience consciously in the construction of an utterance. Similarly, skilled practitioners of literature work by instinct much of the time, their judgment having been so scrupulously trained as to work unconsciously. Again, their conception of the audience's perspective may play little role in their conscious activity and may indeed be indistinguishable from their own perspective. We can say this about all the different kinds of intention that motivate a literary work. The distinctions I have made between communicative, artistic, and practical intentions are conceptually vital but may have little significance for the psychology of the artist.

It is also important to acknowledge that in the processes of thought and communication all of us make assumptions of which we are unaware and that none of us can provide a full account of the things we take for

© The Author(s) 2017
J. Farrell, *The Varieties of Authorial Intention*,
DOI 10.1007/978-3-319-48977-3_4

granted. We struggle to limn the shape of our knowledge and our ignorance, but no degree of vigilance can free us from error. The unconscious intentions and meanings discovered by critics in literary texts using "critique" and the hermeneutics of suspicion are of a different sort, however, from the not consciously articulated intentions embedded in ordinary speech and action. They typically embody a quite definite meaning, even though that meaning is inaccessible to the artist, requiring theory to be extracted. It is one of the ironies of literary theory that the surface intentions of authors have been set out of bounds as inaccessible while unconscious intentions, though inaccessible to the artist, have become routine for theorists to decode.

In this chapter I examine and evaluate the sources of intention located in the major modes of suspicious hermeneutics. Before I do so, however, I would like to address an issue that is raised by the apparent co-existence of so many modes and levels of interpretation: how do they relate to each other and do we need to choose among them when interpreting a work? Is there, in other words, a single right interpretation?

To make progress with this question, it is important to specify more precisely what we mean by interpretation. So far, I have been discussing interpretation as the attempt to understand what a work is saying, a process quite analogous to the one we perform in everyday conversation. The term "interpretation," however, covers many other activities besides the recovery of the work's meaning. Literary appreciations, historical arguments about the place of a work in its tradition, its contribution to the development of its genre, and so on, also come under the rubric of interpretation. And, of course, one of the most important functions of literary interpretation is the attempt to assess the value and impact of literary works by setting them in relation to other phenomena that may be important to the reader—to show, for instance, that they have contributed to the progress of feminism or democracy or class struggle. This is one way for their value to be enhanced. As we have seen, the impact of literary works, like other utterances, depends upon the perspective of the observer and can change with time. The question of what impact works should have is subject to perennial contest and negotiation—a negotiation that virtually defines the field of literary scholarship. As long as a work of literature is alive or there is someone willing to revive it, the question of its impact can never be put to rest, nor is there any hard and fast limit upon the considerations that can be brought to bear.

The multiplicity of aims and practices that go under the name inter-pretation guarantee that interpretation is multiple and endless, that there will never be a single, correct or complete interpretation of any work. But this should not obscure the fact that few literary critics are willing to say that they decide what the works they write about are *saying* based upon such goals as making them aesthetically attractive, politically significant, artistically innovative, or influential. Except for determined relativists like Stanley Fish, most literary critics base their arguments about history, artistry, and politics upon the meaning of the work as grounded in the text in the attempt to do justice, by whatever methodological lights, to what is there. This is even true of deconstructionists, who start with the apparent meaning of the text to find its deeper indeterminacy. Freudians and Marxists distinguish between surface and latent meanings and take the surface meanings as given in order to refigure them at a deeper level.

This discussion shows the value of the distinction I have drawn between meaning and impact in illuminating the diversity of literary interpretation. Meaning, grounded in communicative intentions, provides a core around which we constantly negotiate about the impact and value of literary works. Diverse critical methods need not be in contradiction; they can also feed and motivate each other. The kinds of stories we tell about a work's reception history, for example, may influence the kinds of story we want to tell about its artistic value or its political implications. For all of this our reading of the work's meaning provides a basis. The stability of meaning, grounded upon authorial intention in context, does not imperil the variety of practices that go under the name of interpretation. Rather, it makes them possible, for if every critique of a literary work addressed a different set of meanings and intentions, every critique would be addres-sing a different work. In such case the further purposes of literary inter-pretation would be entirely blunted, for no two critics would be talking about the same object. It would be impossible for them to disagree in a mutually relevant way.

It would be naïve, though, to think that our interpretation of a work's meaning could remain unaffected by the maelstrom of conflicts that surround the question of its value in an ever-changing world. Arguments about the truth, justice, impact, and quality of a literary work inevitably affect the direction and intensity of our search for its meaning. Let us take as an example Chinua Achebe's famous essay on *Heart of Darkness.*[1] In concise and devastating fashion, Achebe demonstrates that Conrad's novella, universally accepted as one of the great works of English literature, systematically portrays Africa as Europe's degraded other, the symbol of a primitive, superseded past, the horror of the story being the "lurking hint of kinship" between British whites and black Africans. In Achebe's account, Conrad is a "thoroughgoing racist" (in the first version a "bloody racist") whose work dehumanizes the people of an entire continent.

Achebe's aim is not to reinterpret Conrad in the sense of finding a new meaning in his words. Rather he is assessing the *impact* of these words based on the way they portray the world and the people in it, with the clear implication that this impact undermines the value of the work. His aim is not to maximize the story's value, as critics often do, but to reduce it, not by changing what it means but by clarifying the ethical import of its message. In doing so, Achebe is reflecting directly upon the author and his action in writing the story. He draws attention not to new meanings or ones that appear only through a special practice but to meanings that were always there in plain sight but which he has highlighted with new clarity. Thanks to Achebe, Conrad's artistic practices also appear in a different light, especially the potentially manipulative vagueness of his emotionally charged grandiloquence. Achebe's complaint against Conrad would have no purpose if his method of interpretation created the meanings it denounces. He has no interest in undermining his opponent's success in conveying his vision. It is the vision itself that concerns him. Further, it would be absurd for him to make the standard poststructuralist move of assuming that the text somehow already knows that the opposition Europe/Africa is an arbitrary reflex of language. What Achebe does is to stand up to Conrad and his admirers and tell them they are wrong. The story may have more virtues than Achebe recognizes, but those who are convinced by his account will no longer be able to see a definitive understanding of race as one of them.

Though Achebe is reading the text as written, showing what it was always saying, there is no doubt that once we have read his essay we understand the story differently. He has revealed the way the Europe/Africa distinction is a stand-in for the civilized/savage distinction; the theme of the story is clarified in a manner that Conrad's overwhelming rhetoric tends to diffuse. And this undoubtedly focuses our attention on a different level of detail and in a different direction than would have otherwise been the case. Achebe does not mention Kurtz, for instance, the story's linking figure between civilization and barbarism, and the reader is challenged to integrate Achebe's insights with the complications created by that character. In the long run, Achebe's attack has led to a better and more historically informed recognition that while Conrad's story represents an important attack upon imperialism and the most significant literary response to the atrocities in the Belgian Congo, it is also couched in terms that are tainted with the late-nineteenth-century version of racism.[2]

It seems clear, then, that the answer to our question is that if we take interpretation in the broad sense as the attempt to determine the various kinds of impact and significance a work can have, to set it in relation to other things we care about, assess its artistic or historical importance or the way it has been received, excerpted, marketed, redacted, and redeployed, then there can be no single correct interpretation. Probably none of these different kinds of interpretation is susceptible to final answers. Each involves considerations that go beyond the meaning that belongs to the work in its original setting. At the same time, there must be a core of meaning, in the proper sense, to give all these other practices point and purpose, and if this cannot be thought of as fixed then the surrounding discussion loses its purchase.

That still leaves us with the issue of interpretation in the narrower sense of discovering the text's meaning—can there be a single correct interpretation there? My earlier discussion of intentionality has attempted to settle the question with regard to the author's deliberate intentions. However difficult it may be to discover what the author intended, his intentions do provide a stable object for interpretation, and interpretations that do not accommodate that intention cannot be correct. There remains, nonetheless, the question about how to fit unconscious intentions, however we conceptualize them, into this picture. It is also important to recognize that not all interpretations that go beyond the factual content of the text require the positing of unconscious meaning. It is to the issue of interpretive levels that I now turn.

LEVELS OF INTERPRETATION

There are, I will propose, three levels of meaning-oriented interpretation for literary texts: surface, deep, and interlinear. The *surface level of interpretation* is the one we have primarily been dealing with in our discussion of intentionality, the level of what the author is explicitly saying and implying. It supplies the basic facts of the story, basic attitudes toward those facts, and an overall sense of point. With regard to *Hamlet*, for example, it reveals that Hamlet is the prince of Denmark, that his father is dead and mother remarried, that he kills Polonius, that Horatio is his friend, and that his eventual death is a tragic loss. Further interpretations of the play depend upon the truth of these basic facts and others like them, so we can say that there is a single right interpretation of the play in the sense that there is a correct way of describing what actually happens in the most fundamental sense. Interpretations that contradict each other about the surface of the work cannot jointly be right, though some interpretations may reinterpret works in a way that alters their face value.

In spite of the stability of surface meaning, it would not do, however, to associate the author's intention with a *single* correct interpretation, rather than a set of correct interpretations, since literary practice itself tends to militate against simplicity and clarity of that sort. For the most part, authors do not content themselves with providing a single, univocal meaning. In the case of *Hamlet*, the explicit facts of the story have given rise to centuries of speculation as to their true import and how we should feel about them. Authors leave a great deal of room for readers to fill in the details of a narrative and to grasp its implications. Literary symbols, indeed figures of all kinds, are a particular source of ambiguity and suggestiveness. So there is no need to associate the presence of authorial intention with singleness of meaning, even when we talk about the surface of the text. I have stressed the fact that language does not contain meanings that can be extracted whole; rather it offers prompts for the reader's inference. Literature exemplifies this in the extreme. It does not offer us meanings pure and simple (whatever that might entail) but an invitation to discover meanings along with the resources on which to work. Sometimes the experience of discovering, or failing to discover, meaning is more important than the meaning itself.

When Robert Frost entitles a poem "Mending Wall" he provides a puzzle for the reader since the phrase is ungrammatical. It sounds like the language of the "old-stone savage armed" mentioned by the poem's speaker. Does the title mean "mending the wall," with "mending" as a participle, or does it mean "the mending wall," with "mending" as an adjective? The first reading makes straightforward sense since the mending of the wall is going on in the poem while the second one offers a more interesting suggestion, that though the wall separates the two characters it also mends them by bringing them together in the act of repair. Perhaps there is a glance at the idiom "mending fences." We cannot be certain that

Frost had these possibilities in mind when he chose his title, but they are highly relevant, and there is no better explanation for the oddity of the phrase "mending wall." Like everything else in the poem, the title seems designed to teeter between perfectly balanced options, leaving the reader with no simple answer. This ambiguity cannot be accounted for as merely characteristic of literary language or language itself when it is an effect skillfully calculated by the poet. What we have is not a single correct meaning but a set of relevant ones.

It is also important to recognize that authors can intentionally flout the expectation that their words have a relevant interpretation. Throughout this book I have been talking about the principle of relevance as an enabling element of communication, but the presumption of relevance has other literary uses. Here is a paragraph from Gertrude Stein's *Tender Buttons*:

> A sad size a size that is not sad is blue as every bit of blue is precocious. A kind of green a game in green and nothing flat nothing quite flat and more round, nothing a particular color strangely, nothing breaking the losing of no little piece.[3]

This paragraph has no correct interpretation and could be described as nonsense, yet it is nonsense calculated to engage our search for relevance and thus provides a certain kind of experience. Only the fact that it has been framed within a work of literature assures us that we should give it appreciative attention. Indeed, its whimsically intentional literary quality is enhanced by its very lack of relevance. It is not when literary works are straightforwardly interpretable on the surface that intentionality becomes most visible but when the surface is most opaque. So again, even when we are dealing only with the surface meanings of a text, the association of intention with singleness and clarity of meaning is a false one.

A second kind of interpretation is what, borrowing from Arthur Danto, I will call *deep interpretation*.[4] Such methods address the already interpreted text, taking the surface as a way of entry toward some more valuable or explanatory level of meaning. Some literary works—allegories in particular—call for this kind of interpretation in order to grasp the author's intention, but deep interpretations in the standard mode of "critique"—Marxism, psychoanalysis, some forms of structuralism, and myth criticism—focus upon unconscious sources of meaning, sources that are inaccessible to the author. Such readings leave the surface meanings of the text in place. In fact, they depend upon them while seeking to resituate them in the context of a larger or more causally explanatory meaning. I will deal with the subject of unconscious intentions and meanings in the next section, but here it will be enough to point out that, to the degree that these methods of reading are valid, there is no reason to see them as conflicting with each other. They simply address different aspects of the work in question—sexual, political, structural, and so on. There is also the further issue of whether or not there can be only one correct deep interpretation of a particular kind, but here the answer must be mixed. Obviously Marxist critics may offer contradictory arguments about the class determinants of a literary work, but they can also build on each other's arguments. Psychoanalytic arguments have a narrower scope and therefore tend more often to conflict, but such judgments can only be made on a case by case basis.

Finally, there is what I will call *interlinear interpretation*, what we find while "reading between the lines." Some interpretations of this sort take place with the author's intentions in mind. It may be, for instance, that the repeated references in the works of Sophocles to the distinction between human and animal constitute a deliberate motif intended by the author, part of what we might think of as the argument of his work. On the other hand, the motif may represent a complex of associations of which he is barely aware, evidence of a tendency in ancient Greek thought larger than one work or one author. Literary scholars constantly confront issues of this kind, issues about the degree to which the text is saturated with the author's personal intentionality. *Degree of saturation* is often correlated with formal complexity, and the more distinct units of composition—chapters, stanzas, scenes—a work has, the more intentionally concerted is the meaning. There is almost no limit to the intentional saturation we can attribute to authors like Dante, Spenser, Milton, and Joyce.

When we say that surface interpretation provides us with the basic facts of what happens in the story there remains another question—how should those facts be correctly described? One of the most common forms of interlinear interpretation is what we might call *thematic interpretation*, where characters and situations in the work are fitted significantly into general categories, even if these categories are not explicitly mentioned in the work. This aspect of literary intelligence was noted by Aristotle, who asserted the superiority of poetry to history on account of its ability to present not just what happens to happen but what tends to happen. The territory of poetry, he believes, is the probable and the typical. This aspect of literature is hard to ignore. If a novelist presents the members of a disadvantaged or oppressed group in a way that seems to validate negative stereotypes, for example, it is no excuse to say that he is only portraying individuals. We inevitably take the author's portrayal as being typical. Particular characters are never portrayed merely as themselves. They are always seen under an aspect, as an example of something. Here is a limit to the literary author's intentional license. He cannot offer the merely particular as particular. That is the purview of history and memoir, and even there the magnetism of the general is strongly felt.

If the author's vocation is to particularize and investigate the general in the particular, as Aristotle believed, the critic's task is often to identify the general significance in the particular, to see the particulars, in other words, aspectivally. And here great judgment is required. Is it more important to see Hamlet as a dilatory avenger, a demoralized philosopher, a victim of melancholy, a disappointed son, or a disenfranchised prince? He might be all of these things, which is to say that, in the world of the play, he has the aspect, falls into the type, of all of them. But which of these descriptions, if any, is most explanatory of his situation and behavior? Here we may take "explanatory" as being relative to the author's intention or to the cultural context (though these need not be separate). Figuring out under what descriptions we should regard the actions, characters, and situations of a literary work is often a matter of deep historical research and may take us to concepts that the author would have simply taken for granted in the minds of his audience or ones that both he and they would not have been explicitly aware of.

It is in making thematic interpretations that much of the productiveness and interest of literary criticism lies and also much of the risk. The problematic element is that there are many true descriptions that can be applied to the elements of a work which have the appearance of being highly significant but which might never have occurred to the author in the same terms that we are using. It is true to say, for instance, that when Hamlet kills Polonius, he kills the other most loquacious character in the play. Shakespeare does not make a point of this and might not have been thinking in the same terms, but some readers might still find this fact to be telling. Hamlet, after all, is much concerned with the emptiness of words. At his death, "The rest is silence," and the irritation caused by Polonius's infuriatingly prolix interference might be thought to feed into the alacrity with which Hamlet slays the listener behind the arras. Do these facts have genuine relevance for our understanding of the play? Must we believe that Shakespeare was making the fact that Hamlet kills the most loquacious character in the play salient for us *in those very terms* in order to motivate our interest in this fact?

This is the kind of question about which critics' intuitions will differ, and it would perhaps be premature to judge the case without actually trying to interpret the play along the suggested lines. But I would venture to say that most practitioners of literary interpretation would not require that Shakespeare consciously intended to make relevant Hamlet's killing the most loquacious character under that very description in order to find the fact that he does so meaningful in the context of the entire play. Such interpretations constitute an important part of literary criticism in its classic form. The source of their authority is the overall coherence of Shakespeare's vision rather than a discrete intention. If this is right, then literary texts have a meaningfulness that depends to some degree upon the indirect implications of what the author intended. The hard part is deciding how far we can go beyond the explicit terms of the work to understand its thematic implications.

When we make such interlinear interpretations, are we discovering something about the play that the author did not know? Some of the difficulty here lies in the subtlety of the word *know*. When you started this paragraph, did you know that Jefferson never dined with Kublai Khan, that Marx never watched TV, and that the Bible is longer than the Gettysburg Address? In a real sense, you almost certainly did, but it is unlikely that you ever brought any of them to mind before I mentioned them. You can be said to have known them because they are instantly derivable implications from things you do know, and we commonly consider such implications part of our knowledge even though there are no conscious or even unconscious mental states involved. Such facts can be said to be unconscious only because, until asked, we did not know we knew them in the sense of having them consciously in mind, even though we can state them off the top of our heads, so to speak—which is, by the way, a funny place to put unconscious knowledge. That Jefferson could not have dined with the Khan, and that people born in the twelfth century could not have met people who lived in the eighteenth are facts that play a role in our thinking whether we are consciously aware of them or not.

Now what if someone had asked the poet of *The Iliad* if he knew that Achilles is the only character in the poem who performs human sacrifice?

This is a more interesting fact than the ones about Jefferson, Marx, and the Bible. Certainly, the poet would know the answer as soon as asked and might have consciously decided to distinguish Achilles in this way even though he does not make a point of it in the poem. (Nobody says, "Only you, Achilles, would do such a thing.") But even if he never consciously considered the fact that only Achilles performs human sacrifice, neither the poet nor anyone else could deny that, once pointed out, it is an important thing to know about the poem and points toward an important aspect of Achilles' character. Whether it was inserted into the narrative to make this point or not, it is part of what makes Achilles different from other characters, part of what makes him special. Achilles is the kind of person who would commit human sacrifice, whereas it is hard to imagine Odysseus bothering to do so; or, to put it more aptly, it would be better to use another type of character than Odysseus as the protagonist of a story about human sacrifice. Achilles, of course, is just the type to undertake such a grand action and to do so on the grandest possible stage, whereas Odysseus is more comfortable with unceremonious slaughter at home.

Such distinctions make an important contribution to the poem's "world." Indeed, this is what it means for a poem or a novel to have a "world." It is for the author and the audience to have a non-explicit background, a sense of how things would go in situations that do not actually arise in the work. Both the author and the audience are in constant contact with this background of counterfactual implication, which is closely connected to the cognitive background the author calls upon simply to make his intended meanings comprehensible. It is, in a sense, the background he creates, melding vaguely into the real world that unites author and audience. The artist creates a world as part of the process of telling his story, a world not created for its own sake but for the purposes of the work. This world comes into being piece by piece as the story progresses, with characters and settings becoming more and more clearly defined, more narrowly predictable and typical—and therefore potentially more surprising. One way of thinking of the critic's job is to become the philosopher or scientist of such imaginary worlds, the observer of their patterns and decoder of their rules. What precisely is the world subtended by the work? How should its events, characters, and situations be relevantly described? How does this world differ from the ones imagined by other, relevantly similar worlds subtended by other works—works by the same author or by different authors? How does it relate to the world in which the author and his original audience lived and how do we account for these differences? Which of these are due to cultural factors, which to matters of genre, and which reveal the mark of a particular author? How does it differ from our world or the world as it should be? These are all questions upon which critics can claim an authority that competes with the author's.

Reading between the lines does not happen, of course, only in literature. Other people often understand us and our actions better than we do. They may have a better analytic vocabulary at their disposal than we do, benefit by being free of the positive bias most of us apply to ourselves, invest more effort into understanding us than we do, or simply be more observant and acute. This applies all the more to understanding the creation of works of art, where critics have the fullness of time to analyze what an artist may have written in a single day.

The multi-dimensional nature of the artistic task also adds to the complexities of literary interpretation. The author is working within a literary genre that provides constraints upon meaning, structure, and tone. He aims at a general effect and wants the work to have point, enough to keep the audience engaged. This means that his choices, though intentional, do not all have the same weight of agency attached to them. This is again a wider aspect of agency. Even things we do intentionally have implications or effects we do not strictly speaking intend or intend in the full sense. Let us return to an earlier example: I give you a shove to get you out of the way of an oncoming car. I shove you intentionally and know I am going to hurt you when I do it, but I do not intend to hurt you. I intend to save you from being hurt. An adequate critique of my action must take this into account. So it is with the composition of a literary work, where many things are done for the sake of other things. An epic needs lots of slaughter, for instance, so if you want to write one you cannot neglect it, though some authors—Milton, for example—might have preferred to skip the mayhem. Once an author has chosen to compose in a certain literary form he has no choice but to satisfy its needs. It is up to him how he does so, but the fact of his attempt does not belong to the author in the same way as his more idiosyncratic choices. Readers may be in a better position than the author to judge the compromises involved between his abilities and inclinations and the needs of the genre, how an author tends to manage artistic challenges, what his typical solutions are. So interpreting the meaning of a work and its thematic emphasis also means taking into account the artistic instruments the author is working with, their characteristic possibilities and constraints.

In this domain, of course, the critic has a wider field of comparison for the author's practice than the author could anticipate, and has access to different terms of understanding. There was no reason for Austen, Flaubert, or Dostoevsky, for instance, to analyze their own virtuosic use of what we call "free indirect discourse" or to compare it with that of other writers, as the critic Roy Pascal has done.[5] These authors might not even have had a distinct concept of the technique, an analysis of which might have taken them by surprise. Yet, undoubtedly, they employed it intentionally and would have recognized its significance if it had been pointed out. This is what happened to Monsieur Jourdain when he found out that all his life he had been speaking prose.

An increase in our understanding of an artist's techniques and skills does not change the meaning of the work, but it can change its impact, make us value it differently. One thing it does is to help us locate the originality of the author based on the weight of agency. Kendall Walton poses an intriguing thought experiment that clarifies this point. What if there was a culture where Picasso's *Guernica* had become the basis for a genre?[6] Painters paint "*guernicas*" all the time, with the same iconographic features and roughly the same meaning as the original, but the works differ in matters of tone and shading and can even be in three dimensions. A person seeing any of these *guernicas* for the first time would be struck by their marvelous iconography but, after a few more *guernicas*, she would soon come to realize that this was simply a generic feature, not to be attributed specifically to the work or author in question. In that case it might turn out to be a not terribly interesting *guernica*, or if it was an interesting one, its interest would lie in what set it apart from other *guernicas*, not the features it shares. And of course Picasso's original *Guernica*, flat and dull as it was, would probably look rather shabby. We find value in the particular contribution an author brings to a genre, not the work's generic features.

The strangeness of the *guernica* scenario is clarifying, but we can think of less exotic examples. In medieval and early modern art, annunciations, crucifixions, and other subjects have a similar generic quality. The artist's task is to make the individual work distinctive. Some of the sources of that distinction may be completely self-conscious. Artists can diverge deliberately from the practice of others, and that can be part of the meaning and point of the work. But not all divergences are of this kind, and even deliberate innovations are difficult to characterize precisely. That is part of the critic's domain. When investigating the world of the work, the critic is always in the position of deciding how much of that world is subtended by the genre the author has chosen, how much simply belongs to the world the author and his audience take for granted, and how much is the author's specific imaginative contribution. Such considerations come into play both in the interpretation of the work's meaning and accounting for its impact—its ethical, artistic, political, and historical significance.

In the case of the latter, it is well within the purview of the critic to put to the work questions the author never directly considered or made a distinct concern. In the writing of his plays, for example, Shakespeare created for his boy actors a wide array of female characters in many conditions of life, from Cleopatra to Portia to Juliet's nurse, but it is unlikely that he ever set himself the task of examining either the nature or condition of women, even if one could cite many speeches where distinctions of gender are crucially made. Nonetheless, we can draw an interesting set of implications about the nature and condition of women from Shakespeare's plays. We can ask such questions as Shakespeare in his time would not have asked. And from our vantage point we can assess the answers with a better sense of their historical specificity than Shakespeare from his vantage point could have done.

There is nothing unfair or odd in putting questions to the author that he never intended to answer, because works of art often ask us to share their view of the world. They seek to persuade us that things are a certain way and not another. They emphasize some aspects and take others for granted, but they submit all of them to our contemplation as we become absorbed in the work's point of view. This is where the ethical and political value of the distinction between meaning and impact becomes clear. We enter the world of the work in order to know it, and in order to know it we enter imaginatively into the world in which it was made. We are interested in what belongs to the author and what was the common possession of his time and place. But as we understand we also reserve our judgment. Again, I return to the point that the making of a literary work is not simply the extrusion of a text but a human action. Its impact cannot be left up entirely to the author's intentions any more than the impact of any other human action. To revert to the standard ethical vocabulary, the agent's intentions do not exhaust the significance of what she has done. Its impact is still to be known. If this were not so, historical investigation would have little point. There would be nothing more for the historian to do than chronicle the intentions with which people acted, without commenting on their impact on other people of the time and their value for us.

Much of the reluctance of literary critics, especially those in the Barthesian vein, to accept the fixity of surface meaning and the largely intentional basis of interlinear interpretation is grounded in the notion that if we cannot change the meaning of texts inherited from the past we cannot escape their influence. We remain ruled by them. There is a deep metaphysical problem with this idea, for the implication is that if we cannot change the past we cannot act in an effective way regarding the future. But if we know anything for sure, it is that we cannot change the past. Fortunately, as the example of Achebe suggests, we do not have to change the meaning of the literature of the past in order to change our view of it. Let me give one more example that shows this, one that depends upon the aspectual dimension of interlinear reading I discussed above. *Great Expectations* contains the lovable character Joe Gargery, who is married to the hero's abusive sister and does his best to soften the effect of her treatment on the boy. Joe is more like a child under his wife's thumb than a husband. He is good-natured, gentle, and humorous, a fine example of what might in a broad sense be called Christian patience. But readers in the twenty-first century are less likely to admire Christian patience than Dickens and his Victorian audience. Dickens's willingess to preach the acceptance of the hard conditions of life now looks like a symptom of his conservative social attitude. Still more discouraging, undergraduate readers of today quickly recognize poor Joe as an "enabler," a person who in spite of good intentions helps perpetuate an abusive situation. The introduction of this therapeutic vocabulary into Dickens' thoroughly moralized world threatens to undermine the meaning of that world altogether. Joe's moral virtue becomes complicit with social and personal pathology.

Based on the facts of the story, Joe Gargery fits the category of an enabler perfectly well, yet in the world of the story, this does not make him one because Dickens does not invoke that category, nor can the socio-therapeutic attitude associated with the term *enabler* be considered a source of relevant implications in Dickens' world. It is probably fair to say that the enabler category was not available to Dickens, but even if it had been, he might not have been willing to invoke it. If we wish to invoke it, what we are doing is disagreeing with Dickens, and perhaps his culture, about how people like Joe should be regarded. Should we think of them as enablers or examples of Christian patience? The answer to this question may affect the impact and value of the novel for us, but it does not change its meaning. In Dickens' world, Joe is an admirable example of Christian patience. Only by recognizing that meaning can we register our difference with Dickens.[7]

What are the implications of all this for the question we began with in its slightly amended form: Is there a single set of correct interpretations of a literary work? If directed to the *surface content* of the work, the answer is more or less yes. The original charge of information in the work is fixed, however difficult it may be to gain access to it. There may be surface aspects of a work that are relevant but still ambiguous, either accidentally or deliberately so, leaving room for interpretation, but that room can itself be delineated. Frost's title gives us a lot to play with, but "Mending Wall" cannot mean "See you next Tuesday." This is not to say, of course, that we cannot be wrong about the surface meaning of all or part of a work. But the fact that we can be wrong about it comes along with the fact that we can be right about it. As we have seen, critics who seek to destabilize the surface meaning of the text need to get the author at least partially out of the picture.

Deep interpretations take the surface meaning of the work for granted, so their readings do not conflict with it. They may find the surface meaning highly conflicted and ambiguous in itself, but they will resolve such contradictions on a different level. As for *interlinear readings* of the various kinds I have sketched, to the extent that they focus on different themes they need not conflict. Valid readings can multiply, except in the sense that such readings tend to attribute a weight of importance to the theme or aspect they specify at the expense of others. Such weighting requires critical judgment about the author's intentions but is not constrained by or limited to the author's own terms of understanding. The critic's project is for her to choose and justify.

FREUD

It would seem puzzling that psychoanalysis has been able to thrive in the text-centered era given the method's obviously author-directed focus, but the puzzle is easily solved. The true target of anti-intentionalist irony and its elevation of text over author is the rational bourgeois subject. Exposing the hidden irrationality of that subject in the Freudian manner is as good a way of displacing it as denying its norm-governed employment of language. But this leads directly to another puzzle, for, as I have explained, intentional psychology requires a principle of rationality, albeit a limited one. To see something as intentional, even unconsciously intentional, is to attribute to it a fit between desire, belief, and action. So, by discovering intentions hidden from the author in the unconscious mind, psychoanalysis extends the domain of what is rationally comprehensible, which is to say it extends the domain of the rational subject itself. Freud's final version of the psyche actually involves, at a minimum, three sources of intentionality working independently. There is the id, with its desires and goals; then the superego, with its need to contain and punish the id; and finally the ego which, in the case of dreams and symptoms, must contrive symbols that can be understood by one audience, the id, while passing by the censorship of another, the superego. The unconscious mind must triply satisfy the paradigm of rational fit between desire, belief, and action that characterizes all intentional activity. Describing Freud's topology of the mind this way, we can see that what he has done is attribute agency and a dramatic situation to these intrapsychic characters, allowing us to grasp their intentions against the background of the situation he has described. The id is the driving force of Eros, the superego the punisher of Eros, and the ego the compromiser. Both the notion of Eros itself and the three characters surrounding it were, like so much of psychoanalysis, adapted from Plato.[8] The model is enriched with further elements of intentionality by the addition of the Oedipus myth.

Only by making mental forces into characters could Freud's mechanistic explanatory scheme also function as an interpretive one. So Freud the prophet of hidden intentionality was also the prophet of hidden agency and covert rationality. If psychoanalysis had turned out to be a persuasive theory of the mind, it would have had genuine implications about the meaning of literary works and the sources of their appeal. Its implications are radical indeed. Unfortunately, the fact that psychoanalysis asks for such a radical revision of our understanding both of everyday psychology and of literary texts turns out to be one of its many liabilities. Contrary to Freud's vision of human beings as swaddled in false innocence, the trickiness, greed, sensuality, and selfishness that Freud saw concealed in the unconscious are quite apparent on the surface of our thought and behavior.

The need of psychoanalysis to endow the mind with multiple homunculi possessing intentions of their own has led many to question its validity. Freud's way of combining rational and mechanical explanation has been regarded by some as a mark of incoherence and by others as a crucial break-through.[9] For our purposes, there are two points to be emphasized. The first is that psychoanalysis is, indeed, inescapably an intentionalist theory. In fact, it is an intentionalist theory not only in regard to the issue of textual meaning which we have been pursuing but also in the older vein of Romantic psychology, seeing the literary work as a deep and total expression of the author's psyche. Freud was a full-blown practitioner of the "Intentional Fallacy" in its most naïve, even if most labyrinthine, form. The second point is that the systems of unconscious intentions of the kind Freud claimed to discover are different from the conscious intentions we discover in every-day life precisely in being hidden and therefore requiring theory to be recovered. In order to practice psychoanalysis, we cannot depend simply upon our ability to make psychoanalytic interpretations. We need to make many additional assumptions, not only about the rational homunculi but about the relations between them and the forces that govern human motiva-tion in general. This is a point that Freud did not understand. He consistently held that applications of psychoanalysis could serve as proofs of its validity. Based on his self-analysis and his experience with a few dozen patients in fin-de-siècle Vienna, he offered us a grand account of universal human psychol-ogy rooted in a highly speculative topographical and hydraulic description of the mind and of human evolution. Few who have engaged seriously with the issues raised by Freud's logic and the failure of experimental validation for Freud's science will come away endorsing many of his distinctive claims.[10] We would need to be able to accept as valid at least a significant percentage of Freud's evidence for his theory—his accounts of dreams, parapraxes, neurotic symptoms, and so on—in order to use it plausibly as a mode of interpreta-tion, and that validation has not been forthcoming.

It is also important to recognize the scope of psychoanalytic teaching, how much it asks us to believe not only about the mind but about human life and history. It is clearly a historical ideology. For psychoanalysis, each of us in the course of our maturation has to struggle with the indulgence of the pleasure principle, infantile narcissism, and the Oedipal dangers that kept past generations in thrall to religion and other premodern delusions. Those who cannot do so wind up developing neurotic or psychotic conditions that are the private versions of ancient systems of fantasy. Adjustment to psychological modernity and its ideology is the norm and goal of psychoanalysis.[11] The existence of this ideological dimension does not disprove its claims, but it helps explain some of its appeal for those who have not questioned its scientific standing.

This is not the place to reiterate the critique of psychoanalysis which has significantly undermined its credibility after a hundred years of cultural dominance, but it is remarkable that in a century in which the influence of science steadily increased, a theory rooted in Victorian biology and hinging upon a universal desire for incest should have lasted so long. Freud argued that the prevalence of an incest taboo confirmed the existence of a desire to break it. He might as well have argued that the existence of grammatical rules implies a desire to speak ungrammatically.

Despite the obvious weaknesses of psychoanalysis as a psychological and biological theory, there are properly artistic reasons for its extended currency. Just as attitudes toward intentionality have been shaped by new forms of artistic practice as well as by theoretical arguments, so certain theories have an imaginative character that makes them appealing not only to artists but to critics as well. This is supremely true of psychoanalysis. It made possible a counter-cultural stance at once underwritten by science yet providing a rich connection to ancient and foregone cultural practices and materials. The Freudian unconscious was the reservoir of uncontrollable forces and conflicts, primal dreams and mythologies, traces and residues of the entire human past inflected in the infantile experience of each individual. Psychoanalysis proved supremely adaptable to twentieth-century art in a way that validated the fine literary sensibility of its founder and his claim that he learned everything he knew from the poets. Indeed, what separated the first generation of psychoanalysts like Freud, Jung, and Rank from their successors was not only their creativity but their immersion in the classics, literary culture, and the arts. They borrowed richly from the poets and paid back their debt in kind.

The imaginative quality of psychoanalytic theory itself and of Freud's readings, especially of his own dreams, is one of the great sources of their appeal. Psychoanalysis is one of the most interesting theories ever invented. The idea that each of us has a secret life which harbors all our mysteries and to which a therapeutic shaman has the key is a doctrine that, as Nabokov somewhere observed, makes us interesting to ourselves. Most scholars who continue to apply psychoanalysis to the study of literature do not do so because they endorse it as science but because it has a fundamentally compelling quality—because it is *interesting*. There is a certain irony, though, in the emergence of interestingness as a criterion of the value of literary readings over the last two or three generations of critics because interestingness is self-evidently an aesthetic criterion and there is no concept toward which these generations have been more skeptical than the notion of the aesthetic; yet they are strongly inclined to support their own work employing this unambiguously aesthetic criterion.

MARX

The other explanatory theory that offers a full apparatus for the interpretation of literature is Marxism, and so we can ask once again what is the hidden source of intentionality that allows interpretations which go beyond the intentions of the author. The answer, of course, is history. History itself has a meaning and a direction of its own, observable in the dialectic of class conflict. Again, the identification even of a hidden intention requires the assumption of rational agency at work, and this is the point that now makes Marxism so difficult to defend. It is not just that history is taking too long to get to its goal or that it is taking too messy a route to be counted rational. It is that the theological basis of Marxian teleology is all too clear. What Fredric Jameson calls "the Pascalian wager of Marxism"—that "History is meaningful, however absurd organic life may happen to be"—leaves us asking who is the intentional agent behind this history. Otherwise both the meaningfulness of "History" and the consignment of "organic life" to absurdity look like bare gestures of faith.[12] The mere similarity of Marxism to religion has, of course, been often observed, and Marxism's claims cannot be disproved simply because they resemble those of religion. What it does make clear, though, is that to endorse anything like classic Marxism we must posit a hidden source of intentions.

Marxism survives in academic discourse as a talisman of political commitment to historically left causes. What is most striking about the Marxist form of argument, however, is how little it ultimately freed itself from either of its original enemies, capitalism or religion. Religion, via Hegel, supplied the hidden providence. British economists like Adam Smith supplied the notion of a grand economic system with a logic of its own which, if allowed to take its own course, will by the working of an invisible hand bring about the predetermined best result for all. Operating within the parameters set by these hidden agencies and unintended systemic consequences, Marxists have perennially struggled to find a place for conscious and deliberate political action or even a standpoint for analysis that has not already been reduced to a symptom of class.[13] The space of intentional human action, where artistic works are created, tends to be eclipsed.

Again, this is no place to take up the discussion about whether classes and economic forces are the true motors of history that Marx took them to be. The point that is essential for our purposes is that to interpret texts in the Marxian manner is to alter their impact rather than their communicative point. It is to see behind the meaning of a work to its role in a larger account of events, what Jameson follows Marx in calling "the collective struggle to wrest a realm of Freedom from a realm of Necessity" (19).[14] It does not touch upon the issue of a work's meaning per se. Rather, it takes that meaning for granted as a starting point. And as with psychoanalysis, Marxian interpretation requires that we take on board a wide range of intellectual assumptions going far beyond what is embodied in the text. Marxist criticism cannot be sustained merely by its ability to produce brilliant readings of literary works unless, once again, one is willing to adopt merely aesthetic criteria for the justification of scholarly arguments.

Nevertheless, Marxist studies of literature have contributed widely to our understanding of the literary past and its connection with historical and economic trends, which, unlike Freudian unconscious drives, surely do exist even if not in the all-determining form Marx assumed. On the other hand, history and class conflict lack the spooky, uncanny dimension of the unconscious which made psychoanalysis so congenial a resource for twentieth-century art. The artistic influence of Marxism has generally been to restrict the imagination to Marxist conceptions of what is real and to follow Hegel's example in describing art and the imagination as offering preliminary or retrograde compensations. There is also a utopian dimension in the work of Marxist critics like Ernst Bloch and Fredric Jameson, but its grounds are extraordinarily abstract and futuristic, too much so to be an influence upon aesthetic practice.

The fact that history is not a rational agent does not, of course, mean that history is irrelevant to our understanding of literature, even after we have done our best to understand the work in its own terms. For once we have understood the work as a verbal utterance we still have the deeper task of understanding it as a human action, which is to say as an ethical and political gesture and an artistic accomplishment, and this means putting it in the wider context of its time and place, connecting it with and distinguishing it from our own. History may not have a project-like direction of its own, but it is the aggregate of many human projects moving in many directions, interacting complexly and unpredictably against the background of shifting natural and social conditions. Some of these projects are local and personal, others have a truly historical force like the struggle for racial justice, the equality of women, or the establishment of democracy. It is in the context of these larger historical projects that literary criticism finds its ethical, political, and historical vocation. It can truly be said that, on account of Marx's influence, never again will we take up questions about the production of literary works without considering the material and social conditions of their making.

FOUCAULT AND GREENBLATT

There is another source of transindividual intentions that has come into play in literary studies—Michel Foucault's conception of power, derived from the philosophy of Friedrich Nietzsche. Nietzsche's conception of power referred to the biologically driven impulse of individuals and groups to impose beliefs and practices upon others that are life-enhancing for themselves. In Foucault's formulation, however, this power works somehow above and through the localizable forms of agency and their conscious or explicit intentions, creating institutions, practices, and forms of discourse. Attempts to resist power have already been co-opted back into its workings. In order to observe power in action, all one has to do is chart the functioning of institutions and practices as they regulate the activities of those who perform them and those they are performed upon, as Foucault did in studies of major social institutions in the 1960s and 1970s. In these books, we see the completed pendulum swing of French theory from Durkheim's idealization of society in the early twentieth century back to Rousseau's full-blown paranoia about the evils of society per se. Jean-Paul Sartre prepared the way with his theory of the gaze, but Foucault showed how narrating the depredations of the social other could become the basis of standard practice for historians and critics.

To understand the strange force of Foucault's influence, consider the much-celebrated coup he achieved in the first volume of *The History of Sexuality* when he observed that the discourse of psychoanalysis posited culture as a form of repression whereas in Foucault's account this very notion of repression is itself a form of power that permits the creation and circulation of more and more discourse about sex. The discourse of "repression," Foucault asserts, is part of the culture it claims to liberate.[15] He had discovered that power was not just prohibitive, not just a check upon freedom, but that it could actually be *productive*. This has been a guiding academic insight over several decades.

What is odd about this story is that scholars could be shocked to discover that power is productive, for what is power, after all, but the ability to do and make things? This would only have come as a surprise to those who have become so accustomed to thinking of power as elsewhere, and human beings as objects of external determination, that the notion of power as productive was truly unfamiliar. At the same time that Foucauldian power acquired an active and positive character, remarkably extending its scope, it remained no less hostile to human wishes. The return of power to the productive side of the equation completed a long-developing alienation of agency.

Freud's theory of unconscious intentions was an empirical hypothesis subject to disconfirmation. Marx's concept of history was a reductive gesture that produced important insights but eventually showed its limits. Foucault's conception of power was based on a simple gestalt switch, from a concept of agency that belongs positively to individuals and groups in potential harmony or conflict, to a concept of agency for which all local choice is an illusion, the projection of a faceless and malign collectivity. Foucault led inquirers toward empirically rich studies of areas of culture and modes of discourse that had not engaged literary critics in the past, and his work was the vehicle for exposing genuine abuses of power, particularly in the psychiatric establishment of the 1960s. But, as a conception of agency, it leads to a hopeless and truly paranoid bind, a complete alienation in which one's own critical activities have no ground to stand on.

Foucault's notion of power has been widely influential in many areas of literary theory, too many to be surveyed here. Stephen Greenblatt adapted Foucault's use of the anecdote to create the New Historicist essay, a way of deploying the concept of power in a case study without the obligation to provide an elaborate historical background in the manner of Foucault. But despite Greenblatt's reliance on a transindividual conception of agency, he actually employs a rich vocabulary of individual agency as well. His authors negotiate, exchange, appropriate, co-opt, and undertake many other social, political, and cultural activities. This is true even after the period when he focused on "self-fashioning." He also lends credit to group actors more localizable than Foucault's abstract power—the elites, for example, that use Shakespeare's theater as a site of struggle for authority as shown in "Shakespeare and the Exorcists," Greenblatt's superb essay on *King Lear*.[16] With his sharp eye for the subtleties of literary making, Greenblatt often sounds like an older humanistic or aesthetically minded critic, with formulas like "resonance and wonder" setting aesthetic appeal on an equal footing with historical interest.[17] In approaching Early Modern culture, he seems closer in spirit to Clifford Geertz than Foucault, extending literary critical habits of reading beyond the literary sphere and creating what he calls a "cultural poetics" rather than importing a method from outside (5). Nevertheless, the New Historicist mode always has at its disposal the guaranteed relevance which comes of an exposition of Foucauldian power.

As its own practitioners have often observed, New Historicism is too protean a methodological attitude to allow precise characterization. Here I will make two observations about it. One is that it tends toward a deep interpretation of the political and cultural struggles of the past by allegorizing them in terms of subversion and containment. Greenblatt himself admits that these categories may only serve as projections of how we would respond to the entities we characterize in this way if they were active in the present day. "We find 'subversive' in the past," he writes, "precisely those things that are *not* subversive to ourselves, that pose no threat to the order in which we live and allocate resources" (39). This way of imposing meaning upon the past is strikingly similar to the progressive/ reactionary mode of Whig history and not likely to be any more objective or free of anachronism. Greenblatt's willingness to make admissions of this kind seems like an ingenious application of the very technique of rhetoric he finds in his sources, arousing subversive doubts in order to contain them, expressing nihilism about the claims underlying his own strategies in order to show they maintain their power in spite of it. At the end of "Shakespeare and the Exorcists," when he notes that under the influence of Lamb and Coleridge, the charismatic energy of Shakespeare's theater was transferred to the silent experience of readers—"the commercial contingency of the theater" giving way to the "philosophical necessity of literature" (128)—one feels that Greenblatt should add his own rhetorical achievement—the rhetoric of power and history reclaiming the social energy of the stage for the critic's own voice.

As for the second point, I have mentioned that New Historicists like Greenblatt do frequently engage in intentional explanations about what is happening in and through literary works. But the conception of Foucauldian power that remains in the background and often underwrites the subversion/containment narrative is not an intentional but a functional form of explanation. This is only one of its weaknesses, but it is an instructive one, all the more so for being shared by Marxist ideology critique.[18] A functional explanation appeals to what things do once they already exist. Hence it cannot explain how they came to be in the first place. Thus, it is useless when applied to individual cases like literary works; what they do later is irrelevant to how they came about in the act of creation unless there is an intention involved. Successful functional explanations like Darwinian natural selection deal not with individuals but with types; the adaptations that shape Darwinian species come about by accident and are integrated into the type by a feedback loop involving gene frequencies in changing environments. Functional explanations cannot cope with the individual aspects of production, including the activities of authors; and when we are dealing with complex economic, social, and cultural phenomena, the kind of feedback loop sustaining a Darwinian type will not be easy to find. To be valid, functional explanations of literature must specify not only what advantages a type of literary work might provide but also how those advantages helped it be preserved and transmitted. Vague terms like "power"—not much more than another name for function—do not help, and the functional explanations offered by literary critics, when they are not completely blind to these issues, almost always turn out to depend on the intentions of authors and audiences.

STRUCTURALISM

We have seen that intentional interpretations stand or fall on the basis of how well they account for the meaning of the texts they address, but non-intentional explanations and explanations that involve unconscious or hidden intentionality like those of Marxism and psychoanalysis stand or fall on the basis of how well they account for a much wider range of data. The most basic reason for this is that the sources of intentionality they evoke lack something that is always present in conscious communication—the ostensive signaling by speakers or authors that, by the very construction of an utterance, they are giving evidence of an intention that is worth our while to retrieve. Neither the unconscious nor history can be said to signal us in this way. They do not make an utterance. That is why we need a theoretical justification to look for meaning in them. But what about theories of language itself, theories with an explicit semantics of their own? Is it not to be expected that they would alter the surface meaning of the literary text in a way that is relevant to the critic?

The fact that a theory of language alters the meaning of the texts to which it is applied or, indeed, the fact that it can be "applied" at all to individual texts, is a reason to be suspicious of it, for the primary aim of a theory is to explain what we are already doing in general, not to change it or make particular applications. Sperber and Wilson's theory of relevance, which I have proposed as a candidate for understanding language as communication, has the advantage that it suggests no new meanings for literary texts or utterances in general. It merely attempts to explain how we arrive at the ones they would normally have. If literary texts are not as immediately graspable as more ordinary acts of communication, that is only because they aim at larger, more subtle and complex effects than ordinary utterances, not because they are using a fundamentally different instrument or because they can only be grasped on some deeper level. Theories like New Criticism that make literary language fundamentally different from ordinary language do change the meanings of texts. In the hands of New Critical readers, literary texts become by nature ambiguous and ironic (in a special, idiosyncratic sense) and their most essential content and function becomes the demonstration of these qualities. Deconstruction has the same self-referential bias. Language itself becomes the subject of its own operations, the agent of its own deconstruction. As we have seen, it is only by removing or qualifying the guarantee of relevance provided by the author that such linguistic theories can liberate language for the new tasks to which they recruit it.

Historically speaking, the development of literary linguistics was part of the reaction against the mistrust of language and imagination that per-vaded Enlightenment culture and became a firm dogma in the various positivisms that dominated Anglo-American culture from the late nine-teenth century into the mid-twentieth. From the positivist point of view, literary language, compared to the language of science, consisted of mere "pseudo-statements," to use I. A. Richards' term.[19] The same brush was used to tar ethical and political statements and, indeed, value judgments of any kind, often taken to be expressions of mere feeling. The New Critical move was to turn the tables on the positivist by asserting that the very qualities which make literary language different from practical and scien-tific language—its complexity, ambiguity, penchant for irony, opacity, and unparaphrasability—make it superior in its own domain. In fact, they make literary language an antidote to the numbing qualities of ordinary lan-guage. Stanley Fish has neatly diagnosed the problem of this argumenta-tive strategy. If we begin by accepting an impoverishment of ordinary language as a human instrument and then define literary language as a deviation from that already devalued instrument, the result is to devalue both. A double alienation is achieved. "Deviation theories," as Fish puts it, "always trivialize the original and therefore trivialize everything else."[20] In the model of the New Critics, the primary value of literature lies not in any virtues of its own but in the way it deviates from ordinary language, and this becomes the monotonous meaning of the individual works to which it is applied.

Structuralism was another form of explanation that changed the meanings of the texts it was meant to explain. Instead of isolating the text, as formalist readings tended to do, structuralists tended to see them as part of a signifying system that encloses the author and his culture and constitutes its reality. The best structuralist critics produced superb analyses of the cultural vocabularies informing the texts they studied. I am thinking especially of the invaluable work on ancient Greek culture produced under the influence of Claude Lévi-Strauss by Jean-Pierre Vernant, Pierre Vidal-Naquet, and especially Charles Segal. Segal's close analysis of the systemic resonances of Sophocles' vocabulary, for instance, focuses insightfully on key binarisms like nature/culture, raw/cooked, man/beast, and tame/wild.[21] The effect is genuinely illuminating. Still, in order to produce sufficiently interesting interpretations of individual works, it was necessary for structuralist critics to devise larger cultural narratives to support their textual readings—to look behind the vocabulary of the classical Greeks, for example, to a larger and ongoing story of the overcoming of Nature by Civilization, represented in the confrontation and vanquishing by the Greek heroes—Hercules, Oedipus—of the uncanny and monstrous enemies of the polis like the Sphinx. This is in line with Lévi-Strauss's dictum that we can find in myth imaginary solutions to real problems, problems that arise from contradictions or antinomies within a culture's conceptual vocabulary.[22] The resonance of Hegel is obvious, and this way of interpreting culture as myth has been especially attractive to Marxists because, as with Marx, there is a collective mind operating here on a transindividual level. We should also recall structuralism's origins in the heyday of Durkheimian functionalism, in which the good of society was the all-explaining factor in cultural development.

There was something undeniably valuable about the attention that structuralists brought to the conceptual vocabularies employed by the cultures they studied. It is a basic part of the task of thinking to become self-conscious about the unexamined assumptions we make and the meanings of the terms we use, the way we frame the subjects of our thinking before we have even begun to inquire. Structuralism provides resources for doing that when we study distant cultures and for turning the lens back upon ourselves. But structuralism tended to displace the locus of thought from the thinker to the instrument, from *parole* to *langue*, to see thinking not as enabled but as determined by language. It tells us that it is language which speaks, not the person who uses it. And so we encounter the same problem we did in the cases of Freud and Marx, that meaning is attributed to an entity to which communication has no relevance. Language, after all, has no aims or goals of its own, no local context or situation in which we could ground our understanding of its motives or purposes. It cannot *act*. And as we have seen, contrary to the structuralist sense of its autonomy, the fabric of language is radically incomplete, its underdeterminacy requiring a complex system of inference on the part of its users.

DOES LITERARY DARWINISM POINT TOWARD HIDDEN INTENTIONS?

Interpreting the meaning of a literary text is one way of explaining why it has the features that it does, but not all explanations are interpretive and directed toward the author's meaning. As we have seen, some adopt a wider explanatory framework that provides meanings not available to the author, Marxism, psychoanalysis, and structuralism being the prime examples. And some frameworks of explanation do not bear upon the meanings of individual works at all. A case in point is the recent scholarship that examines the implications of evolutionary psychology for literature.

One might think that the Darwinian understanding of human nature would change our sense of the content of literary works because there is a kind of general irony that operates in Darwinian explanations of human behavior. Through a Darwinian lens we see that many of our ways of feeling and behaving have functions of which we are not immediately conscious and which stem from primary biological needs. In this perspective, romantic love can look like a delusion motivated by the need for our genes to copy themselves; obesity becomes a sign of our inability to adjust our appetites from a situation of scarcity to one of abundance; and our tendency to compete and quarrel over every inch of interpersonal territory, measured in real or symbolic terms, barely needs a Darwinian framework to suggest that human beings of the twenty-first century are still only a step off the savannah, acting out of competitive urges that no longer fit the present conditions of life. Where Christianity saw original sin as the explanation for this unaccountable irrationality, Darwin found our only slightly adapted animal nature.

Looking at literature through an evolutionary lens is bound to change our general understanding of it because it changes our general understanding of life. It points to some of the same causes as other explanatory models but puts them in a different relation to each other. Whereas the thinkers of the nineteenth and early twentieth centuries tended to isolate one of the key motivations of human behavior—the drive for sex, economic resources, status, or power—the evolutionary perspective invites us to see these as mutually fungible. Sex, power, wealth, and status are different issues in the same currency, all of them ultimately to be traded for reproductive advantage.

This updated version of Darwin provides an account of the human motivational system that integrates the elements stressed by Marx, Nietzsche, Freud, Veblen, Mauss, and others. The implications for our understanding of society and history as well as literature are profound. When we look at the preoccupations of the standard literary genres, we find just the features that Darwinian theory would lead us to expect—the drama of sexual selection between male and female, competition among males or groups of males for power, prestige, wealth, status, and sexual opportunities, the subtleties of human maneuvering of all kinds, and the difficulty of knowing what other people are really up to. The power of the most enduring writers—Homer, Shakespeare, Austen, Melville, Balzac— stands out more clearly for their concentration on these themes. Darwinian theory also provides insight into the motivations of authors and readers. Its stress on our deep and continuous need for mutual assessment casts in a vivid light our fascination with literary portrayals of imaginary characters, which give us the opportunity to observe the behavior of other "people" with a clarity rarely possible in life.[23] It also explains our need to connect a work with its author, which goes beyond our reception of its meaning and always involves the evaluation of a performance.[24]

Darwinian theory helps us make sense of our interest in literature and is bound to affect our sense of the impact and value of literary works but, in spite of all this, it does not change the meaning of those works. A person who takes up the Darwinian frame of mind may find Frost's view of nature, for instance, more congenial than Wordsworth's, but this, of course, is only because Frost has been influenced by Darwin.[25] It does not mean that either Frost's or Wordsworth's poems change their meaning when considered by a person who takes a Darwinian perspective. And this is entirely to the credit of the theory. It is to the advantage of Darwinism as a perspective on everyday human psychology that it does not change our sense of that psychology in a radical way. It does not ask us to believe in submerged intentions, unconscious drives, or hidden forces of history. It merely highlights the continuity of some fundamental motives through the vast diversity of cultures, thus explaining why the advances of modernity have not caused us to outgrow the appeal of the premodern imagination.

I have been stressing that the discovery of unconscious meanings requires extra theoretical assumptions beyond those involved in ordinary communication, assumptions that must provide controversial new sources of rationality and intention because the communicative situation, in which one agent provides another with an utterance as a prompt for inference, cannot exist when the intentions are unconscious. The process of mutual anticipation cannot operate on that basis. My own belief is that the extra theoretical assumptions that sustain the models of unconscious intention employed by literary critics do not stand up to scrutiny, but that is a question readers will have to pursue for themselves.

Is Actor-Network Theory the Antidote to the Totalizing Modes of "Critique"?

Except for Darwinism, the forms of deep interpretation I have been discussing in this chapter are seminal examples of the hermeneutics of suspicion recently described by Rita Felski in *The Limits of Critique*. As I mentioned in the Preface, Felski's admirable reconsideration of critique has a striking limit of its own. Though she is aware that critique undermines the agency of individuals and marginalizes the responsibility of authors, the one element of critique that she herself remains attached to is the taboo on authorial intention. It is an element that critique preserved from the New Critical vogue that preceded it. Despite the passing of critique, it is still "texts" and the impact of their distinctive qualities to which she hopes to regain access, as well as the social process of their interaction with readers. The productive agency of literature and the role of the author remain out of bounds, so the social nature of literature does not come fully into view. Felski complains that critique reduces text to context (183), but she does not bring the author, the mediating figure between text and context, back into focus. Instead, she looks to another grand theory, Actor-Network Theory, propounded by the French sociologist of science Bruno Latour, to guide scholars out of the labyrinth of critique. Does Latour provide the answer to critique that Felski is looking for?

In some ways, Actor-Network Theory looks like quite a suitable antidote to paranoid criticism. It is based upon its own critique of standard social science as reducing "the social" to some grand, unlocatable agency like Society or Capital. Latour is ironic toward a way of thinking that explains the entire social dimension with reference to nothing other than a hypostasized version of itself. The very project of explaining the social in other social terms seems to him fundamentally misguided. Rather, the way to understand social activity is not to explain it but to describe the novel entities and activities it brings into being, the networks between disparate objects it creates. In describing these objects, Latour believes there is no reason to insist on the distinction between human and non-human ones, both of which he calls "actors." He sees the need to make such a distinction as an unsatisfiable demand of being "modern."[26] In Latour's vocabulary, an "actor" is anything that can "modify a state of affairs by making a difference."[27] It can be a human agent or a speed bump. And while he does not explicitly rule out intentional human actors as part of social activity, he puts them on the same footing as the "non-human actors." Latour provides an elaborate, quasi-scholastic metaphysics to back up his ontology of pure relations, networks, actors, and events, but his method would look more at home in the positivistic and behavioristic mid-twentieth century than in the twenty-first.[28]

The intellectual adjustments required to get one's mind around Actor-Network Theory and grasp the value of its non-explanatory but exhaustive mode of description have led Latour on a career of endless polemic and tireless re-explanation.[29] But the critique-occulted insight that Felski hopes to ground using Latour's theory is really a very simple one—that the distinctive qualities of "texts" (I would say "literary works") play a role in determining what kind of networks they generate (167). In other words, the qualities of the works themselves actually matter. And this makes what they have to say worth listening to: "past texts have things to say on questions that matter to us" (160). In my view, this is not something we need a special theory to establish. It could only have seemed so for scholars who have been trained in a very systematic alienation by means of a long-enforced taboo. Felski hopes that Actor-Network Theory might widen scholars' perspectives beyond the reader–text relationship and help them see reading once more as a relationship between "actors." It might make them skeptical about the period divisions that guide professional activity. These goals are certainly to be promoted, but in my view the price is high. The text is cut off from one of the most important actors, becoming uncannily a kind of actor itself. "The fate of literary works," Felski writes from the point of view of Actor-Network Theory as adapted to her own agenda, is "tied to countless agents: publishers, reviewers, [literary] agents, bookstores, technologies of consumption (e-readers, Amazon.com), institutional frames (women's and ethnic studies, for examples), forms of adaptation and translation, the physical and material properties of books ranging from fonts to photographs, and so on" (183–84). In a list of "agents" as multifarious as this, the absence of authors is striking. The literary text is being given the uncanny status of a first cause, an unmoved mover which sets everything else in motion. The exclusion of the author is a guarantee that intentions will not enter the process, but then how will the activities of publishers, reviewers, and scholars of women's and ethnic studies, or even the activities of Actor-Network theorists themselves, enter the picture? These are intentional actors too. In adopting Latour's non-intention-based notion of an "actor," Felski is taking on board Latour's own borrowing from structuralist semiotics.[30] Thus she is importing back to literary criticism an element of the very mode of critique she hopes to leave behind.

THEN HOW SHOULD WE READ AFTER ALL?

Latour's provocation does direct the scholar's attention to the remarkable array of things and people that are involved in the production, mediation, and consumption of literature—three fuzzy and overlapping categories which I take to capture most if not all of what literary scholars study. Under the *production* of a work I would place not just authorial activity but the literary institutions of the time, the political, intellectual, and social context, the media and technology of production and dissemination, including the material creation of the book, play, or poem. Readers will be able to add further items. Under *mediation* I think of the way works are advertised, redacted, censored, anthologized, restaged, remade, theorized about, appropriated in other works, responded to, and so on. Since the eighteenth century, just about every change of artistic practices has been mediated by a preface, a trend, a manifesto, a movement, or a theory.

Authors, of course, do a lot of their own mediating, and some of them are supremely good at it, Dickens, Yeats, and Pound being prominent examples. Finally, under *consumption* I would place the history of reading and rereading, reinterpreting, and the long, sometimes inspiring and sometimes discouraging story of whatever it is that literature may be said to accomplish.

Interpretation, for decades now the literary-critical practice par excellence, belongs not only to studies of production but also to the fields of mediation and consumption; it can aim at the original meaning of the work, the way it was reframed in later transmissions and redactions, or the way it was subsequently received up to our own day. And criticism itself plays a role in all three spheres of literary activity, altering the way works are made, thought about, and experienced. I see no disadvantage to regarding its concerns and methods as taking the form of a wide-ranging pluralism. None of the fields of interest I have sketched need be rivals to each other, though not every scholarly endeavor will deal with all three. Just about every grand theory tends to emphasize one or the other, though, marginalizing the rest. Since production and original meaning were the great preoccupations of traditional scholarship, during the phase of critique the study of production became a foil for the newer subjects of mediation and consumption. The deauthorized conception of the "text" was a neat way of focusing scholarship on later appropriations while the availability of unconscious intentions kept the author's mind in play as the locus of intentions visible only to the critic. The superiority of the critic over the text emphasized by Felski also permitted the establishment of status inequality among critics, giving an advantage in professional standing to the practitioners of critique as opposed to their more staid author-centered and text-editing colleagues. Actor-Network Theory seems like the most unprescriptive, promiscuously empirical theory imaginable, but it still has its protocols and prohibitions, and its claim to be a general way of gaining social knowledge would still give it a status appeal in contrast with other ways of doing things.

So, do we need a sweeping new hegemonic theory to undergird the kind of pluralistic outlook imagined above, an outlook that accepts the worth of a great deal of what actually goes on in scholarship without establishing an a priori hierarchy supported by theory? Not if we can once again have recourse to the everyday notion of intention. Granted that notion, we can simply accept that both the objects of literary study and the study itself are intentional activities, and we can approach them on that basis. We can acknowledge the contributions of individuals to literature—authors, printers, publishers, critics—while recognizing the social nature of the endeavor. As we have seen, linguistic intentions are essentially social in nature, involving mutual knowledge and anticipation on the part of speaker or author and audience. The artistic aims that animate a work involve mastery of pre-existing forms and literary resources created by others and are other-directed in character. And when we get to the practical sphere, the social nature of literature is even more undeniable. Writers inevitably put forward a point of view and contribute to social projects beyond the mere creation of literary works. Literary institutions provide the enabling and co-ordinating frameworks for the intentional activities of multiple and diverse individuals in every sphere of literary activity. Material, technological, and social conditions constrain and enable literary work. They are not intentional in themselves but they must be contended with in intentional terms by the participants in literary work and by those who study literature. They cannot be treated as brute material constraints, but neither can they be made into agents in their own right.

Finally, when conceptualizing the social nature of intentionality in broad historical but secular terms, let me return to the key notion of the *project*. Like the institutions to which they are often connected, projects are transindividual intentional structures defined by shared motives and goals that co-ordinate the actions of many agents, often over long stretches of time. Feminism is a good example. The improvement of the position of women in society has been a recognizable goal of many people and institutions since the late eighteenth century, with antecedents stretching much further back. It is a purpose intentionally shared among many agents with common views and motives and has made an important mark upon history. That does not mean, of course, that it is a goal of History or the product of a zeitgeist. The progress it makes should not be the subject of a "master narrative." Its success is contingent at every moment, including the present, because it depends not only upon the validity of its claims and the appeal of its values but also upon the continuing efforts of those who promote it. Projects, of course, also generate resistance, which is to say, counter-projects and rival projects. Projects as substantial and long-lasting as feminism become internally diverse and can be seen as a sequence of smaller projects or a competition among them. Projects need to define themselves from the start and such definitions will always be a matter of contest.

The value of feminist criticism depends on the way it does justice to the larger feminist project and the value of the project itself, and these are matters than cannot be resolved theoretically. They depend upon ultimate ethical and political commitments. The study of literature itself is a hybrid of many intellectual and social projects, some knowledge-based and some more explicitly ethical or political in nature. It is up to the critics to defend their choices. Not all projects, of course, are political in nature; there are literary movements as well. No literary theory or simple fact about literature will ever be able to settle a priori which projects or movements should provide the impetus for literary investigation or which methods will prove useful for its pursuit. But we are hopeless to grapple with these issues without notions like intention and project. Deep questions of value are at the heart of them, questions that cannot be settled from the point of view of literature alone. But works of literature can contribute to the discussion if we can respond to them as something more than mere texts.

NOTES

1. Chinua Achebe, "An Image of Africa: Racism in Conrad's *Heart of Darkness*," in Vincent B. Leitch, ed., *The Norton Anthology of Theory and Criticism*, 2nd ed. (New York: W. W. Norton & Co., 2010), 1612–27.

2. See Patrick Brantlinger, *Rule of Darkness: British Literature and Imperialism, 1830–1914* (Ithaca, NY: Cornell University Press, 1988), chapter 9.

3. Gertrude Stein, *Selected Writings of Gertrude Stein*, ed. Carl van Vechten (New York: Vintage, 1990), 466.

4. Arthur Danto, *The Philosophical Disenfranchisement of Art* (New York: Columbia University Press, 1986), 50–51.

5. Roy Pascal, *The Dual Voice: Free Indirect Speech and Its Functioning in the Nineteenth-Century European Novel* (Manchester, UK: Manchester University Press, 1977).

6. Kendall Walton, "Categories of Art," in Peter Lamarque and Stein Haugum Olsen, eds., *Aesthetics and the Philosophy of Art* (Malden, MA: Blackwell, 2004; rptd. from *Philosophical Review* 79 [1970], 334–67), 147.

7. Stephen Blackpool from *Hard Times* and Harriet Beecher Stowe's Uncle Tom pose the same set of issues. The derogatory use of "Uncle Tom" applies to the viewpoint of the novel rather than a mere character.

8. John Farrell, "The Birth of the Psychoanalytic Hero: Freud's Platonic Leonardo," *Philosophy and Literature* 31, no. 2 (October 2007): 233–254.

9. See Paul Ricoeur, *Freud and Philosophy: An Essay on Interpretation*, trans. Denis Savage (New Haven, CT: Yale University Press, 1970), Book 2, part 1. For an interesting treatment with references to the literature see Donald Davidson, "Paradoxes of Irrationality," in *Problems of Rationality* (New York: Oxford University Press, 2004), 169–187.

10. See, for example, Edward Erwin, *A Final Accounting: Philosophical and Empirical Issues in Freudian Psychology* (Cambridge, MA: MIT Press, 1996) and Frederick Crews, ed., *Unauthorized Freud: Doubters Confront a Legend* (New York: Viking, 1998).

11. For a fuller account see John Farrell, *Freud's Paranoid Quest: Psychoanalysis and Modern Suspicion* (New York: New York University Press, 1996), chapters 1–3.

12. Fredric Jameson, *The Political Unconscious: Narrative as a Socially Symbolic Act* (Ithaca, NY: Cornell University Press, 1981), 164.

13. John Farrell, *Paranoia and Modernity: Cervantes to Rousseau* (Ithaca: Cornell University Press, 2006), 248–250.

14. Jameson, Political Unconscious, 19.

15. Michel Foucault, *The History of Sexuality*, vol. 1, trans. Robert Hurley (New York: Vintage, 1978), 10.

16. Stephen Greenblatt, *Shakespearean Negotiations: The Circulation of Social Energy in Renaissance England* (Berkeley: University of California Press, 1988), chapter 4.

17. See Stephen Greenblatt, "Resonance and Wonder," in *Marvelous Possessions: The Wonder of the New World* (Chicago: University of Chicago Press, 1992), chapter 3.

18. On the problems of Marx's functionalism see Jon Elster, *An Introduction to Marx* (Cambridge: Cambridge University Press, 1986), 31–34.

19. I. A. Richards, *Science and Poetry* (New York: Norton, 1926), 67.

20. Stanley E. Fish, "How Ordinary is Ordinary Language?" in *Is There a Text in This Class? The Authority of Interpretive Communities* (Cambridge, MA: Harvard University Press, 1980), 101.

21. See Charles Segal, *Tragedy and Civilization: An Interpretation of Sophocles* (Norman, OK: University of Oklahoma Press, 1999), 20.

22. Claude Lévi-Strauss, "The Structural Study of Myth," in *Structural Anthropology*, trans. Claire Jacobson and Brooke Grundfest Schoepf (New York: Basic Books, 1963), 226–227.

23. See, for example, William Flesch, *Comeuppance: Costly Signaling, Altruistic Punishment, and Other Biological Components of Fiction* (Cambridge, MA: Harvard University Press, 2007); Brian Boyd, *On the Origin of Stories: Evolution, Cognition, and Fiction* (Cambridge, MA: Harvard University

Press, 2009); and Blakey Vermeule, *Why Do We Care about Literary Characters?* (Baltimore, MD: The Johns Hopkins University, 2010).

24. Denis Dutton, *The Art Instinct: Beauty, Pleasure, and Human Evolution.* (New York: Bloomsbury Press, 2010), 177–192.

25. Robert Faggen, *Robert Frost and the Challenge of Darwin* (Ann Arbor: University of Michigan Press, 1997).

26. Bruno Latour, *We Have Never Been Modern* (Cambridge, MA: Harvard University Press, 1994).

27. Bruno Latour, *Reassembling the Social: An Introduction to Actor-Network Theory* (Oxford: Oxford University Press, 2006), 71. The phrase "making a difference" suggests the central problem of Latour's attempt to promote ordinary objects into actors. Without the goal provided by an intentional framework, what do they make a difference to?

28. Latour's metaphysics has been summarized in Graham Harman, *The Prince of Networks: Bruno Latour and Metaphysics* (Prahran, VIC: Re.press, 2009).

29. To get the flavor see "On the Difficulty of Being an ANT: An Interlude in the Form of a Dialog," in which Latour stages a lengthy interchange between himself and a baffled graduate student who cannot grasp the point of doing Actor-Network Theory. *Reassembling the Social*, 141–156.

30. Latour, *Reassembling the Social*, 54. In place of *actor* Latour often uses Greimas's term *actant*.

CHAPTER 5

Authorship and Literary Value

THE GENERAL PLURALITY OF VALUES

The term "value" has been one of the great skeptical weapons of modern culture. The lingering legacy of positivism tells us that values are subjective and hazy or merely emotive while facts are solid and objective. This legacy has often been attacked, especially by philosophers of science who are aware that facts and values, insofar as the distinction holds up at all, are complexly "entangled" in just about everything we do and that there is no absolute perspective upon reality which does not take some epistemic values for granted.[1] In an earlier chapter I raised the possibility that values are so much a part of our daily thinking that we cannot set them at an interrogative distance; every time we decide that one action or one view of a question is better than another we are making a judgment of value. In discussions of literature, value judgments are typically regarded as something that only comes after the work has been encountered rather than as part of the experience of reading it, but this attitude is hard to justify. The pleasure we take in reading a work of literature is based upon an implicit value judgment, made sentence by sentence, that this is something vital and interesting, stimulating to us in a way that is worth our time in comparison with other literary experiences we have had and other things we could be doing. The perception of value keeps us reading. It is not as if we experience the pleasure provided by the work and then evaluate the work by judging that pleasure. Rather, our pleasure itself involves an

© The Author(s) 2017
J. Farrell, *The Varieties of Authorial Intention*,
DOI 10.1007/978-3-319-48977-3_5

implicit judgment that the work has value, that it is doing something unexpectedly well, or well enough to keep us going. By the same token, authors cannot simply aim to engage or stimulate an audience directly. They must try to do something stimulating with words—tell a story, for example—and by doing that well they provide pleasure. Literary value is a quality of the work, not merely a quality of the experience the work provides.[2]

Of course, when talking about literary value, it is important to recognize from the start that literary works can have many other kinds of value— religious, political, social, economic, psychological, or cultural. They also have value for the way they develop the techniques or extend the subject matter of the art. For several decades, literary scholars have typically discussed the question of value primarily in terms of canon formation, the process by which books are selected to be taught and discussed in the academy. The governing assumption is that this process is importantly determined by the political, social, or economic interests of the canonizers; the value of the experience the works provide for its own sake has largely been set aside. The prevalence of the notion that literary works have no stable meaning, that their meaning is indeterminate, or determined by the interpreter's framework, has tended to discourage the sense that works can have a stable literary value as well.

The habit of talking about literature in terms of *the* canon can obscure the range of values and interests literature serves; in principle there could be many literary canons, each centered upon a different value. That, of course, would be too tidy a way of handling the question as to how these values should play against each other. The loose assemblage we now call the canon, as represented in the academic study of literature, does not foster a single value. Instead, it is a continuously negotiated compromise among competing values and interests, one that keeps the issue of how they should be balanced constantly alive. This is as it should be. But recognizing the variety of purposes and values that can be served by literary works need not undermine the sense that literary works do have a distinct purpose as literary works and that they can be evaluated as to how well they achieve it. That purpose is to provide a valuable experience for the reader—pleasure or some other kind of stimulation. Most authors may have ulterior designs upon their readers in providing such experiences, but the distinctively literary aim remains, and since purposive human activities must have criteria for success, it would be strange if works of literature were an exception and lacked this normative dimension.

The fact that literature can have many kinds of value and that it can be judged by many criteria other than the experience it offers does not mean that literary value derives from merely "aesthetic" or formal elements. If a writer can express a profound view of the world or of human behavior, provide deep political or ethical insight, or involve us in quests, puzzles, and mysteries, all of these contribute to our experience, thus enhancing the literary value of the work and testifying to the author's skill and power. Such qualities are certainly no less important than the gifts of style and form. All of them give substance and reality to literary works and make some of them superior to others of their kind. When we are talking about the literary value of a work, we are talking about the total experience it provides, not merely its formal properties.

The great question about literary value is *value for whom?* Who is the proper judge of literary value? If we are willing to weigh everyone's experience equally in the balance, we can identify the best literary works simply by comparing sales. This approach is akin to utilitarianism in ethics, an application of the hedonistic calculus to derive the greatest happiness of the greatest number. The winners in such a contest will inevitably be pop fiction writers like James Patterson, who pumps out bestsellers by the month with the help of a stable of co-authors. Making as few demands upon his readers as possible, Patterson outsells the classics and undoubtedly gives more pleasure by the year than Shakespeare or Jane Austen. In the same way, acts like the Three Tenors, which was popular a few years ago, give more net pleasure per annum than fully staged operas by Wagner and Verdi because of the size of the audience to which they appeal. Given the sheer massiveness of modern consumer populations, it is likely that current bestselling authors have given more hours of pleasure than most classic authors have *ever* given through all the centuries of their existence.

The alternative to the utilitarian approach commonly goes under the name of *criticism*, a term which implies that acts of literary creation call for judgment as to how well they have been made. The ethical analogue is the view that actions cannot be judged entirely by their net effects, but that some things are intrinsically right or wrong, better or worse. For literature, this approach requires a form of expertise that can judge works based on their artistic qualities. Such an approach would ask not simply how much pleasure a work gives but how well it does those things which allow it to give pleasure, how well the author chooses, invents, or arranges words, themes, and narrated events to construct the work. From this point of view, the pleasure one takes in a work of literature involves a judgment of the skill that went into its construction, a judgment that we make moment by moment, not only when the reading is done.[3]

If the utilitarian approach is correct, identifying the best works is quite simple. We can learn about the comparative literary value of works of literature by simple, empirical means, then go on to consider whatever other, extraliterary kinds of value they may have. But if the work itself is the object of evaluation, along with the act of creation that produced it, then matters are more complicated and the notion of expertise enters the picture. Who is the proper judge of a literary work, the average person considered in the mass or the person who has intimate knowledge of the art? The first answer seems like the more democratic one until we recognize that the comparison of artists, athletes, and performers of all kinds is also one of the most popular, indeed ubiquitous, of all human activities. Discussions about value are a universally enjoyed form of sharing. The expertise it demands can hardly be called elite. Applying the utilitarian criterion of artistic value, on the other hand, making literary value identical with gross pleasure, would require a severe reform of our everyday vocabulary. It is deeply, inextricably embedded in the traditions of literature to believe that when we are judging literary or artistic value, we are assessing the performance of the artist as it appears to those who can compare it with others of the same kind.

This picture of literary valuation makes it look like our way of judging human activities more generally, and it dovetails with the account of meaning I have given in previous chapters by emphasizing the necessity of refering to the author's performance if we are to understand and evaluate a work. Works that succeed by utilitarian criteria can do so by accident. Accounts of their value need not refer to anything beyond the work alone. But works that are judged in comparison with the standards of performance set by other authors and by our general estimate of human ability cannot succeed by accident or by the qualities of the work considered merely in itself. Intention is required and more than intention, skill, as displayed in practice. The display of authorial skill may not provide us with a sufficient criterion for establishing the nature of a work of art and what makes it a good one, but it is a necessary element. Once again, the work alone, considered as a mere object, cannot suffice.[4] Just as we interpret the meaning of a work as an utterance in context, so we judge the value of a work as a performance in context.

The philosopher Malcolm Budd has defined the literary critic's task as "the attempt to describe works of art in ways that justify our response to them; it is the rational appreciation of works of art."[5] Such notions as "rational appreciation" now have an alien, antique ring to the ears of literary critics, comparisons and justifications of literary value being beside the point of most literary scholarship as it is currently practiced. Indeed, the term "criticism" itself has become something of an anachronism in light of what scholars actually do. Much scholarship seeks to assess works of literature for their cultural or political effects without necessarily implying that they have a specifically literary or artistic value at all.

Nonetheless, many of the historical and analytic judgments that scholars make about literary works are also implicit judgments of literary value, and the literary status of works remains one of the key factors that makes them worth discussing in the first place. Shakespeare's politics is more compelling as a subject for scholarship than Marlowe's politics on grounds that are literary and cultural, not political. More importantly, judgments of literary value do not play their role merely in setting works and authors against each other. Their principle use is to direct us toward the works that are important, and especially toward what is important in each work, its "specific characteristics."[6] Judgments about the way the elements of a literary work function are typically judgments of evaluation, and a criticism that cannot assess literary works in literary terms will not be able to see how they create their effects or contribute to other kinds of value. It will not be able to balance instrumental concerns against the literary ones that were surely there from the start. Whatever theoretical approach they take, then, scholars need to make use of their literary responses, and it is unlikely that they can do this from a strictly non-evaluative point of view. Our basic understanding of literary works seems inseparable from our judgments about the effect of each chosen word.

Naturally, there is always a certain risk in using one's personal responses as the basis for scholarly judgments. Barbara Herrnstein-Smith begins her well-known book *Contingencies of Value* by narrating her career-long vacillation over the worth of Shakespeare's sonnets.[7] Such vacillations are familiar. They are a hazard for scholars who live many years with their subjects and identify intensely with them. We can easily invest too familiar authors and works with all the ambivalence we feel toward our own professional selves. Partly on the basis of her experience, Herrnstein-Smith characterizes the value we attribute to literary works as entirely subjective and contingent. Value *creates* value, she argues, meaning that one act of valuation tends to beget another, leading to the appearance of an artificial consensus which is really based on the power of suggestion (10). True to her belief that thought in general is a process of

Heraclitean flux, Herrnstein-Smith concludes her book with the concession that her own preference for the argument that literary judgment is entirely a contingent matter of personal taste is itself entirely a contingent matter of personal taste (151).

Even if we accepted this argument about the source of Herrnstein-Smith's own preference, doing so would discourage us from adopting her position. Instead I am going to argue that literary judgment has some objective basis, at least within each genre, medium, and mode, defining these in the loosest possible way, and that the consensus which forms about the value of literary works is too stable to be understood merely as an accidental coalescence of subjectivities. The belief in the indeterminacy of meaning in recent decades has not strengthened, of course, the sense that literary works have a value all readers should be able agree upon. Indeed, readers who interpret works differently can be thought of as actually evaluating different works. What is more striking, though, is that there are many works of literature whose value seems to remain stable despite or even because of the diversity of readings they inspire. If I am correct that the pleasure we experience in a work of literature is an implicit value judgment about the quality of the work as a creation of the author, then our pleasure in a sense commits us to an objective claim about its worth, no matter how interminable the discussions about that claim may be.

AFICIÓN

The first time you attend the bullfight or the ballet you witness daring and agility of a remarkable sort, things that you have never seen before. The feats of the matadors and ballerinas may fill you with dread or delight, but you are not ready to appreciate them as art. Without experience as a spectator, you cannot tell which accomplishments are common to all matadors or ballerinas and which are special to the performers in front of you. You have no grounds of comparison other than your sense of what the average person could do. The individuality and distinctiveness of the performers' styles are more or less invisible. You lack, in other words, what Ernest Hemingway, in his writings on the bullfight, calls *afición*, a term that, in his usage, implies not only passion but well-informed appreciation for the spectacle in question. Only the viewer who has some measure of *afición* can appreciate the artistic value of a performance.

Afición does not come of itself. It requires devotion and training of a kind parallel with, though not the same as, the devotion and training required for practice of the art. Perhaps the greatest *afición*, the greatest capacity for passionate appreciation, does most often belong to distinguished practitioners themselves, but the ability to express and share *afición*, to identify and describe the techniques of the art and identify the marks of success and failure, is a skill quite separate from the artist's ability to create or perform. The attraction of the term *afición* is that it combines amateur and professional activities. Literary critics, insofar as they are concerned with the value of works of art, need *afición*. It is not the only form of critical expertise, but it is the classic form. Literary critics know what categories of judgment artists and other critics will apply to works in the various genres and types of literary performance. They strive to develop a refined sense of the expectations appropriate to each genre and type. Many of their judgments appear to have an inevitable quality. When comparing Shakespeare's tragedies, few experienced readers will consider *Titus Andronicus*, with its relentlessly hyperbolic gore, to be the equal of *King Lear*, with its sublime poetry, humor, and depth of insight into human feelings. The superiority of *King Lear* seems so obvious that it is barely worth discussing. And if the differences between *Titus Andronicus* and *King Lear* are not clear enough, compare *Lear* with Nahum Tate's version of the play, or with Dryden's *Conquest of Granada*, with its ridiculous bombast, or with Samuel Johnson's limp tragedy, *Irene*.

Examples like the *Lear/Titus* contrast are particularly compelling because they suggest that we experience differences in impact and value among works to which we have more or less the same relation of every other kind, works that come from the same source and reflect roughly the same worldview in the same genre but which still affect us differently on account of their artistic qualities. If to our eyes not all Petrarchan sonnets or Quattrocento madonnas have been created equal, the explanation would seem to lie not with the differences in ideological resonance among them, if there are any, or with differences in the status benefits they confer on the audience, which are nonexistent, but with their peculiar contents and the ways they have been put together, ways that give value to the experience they provide. While comparisons between the most admired authors are always difficult, it seems relatively easy to see that some works of literature are simply inferior to others. I would venture to say that most qualified readers of Shakespeare would not only find *Lear* superior to *Titus* but that they would place *Julius Caesar* somewhere in between. The consensus that accompanies such judgments seems to be more than a matter of chance. And if we find it hard to identify the precise grounds of *King Lear*'s superiority to other plays except by using superlatives that themselves will be hard to define, it is much easier to say why *Titus Andronicus* is not a good play. We are always on surer ground saying why literary efforts fail than why they succeed. The reason for this is an interesting one to which I will return.

The critical thinking that we exercise in judging literary works is not special to the arts. It applies to just about any purposive activity that can be carried out well or badly. We judge a good job of plumbing and a good mathematical proof with the same question in mind—how well does it achieve its goals? It would be strange if art were the only sort of making or doing that cannot be reliably evaluated in this way. The fact that acquiring *afición* even for ordinary skills requires a gradual and somewhat painstaking education also seems to guarantee that something solid is being learned, that the student of the art as she progresses is getting closer and closer to an object of knowledge.

There is more than a touch of irony, however, regarding the increase in certainty that comes from expert knowledge, for this increase in certainty does not necessarily move those who have it toward unanimity. At most there is consensus within a certain range of opinion. Aficionados of every kind of performance, no matter how subtle or minute their appreciation, still manage to disagree about what constitutes the finest performances and who are the best performers. Joselito or Juan Belmonte in the bullring? Callas or Tebaldi on the opera stage? And in the novel, Tolstoy or Dostoyevsky, Hemingway or Nabokov? These questions can never finally be settled. In judging the arts, greater knowledge narrows the field of disagreement but also sharpens its focus. The most passionate investment in artistic expertise leads not to unanimity but to discord.

It may be that critical disagreement becomes inevitable when people invest so much energy in the making of subtle discriminations, and the interminability of disagreement seems, in fact, both to be one of the pleasures of *afición* and one of the things that makes it seem unprofessional. But it should not be forgotten that criticism as an evaluative art is competitive just like criticism as an interpretive art. The genre prohibits the critic from simply rearticulating a known consensus. In order to have something worth saying, critics must either disagree with judgments already known or at least find new reasons for supporting them. They are in the bullring too.

Still, despite all these motives for contentiousness, there is a peculiarly inconclusive quality to the explanations we give of why a literary work succeeds, one which cannot be accounted for by the pleasures and imperatives of disagreement. Expert critics can point to the features of a work that constitute its attractions. They can point out the lines and shapes in a painting that account for its gracefulness and the contrasts of light and dark that make it dramatic; they can highlight the bold metaphors that make a poem vivid. But they cannot provide rules for producing any of these effects. No merely technical recipe can be advanced for effects like grace, dramatic intensity, or vividness. We can see how techniques function when they work, but the explanations cannot be generalized. Evaluative terms like gracefulness or vividness cannot be defined in non-evaluative terms; they cannot be reduced to the merely technical. And the same relationship holds between the evaluative descriptions we give of a work and our general appraisal of its value. Being told that a work is graceful or disturbing or tranquil does not tell us if these effects have been successfully integrated into the total impression that it makes. Grace and tranquility are marvelous qualities in Raphael's paintings but insipid in the works of Guido Reni. Critics may have a certain authority about the valuable qualities literary works possess, but they cannot make reliable predictions about whether or not their fellow experts will find a work valuable on the basis of those qualities.[8]

The success of works of art does not seem to be reducible in any straightforward way, and the elements to which we might reduce it—grace, humor, ingenuity—are equally elusive, but other reductive accounts of aesthetic judgment are in no better shape. Knowing that a literary work tends to confirm some aspect of a class ideology does not tell you that the members of that class will actually value or enjoy it any more than knowing that a work challenges some aspect of class ideology tells you that members of that class will fail to enjoy it. Some types of art tend to appeal to members of one class or another, but this appeal will never be exclusive. There will always be people who cross the lines of taste and escape the pigeonholes of distinction. And knowing that a form of art—opera, rap, or country—tends to appeal to one group of people rather than another does not tell you anything about the relative value of individual works in that form.

In ascribing artistic value, then, we are always working backwards from our responses. Only after we experience a work as valuable or faulty can we attempt to grasp how its peculiar qualities contribute to its value or lack of it. And only once we experience the presence of these qualities can we observe how they have been technically achieved. This account of value is sometimes called *aesthetic holism*.[9] It discourages us from thinking that aesthetic judgment can be grounded in or reduced to anything else. This does not necessarily mean, of course, that our aesthetic explanations for literary value are false or empty, but it does mean that they are inherently open-ended. Room for disagreement always remains. Whenever we point to a quality that gives us pleasure in a literary work and offer that as a reason for why others should take pleasure in it too, we are always vulnerable to the reply that the work does not actually possess that quality, that it does not actually give pleasure, or that it gives pleasure on account of a quality different from the one we have identified. In their holistic aspect, works of art turn out to be rather like people. No matter how many admirable or charming qualities we judge them to have, and no matter how disinterestedly we view them, the question of whether or not we will actually find value in their company, their behavior, or even in their existence remains, all things considered, an open one.

The holistic aspect of aesthetic judgment casts an ironic light not only upon the exercise of critical expertise but also upon the history of speculation about the arts as reflected in the prefaces and manifestos of authors themselves. Much of the history of literary theory consists of attempts on the part of artists to rationalize their practices. Especially since the late eighteenth century, artists in just about every medium have advanced theoretical explanations to justify their artistic experiments. Typically, these explanations depend upon some claim about the essential nature of the art in question and how a recognition of this nature can guide artistic practice, partly by stripping away the unnecessary accoutrements wrongly preserved by tradition in the mistaken belief they were essential. Were these revisionary diagnoses valid and capable of guiding practice, aesthetic holism would be undermined and artists could proceed by recipe to produce fine works of art. But that has hardly proven to be the case. Instead, each generation overthrows the theory about the secret of art provided by the previous one, and each finds itself overthrown in its turn. All of the talk about the true nature of an art depending upon expressing emotions or corresponding with social realities, estrangement effects, or objective correlatives, was destined from its birth to be fodder for the literary historian, providing background for the explication of artistic intentions but without the explanatory force the authors intended. The great artists turn out to be powerful in their experiments but fragile in their theories. The theoretical discourse of artistic practice assumes that there is a true way for the artist to proceed and that art can make progress by taking that way, but the true way always turns out to be just another temporary expedient, useful but limited and subject to correction in the next generation. The critique of past art provided by artist-critics may be entirely valid; we may fully endorse, for instance, Wordsworth's complaints about the poetic diction of the late eighteenth century. But the validity of these complaints does not make them a useful guide to artistic practice—unless you happen to have the Wordsworth's talent for writing poems.[10]

In addition to aesthetic holism, there is another limit upon our explanations of artistic value. Each artistic medium and each artistic genre has its own sources of value, and there is no common standard by which they can be compared. Artistic value is inherently pluralistic. The things that make a fine lyric and a fine satire, or fine pop song and a fine sonata, are truly incommensurable, and the effect is only more obvious in comparisons between media. Each genre in each medium has its own audience and its own way of interpreting the values of performance. Some cross-over may be possible. Some aesthetic qualities—gracefulness, beauty, wit—may extend over the lines between media. And perhaps we can say that figures like Beethoven, Shakespeare, and Michelangelo occupy a similar status position in their respective media, but that is a comparison not of authors, only of judgments about authors.

To call something pluralistic is to say that it takes different forms in different contexts. To call something holistic is to say that it is difficult to explain in other terms. Neither pluralism nor holism about literary value imply that it does not exist. The explanatory elusiveness and pluralistic nature of literary value seem to me not contingent to our understanding of its nature but essential, and they are both connected to the notion that when we are judging a literary work we are judging it as the result of a competitive human activity. To appreciate it we must be able to judge it as a performance that could not be predicted on the basis of existing models. The author's contribution cannot be assessed merely on the basis of the work itself. The context of performance is required. Since much of the serious thinking about literary value in the past has tended to start with the assumption that it is due to a "mimetic" relation to other objects or an "aesthetic" quality inhering in the works themselves, both qualities that can be appreciated apart from their makers, it is important to see where these views go wrong.

Mimetic and Aesthetic Theories

In the twentieth century, literary critics often depended upon the notion of a special, literary language to define what was distinctive about literature and explain its value, but as I tried to show in Chapter 2, literary language and ordinary language are much the same. It is not the nature of the

instrument but the purposes to which it is put that makes literature different. More traditional attempts to define literature tended to focus on a
distinctive quality attributed to literary objects. So the Platonic conception
of *mimesis*, adapted and applied to poetry by Aristotle, identified the distinction of poetry in the likeness between the work and what it represents.
This conception has a deep intuitive appeal, especially when applied to the
visual arts, but it also has some obvious drawbacks. As Nelson Goodman
pointed out, the likeness relation is usually thought of as a reflexive one.[11] If
I am like you then you are like me in the same way. With works of art,
though, we do not see the likeness going both ways. If we could meet the
woman Mona Lisa we would not admire her according to how well she
resembled *La Gioconda*, even if seeing her would be an uncanny experience
and might enhance our appreciation of Leonardo's skill as a painter. More
to the point, we do not judge the value of *La Gioconda* itself based on its
likeness to Mona Lisa because we have no idea what Mona Lisa actually
looked like apart from the painting that presents her image. The painting
La Gioconda provides the impression of a presence that is not actually there
for comparison. Whatever the painting's original function was meant to be,
it impresses us not as the likeness of its original model but as presenting a
subject that stands before us *as if real*. It is the illusion of presence that
fascinates, as Ernst Gombrich so tellingly explained, an illusion which begins
with an act of creation according to a set of schemas that Western painters,
mastering their craft over the centuries, gradually learned to make more and
more concrete and convincing to the eye.[12] Aristotle's observation that
poetry aims at the probable rather than the actual or historical, that it is
more philosophical than history, accords with Gombrich's insight that
creation begins with types and the adding of detail. But the copying of
types is no longer truly copying unless we think of these types as actually
existing objects the way Aristotle did, and even then it is not clear how one
copies a type which has no particulars.[13]

So the *mimesis* theory seems ultimately unhelpful. In Gombrich's
account, what the visual artist does is exploit our habits of perception,
developed both in life and art, to turn truly indeterminate visual information
into recognizable patterns of shape and motion. It is not so much a matter of
copying as it is of creating a world from scratch, for, as Gombrich observes,
drawing on the work of Karl Popper, once we realize how much of our
ordinary visual experience depends upon filling out partial data to create an
enhanced experience of "reality," the distinction between perception and
illusion gets rather thin (29). Viewing a painting in the realist mode, we

convert the ambiguous sensory information it provides into a firm illusion of presence in much the same way we do with the equally ambiguous information that comes to us from the real world. In a sense, Plato's complaint that both art and the world it copies are illusions is justified by Gombrich's empirically rich and fascinating account.

The application of the mimesis theory to literature is even more difficult than its application to visual art, but Gombrich's opposing account of art and illusion is strikingly similar to the relevance-based account of how language works that I have outlined in earlier chapters. Visual artists, poets, and speakers in everyday conversation all anticipate how their listeners will turn the radically underdetermined stimuli they provide into interpreted sentences or images, giving rise, as Gombrich says, to "the panorama of illusions that may be evoked by the indeterminate" (225).

Because artistic realism in painting does not come to us as naturally as speaking or story-telling—indeed, it need not be the primary goal of artistic activity—visual artists had to make considerable progress experimenting with the techniques of illusion-making before they could reach anything near the vividness of verbal practice, not to mention that of literary art. Gombrich, in fact, sees the revolutionary impulse toward realism in the visual arts of the Greeks as due to the influence of literary narrative (129–33). In any case, like painting, literature and its companion-art, rhetoric, also have a long history of experiment with manipulating the verbal medium in a way that exploits the imaginative capacity of the audience to turn underdetermined information into powerful impressions of experience. In both cases, what we admire is the power of the illusion that the artist can produce. We know what we are experiencing is an illusion of presence, and we enjoy and appreciate its force.

It was in reaction against this illusionistic battery of poetic and rhetorical practices that the Romantic doctrine of expression emerged, a rejection of artifice on the grounds that the nature and function of art is not to imitate the world but to express the feelings of its maker. But where the mimesis theory eliminates the artist and sees the artwork as a detached object standing in an essential relation to another object which it represents, the expression theory ties the work too closely to the artist. Though it may well be that many works of literature seek to express the feelings and experiences of their authors, it is just as obvious that many of them do not and that having feelings is neither necessary nor sufficient for the creation of a work that readers will find expressive. And while the lack of sincerity may in some cases be a literary fault, mere sincerity in itself is hardly a literary virtue. The transparency of the author's emotions is often, in fact, a drawback in a literary work.

T. S. Eliot argued that it was not the intensity of the emotions invested in a poem but the intensity of the artistic process that contributes to its value. This seems only a little closer to the truth. One suspects that many of the finest passages of Shakespeare and Goethe were written with less fever and fret than the weaker poems of Rilke or Hart Crane, not to mention Eliot himself. It is the *impression* of intensity, among other things, that artists aim at. They may do so cold-bloodedly, à la Nabokov, and most of the time we have no way of telling how much of what they express comes from their own mental life and how much is imagination. And we do not have to know. Merely that the artist felt them need not make them valuable for us.

The skepticism about intentionality that I have discussed in previous chapters was evoked in reaction to the Romantic cult of expression, but it often served the defense of another approach which has given its name to the problem of "aesthetic value." There are many versions of the doctrines of "taste" and "aesthetic judgment," from Hume and Kant to Pater and Beardsley, with varying degrees of moralism or immoralism attached. In general the notion is that we have a pleasurable receptivity to certain qualities in our experience of the world and that the artist endows the work of art with similar qualities. So we can explain the pleasures of art in the same terms as the pleasure we take in other objects of experience. Art is just one source of aesthetic pleasure. The capacity to experience such pleasure in response to certain experiences may depend upon contingent features of our peculiar human subjectivity, but it is a subjectivity that we share. The use of the term "taste" to denote aesthetic judgment emphasizes its kinship to sensual experience, but beauty is the aesthetic quality par excellence, and the emphasis on this quality gives some versions of aestheticism a quasi-Platonic aspect. In general, what aesthetic approaches tend to share is the idea that the author gives aesthetically attractive qualities to the work and readers respond to them as they would to any other aesthetically attractive object. The author is the cause and source of what is interesting in the object, but once the object has been created, there is no further need to refer to the author than there would be to the source of a natural object when considering it aesthetically. And since the text is thought of as being like a natural object, possessing preeminently a form given to experience, the cognitive elements of the aesthetic experience tend to be discounted or, in the vein of "aestheticism," excluded from consideration altogether. Art should be for its own sake. It is not *about* anything. It does not represent or express anything but itself.

The aesthetic point of view has its attractions. It seems natural to connect the pleasure we experience of the natural world with the pleasure we experience of natural things in art because artists have so often taken as subjects those people and things that strike us with their beauty, grace, and elegance in life. The insistence on the disinterested character of aesthetic appreciation, as we have noted, also seems instructive in this context. Our everyday perceptions of gracefulness, delicacy, and wit are not obviously related to our practical interests in any definite way (especially if we leave out sexual attraction), yet we are not inclined to regard them as merely subjective. We expect other people to share them, and if they do not immediately do so we can point them toward the features of our experience that bring them about, the ones that not only explain but justify our aesthetic responses.

The fact that aesthetic response is describable and sharable and does not depend upon practical commitments contributes to our sense that it depends upon something external and beyond our control, something that is available from a third-person perspective. If others do not share our response, we suspect them of insensitivity or bias. So for theorists like Hume who defend the objectivity of taste, practical interests play an important but negative explanatory role. Practical interests, along with ideological biases, arbitrary associations, and personal defects, serve to explain the persistence of discord in aesthetic judgment. To be able to expel them from consideration as obstacles of aesthetic experience is a great benefit from that point of view.

In spite of the enormous intellectual and artistic talent that has gone into articulating and defending the aesthetic account of value, its problems have become clearer and clearer, not least of them the difficulty of saying just what the essential aesthetic qualities are. The mere diversity of the candidates is discouraging—unity, complexity, intensity, unity-in-multeity, beauty (of style, of form, etc.), sublimity, truth, coherence, elegance, wit, ingenuity, unpredictability, suspensefulness, poetic justice, sincerity, absence of insincerity, vividness, originality, surprisingness, defamiliarization, propriety of moral judgment, absence of moral repugnancy. All of these, no doubt, can be an advantage to a work of art, but none of them, even in combination, can guarantee its value. Then there is the fact that our interest in literary experience is not confined to what is "aesthetically" pleasing. Literature presents us with spectacles that if real would bring horror and disgust. Modern art in particular has explored the negative dimension of the aesthetic, but there are ancient examples as well, tragedy being the foremost. Negative aesthetic experiences are aesthetic nonetheless, of course, but we cannot rely upon their being aesthetic in character to explain why we find them valuable in literature even though repulsive in life.

The aesthetic point of view also fails to do justice to the undeniable cognitive pleasures offered by art. Though the mimesis theory does not succeed in providing an adequate account of the nature of literature, there is no doubt that works of literature, however loosely we must interpret the metaphor, do provide us with a view of the world, and that is part of their interest. Many works of literature can be usefully thought of as providing a theory about some aspect of existence along with a picture of what the evidence to support it would look like, while leaving the investigation itself to the reader. And there are other aspects of the literary experience which are even more unambiguously cognitive in character and which provide intense pleasure to readers properly inclined. An example would be the invitations to puzzle-solving and decoding provided by authors like Dante, Spenser, Joyce, and Nabokov. Metaphor and irony also make cognitive demands that contribute to literary value. In fact, the process of interpretation, indeed of reading itself, which is the basis of literary experience, is so undeniably cognitive in character that it seems impossible to eliminate cognitive considerations from our understanding of literary value. It is also interesting to note that the experience of ambiguity, which is clearly of a cognitive sort, is one of those things which give us pleasure in literature but tend to annoy us in life.[14]

Artistic versus Aesthetic Value

Pointing out the weaknesses of the aesthetic account of art does not necessarily lead us to accept a more author-based account, but the author-based understanding of literary value that I am going to recommend is one that I believe accords more closely with the facts about how we evaluate literature and other works of art than any of those discussed in the previous section, and it goes back to the principle that the creation of a literary work of art is a human action. Although it is not one of the pre-eminent traditional theories of literary value, it has been the byword of the practical critic. It was stated by Samuel Johnson in terms that can hardly be bettered:

> Every man's performances, to be rightly estimated, must be compared with the state of the age in which he lived, and with his own particular

opportunities; and though to the reader a book be not worse or better for the circumstances of the author, yet as there is always a silent reference of human works to human abilities, and as the enquiry, how far man may extend his designs, or how high he may rate his native force, is of far greater dignity than in what rank we shall place any particular performance, curiosity is always busy to discover the instruments, as well as to survey the workmanship, to know how much is to be ascribed to original powers, and how much to casual and adventitious help. The palaces of *Peru* or *Mexico* were certainly mean and incommodious habitations, if compared to the houses of *European* monarchs; yet who could forbear to view them with astonishment, who remembered that they were built without the use of iron?[15]

The suggestion I want to develop here is that when we respond to a work of art we are responding to and valuing it with a particular understanding of it as an action, which allows us to appreciate it as a display of skill, wit, imagination, wisdom, or whatever else tends to evoke our admiration.[16] We attend to the work as an experience and value the experience it provides us, but we value it as one that has been created by another human being in a particular way, and we judge it in those terms. We are keenly sensitive to its originality and eager to understand, as Johnson says, "how much is to be ascribed to original powers, and how much to casual and adventitious help." Our sense of the historical context in which a work was created is essential not only to the way we understand it but also to the way we experience it. A work with a distinctive new style is better than one that borrows its style from elsewhere. The style may be as well-employed in its borrowed version as in the original source, but the borrowed will never evoke the same admiration as the new. Its qualities can be too easily explained. The early style of Cormac McCarthy, too closely indebted to Faulkner as it is, will always pale next to the original, and Isabel Allende's imitation of Marquez in *The House of the Spirits*, which is more uncannily perfect both in subject and in style, seems all the stranger and weaker for that. Even Melville seems to falter when, in the middle of *Moby-Dick*, he slips into a pastiche of *King Lear*. The writing is splendid but it is no longer really his own.

Very recently a number of philosophers have proposed replacing the label *aesthetic value* with *artistic value* to denote the value that belongs to the work as an action and that cannot be attributed to it as a mere object or work.[17] One advantage of this choice is that it has a clarifying effect on the aspect of literary value that I have been calling *aesthetic holism*, a term I can now recast as *artistic holism*. The fact that there is and can be no recipe or algorithm for producing a work of art is directly connected to the fact that artists cannot hold an audience simply by repeating what their predecessors have done, producing similar objects but by a different, more imitative process. Whatever the state of the artistic game, the artist must find a way either to exploit the rules to the maximal extent, change them, or flout them to his advantage. To imitate is to be predictable—in other words, causally transparent. Instead of being surprised by the author's performance, the imitator's audience is always two steps ahead of him. He seems to disappear behind his model, of which he presents a comically distorted mirror image. Emerson's maxim "Imitation is suicide" may be absurd as a guide to life, but it is perfectly reasonable for the artist. Originality may be a peculiarly modern point of emphasis, but in the centuries before the artist became responsible for the content of art there was still a premium on "invention" and on "things unattempted yet."

Here, however, it is important to issue a caveat. When I say that our appreciation of art is directed at the performance of the artist, I do not mean to imply that what we are somehow experiencing is the artistic process itself. What we are experiencing is the work that has resulted from that process. In a successful work we do not fully understand the process of creation, and that is an essential part of its success. The process remains at least partly invisible and irreducible to its models, and that is necessary to its value. Works that fail to rise above convention or that betray their origins in the work of other writers expose the artistic process too nakedly to the expert reader's view and in doing so they lose their hold on our attention. Whether they aim at illusionistic absorption or self-demystification, the inability of artists to transcend their sources is always deflating.

The paradox, then, is that we most appreciate the artist's performance when we cannot fully account for its character based on our understanding of the contemporary state of the art. Our response to art depends essentially on the originality, unpredictability, and inimitability of human performance. These are necessary, though not sufficient, for its value. If art could be confected by recipe, it would not be worth doing. This is where it differs from the "aesthetic" felicities of nature. We do not tire of the sources of natural beauty nor do we require them to be unpredictable or surprising. We need not compare them with each other, and though the pleasure we take in some of them may diminish as our experience of nature widens, their value cannot entirely fade because there are no standards of performance attached to them. If artists could give their works the same kind of non-competitive appeal, we would not care if that appeal was achieved by means already perfected by other artists. But that is not the case. We require art, unlike nature, to surprise us with its quality.

Of course we also value originality insofar as it enriches the techniques of art or expands its range of subjects; we ascribe historical value to works that depart from established practices and become a model for other writers. This is another respect in which our judgment of value is action-focused rather than object-focused. But the point I am making is a different one, that as well-informed critics we actually *experience* the works differently when they are artistically original. They have different artistic qualities and value than they do when we recognize an imitated source. The process by which they have been created is essential to the identity and power of the work. We are assessing it as an action, not just as a structure of words.

Perhaps this is even clearer in the visual arts than in literature. When we look at a painting by Jan van Eyck, we are stunned that anyone could produce an image of reality with so much sharpness of detail. It is not the sharpness of detail in itself that impresses us; that we are used to from our own visual experience, and now from photography, which exceeds even van Eyck's verisimilitude. Rather, it is the fact that the sharpness was made by hand that makes it thrilling in comparison with what other hands can do. As for photographs, we have learned to value them not for their level of detail, which belongs to the camera, but for the brilliance with which they capture a particular moment. We value them, in other words, for the aspect of the performance that shows the artist's skill.

The identification of skill as a necessary component of artistic value also helps us make the distinction between those things that have literary or artistic value and those things that do not. It can stand in, in other words, for *disinterestedness*, which was the identifying marker of art in the aesthetic model. Many kinds of discourse provide us with pleasure either, for example, by giving us good news, by expressing congenial sentiments, or because of the sheer pleasure of the thought involved. But only discourse that provides us with a valuable experience through the skill it exhibits counts as artistic. It is the exercise of skill, not the absence of practical interest, that distinguishes works with literary value from other kinds of writing. This is why works like Gibbon's *Decline and Fall*, Emerson's *Essays*, and Augustine's *Confessions* can be recognized as literature even though there were not undertaken solely with a literary purpose in mind. What they were undertaken to do, not primarily but among other things, was to provide a valuable reading experience through the choice, invention, or arrangement of words, themes, or narrated events.

That fact that we respond to a work and judge it not simply as a work but as an artistic performance does not mean, of course, that the author was conscious of every element of his achievement. What it took to write part one of *Don Quixote* in 1605 is not something of which we can expect Cervantes to have definitive knowledge even though he was the one who carried it out. But when we experience the work of art, what we experience is his creation in the context of his time and with the resources and precedents then available. Our very experience of the work is historical in this important sense. Borges illustrates this point in the story "Pierre Ménard, Author of the Quixote." When the twentieth-century author Pierre Ménard "writes" the apostrophe to time that originally appeared in Cervantes' work, it is not only different in meaning from Cervantes' original apostrophe; it is also superior in value because the sentiments it contains are more surprising in the mouth of the twentieth-century author than they would have been if written in the seventeenth century.

Of course Borges is bracketing the fact that Ménard "wrote" these words in a very different sense from the way in which Cervantes wrote them. What he actually did was to use a string of sentences identical with Quixote's as the linguistic material for his own utterance. Given the fact that in the story Pierre Ménard arrived at his utterance by immersing himself in Cervantes' world, it should actually have had the same meaning that it had in Cervantes' world, with the added wrinkle that it was being produced in the twentieth century. But what is really different about Ménard's performance is the kind of ability it shows. Ménard is a different kind of artist from Cervantes. His performance, an uncanny kind of historical ventriloquism, if it were actually possible, would be remarkable, but it would be a different performance from Cervantes' and have a very different kind of value, even though the passages he "produced" were identical with the passages of *Don Quixote*.

Let me make this point even more vivid with a hypothetical example. Imagine that Emily Dickinson's poem "Because I could not stop for death" had been misplaced during her lifetime and found its way into a scholar's attic where it was belatedly discovered. If this really happened, the effect of its publication would be sensational. But let us imagine that the lucky scholar is, unfortunately, a frustrated poet, so instead of giving it to the world as an unfamiliar and wonderful Emily Dickinson poem he decides to publish it under his own name. In this case the effect would be very different. Readers might be amazed that anyone could mimic Dickinson so uncannily, some would find it a parody, and some might even wonder if the poem might actually be by Dickinson, but under our poet's signature it would not have the same value that it would have had under hers even though the text was identical with Dickinson's own. The reason its value would be less would be that the artistic process that readers would be assuming had produced it would be far less admirable than the process by which Dickinson produced it. Dickinson, for instance, was thinking about death and eternity, and writing about them in a style all her own, whereas our poet *manqué* would seem to be thinking almost entirely about Dickinson. It would not help, furthermore, if he made this explicit by giving it the title "A New Poem by Emily Dickinson, Discovered in My Attic Last Week." That would return the poem, in a sense, to its nine-teenth-century context but still confess that it was written as pastiche. The result would be a diverting but minor exercise even in an artistic milieu well accustomed to postmodern game-playing and pastiche. Clearly the artistic process by which a work is produced is essential to the value of the work and plays an important role in determining its artistic qualities. A shift in our conception of the author's identity and situation make the poem a different poem. What makes this hard to see is that we do not have access to the artistic process unless we can infer it from our knowledge of its undi-gested sources, and then the effect is for the worse. The work is valuable to the extent that the process which produced it remains beyond our analysis and defies straightforward explanation. The moment it becomes truly explainable, it loses value.

Such disorienting shifts occur, as Denis Dutton points out, whenever we discover that a work we believed to be by one person turns out to be a forgery created by somebody else.[18] This discovery does not alter the textual object in question in the least, but it decisively alters the identity and quality of the work. Whereas we had mistaken it for an original production created in a certain context, showing certain powers of obser-vation and invention and an individual style, now we see it as the product of mere imitation, requiring powers of observation not of the world but of another person's work. Different abilities create different values. By the same token, the fact that a pianist's dexterity has been enhanced electro-nically leads to a similar disenchantment. In fact most people do not seem to find electronic music really satisfying. As Kendall Walton observes, when we know that music has been produced electronically, the rapidity of its precisely spaced notes does not seem like speed; it does not make the impression of approaching a limit.[19] The limit in question, of course, is the human limit on how fast fingers can move.

Our responses to the exposure of forgery and plagiarism may have a moral component, but they are not merely moral. They are also matters of aesthetic response, showing in a vivid way how a single text or object becomes a different work, the product of a different action, when our understanding of the circumstances of its composition changes. The qualities of a work do not inhere in the text alone any more than its meaning does. They depend upon the circumstances in which it was produced. We are enjoying an act of creation, not a mere text.

Appreciating and evaluating artistic performances is just one aspect of our general interest in observing and assessing the behavior and capacities of other human beings, and in art as in other areas of life we take interest not only in surprisingly fine ones but also in surprisingly bad ones. Such spectacles are superior in interest to the merely routine: even art we enjoy as "camp" is superior to the efforts of the mere imitator because it takes us by surprise. Though the camp effect may be infelicitous, we still admire its unexpectedness—*You couldn't make this up!* The pleasure we take in camp and in laughably bad art—the films of Ed Wood, the poems of William McGonagall—is yet another source of evidence that what we are responding to in art is the artistic performance, not merely the object itself, since these works have no artistic value in the proper sense. As Susan Sontag observed, camp exposes the inflated ambitions and naïve goodwill of the artist, which would normally amount to simple failure but toward which the camp sensibility takes a peculiarly appreciative stance. Sontag proposes camp as a third aesthetic, to be added to the ones she calls "serious" and "avant-garde," but as her remarks make clear, camp cannot establish its own standards. They are necessarily the most traditional ones. "In naïve, or pure, Camp," Sontag says, "the essential element is seriousness, a seriousness that fails."[20] It is not the value of the work per se that engages us but the thought that it was considered worth making and the inimitable way this thought has been carried out.

Our interest in camp and in egregiously bad art is of a piece with the delight we take in inspiredly bad performances in just about any area of life. There is nothing more amusing than a person being misled by a naïve impulse toward self-display and a simple-minded recipe for carrying it out. The inadvertent charm of the "cross-gartered" Malvolio and the "rude mechanicals" will never fade. Obviously, the element of surprise I have been discussing here is not sufficient to account for the value of a fine work of art because camp art is precisely not that. But it shares the holistically irreducible quality of fine art and gives us pleasure on that basis. True camp cannot be aimed at by imitation any more than you can amuse people by attempting to be stupid.

A New Aspect of Levels of Intention

Judgments of meaning and judgments of value have a lot in common, both applying pre-eminently to the act of creation in its original context. The textual fallacy is equally untenable in both cases. Yet differences remain. As I have pointed out, communicative intentions succeed simply when the audience is able to recognize what they are, while artistic intentions often succeed only in spite of our recognition of the author's intention. The communicative intentions embodied in a work can succeed completely while at the same time the artistic intentions behind them can fail utterly.

In an earlier discussion, I argued that just as the artistic effectiveness of a work depends upon its communicative content, so we might also say that the extrinsic, practical effectiveness of the work depends both upon its intrinsic communicative and artistic effects. This way of putting it envisions a kind of pyramid structure, the artistic success of a work depending upon its communicative success, and its practical success depending upon its artistic success. The embedding of levels of intention in a literary work is not as neat as the embedding of a pragmatic action like raising my hand to vote, but the generally pyramidal structure is there. In another sense, however, the varying intentions that motivate a work tend to be in competition, with each operating as a constraint upon the others. This is why the more that readers are conscious of the author's artistic goals—to move, shock, or amuse—the more difficult it is for author to achieve them.

Consider Shakespeare's decision to stage Cordelia's death at the end of *King Lear*. The deaths of Lear and Gloucester would have more than sufficed for a tragic ending, and Cordelia would have made a poignant witness to her father's last agony, but Shakespeare decided that she should die on stage and that her father should witness her death before his own. Did Shakespeare kill off Cordelia because only such an ending would be consistent with the play's governing bleakness—in other words, in a way that simply completed the play's vision of the world? Or did he do it in the same spirit that Dickens killed off Little Nell, because he knew the audience had been set up for a shock and that such a shock would deepen the impact of the ending? Lurking behind such artistic motives, of course, we can always glimpse the practical one of earning the world's acclaim and reward.

The issue is decided, of course, not by interrogating Shakespeare's private motives, if that were possible, but by examining the play. Fortunately, in the case of *Lear* there is no doubt that Shakespeare has earned his ending, that after Gloucester's eyes have been put out on the stage with such brilliantly realized horror, there is no spectacle of grimness that would be incongruous with the vision of this play. So we do not feel that Shakespeare is constructing his horrific ending primarily to manipulate the audience. Matters are different with the death of Little Nell. Here the practical, manipulative dimension of the work seems paramount over the value of the story itself. The impression that artistic or theatrical considerations are overriding the consistency of vision tends to undermine our sense of its integrity and seriousness. If we continue to enjoy it, we do so partly in the vein of camp.

What Is Literature?

Unlike the aesthetic point of view, the artistic view I have offered puts literature on a continuum not with natural objects but with other verbal performances—minor ones such as jokes, puns, metaphors, vernacular storytelling, bits of repartee and *bons mots*—but also more substantial and pre-concerted performances—history writing, for instance, autobiography, and oratory. All of these seek to engage, surprise, and impress an audience with displays of skill in the use of words.

There is a clarifying and simplifying benefit in locating artistic value in the performance of an activity rather than the mere perception of an object because it relieves us of the seemingly impossible task of identifying the common experiential or "aesthetic" qualities that unify the art. It is not my purpose here to propose a new definition of art. So many fine minds have foundered in the attempt to define basic philosophical terms that the value of definitions themselves has come into question.[21] But the line of argument I have been pursuing suggests that the best prospects for locating the place of the arts will be among the many displays of skill of which human beings are capable, while distinguishing them by the medium they use. Literature, then, as I have suggested, would consist of displays of skill in the choice, invention, or arrangement of words, themes, or narrated events. This approach would jettison the modern conception of aesthetics, which works from the passive point of view of the spectator, and take up the active one of the practitioner and his craft. Verbal and literary performances belong quite properly among the many things we do for their own sake while also doing them for something else. Literary works aim at the values that permit effective literary performance understood in the contemporary context of their medium and genre, and we seek to appreciate them in that context. Both interpretation and evaluation require historical perspective relative to genre and style, and the modern proliferation of genres and styles in movies, music, and literature shows how narrowly and specifically our *afición* can be focused. Because there are many media and many skills that human beings can display, value takes as many forms in art as it does in other areas of life. It is inherently pluralistic and open-ended; we can recognize the originality, skill, and surprisingness of performances as different as those of Skelton, Swinburne, and Celan.

But if the defining mark of literary value is the display and recognition of performance with the written word, how should we conceive of literature as an institution? The answer to this question highlights one of the great advantages of taking the artistic point of view rather than looking for something that is in common among literary works themselves. Here I would like to discuss one of the reasons for the recent interest in defining art in terms of the artist's achievement, the long-percolating effect of Arthur Danto's argument from indiscernibles.[22] Danto pointed out that if we think only of the object there before us, Duchamp's *Fountain* and other ready-mades are indistinguishable from their perfect duplicates in the department store. How can one of them be a work of art while its identical twin is not? As we saw in Chapter 1, the difference lies in the artist's gesture of assigning one of them to the category of art. This gesture gives the ready-made qualities it did not have before and that are not shared by its banausic look-alikes—wit, for instance, ingenuity, and, undoubtedly, impudence. The qualities they acquire in this way alter their very identity and make them viewable as art.

Stimulated by Danto's insight, George Dickie developed the widely-discussed "Institutional Theory of Art," which claims that a work of art can be defined simply as what an artist presents as an artwork to what Danto called the "Artworld."[23] Dickie's theory goes to the opposite extreme from theories that concentrate on the aesthetic object, leaving all to the artist's intentional action, though it is surprising that Duchamp's original gesture of freedom from the institutional canons of taste should have led to a theory that emphasizes the artist's attachment to an institutional setting as the defining characteristic of art.

Dickie's definition of art has a jauntily circular aspect, but it does not seem to answer the question of what makes the Artworld an *Art*world, the institution an institution of *art*. And since it ascribes to art no particular function, it has nothing to say about its value. Though Dickie's definition of an artist specifies a person who participates "with understanding" in the making of a work of art (92), it would be beside his point to say what that understanding must be. Dickie's theory does have one advantage, though, which is that it separates the issue of what defines a work of art from what makes it good art. He associates the institutional setting entirely with the first issue, that of defining art. I, however, would shift the balance toward the second, that of value. Particularly regarding literature, if we can establish its nature as being defined by the skill-displaying, admiration-attracting, and norm-governed character of all human expression as it is invested in verbal performance, then the institutions of art can be identified as what it seems to me they are—dedicated settings for the recognition and enhancement of activities that already have a performance-oriented character.

This helps us make sense of one of the central puzzles of the way we use the concept of literary value—the way we apply it to works that were not undertaken with the primary intention of being literary works. Here the focus on literature instead of visual art is clarifying. There is something both magical and scandalous about the way ordinary and banal objects like *Fountain* can be elevated to the level of art merely by being exhibited, but, as we have seen, it is much less jarring to recognize the literary value of the writings of Gibbon, Emerson, or Augustine. Even purely scientific works like Darwin's *Origin of Species* have literary value in spite of their clearly utilitarian primary purpose. This is because their authors, though they were not working in strictly literary genres, nevertheless succeeded in engaging their audience by means of literary skill. Indeed the concept of the purely literary is a relatively recent one, associated especially with fiction and lyric poetry. Most ancient genres assumed the burden of instruction as well as delight. To recognize the literary character of any piece of writing, however practical its purpose, is only to insist on its success in giving pleasure beyond the value of the mere information it conveys.

We can think of the institution of literature, then, not as constituting the site where literary objects are constituted but as a historically evolving framework for their display in the pursuit of a variety of goals; it fosters a set of games that is always evolving and changing, providing new opportunities for engaging an audience. But it is only the most saliently dedicated arena for our verbal talents, not the only one. To mark something as literature is not to say that it has been created according to the rules of a literary game for its own sake but rather to make a value judgment about it as a display of skill in the written word such that it can be appreciated for its own sake aside from its utilitarian value. The author need not have intended to create a literary work in order for us to think of it as literature. All he need have done is to use words in a sufficiently skillful way. So we are able to canonize works of mythology, theology, devotion, oratory, history, and even science on account of their literary value, the skill they display in engaging the attention of their audience through the medium of words. And if jokes, *bon mots*, witticisms, and everyday eloquence, however brilliant, cannot rise to the level of the literary, it is only because they are too brief and wedded to their transitory, local contexts to be worth preserving in written form. But this does not keep them from becoming the stuff of literature. Literary artists depict them constantly in a way that calls upon the same charm and interest that they have in their vernacular contexts. In this regard it is not surprising that so much literature mimics historical narrative, oral storytelling, and conversational repartee. As the work of Mikhail Bakhtin would suggest, heteroglossia and the multiplicity of speech genres are conditions of life as much as they are conditions of literature.

This is a good place to recall the distinction between literature in general and literary fiction because they differ from each other in that fiction demands the recognition on the part of the audience that a particular kind of literary game is being played. The fictive stance allows writers of fiction to mimic ordinary forms of discourse and exploit their imaginative potential without being mistaken for truth-relevant. With the growth of modern skepticism about other kinds of narrative, fiction has gradually increased its territory. It appropriates history, myth, and chronicle, and even ingests fictions from other media such as film.[24] In doing so it borrows their literary and artistic potentials. When Thomas Mann in *Doctor Faustus* borrows the voice of his protagonist's biographer, or when Mark Twain impersonates Huck Finn, what he is doing is not merely adding a literary dimension to what would otherwise be a merely instrumental type of performance. He is exploiting the expressive and artistic potentials that are already part of that type of performance. We are always sensitive to the impression we make on others in our verbal performances, and we know that our ability to communicate with others, to gain their cooperation and admiration, is often due as much to the way we express our ideas as it is to the ideas themselves. Fiction's concentration on the experiential qualities of language only heightens this aspect of everyday life. Indeed, it is only because our ordinary speech is full of whimsy, ingenuity, beauty, and sometimes even poetry that we can appreciate the enhancement of those qualities in fiction.

Fiction is often taken to be the literary phenomenon par excellence, and non-fictive forms of narrative like history, autobiography, and memoir seem to have a secondary literary status. Poststructuralist critics like Paul de Man even insist that "All literatures, including the literature of Greece, have always designated themselves as existing in the mode of fiction."[25] But fiction's need to mimic other forms of discourse and to make an art of them suggests that it is the secondary form, a dedicated framework for intensifying and purifying the pleasures of verbal performance by delivering them from their everyday duties. This way of seeing the difference between literature and fiction keeps us from the temptation to make a strong distinction between speech and writing or between literary and oral imagination. Literary institutions are a way of giving prominence to the expressive aspect of language which animates writing and speaking generally.

By suggesting that fiction builds upon, intensifies, and purifies the imaginative value of a wider range of linguistic behavior it may seem that I am making too close a connection between the imaginative qualities of fiction and the imaginative qualities of the materials it works on. After all, in writing *The Adventures of Huckleberry Finn*, Mark Twain did not simply imagine a fine performance of a vernacular kind and submit it to the reader as his own. The sense of Huck's difference is primary; in reading the tale we have the peculiar qualities of Twain's narrator constantly in mind. We recognize Huck's expressiveness and mother wit, but we are also amused by the misunderstandings and distortions that come with the limits of his perspective. We take pleasure both in the colorful felicities and in the flaws of Huck's way of speaking and thinking. While the literary value of Twain's performance is built upon Huck's performance, it clearly differs from it in value. Nevertheless, it is essential to the value of the work that Huck's way of speaking and the process of thought behind it is itself subject to evaluation. Without that fact we would not be sensitive either to the felicities of his narrative or to the interest of its failings. As we have seen, both the felicities and the failings of performances of all kinds can have value for the spectator and therefore for the artist as well.

The Diversity of the Literary Market

Taking the artistic rather than the aesthetic point of view also helps us address a question raised by the pluralistic dimension of literature and the utilitarian versus critical issue I raised earlier. Since there are many genres and styles in the literary marketplace, each with its own audience and standards of performance, how should they be divided and can they be distinguished on account of their value? It seems clear enough, for instance, that jazz and classical are different kinds of music and for most purposes should be evaluated in their own terms, but should we separate fiction as an art from pulp fiction in the same way, ascribing to each its own standards of performance? Can we say that the novels of Flaubert and Joyce are simply things of a different kind from the novels produced by James Patterson and his stable of co-authors at the rate of a dozen or so per year? Or do we have some basis for ascribing superior value to so-called literary over pulp fiction?

The sociology of Pierre Bourdieu offers a well-known answer—that reading is a status-based activity and that readers acquire their taste in art as part of their class identity.[26] The superior difficulty and expense of elite art, then, are motivated by the upper-class audience's need for distinction. This explanation has some point. Elite culture tends to demand greater financial and cognitive resources than popular culture, and this seems to be a part of its appeal. The difference between opera and jazz is one of social milieu as well as musical style, and we can say the same for literary as opposed to pulp fiction. But this only takes us so far, since, as I have pointed out, there are many people who go from reading Proust in the morning to detective fiction in the evening. The superior demands of fine art are not always welcome even for those who accord them the greatest worth.[27] We see here the same general problem that bedevils the economic analysis of preference—that people drink coffee in the morning, soda in the afternoon, and wine in the evening. Unless you can factor in the causes for these shifts in taste, the order of preferences you can deduce from their behavior looks simply irrational. There seems to be little hope of understanding the differences in status among different literary or artistic forms by reducing them to differences in the status of their audiences.

The eminence of the fine arts in the hierarchy of taste has sometimes been justified on the grounds that no one goes from preferring the lower versions of an art to the higher ones—that people who love Proust do not switch to Mickey Spillane.[28] This, however, is also empirically doubtful, for reasons I have just given. And it is rather simplistic to think of people as preferring one genre to another *tout court*. A good example of any genre should be more valuable to any reader than a bad example of another. Here is where the artist-oriented point of view shows its value by helping us locate a distinction between elite and popular which is less doubtful than the ones based on the analysis of consumption. Fine art makes demands on the artists themselves that lesser genres simply do not make. So while the same readers might be able to move appreciatively from Mickey Spillane to James Joyce and back, it is highly unlikely that Spillane could have succeeded in writing a novel in the manner of Joyce (or, indeed, in any of his manners), whereas it is easy to imagine that Joyce could have written a novel in the manner of Spillane. It is not only that reading Joyce requires more training and effort from the reader. These things need not contribute to literary value. But there is no doubt that the writing of his books requires a talent that resembles but exceeds that of the authors of genre fiction. This seems the most reasonable way of explaining why we elevate certain genres and styles over others. They embody a more difficult and demanding performance. Again this is a quality that links our way of judging art with other kinds of performance. The more rare and difficult they are, the more they surprise us and the more we enjoy them.

Let me be clear that I am not returning here to T. S. Eliot's notion that the value of art can be explained by the intensity of the artistic process itself. I am using "difficult" in a normative rather than the psychological sense. It is the rarity in the achievement of the writing of *Ulysses* as experienced by its readers that makes it valuable, the fact that it does things that other books simply do not do, not the psychological facts about Joyce's process of composition. Similarly, it is the factory-like regularity with which pulp fiction can be written that explains its relative lack of literary value. Writing pulp fiction demonstrates no special capacity, while the writing of *Ulysses* shows unusual capacity, and we recognize that capacity on account of the experience we are having. Of course it is hard to imagine an artist like Joyce actually writing a work of genre fiction without the malicious mimicry he sometimes practices, but what he lacks is not the capacity for the job, just the stomach.

It is the focus on capacity that sets apart the enduring achievements in literature from ones that can be mass-produced according to formula, and it is in evidence long before the split in audience between mass and elite culture. That split in itself is a product of artists' need to develop ever more novel ways of displaying literary talent. Distancing themselves from their fellow practitioners, they have often left a good part of the audience behind. This is particularly evident in the modern visual arts, which have been deprived of many of their traditional functions; the decline of illusionistic art has only heightened the competitive demand for innovation and led to more and more novel, demanding, extreme, or abstract performances.

The more unpredictable, original, and skillful a work of art seems to be, and the more it improves upon or departs from precedent, the more it benefits from Johnson's "silent reference of human works to human abilities." The resistance of art to reductive formulas is the very condition of its possibility as a mode of innovative display, and the inability of the most intensely engaged audiences, audiences of the highest *afición*, to agree on which are the best performances and even the values that distinguish them is a related phenomenon, for part of the intimacy of aesthetic response depends upon a certain freedom within the constraints of judgment. The freedom and inherently experimental nature of art, the constant need to rework, extend, and break with convention, seems to lead inevitably to a fracturing of the audience as it grows. Here the themes of artistic holism and pluralism come together. Nature is predictable; art is not, nor is the judgment of artistic value, except in the very long run.

I mentioned above that many attempts have been made to identify the defining sources of artistic value. In the mid-1950s, the philosopher Morris Weitz challenged the definability of art in the classic sense of identifying its necessary and sufficient conditions. Weitz argued that the forms of art could have no more than a Wittgensteinian "family resemblance," art being an inherently "open" concept because future practitioners will deliberately flaunt their departure from any reigning conception of art they can identify.[29] Changing the game, we might say, is the name of the game. Weitz's skepticism, instead of making us hopeless about understanding the nature of art, draws our attention to one of its fundamental qualities—that it is a competitive activity on the part of those who practice it, an activity which rewards the crossing of boundaries and the overthrow of expectations. We will never be able to understand the nature of art by attempting to define the artwork as an abstract set of constraints or qualities apart from the artist himself. Part of the freedom of art is its need for constraints, but part of the value of those constraints is that they can be broken as well as obeyed. It is significant in this context that of all the qualities that have been suggested as necessary to aesthetic experience, surprise and unpredictability are the ones that stand up the best because they are always relative to previous experience and expectations. The experience of surprise is essentially historical and comparative, and points toward the distinctiveness of the artist. While not an open concept in itself, the set of things that produce it could not be more so. Not all surprises are to be cherished, of course, but the absence of surprise does seem to exclude genuine literary value. Surprise must not be defined too broadly, however. It would not be helpful to say that valuable works must surprise us by how good they are. That would be still to depend upon a prior judgment of excellence. The work must surprise us with its qualities in comparison with other works of the same type.

The near emptiness and relativity of surprise and unpredictability as concepts shows how little we can say about what makes literary works in general valuable, but their centrality to the discussion of literary value and the irreducibility and holistic nature of literary performance are connected to one of the perplexing characteristics of literary judgment—that we are much more sure of ourselves in saying why a work is bad than why it is good. We can easily identify elements of a work that disqualify it—elements that make it either predictable or simply unsuited to create the effects it is striving for—while the qualities we cite as a successful work's virtues are bound to be a subject of controversy, and, as we have seen, will not stand up as the basis for binding rules of art. Its connection with predictability makes failure in art fundamentally more explainable than success, which always involves the sense that the artist has done something which could not have been predicted given the means at his disposal. The artist's contribution has to play a role in the explanation of a work of art, but it is a role that paradoxically defies straightforward explanation. It points toward a capacity and not a mere action. Here is the slender truth behind the Romantic conception of genius as a power to create without rules.

AUTHOR VERSUS WORK

Readers may be wondering at this point if my account of author-focused literary value really does justice to the experience of literature. They might assent to the notion that our experience of literary value takes certain things about the process by which the work was created for granted—that, for example, the author is responsible for the experiential qualities of the work, which are not borrowed from others by imitation, forgery, or plagiarism in a way that makes them evidence for something other than skill. They might also agree that the author should stand behind the perspective provided by the work; as I mentioned in an earlier discussion, while sincerity is not a literary virtue, its conspicuous absence can diminish our appreciation. But these conditions might seem more like the absence of distraction than positive qualities of the work, which in classic, illusionistic art we value for its power to absorb us and make us forget the real world in favor of the world it opens before us. Here the narratological distinction between internal and external perspectives is a useful one. The internal perspective of a story or fiction is the one inside the world it conjures up for us—containing people, events, and situations—whereas the external perspective views the story from our own world, where it is only a discourse containing descriptions and observations about characters in the literary sense, types of people and events created by an author for the benefit of an audience. It is from the external perspective that we glimpse the presence of an author and understand the nature of his performance.[30]

It would be wrong to think of all artistic performances as making their impact on the reader only from the internal point of view. Many works depend upon being able to balance an internal and external perspective. Metafiction is particularly salient in this regard. But even when we are experiencing a work with total absorption in the world it creates, we are still aware that it is imaginary, that it is being prompted by the intentional activity of an author. We are being surprised, in fact, by the liveliness and power of its illusion, how consistently it seems to derive from an experience either of the world or of the mind rather than from others' words. This is the case even with the most conventional art, for the fulfilling of conventions is never enough. Conventions must be animated in order to keep us from regarding them in a merely external way, as well-known patterns of words and ideas. Failures of imagination on the part of the author betray his presence; they let the reader fall back into the external perspective in a deflating and disappointing way. So for forms of art that invite absorption in the internal perspective, the absence of the author's presence is the very sign of his success; as such works progress, our appreciation grows as the author shows his ability either to remain within the conventions of the genre without exposing them as mere conventions or his ability to flout the conventions without merely deflating them.

The dynamics of reading as described by reader response critics like Wolfgang Iser are quite instructive in this regard.[31] In the course of engaging with a literary work, the reader is being drawn into a continuous process of anticipation, confirmation, and correction and well as amplification and inference, and these complex cognitive operations have to be prompted by the work in a way that preserves its coherence. The reader of a narrative is caught up in a particular moment but looking backward and forward at the same time. Successful narratives achieve a certain rhythm of inferential progress. The movement is like a dance in which both partners must keep up, and the failure of the author to keep up with the reader, to stay ahead of her anticipations, to continue to fulfill them at the right moment, or to correct them meaningfully, brings the pleasure of reading to an end. The same thing happens when the author gets ahead of the reader, though difficulties of this kind can also be a literary resource. This description of reading works best with the novel in mind, but some version of it must be applicable to other genres as well.

It is in similar terms that we can explain the role that expertise plays in the experiences of literary readers as opposed to readers of pulp fiction. It is much more difficult for expert readers than for neophytes to find value in the internal worlds of pulp fiction because expert readers are too familiar with the literary formulas from which they are composed. Joycean readers of James Patterson will likely be able to regard the work only from an external perspective, finding it too easily predictable from that point of view. Expert readers are delighted and surprised whenever they discover an author who can sustain the internal perspective without showing the seams that hold it together. They experience the intensity with which the internal perspective is sustained as an achievement of the author. Pulp readers, on the other hand, may not have the resources to enter the imaginative worlds of literary fiction without exerting more effort than the experience is worth. They do have, however, a compensating advantage, which is the ability to enjoy the worlds conjured up by pulp authors without taking up an external, deflating perspective about how they are sustained.

Literary power of the absorptive kind, then, stems from the ability of the work to sustain the interest of its internal perspective in competition with the external perspective *at whatever level the reader may be able to occupy it.* The relation is a proportional one. For the expert reader, the internal perspective can win out only on the basis of its genuinely surprising power, which deflects the external critique at least long enough to let it have its sway, while for the pulp reader, the internal perspective can win out by virtue of how weakly the reader occupies the external perspective itself. In either case the appeal of the work derives from its inexplicable, irreducible power to defy the critical scrutiny of the reader.

The external/internal distinction also offers a wider view of the difference between popular and literary judgment based on how the audience relates to the artist. Neophyte readers (such as undergraduates) diverge from the cultivated taste of *aficiónados* in two directions. At one extreme they focus too heavily on the external lives of authors for their own sakes at the expense of the work, reducing it to biographical themes. At the other extreme they become absorbed entirely in the internal perspective of the work, without a critical awareness of the manner of its making. The critical perspective seeks a balance between these two, neither reducing the work to the life nor confusing the work with life, but instead appreciating the work as a human performance, one that either displays the imagination of the author in a way that rewards the reader's attention from an external perspective or invests it in an internal world whose illusory power testifies to the author's hidden presence. *Afición* balances between internal absorption and external appreciation, and does so in the context of other performances of the same kind. Its critical nature highlights the fact that literary creation is a competitive activity. From the point of view of any work of art which seeks to create its own internal world, other artists belong to the rival and deflating power of the external world.

VALUE AND MEANING

Throughout this book I have been stressing the distinction between communicative and artistic intentions and particularly the different roles they play in their respective spheres. In attempting to understand the communicative content of the work, the author's intention is essential, whereas in attempting to understand the artistic achievement of the work, it is informative but by no means definitive. Underlying this difference, however, there is a perhaps more crucial similarity—that in either case there is a need for finesse both on the part of the author and the audience. Neither meaning nor artistic value can be created simply on the basis of existing practice, its rules and conventions. On an everyday basis, the vocabulary of a language is constantly being bent from the patterns of established usage, and speakers and writers are constantly using their skills to provide their audience with novel experience through the use of language. The need for innovation is both verbal and artistic. The institutions of literature feed upon novelty and skill of both kinds and enhance them. It is the elusiveness and unpredictability of literary performance, both in communicative and artistic terms, that gives license to the various kinds of skepticism about meaning and value I have been discussing in this book, but this elusiveness and unpredictability are the very conditions both of the meaning and the value of literature. They are the signs not of its weakness or unreliability but of its continuing power to engage us.

There is also an important convergence in the nature of the mistakes about meaning and value that I have been attempting to counteract. Both the textual fallacy and the theory of the aesthetic turn the work into a detached object separate from the person who brought it into being. In both cases its character as an action—linguistic, artistic, ethical, and political—is occluded or rendered uncanny. And so is the relation between the work and its audience, the people to whom it was originally directed. A consistent application of the textual fallacy would make reinterpretations of the original work equally inaccessible.

The textual fallacy originated with the impulse to purify the realm of literature, to free it from the messiness of its human origins, but the account of literary making and reception that I have provided leaves it in an impure and messy state. The meaningfulness of literary works depends not only upon detached, objective linguistic resources but upon the fragile power of authors to anticipate what an audience will make of their words. Risk is inherent to the endeavor, and communicative failure is to be expected, though the ability of many works to command the interest of audiences over the centuries testifies to the power with which authors do indeed understand how the words on the page will be construed and felt. When we turn to the matter of artistic accomplishment, the qualities that make works valuable do not belong entirely to the works themselves. To have their full effect, they must have been executed in a certain way (invented rather than borrowed) and with a certain spirit (imagined in good faith rather than with manipulative calculation). Works fail when we can see too easily through the process of their construction, making failure more explicable than success, a strange asymmetry. It is ultimately not the detached work in itself but the author's performance against the standards established by other works and our general sense of human ability that impresses us. And if this picture were not messy enough, add the fact that literature itself engages in every kind of religious, ethical, and political issue and that its artistic forms are connected to its many cultural functions. Rarely are its concerns merely literary or artistic; it aims not only at meaning but at impact and value. Further impurity arises with the continuing mediation, repackaging, and reinterpretation of long-existing works, making our relations to them always richer but also messier and more complex. In responding to literature we are responding to experiences that have been contrived at least in part to serve ends most of which cannot be our own and that have already been recruited into many subsequent polemical contexts, forcing us to respond not only to the original act of creation but to what others have made of it. Yet in order to truly engage with such works, we must be able to experience their artistic value word by word. We still need *afición*, and in my mind the slightly embarrassing connotations of that word—borrowed from Ernest Hemingway—are an appropriate admission. It is no wonder so many critics are drawn to the notion that literary value is merely subjective or that it can be reduced to something else, even though our own responses tell us otherwise—tell us insistently that the person who thinks James Patterson writes better novels than Jane Austen or that Rod McKuen writes better poems than W. B. Yeats is simply making a mistake.

NOTES

1. The metaphor is Hilary Putnam's. See "The Entanglement of Fact and Value," in *The Collapse of the Fact/Value Dichotomy and Other Essays* (Cambridge, MA: Harvard University Press, 2002), chapter 2.

2. Pleasure, of course, is not the only kind of value that literature or art provides. The twentieth century has vastly expanded the range of experiences that are found valuable in art. I use "pleasure" here as a stand-in for all of the other forms of stimulation that give value to literature.

3. A related approach is the "test of time" argument, which takes the fact that certain works endure as a testament to their artistic merits because all the local and temporary contingencies that can stimulate a contemporary reader's interest have faded away. The test of time argument highlights the temporal range of the audience rather than its numbers. Like the utilitarian view, it can be applied by an empirical study of the audience, but it does propose a privileged point of view for the assessment of a work, which makes it more akin to the critical than the utilitarian approach. See, for instance, Anthony Saville, *The Test of Time: An Essay in Philosophical Aesthetics* (New York: Oxford University Press, 1982).

4. For an account of the relation between admiration and aesthetic value compatible with mine see Kendall L. Walton, "'How Marvelous!': Toward a Theory of Aesthetic Value," in *Marvelous Images: On Values and the Arts* (New York: Oxford University Press, 2008), 3–22.

5. Malcolm Budd, *Values of Art: Pictures, Poetry and Music* (London: Allen Lane, 1995), 40.

6. Nelson Goodman, "Merit as Means," in *Problems and Projects* (Indianapolis, IN: Bobbs-Merrill, 1972), 120.

7. Barbara Herrnstein-Smith, *Contingencies of Value: Alternative Perspectives for Literary Theory* (Cambridge, MA: Harvard University Press, 1988), 1–8.

8. For two classic statements of this position see Arnold Isenberg, "Critical Communication," *Philosophical Review* 58 (1949), 330–42, and Frank Sibley, "Aesthetic Concepts," chapter 1 of his *Approach to Aesthetics: Papers on Philosophical Aesthetics*, ed. John Benson, Betty Redfern, and Jeremy Roxbee Cox (Oxford: Clarendon Press, 2001).

9. Alan H. Goldman, *Aesthetic Value* (Boulder, CO: Westview Press, 1995), 135.

10. The frailty of artistic theorizing is another symptom of the difference between communicative and artistic intentions.

11. Nelson Goodman, *Languages of Art: An Approach to a Theory of Symbols* (Indianapolis, IN: Bobbs-Merrill, 1968), 4.

12. E. H. Gombrich, *Art and Illusion: A Study in the Psychology of Pictorial Representation*, 2nd ed. (Princeton, NJ: Princeton University Press, 1960), 28.

13. Of course he did not think of them the way Plato did, as independently existing, but rather as the formal principles of individuals that make them the kind of thing they are.

14. J. D. Cohen and G. Aston-Jones, "Decision and Uncertainty," *Nature* 436 (2005), 472, discussed in Michael McGuire, *Believing: The Neuroscience of Fantasies, Fears, and Convictions* (New York: Prometheus Books, 2013), 152.

15. Samuel Johnson, "Preface to *Shakespeare*" (1763) in Vincent B Leitch, general ed., *The Norton Anthology of Theory and Criticism*, 2nd ed. (New York: Norton, 2010), 385–86.

16. For one of the fullest defenses of this view see Gregory Currie, "Art Works as Action Types," in *An Ontology of Art* (London: Macmillan, 1989), chapter 3.

17. For an introduction to the discussion, see Dominic McIver Lopes, "The Myth of (Non-Aesthetic) Artistic Value," *The Philosophical Quarterly* 61, no. 244 (July 2011), 518–36; Robert Stecker, "Artistic Value Defended," in *Journal of Aesthetics and Art Criticism* 70, no. 4 (Fall 2012), 355–62; and Louise Hanson, "The Reality of (Non-Aesthetic) Artistic Values," *The Philosophical Quarterly* 63, no. 252 (July 2013), 492–508.

18. Denis Dutton, *The Art Instinct: Beauty, Pleasure, and Human Evolution* (New York: Bloomsbury Press, 2009), 177–88.

19. Kendall Walton, "Categories of Art," in Lamarque and Olsen, eds., *The Philosophy of Literature* (Malden, MA: Blackwell Pub., 2009), 149.

20. "Notes on 'Camp'," in David Rieff, ed., *Susan Sontag: Essays of the 60's and 70's* (New York: Library of America, 2013), 266.

21. For a recent discussion see Robert Stecker, "Is It Reasonable to Attempt to Define Art," in Noël Carroll, ed., *Theories of Art Today* (Madison, WI: University of Wisconsin Press, 2000), 45–64.

22. Indiscernibles are the governing theme of Arthur C. Danto, *The Transfiguration of the Commonplace: A Philosophy of Art* (Cambridge, MA: Harvard University Press, 1981).

23. George Dickie, *Introduction to Aesthetics: An Analytic Approach* (New York: Oxford University Press, 1997), 83. I have simplified Dickie's early version of the theory. His later version omits the notion of "appreciation" and leaves the concept of the artist as implied in the notion of an artworld itself: "A work of art is an artifact of a kind created to be presented to an artworld public" (92).

24. I am thinking especially of books like Thomas Pynchon's *Gravity's Rainbow* or Manuel Puig's *Kiss of the Spider Woman*.

25. Paul de Man, *Blindness and Insight: Essays in the Rhetoric of Contemporary Criticism* (Minneapolis, MN: University of Minnesota Press, 1983), 17. See the discussion by Peter Lamarque and Stein Haugom Olsen in chapter 6 of *Truth, Fiction, and Literature: A Philosophical Perspective* (New York: Oxford University Press, 1994), 273–75.

26. Pierre Bourdieu, *Distinction: A Social Critique of the Judgment of Taste* (Cambridge, MA: Harvard University Press, 1984).

27. "Serious" fiction not only makes greater demands upon the reader but also poses greater risks. You may curl up with a novel by Iris Murdoch only to discover it is not as good as the ones you have already read, whereas thrillers and detective novels offer relatively predictable pleasures.

28. See Goldman, *Aesthetic Value*, 173.

29. Morris Weitz, "The Role of Theory in Aesthetics," *Journal of Aesthetics and Art Criticism*, 15 (1956), 27–35.

30. The distinction is close to the classic narratological one between story and discourse, as explained, for instance, in Seymour Chatman, *Story and Discourse: Narrative Structure in Fiction and Film* (Ithaca, NY: Cornell University Press, 1978). Its use in philosophy is especially associated with Thomas Nagel's *The View from Nowhere* (New York: Oxford University Press, 1986), and its value for issues of literary theory is explored in Lamarque and Olsen, *Truth, Fiction, and Literature*, chapter 6.

31. Wolfgang Iser, *The Implied Reader: Patterns of Communication in Prose Fiction from Bunyan to Beckett* (Baltimore, MD: Johns Hopkins University Press, 1978).

CHAPTER 6

Conclusion

The basic insight I have highlighted in the title of this book—that there are varieties of authorial intention—suggests a reframing of the task of scholarship and criticism—that we should respond to each kind of intention in a different way. To grasp the meaning of an author's work we need an openness to his communicative intentions, a willingness to take the place of his original audience. His artistic efforts, by contrast, ask us to respond to the power of the work in the context of the art and life of the time, whether deriving from the author's intended efforts or not. We do so with the benefit of our entire experience of reading, and our responses are not necessarily any more consciously explicable to us than the author's intentions are to him. Finally, the ulterior, practical effects of the work which constitute its impact—again, whether they were intended or not—challenge us to understand and judge from our own point of view. The separation of these three operations will never be complete or perfect, but it can help avoid the confusion that comes from the taboo on authorial intentions, when meaning becomes unstable or arbitrary, artistic value no longer has a stable work to belong to, and the practical agency that was denied to authors migrates to occult, transindividual entities in paranoid fashion.

In the writing of this book and in conversations with my fellow scholars about its subject I have been acutely aware how attached they are to the textualist attitude and how enormously resistant to the very notion of intention. Renouncing the clean crisp word *text* in favor of the laborious word *work*, which demands adjectives such as *literary* and seems to give the scholar's

© The Author(s) 2017
J. Farrell, *The Varieties of Authorial Intention*,
DOI 10.1007/978-3-319-48977-3_6

mouth a day's labor, is hardly a congenial idea; in the classroom I myself speak mostly of the *text*. For many scholars, the fact that a literary work is grounded in stable authorial intentions seems to portend the closing off of possibilities, and the fact that authors create the substance which later interpreters work upon threatens to devalue studies of mediation and reception. I am acutely aware how difficult it is to dispel the sense that intention is a recklessly Cartesian concept, incompatible with the subtleties and velleities of reading. Most striking to me, though, has been the way the stability of literary meaning seems to many like a threat to political freedom, an undesirable form of submission to authority. To give an example, François Cusset, in the preface to the English edition of his richly informative book *French Theory: How Foucault, Derrida, Deleuze & Co. Transformed the Intellectual Life of the United States* (2008) pronounces the following credo. "Nothing may be more essential to political resistance and intellectual autonomy today than *not* taking for granted texts and discourses, from literature to ideological propaganda. Grounds for action and subversion will be found in the undecidability of meaning, in the construction of a text by the ever-changing community of its readers, in the leeway still to be found in interpreting a canonical work, even in the deliberate stretching of the gap between text and context, signifier and uses, the worship of classics, and the tricks of hermeneutical action." I am not quite sure what Cusset means by "the tricks of hermeneutical action," whether they are among the sources of our "intellectual autonomy" or part of what we should oppose, but he goes on to make it clear where the enemy lies.

> Reactionary politics and the locking up of the existing social order will always require a submission to essentialized texts, to unquestioned canons, to interpretation understood as the revelation by others of a one-sided meaning. Where interpretation is obvious, where it is *not* a question, power reigns supreme; where it is wavering, flickering, opening its uncertainty to unpredictable uses, empowerment of the powerless may be finally possible.[1]

In this paragraph Cusset expresses a set of attitudes precisely the opposite of the ones that inspired this book, but he shows why they are hard to give up. He associates stability of meaning with political power and stasis, and resistance with uncertainty and undecidability. He does not imagine that interpreters of the present can stand up to the language of the past on an equal footing. There is a troublingly undemocratic implication behind Cusset's undoubtedly idealistic concern. What he implies is that the past, or really anyone with whom we disagree, cannot be allowed to speak in a clear and stable way, for once they do so we will not be able to defend ourselves against their power to determine our reality by means of their words. And so the literature and culture of the past—and by implication all the words of others—have to be destabilized, which is to say defused to protect us from their power. Presumably others, now and in the future, will respond to our words in just the same way, hoping to escape from our irresistible linguistic authority.

This is a forlorn and pessimistic point of view, for as I have said, if there is one thing we know for sure it is that actions taken in the past, including artistic utterances, cannot change, however much our understanding of them—which is to say, our response to their impact—may change. The notion that we can only resist the influence of the past by changing the meaning of the works it left behind rules out the much more hopeful possibility that we might be able to understand the culture of the past in something like its own terms, with however much difficulty and uncertainty, and even while understanding it, still be free to consider how much we want to share its ways and how much we want to resist them. In the course of this book I have tried to suggest the basis for believing this is possible. To give up this hope is to undermine the possibility of culture as a dialogue, either with the past or among our contemporaries. The notion that the mere stability of language understood in context is threatening to our freedom is evidence of a profound alienation of agency in modern culture, a susceptibility to the belief that power is always elsewhere and that evasion is the only viable strategy. As I have tried to show in my work on paranoia, such suspicion is the quintessential form of modern credulity.

Mistrust of language is a signature of modernity, but language does not have the autonomous power to shape reality that its theorists often claim. It requires the guarantee of intention behind it in order to license the interpreter's remarkable powers of inference, and these inferences require common knowledge of the world shared by author and audience, the knowledge against the background of which their language developed in the first place. Meaning is a joint affair, not "one-sided" as Cusset assumes. It does not lie entirely in the power either of authors or of readers. The construction of meaning is a mutual process that permits remarkable intimacy. It is an affair of subtle innovation, of constant adjustment and change. The connections we make with literary works in order to grasp their meanings do not commit us to sharing their aims, endorsing their visions, or accepting their values. Mere comprehension does not threaten our intellectual autonomy but is a crucial element of it. We can listen but still disagree. Cusset equates questioning with the displacement of meaning and therefore the lack of understanding, whereas it seems to me that questioning must begin with understanding. Questioning is a part of dialogue.

The benefit of admitting authorial intention back into the critical vocabulary will not be to transform the meanings of literary texts, for, as I noted at the outset, recourse to authorial intention has never really gone away; it has only been disguised and made furtive. The airless textualism of the mid-twentieth century has long dispersed, and historical inquiry has again become the primary concern of literary scholars, but in terms of self-understanding they too often remain confined within the distortions of the textual fallacy and the habits of critique. What Fredric Jameson nicely called "the prison house of language" is actually the theory that language is a prison. Historical studies under the influence of this theory still look too much like a clash of texts and discourses—lately even non-human actors—rather than a struggle involving human agents, and language retains a glamorous halo of reification.

We have every reason to discourage the strange fetishizing of discourse as power and the concomitant elevation of *langue* over *parole* in its various guises, including the notion that there is such a thing as literary language. Literature calls upon the same resources of verbal imagination as other forms of writing and, indeed, the conversational and narrative practices of everyday life. The very notion of there being a language that can be comprehensively understood apart from speakers, the gesture of reification which dominated the twentieth century, is one we would be better off without. And without this notion, there is no reason to think that we are the playthings of language rather than its users. The restoration of authors, their intentions and projects, to full respectability in the theoretical sphere of literary studies should make critics less willing to displace agency and intentionality onto other hidden, unconscious sources like the ones glimpsed by Freud, Marx, Lévi-Strauss, and Foucault; believing in these hidden sources of control requires a great stretch of the imagination, while the recourse to conscious intention as a source of verbal meaning is pragmatically impossible to avoid. And when it comes to questions of value, it is once again a release from paradox to accept the notion that the literary value of a work is intrinsically connected with the author's performance, and that it is with the author that our ethical and political judgments about the historical impact of literary works should begin.

Neither the meanings that constitute works, their precise literary character, nor the literary value they provide can be explained solely with reference to the string of characters that compose the verbal artifact.

When we read literary texts it is people we are trying to understand—people under varying historical circumstances. It is their creative actions we are trying to appreciate, not mere collections of words. These actions come to us having already made their impact on many other people in intervening generations who have inflected them in their own ways. Dealing with people as historical agents is uncomfortable, difficult, exasperating; making judgments about them can be even more so. From a moral and political point of view, it is an inherently troublesome affair. There are reasons why Lewis preferred a "disinfected and severer world" and Foucault wanted to "write in order to have no face." Mere texts could never speak to us in the exciting and often troubling way people do in works of literature. That is the risk, the pleasure, and the profit of reading.

NOTE

1. François Cusset, "Preface to the English Edition" of *French Theory: How Foucault, Derrida, Deleuze & Co., Transformed the Intellectual Life of the United States* (Minneapolis, MN: University of Minnesota Press, 2008), xx–xxi. It is ironic that Cusset's project aims at correcting the way French theory has been interpreted in the course of its "American domestication" (xiii), which is to say he is protecting his chosen authorities from the destabilizing operation they apply to others.

WORKS CITED

Allison, Graham T. and Philip Zelikow. *Essence of Decision: Explaining the Cuban Missile Crisis*. New York: Longman, 1999. Print.

Allt, Peter and Russell K. Alspach. *The Variorum Edition of the Poems of W. B. Yeats*. New York: Macmillan, 1957. Print.

Anderson, Amanda. *The Way We Argue Now: A Study in the Cultures of Theory*. Princeton, NJ: Princeton University Press, 2005. Print.

Anscombe, G. E. M. *Intention*. Cambridge, MA: Harvard University Press, 2000. Print.

Attridge, Derek. *The Singularity of Literature*. New York: Routledge, 2004. Print.

Bakhtin, M. M. *Speech Genres and Other Late Essays*. Trans. Vern W. McGee. Eds. Caryl Emerson and Michael Holquist. Austin, TX: University of Texas Press, 1986. Print.

Baron-Cohen, Simon. *Mindblindness: An Essay on Autism and Theory of Mind*. Cambridge, MA: MIT Press, 1995. Print.

Barthes, Roland. *Sade, Fourier, Loyola*. Trans. Richard Miller. Berkeley: University of California Press, 1976. Print.

———. *Image-Music-Text*. Trans. Stephen Heath. New York: Hill & Wang, 1977. Print.

———. *Roland Barthes by Roland Barthes*. Trans. Richard Howard. New York: Farrar, Strauss, and Giroux, 1977. Print.

Beardsley, Monroe C. *Aesthetics: Problems in the Philosophy of Criticism*. New York: Harcourt, Brace, 1958. Print.

Berkowitz, Luci and Theodore F. Brunner, trans. and eds. *Oedipus Tyrannus*. New York: Norton, 1970. Print.

Birner, Betty J. *Introduction to Pragmatics*. Chichester, West Sussex: Wiley-Blackwell, 2013. Print.

© The Author(s) 2017
J. Farrell, *The Varieties of Authorial Intention*,
DOI 10.1007/978-3-319-48977-3

Booth, Wayne C. *The Rhetoric of Fiction*. Chicago: University of Chicago Press, 1961. Print.

Borges, Jorge Luis. *Labyrinths: Selected Stories and Other Writings*. Ed. Donald A. Yates and James E. Irby. New York: New Directions, 1962. Print.

Bournedal, Peter. *Speech and System*. Copenhagen: Museum Tusculanum Press, 1997. Print.

Boyd, Brian. *On the Origin of Stories: Evolution, Cognition, and Fiction*. Cambridge, MA: Harvard University Press, 2009. Print.

Brantlinger, Patrick. *Rule of Darkness: British Literature and Imperialism, 1830–1914.* Ithaca, NY: Cornell University Press, 1988. Print.

Bratman, Michael. *Intention, Plans, and Practical Reason*. Cambridge, MA: Harvard University Press, 1987. Print.

Buller, David. *Adapting Minds: Evolutionary Psychology and the Persistent Quest for Human Nature*. Cambridge, MA: MIT Press, 2006. Print.

Burke, Seán, ed. *Authorship: From Plato to the Postmodern: A Reader*. Edinburgh: Edinburgh University Press, 1995. Print.

———. *The Death and Return of the Author: Criticism and Subjectivity in Barthes, Foucault, and Derrida*. 3rd ed. Edinburgh: Edinburgh University Press, 2008. Print.

Camfield, William A. *Marcel Duchamp: Fountain*. Houston, TX: Houston Fine Art Press, 1989. Print.

Carston, Robyn. *Thoughts and Utterances: The Pragmatics of Explicit Communication*. Malden, MA: Blackwell Publishers, 2002. Print.

Cavell, Stanley. *Must We Mean What We Say? A Book of Essays*. New York: Cambridge University Press, 1976. Print.

Chatman, Seymour. *Story and Discourse: Narrative Structure in Fiction and Film*. Ithaca, NY.: Cornell University Press, 1978. Print.

Churchland, P. M. "Eliminative Materialism and the Propositional Attitudes." *Journal of Philosophy* 78 (1981): 67–90. Print.

Cioffi, Frank. "Intention and Interpretation in Criticism." *Proceedings of the Aristotelian Society,* New Series 64 (1963–1964): 85–106. Print.

Clark, Katerina and Michael Holquist. *Mikhail Bakhtin*. Cambridge, MA: Harvard University Press, 1984. Print.

Clark, Timothy. *The Theory of Inspiration: Composition as a Crisis of Subjectivity in Romantic and Post-Romantic Writing*. Manchester: Manchester University Press, 1997. Print.

Cohen, J. D. and G. Aston-Jones. "Decision and Uncertainty." *Nature* 436 (2005): 471–72. Print.

Cohen, Michael C. *The Social Lives of Poems in Nineteenth-Century America*. Philadelphia: University of Pennsylvania Press, 2015.

Coleridge, Samuel Taylor. *Biographia Literaria*. 2 vols. Eds. James Engell and Walter Jackson Bate. Princeton, NJ: Princeton University Press, 1983. Print.

Coulson, Seana. *Semantic Leaps: Frame-Shifting and Conceptual Blending in Meaning Construction*. New York: Cambridge University Press, 2001. Print.

Crews, Frederick, ed. *Unauthorized Freud: Doubters Confront a Legend*. New York: Viking, 1998. Print.

Culler, Jonathan. "Lyric, History, and Genre." In Virginia Jackson and Yopie Prins, eds. *The Lyric Theory Reader: A Critical Anthology*. Baltimore, MD: Johns Hopkins University Press, 2014, 63–76. Print.

———. *The Theory of the Lyric*. Cambridge, MA: Harvard University Press, 2015.

Cusset, François. *French Theory: How Foucault, Derrida, Deleuze & Co. Transformed the Intellectual Life of the United States*. Minneapolis, MN: University of Minnesota Press, 2008. Print.

Danto, Arthur. *The Transfiguration of the Commonplace: A Philosophy of Art*. Cambridge, MA: Harvard University Press, 1981. Print.

———. *The Philosophical Disenfranchisement of Art*. New York: Columbia University Press, 1986. Print.

Davidson, Donald. "On the Very Idea of a Conceptual Scheme." In *Inquiries Into Truth and Interpretation*. Oxford: Oxford University Press, 1984, 183–98. Print.

———. "Radical Interpretation." In *Inquiries Into Truth and Interpretation* Oxford: Oxford University Press, 1984, 125–41. Print.

———. "A Coherence Theory of Truth and Knowledge." In Ernest LePore, ed. *Truth and Interpretation: Perspectives on the Philosophy of Donald Davidson*. Oxford: Basil Blackwell, 1986, 307–19. Print.

———. *Subjective, Intersubjective, Objective*. Oxford: Oxford University Press, 2001. Print.

———. "Paradoxes of Irrationality." In *Problems of Rationality*. New York: Oxford University Press, 2004, 169–87. Print.

———. "A Nice Derangement of Epitaphs." In *Truth, Language, and History*. New York: Oxford University Press, 2005, 89–108. Print.

———. "The Folly of Trying to Define Truth." In *Truth, Language, and History*. Print.

De Man, Paul. *Blindness and Insight: Essays in the Rhetoric of Contemporary Criticism*. Minneapolis, MN: University of Minnesota Press, 1983. Print.

———. *The Resistance to Theory*. Minneapolis, MN: University of Minnesota Press, 1987. Print.

Dehaene, Stanislas. *Reading in the Brain: The Science and Evolution of a Human Invention*. New York: Viking, 2009. Print.

Derrida, Jacques. *Of Grammatology*. Trans. Gayatri Spivak. Baltimore, MD: Johns Hopkins University Press, 1976. Print.

———. "Structure, Sign, and Play in the Discourse of the Human Sciences." In *Writing and Difference*. Trans. Alan Bass. Chicago: University of Chicago Press, 1978, 278–94. Print.

———. *Limited Inc*. Evanston, IL: Northwestern University Press, 1988. Print.

DiBattista, Maria. *Imagining Virginia Woolf: An Experiment in Critical Biography*. Princeton, NJ: Princeton University Press, 2009. Print.

Dodds, E. R. "On Misunderstanding the Oedipus Rex." In Berkowitz and Brunner, eds. *Oedipus Tyrannus*. New York: Norton, 1970, 218–29. Rptd. from Greece and Rome 13 (1966), 37–49. Print.

Dreyfus, Laurence. *Wagner and the Erotic Impulse*. Cambridge, MA: Harvard University Press, 2012. Print.

Dutton, Denis. *The Art Instinct: Beauty, Pleasure, and Human Evolution*. New York: Bloomsbury Press, 2010. Print.

Dworkin, Ronald. *Law's Empire*. Cambridge, MA: Harvard University Press, 1986. Print.

Eagleton, Terry. *The Event of Literature*. New Haven, CT: Yale University Press, 2012. Print.

Eliot, T. S. "The Three Voices of Poetry." In Virginia Jackson and Yopie Prins, eds. *The Lyric Theory Reader: A Critical Anthology*. Baltimore, MD: Johns Hopkins University Press, 2014, 192–200. Print.

Elster, Jon. *An Introduction to Marx*. Cambridge, MA: Cambridge University Press, 1986. Print.

Erwin, Edward. *A Final Accounting: Philosophical and Empirical Issues in Freudian Psychology*. Cambridge, MA: MIT Press, 1996. Print.

Faggen, Robert. *Robert Frost and the Challenge of Darwin*. Ann Arbor, MI: University of Michigan Press, 1997. Print.

Farrell, John. *Freud's Paranoid Quest: Psychoanalysis and Modern Suspicion*. New York: New York University Press, 1996, chapters 1–3. Print.

———. *Paranoia and Modernity: Cervantes to Rousseau*. Ithaca, NY: Cornell University Press, 2006. Print.

———. "The Birth of the Psychoanalytic Hero: Freud's Platonic Leonardo." *Philosophy and Literature* 31, no. 2 (October, 2007), 233–54. Print.

———. "Psychoanalysis and Modernism." In Charles Ferrall and Dougal McNeill, eds. *Futility and Anarchy?: British Literature in Transition, 1920–1940*, vol. 2. Cambridge: Cambridge University Press, forthcoming. Print.

Fauconnier, Gilles and Mark Turner. *The Way We Think: Conceptual Blending and the Mind's Hidden Complexities*. New York: Basic Books, 2002. Print.

Faulkner, William. *The Portable Faulkner*. Ed. Malcolm Cowley. New York: Viking, 1946. Print.

Felski, Rita. *The Limits of Critique*. Chicago: The University of Chicago Press, 2015.

Fish, Stanley Eugene. *Is There A Text in This Class? The Authority of Interpretive Communities*. Cambridge, MA: Harvard University Press, 1980. Print.

———. *Versions of Antihumanism: Milton and Others*. Cambridge: Cambridge University Press, 2012. Print.

Flesch, William. *Comeuppance: Costly Signaling, Altruistic Punishment, and Other Biological Components of Fiction.* Cambridge, MA: Harvard University Press, 2007. Print.

Foucault, Michel. *The Archeology of Knowledge.* New York: Pantheon, 1972. Print.

———. *The History of Sexuality,* vol. 1. Trans. Robert Hurley. New York: Vintage, 1978. Print.

———. "What Is an Author?" In *The Foucault Reader,* ed. Paul Rabinow. New York: Pantheon, 1984, 100–20. Print.

Gadamer, Hans-Georg. *Truth and Method. Second,* revised edition. Trans. Joel Weinsheimer and Donald G. Marshall. New York: Continuum, 1975. Print.

Gallop, Jane. *The Deaths of the Author: Reading and Writing in Time.* Durham, NC: Duke University Press, 2011. Print.

Gaskin, Richard. *Language, Truth, and Literature: A Defence of Literary Humanism.* Oxford: Oxford University Press, 2013. Print.

Goffman, Erving. *The Presentation of Self in Everyday Life.* New York: Doubleday, 1959. Print.

Goldman, Alan H. *Aesthetic Value.* Boulder, CO: Westview Press1995, Print.

Gombrich, E. H. *Art and Illusion: A Study in the Psychology of Pictorial Representation.* 2nd ed. Princeton, NJ: Princeton University Press, 1960. Print.

Goodman, Nelson. *Languages of Art: An Approach to a Theory of Symbols.* Indianapolis, IN: Bobbs-Merrill, 1968. Print.

———. *Ways of Worldmaking.* Indianapolis, IN: Hackett Pub. Co., 1978. Print.

Greenblatt, Stephen. *Shakespearean Negotiations: The Circulation of Social Energy in Renaissance England.* Berkeley: University of California Press, 1988. Print.

———. *Learning to Curse: Essays in Early Modern Culture.* New York: Routledge, 1990. Print.

———. *Marvelous Possessions: The Wonder of the New World.* Chicago: University of Chicago Press, 1992.

Grice, Paul. *Studies in the Ways of Words.* Cambridge, MA: Harvard University Press, 1989. Print.

Harman, Graham. *The Prince of Networks: Bruno Latour and Metaphysics.* Prahran, Vic.: Re.press, 2009. Print.

Harris, Wendell. *Literary Meaning: Reclaiming the Study of Literature.* New York: New York University Press, 1996. Print.

Heidegger, Martin. *Being and Time.* Trans. John Macquarrie and Edward Robinson. New York: Harper and Row, 1962. Print.

Herrnstein-Smith, Barbara. *Contingencies of Value: Alternative Perspectives for Literary Theory.* Cambridge, MA: Harvard University Press, 1988. Print.

Hirsch, E. D. *Validity in Interpretation.* New Haven, CT: Yale University Press, 1967. Print.

Irwin, William, ed. *The Death and Resurrection of the Author?* Westport, CT: Greenwood Press, 2002. Print.

Isenberg, Arnold. "Critical Communication." *Philosophical Review* 58 (1949), 330–42. Print.

Iser, Wolfgang. *The Implied Reader: Patterns of Communication in Prose Fiction from Bunyan to Beckett.* Baltimore, MD: Johns Hopkins University Press, 1978. Print.

Jackson, Virginia Walker. *Dickinson's Misery: A Lyric Theory of Reading.* Princeton, NJ: Princeton University Press, 2005. Print.

Jackson, Virginia and Yopie Prins, eds. *The Lyric Theory Reader: A Critical Anthology.* Baltimore, MD: Johns Hopkins University Press, 2014. Print.

Jameson, Fredric. *The Prison-House of Language: A Critical Account of Structuralism and Russian Formalism.* Princeton, NJ: Princeton University Press, 1972. Print.

———. *The Political Unconscious: Narrative as a Socially Symbolic Act.* Ithaca, NY: Cornell University Press, 1981. Print.

———. *Postmodernism, or, The Cultural Logic of Late Capitalism.* Durham, NC: Duke University Press, 1991. Print

Johnson, Samuel. "Preface to Shakespeare" (1763). In Vincent B. Leitch, general ed. *The Norton Anthology of Theory and Criticism.* 2nd ed. New York: Norton, 2010, 385–86. Print.

Johnson, Thomas H. *The Complete Poems of Emily Dickinson.* Boston: Little, Brown, and Company, 1960. Print.

Juhl, P. D. *Interpretation, An Essay in the Philosophy of Literary Criticism.* Princeton, NJ: Princeton University Press, 1980. Print.

Knox, Bernard M.W. *The Heroic Temper: Studies in Sophoclean Tragedy.* Berkeley: University of California Press, 1966. Print.

Kosofsky-Sedgwick, Eve. *Touching Feeling: Affect, Pedagogy, Performativity.* Durham, NC: Duke University Press, 2003. Print.

Lakoff, George and Mark Johnson. *Metaphors We Live By.* Chicago: University of Chicago Press, 1980. Print.

Lamarque, Peter. *The Philosophy of Literature.* Malden, MA: Blackwell Publishers, 2009. Print

Lamarque, Peter and Stein Haugom Olsen. *Truth, Fiction, and Literature: A Philosophical Perspective.* New York: Oxford University Press, 1994. Print.

Latour, Bruno. *We Have Never Been Modern.* Cambridge, MA: Harvard University Press, 1994. Print.

———. "Why Has Critique Run Out of Steam? From Matters of Fact to Matters of Concern." *Critical Inquiry* 30 (2004), 225–48. Print.

———. *Reassembling the Social: An Introdution to Actor-Network Theory.* Oxford: Oxford University Press, 2006. Print.

Leitch, Vincent B., general ed., *The Norton Anthology of Theory and Criticism.* 2nd ed. New York: Norton, 2010. Print.

Levinson, Stephen C. Review of *Relevance: Communication and Cognition,* by Dan Sperber and Deirdre Wilson. Oxford: Basil Blackwell, 1986. In *Journal of Linguistics* 25, no. 2 (September 1989), 455–72. Print.

Lévi-Strauss, Claude. "The Structural Study of Myth." In *Structural Anthropology.* Trans. Claire Jacobson and Brooke Grundfest Schoepf. New York: Basic Books, 1963. Print.

Lewis, C. S. and E. M. W. Tillyard. *The Personal Heresy: A Controversy.* New York: Oxford University Press, 1939. Print.

Livingston, Paisley. *Art and Intention: A Philosophical Study.* New York: Oxford University Press, 2005. Print.

Lotman, Yuri. *The Structure of the Artistic Text.* Ann Arbor, MI: University of Michigan Press, 1977. Print.

Lyas, Colin. "The Relevance of the Author's Sincerity." In Peter Lamarque, ed. *Philosophy and Fiction* Christchurch: Cybereditions, 2000, 32–54. Web.

McGann, Jerome. *The Textual Condition.* Princeton, NJ: Princeton University Press, 1991. Print.

McGuire, Michael. *Believing: The Neuroscience of Fantasies, Fears, and Convictions.* New York: Prometheus Books, 2013.

Maxwell, Nicholas. *The Comprehensibility of the Universe: A New Conception of Science.* Oxford: Clarendon Press, 2003. Print.

Michaels, Walter Benn and Steven Knapp. "Against Theory." *Critical Inquiry* 8, no. 4 (Summer, 1982), 723–42. Print.

Mill, John Stuart. *Essays on Poetry.* Ed. F. Parvin Sharpless. Columbia, SC: University of South Carolina Press, 1976. Print.

Nagel, Thomas. *The View from Nowhere.* New York: Oxford University Press, 1986. Print.

———. "Davidson's New Cogito." In Lewis Edwin Hahn, ed. *The Philosophy of Donald Davidson.* Chicago: Open Court, 1999, 195–205. Print.

Naumann, Francis F. *Marcel Duchamp: The Art of Making Art in the Age of Mechanical Reproduction.* New York: Harry N. Abrams [distributor], 1999. Print.

Ortega Y Gassett, José. *The Dehumanization of Art and Other Writings on Art and Culture.* Trans. Willard R. Trask. New York: Doubleday, 1960. Print.

Pascal, Roy. *The Dual Voice: Free Indirect Speech and Its Functioning in the Nineteenth-Century European Novel.* Manchester: Manchester University Press, 1977. Print.

Pratt, Mary Louise. *Toward a Speech Act Theory of Literary Discourse.* Bloomington: Indiana University Press, 1977. Print.

Price, Leah. *The Anthology and the Rise of the Novel: From Richardson to George Eliot.* Cambridge: Cambridge University Press, 2000. Print.

Putnam, Hilary. *The Collapse of the Fact/Value Dichotomy and Other Essays.* Cambridge, MA: Harvard University Press, 2002. Print.

Quine, W. V. *Ontological Relativity and Other Essays.* New York: Columbia University Press, 1969. Print.

Reddy, Michael J. "The Conduit Metaphor—A Case of Frame Conflict in Our Language about Language." In Andrew Ortony, ed. *Metaphor and Thought.* New York: Cambridge University Press, 1979, 284–324. Print.

Richards, I. A. *Science and Poetry.* New York: Norton, 1926. Print.

Ricoeur, Paul. *Freud and Philosophy: An Essay on Interpretation.* Trans. Denis Savage. New Haven, CT: Yale University Press, 1970. Print.

Rosenberg, Alexander. *The Philosophy of Social Science.* 3rd ed. Boulder, CO: Westview Press, 2008. Print.

Ruddick, Lisa. "When Nothing Is Cool." In Angelica Bammer and Ellen Boetcher Joeres, eds. *The Future of Scholarly Writing.* New York: Palgrave Macmillan, 2015. Print.

Saville. Anthony. *The Test of Time: An Essay in Philosophical Aesthetics.* New York: Oxford University Press, 1982. Print.

Scalia, Antonin. *A Matter of Interpretation: Federal Courts and the Law: An Essay.* With commentary by Amy Gutmann, editor, Gordon Wood, Laurence Tribe, Mary Ann Glendon, and Ronald Dworkin. Princeton, NJ: Princeton University Press, 1997. Print.

Schalkwyk, David. "Giving Intention Its Due?" *Style: A Quarterly Journal of Aesthetics, Poetics, Stylistics, and Literary Criticism* 44, no. 3. (Fall 2010), 311–27. Print.

Schreber, Daniel Paul. *A Memoir of My Nervous Illness.* Trans. Ida MacAlpine and Richard A. Hunter. London: Wm. Dawson and Sons Ltd., 1955. Print.

Scott-Phillips, Thom. *Speaking Our Minds: Why Human Communication Is Different, and How Language Evolved to Make It Special.* New York: Palgrave Macmillan, 2015. Print.

Searle, John. "The Logical Status of Fictional Discourse." In Peter Lamarque and Stein Haugum Olsen, eds. *Aesthetics and the Philosophy of Literature: An Anthology.* Malden, MA: Blackwell Publishers, 2004, 320–27. Print.

Segal, Charles. *Tragedy and Civilization: An Interpretation of Sophocles.* Norman, OK: University of Oklahoma Press, 1999. Print.

Shiner, L. E. *The Invention of Art: A Cultural History.* Chicago: University of Chicago Press, 2001. Print.

Shoptaw, John. "Lyric Cryptography." *Poetics Today* 21, no. 1 (Spring 2000), 221–62. Print.

Sibley, Frank. "Aesthetic Concepts." In John Benson, Betty Redfern, and Jeremy Roxbee Cox, eds. *Approach to Aesthetics: Collected Papers on Philosophical Aesthetics.* Oxford: Clarendon Press, 2001, Chapter 1. Print.

Susan Sontag. "Notes on 'Camp'." *Susan Sontag: Essays of the '60 s and '70 s.* Ed. David Rieff. New York: Library of America, 2013. Print.

Spacks, Patricia Meyer. "Logic and Language in Through the Looking-Glass. In Robert Phillips, ed. *Aspects of Alice: Lewis Carroll's Dreamchild as Seen Though the Critics' Looking-Glasses, 1865–1971* New York: The Vanguard Press, 1971, 267–75. Print.

Sperber, Dan and Deirdre Wilson. *Relevance: Communication and Cognition*. 2nd ed. Cambridge, MA: Blackwell Publishers, 1995. Print.

———. *Meaning and Relevance*. Cambridge: Cambridge University Press, 2012. Print.

Sterelny, Kim. *Thought in a Hostile World: The Evolution of Human Cognition*. Malden, MA: Blackwell Publishers, 2003. Print.

Stroud, Barry. *Engagement and Metaphysical Dissatisfaction: Modality and Value*. New York: Oxford University Press, 2011. Print.

Tanselle, G. Thomas. *A Rationale of Textual Criticism*. Philadelphia: University of Pennsylvania Press, 1989. Print.

Tolstoy, Leo. *Anna Karenina: A Novel in Eight Parts*. Trans. Richard Pevear and Larissa Volokhonsky. New York: Viking, 2001. Print.

Tucker, Herbert E. "Dramatic Monologue and the Overhearing of Lyric." In Virginia Jackson and Yopie Prins, eds. *The Lyric Theory Reader: A Critical Anthology*. Baltimore, MD: Johns Hopkins University Press, 2014, 144–56. Print.

Vermeule, Blakey. *Why Do We Care about Literary Characters?* Baltimore, MD: The Johns Hopkins University, 2010. Print.

Vološinov, V. N. *Marxism and the Philosophy of Language*. Trans. Ladislaw Matejka and I. R. Titunik. Cambridge, MA: Harvard University Press, 1973. Print.

Walton, Kendall. *Mimesis as Make-Believe: On the Foundations of the Representational Arts*. Cambridge, MA: Harvard University Press, 1990. Print.

———. "Categories of Art." In Peter Lamarque and Stein Haugum Olsen, eds. *Aesthetics and the Philosophy of Art*. Malden, MA: Blackwell, 2004, 142–57. Print.

———. "'How Marvelous!': Toward a Theory of Aesthetic Value." In *Marvelous Images: On Values and the Arts*. New York: Oxford University Press, 2008, 3–22. Print.

Widiss, Benjamin. *Obscure Invitations*. Stanford, CA: Stanford University Press, 2011. Print.

Wimsatt, William and Monroe C. Beardsley. "The Intentional Fallacy." In Virginia Jackson and Yopie Prins, eds. *The Lyric Theory Reader: A Critical Anthology*. Baltimore, MD: Johns Hopkins University Press, 2014. 201–10. Print.

Wittgenstein, Ludwig. *Philosophical Investigations*. Trans. G. E. M. Anscombe. 2nd ed. Oxford: Blackwell, 1967. Print.

Wood, Allen. *Kant's Ethical Thought*. New York: Cambridge University Press, 1999. Print.

Yeats, W. B. *Letters*. Ed. Allan Wade. New York: Macmillan, 1954. Print.

Index

Printed in the United States
By Bookmasters